Feel Good

Arthur

Ten Days in August

a novel by

BERNARD FRIZELL

Simon and Schuster

NEW YORK, 1956

First Printing

LIBRARY OF CONGRESS CATALOG CARD NUMBER: 56-6667

MANUFACTURED IN THE UNITED STATES OF AMERICA

BY AMERICAN BOOK—STRATFORD PRESS, INC., NEW YORK

For Lee

Almost all the events described in this novel actually occurred, but the characters, except for those public figures whose true names are used, are of course imaginary. The brief section about General von Choltitz is based on his memoirs as they appeared in *Le Figaro*.

B. F.

CONTENTS

Part One

The Eve

EVERYTHING in the room was black: ceiling, walls, carpeting, even the shiny satin sheets on the spacious bed. Two even-burning candles lighted the darkness; they were black too.

Patrice put on his only suit, a badly cut gray tweed that was too large and made him look even bigger than he was. He had slept long and hard, and now, before leaving, he looked around the small window-less room he had not used for what it was intended and he was not sorry.

He thought of how the Madam had thrown open the door for him and announced, "The black room—for blondes!" He had been so tired he had not even smiled, though the idea, at the first shock, had struck him as elaborately comical. "No blondes," he had said. The Madam had looked at him reproachfully, but beyond that look of disapproval she had not insisted. As such places went, it was a good establishment; and unlike hotels, they asked for no identity papers and made no reports to the police.

Patrice blew out the candles and stepped into the corridor. He passed the erotic frescoes without noticing them. Downstairs, in the big public room, there had been perhaps two dozen girls naked to, or from, the waist, depending on which end was considered more magnetic. The girls were gone. No men were standing at the long bar either, or sitting at the tables around the room. When Patrice had passed through on his way to the black room some of the girls had been dancing with the men or, rather schoolgirlishly, with each other to a tango recording, and one of them had grasped his arm and whispered, *"Une danse d'amour?"* Now the room was empty except for two gray-haired cleaning women, crouched on their knees, washing the floor. The smell of disinfectant had replaced the feminine smell of naked arms and powder. Patrice thought it was very different here in the morning—like an empty theater facing a bare stage, or a night club in the afternoon. At best, he thought, deserted places of entertainment are dreary. The house, in the clear light of morning, had a curdling, hang-overish feel. Its soul of raw gaiety had left it, and the cleaning women scrubbing away might have been morticians preparing the body for display. They looked up spiritlessly as Patrice stepped over their pails and wash rags. Near the door he found the Madam bent over a book. She put it face down, opened to her page, and rose. She was about forty, bird-faced, and slight in a trim black dress.

"Did you have pleasant dreams?" she asked, not without malice.

"The sleep of the virtuous—no dreams," Patrice said. "I left my bag. I may stay again tonight."

She followed his quick glance to the title of her book, *English—The Easy Way*, and smiled.

"They will be in Paris soon," she said. "One must be prepared."

"They" were the American troops in Normandy. Patrice remembered one cloudless June day in 1940, a deserted Paris in the spring, tragic and achingly beautiful, and the butt end of an overheard conversation: "Where are they?" "St. Denis." "The hell with them. I'm not budging." "Me, I'm taking off." In those days "they" were the Germans.

"Will they come here to talk?" Patrice asked.

"They will want to talk too. It helps the illusion. Besides, I must know what they want if I am to serve them well."

"They're a simple people with simple needs. All that's necessary is plenty of girls."

"I will teach them to be less simple."

When Patrice reached the door the Madam added, "I may have to give you another room."

"It's unimportant," he replied. "Without a blonde the color scheme is incomplete anyway."

He found his bicycle in the entranceway. Outside, the sun was bright and Patrice squinted against the glare. His face was angular and gaunt, with deep lines carved in his flat cheeks to the corners of his wide mouth. He was in his middle thirties but looked older, partly because of the premature sprinkle of gray in his black hair but more because he was big and hard. Only his eyes were soft. They were brown and reflective and contradicted the set of the jaw.

He had not pedaled very far when he sensed something peculiar in the air, something unusual. The familiar ball of fear bounced around in his stomach; his muscles were taut; he was ready to bolt. He looked around but saw nothing. Somehow there was something different about the streets. Yet everything looked normal. He marked it down to nervousness and rode on. The nausea, he knew, would pass.

It was early. All along the way the streets were deserted and iron shutters were pulled down across shop fronts. Paris looked like a dead city, presenting an impassive face to the fuzzy, sparkling air. Patrice imagined that the city was as empty as it appeared to be and that he was the only one there. He felt something magnificent and awesome about being the only person in the streets of Paris. The boulevards suddenly seemed enormous and took on the vast sweep of a desert, and the avenues were as silent as forests banked by sheer slopes in the loneliness of the sun and the sky.

Passing a kiosk, Patrice stopped to buy a newspaper and glanced at the headlines: METRO STOPS TOMORROW. FOUNDER OF FRANCO-GERMAN CLUB COMMITS SUICIDE. RACE TRACKS CLOSE. ALLIES LAND IN THE SOUTH OF FRANCE. Patrice felt good reading the last item. Since the Americans had made their break-through at Avranches two weeks before and begun their sweep across France, everything had changed.

Patrice shook his head and looked up. The air was full of ashes. Floating slowly through the bright air, they fell like black snow on his head and shoulders. Four years before he had seen just such a storm on the Quai d'Orsay when Foreign Office employees had burned stacks of documents before fleeing to the south.

He was on the Faubourg St. Honoré and rode slowly to the Place Beauveau. Again he felt something odd about the streets and looked around, perplexed and irritated. The charred paper was falling more thickly here. Facing the Ministry of the Interior, a one-legged beggar was seated on the corner of the Avenue de Marigny squeezing out an air from *La Traviata* on a nickel-plated accordion. The weepy melody rose feebly and pathetically over the square like a wounded bird. Patrice looked down the Rue des Saussaies. Nobody. It was strange. A few doors away stood the headquarters of the Gestapo. Patrice wheeled his bicycle across the square to the beggar.

"I thought you worked the boulevards, One-paw."

"Afternoons."

Patrice dropped five francs into the man's hat. "What's going on?"

"Can't you see? The Gestapo's getting ready to take off. They're burning their records."

Patrice and the beggar exchanged a quick glance. The pathetically sweet air from *La Traviata* took an absurdly sentimental turn under the beggar's satiric phrasing. Patrice could not suppress a grin.

"So they're going to fly."

"Like birds," said the beggar. "They're a people with great qualities."

Still smiling, Patrice pedaled to the Concorde and crossed the big square. It was early-morning empty and the fountains were dry. Between the openmouthed, unslaked bronze gods the obelisk pointed its long slender shadow up the deserted Champs Élysées. The light was blue and vaporous, the air already hot. Patrice turned into the quai of the Seine, where the trees were summer-ripe, hanging full-blown out of the Tuileries and leaning gracefully over the river. It should have made Patrice feel good, as it almost always did, but he scarcely noticed anything around him now because he was thinking ahead of all he had to do that day.

At the Palais-Royal swimming pool, jutting into the Seine, a long line of people waited patiently for a crowded swim. Presently Patrice crossed a bridge and cycled onto the Ile de la Cité. The Prefecture of Police stood on his left, stony-gray and massive. As he passed the building Patrice said aloud, "We have a rendezvous in a few days and I'm going to keep it." But he needed arms, and time was running short. One thing at a time, he thought. First, Danielle.

She was waiting for him in the middle of the St. Michel bridge. Black hair combed back to the shoulders, almond-shaped dark-blue eyes, a good face with strong bones and olive satin skin. He looked at her and wondered why he had been fighting her all these months. What had he been trying to prove? It made little difference now. He had felt last night when he left her what there could be between them; now he felt it again.

They stood beside each other, leaning on the stone parapet of the bridge, and looked across the enigmatic green waters of the Seine at Notre Dame. It was a river for lovers and suicides.

"Well," Patrice asked, "what's your answer?"

"Tell it to me all over again the way you did last night."

He laid it out for her, simple and clear, and the logic of what she had to do and what nobody else could do in her place was inescapable, the way it had been last night.

After a while she said, "All right, I'll do it."

"I knew you would."

It had slipped out and surprised him as much as it did her. She looked at him oddly. She needed no more than that to understand that after all the months she had worked with him he had finally unbent. It had taken her quite a while to unbend, too, following her early suspicions about Patrice's motives. She had unbent all the way over backward, she thought ruefully. But the other thing was too much in her mind for her to be as happy as she might have been about the change in Patrice.

He glanced around. Nobody was in sight.

"Open your bag."

She opened her white bag and he slipped a revolver into it

"You know how to use it?"

She nodded.

"Don't forget the safety. There mustn't be a slip-up."

"There won't be," she said sadly.

†

PATRICE met Lefort at two o'clock on the terrace of the Source, midway up the Boulevard St. Michel.

"Is it all set?"

"A hundred men are spotted in and around the building waiting for the go-ahead."

"How about the guards?"

"You were right. Only two. Four of our men will disarm them."

"Have they got rope?"

Lefort nodded.

"We still have a few minutes," Patrice said, looking at his watch.

They ordered two beers. Glancing at Lefort's *Pariser Zeitung*, Patrice felt a tug at his heart as the black German headlines cried out at him:

WARSAW REVOLT CRUSHED

CITY IN RUINS

TERRORISTS EXTERMINATED

He looked at the two glasses of thin, tasteless beer, then at Lefort, and wondered how anyone that husky could look so cool and sleek on such a hot day. It must be his youth, he thought. Lefort slouched negligently in a chair that was too small for his big body. His close-cropped hair, icy gray eyes, heavy chin and crooked nose, broken while playing soccer as a boy, made him look tough, which he was. Nobody would have guessed he was only twenty-five years old. He was smartly dressed in a double-breasted gray suit, impeccable white shirt and a handsome maroon tie with blue figures. Lefort had the assured air of a man who knew what he wanted and the noncommittal expression of a poker player who would tip off his hand only after the last bet had been made. Patrice wondered what he wanted out of the resistance. The man was not a "pure." You could smell that. Too cynical for a nationalist, not romantic enough for an adventurer. Patrice shrugged. He could not begin to worry about men's motives in the resistance. When they weren't sublime they were human. That covered the gamut.

"Where are they?" Lefort asked.

"All I know is what the BBC tells us. Now that there's a blackout on the line of the Allied advance, that isn't much."

"What they don't tell the Germans they don't tell us," Lefort said without bitterness. "Well, there's good news in Paris anyway."

Wondering what was so strange about the streets, Patrice said distractedly, "I was there this morning. The air was full of ashes. I was covered with them."

"Ashes?"

"At the Rue des Saussaies. The Gestapo is leaving. Isn't that what you meant?"

"Better. The police are on strike." Lefort's eyes glittered. "Even the cops have come out on our side. I just saw a sign on a police station near here: ANNUAL CLOSING. WILL REOPEN WHEN COMPETITORS CLOSE."

So that was what bothered him about the streets, Patrice thought. Naturally! He had not seen any policemen, not a single one. He was amazed that he had forgotten about the strike.

"The cops went out," he said, "but will they stay out?"

"Why not?"

"What will they do if the Boches pick up fifty or a hundred cops and shoot them?"

"The Boches won't have the time," Lefort said. "The insurrection will stop them."

"I hope so."

But he was not sure because nobody knew when, or even if, the insurrection would break upon the occupied city. The basis for an uprising was laid. An instrument had been forged, an army of sorts, that could be used to wedge the Germans out of Paris. The eighty quarters of the city, four to each of the twenty *arrondissements*, were organized for a revolt. So were the suburbs—Pantin, Montrouge, St. Denis, Boulogne-Billancourt and all the rest. Like a huge pie, the vast circle of Paris and its metropolitan area was cut into four slices. Each sector had its general staff. Commanding all of them was the regional staff of the Ile de France, headed by Colonel Rol, a communist. The entire military apparatus was responsible, theoretically at least, to the French Provisional Government's general staff in London.

The chain of command was complete. One command from the top would get down to every man at the lowest echelon, and the insurrection could fly into motion. But there was no agreement at the top. The resistance knew the situation in Paris but did not know the Allied plans; the Provisional Government in London knew the Allied plans but did not know the situation in Paris. While the resistance leadership agreed on the necessity of an insurrection, it was split on who was to precipitate it: London, in co-ordination with the Allied advance on Paris, or itself, when it judged the moment ripe. The split was widened by the antagonism between the resistance and the émigré French in London, with their conflicting mentalities, policies and organizations. Since few resistance leaders believed that London would call for an uprising, if at all, until Allied troops had virtually liberated Paris, the very question of an insurrection was at issue. The issue was already being forced by the communists. Six days before, they had launched a strike of railway workers. The move, catching the Germans by surprise, had paralyzed rail traffic in and out of the French capital. It was the first overt step toward a general strike which would coincide with the insurrection. Like Patrice, a handful of men rode purposefully about the city on bicycles, and beneath the calm surface of Paris, resplendent in the grace of the August sun, the insurrection stirred secretly to life. The machine age, Patrice thought. Insurrection on a bicycle.

"How about arms?" Lefort asked. "Did you get any?"

Patrice shook his head. "I'll be seeing Mignot this afternoon and after him the Dutchman."

"You'll never get anything out of the Dutchman. But when you see him give him this." Lefort handed Patrice a thick envelope. "It's the new code from London. Just got it for him."

Patrice put the envelope into his pocket, looked at his watch and said, "It's time. Let's go."

They finished their beers, paid and got on their bicycles.

"By the way," Patrice said, "Adrien doesn't know where you live, does he?"

"No. Why?"

"He's working for the Gestapo. I had to move fast last night when I found out. To a brothel."

Lefort grinned. "At least you're not living alone any more." He added, "Adrien's being taken care of, I suppose."

"In a few hours," Patrice said grimly, "he'll be ready for the maggots."

They rode to a house in the Rue des Petits Champs, climbed three flights of stairs and were admitted to a cluttered apartment by a bespectacled man of sixty, a professor of the Lycée Henri IV.

"I've been expecting you," he said.

"Is everything ready?"

"Come and see the room we've prepared."

They went into a small bedroom at the end of a long hall. Most of it was filled by a fine old double bed high up from the floor with an iron-barred headrest and a lower iron-barred footboard. The cover was turned down and a corner of fresh white linen gleamed into the plain but comfortable room.

"My wife made it up this morning," the professor said. "We gave the maid ten days off."

"Very good," Patrice said. "You're sure the concierge is all right?"

"Certain. I've known her for twenty years."

The professor cleared his throat. "Our, ah, visitor will be arriving in an hour or so. Perhaps it's time you told me something about him."

Patrice looked at Lefort. "I was coming around to that," he said. "It's Edouard Herriot."

It took the professor a second to register the name; then the surprise leaped across his face.

"The former Premier?"

Patrice nodded. "You'll be entertaining a distinguished guest."

"But he's a prisoner."

"We're going to release him."

"From a German fortress?" the professor asked incredulously.

"He's right here in Paris—at the Hotel de Ville. He's Laval's prisoner, not Hitler's."

"He's still a prisoner. There are—"

"We've planned everything. We're just going to walk him out of the building into a waiting ambulance and whisk him away."

Patrice and Lefort watched the professor's face. The old man looked worried. He knew the escape would be splashed on the front page of every newspaper in the world, that the Germans and Vichy would turn Paris upside down to recapture the ex-Premier. But the professor did not back down.

"It sounds so simple," he said uneasily.

"The best plans," Lefort said, "are the simplest ones."

†

DANIELLE clenched and unclenched her fists. She would have to calm down, calm down.

She took the long way around, skirting the familiar maze of narrow streets, lagging on the broad, imprudent boulevards. Paris had a scrubbed look ; it gleamed under a cloudless sky. The world was bright and unreal, and Danielle felt like a forsaken shadow floating through a sunlit dream. I must not weaken, she told herself. I must do it.

A group of German soldiers in field-green uniforms passed. Their laughter burst and dissolved in the soft air. Danielle heard nothing. Her mind groped in a sudden void and turned upon itself, seeking something to grip. The image of Adrien filled the void. She shivered.

She saw neither the soldiers nor the cyclists scooting by, nor the sun-drenched buildings climbing into the blue Paris sky. The asphalt under her feet throbbed in the early-afternoon heat.

Danielle walked. Her smart white bag was slung over her right shoulder and reflected the hard glare of the August sun. At each step it beat gently at her hip, swung out, beat at her hip.

She could not remember when she had ever been in Paris in August, not even in the past four years of German occupation. Longingly she thought of the sea, the tremulous, light-soaked Mediterranean air hovering over a strip of beach and frothy whitecaps cool and white as snow in the blue and sparkling sea. August meant vegetation : a ravishment of animal heat and sun-tanned indolence, the sting of spray and the smell of pine groves baking in the sun.

A wave of sadness flooded over her. Danielle remembered one August and how she had felt about Adrien, seeing his face with the tender expression, the dark, misted eyes.

The buildings tilted and an expanse of blue sky swung dizzily in an arc. She waited behind burning lids for the world to take shape again.

A pressure on her arm. Caught? Her throat choked with fear.

"Can I help you, madame? You seem to be ill."

The street was sunny-bright again as Danielle opened her eyes. At first the man's face, too close to her own, was a blur, but then the fuzziness disappeared and she saw that he was a middle-aged man with sunken cheeks and terribly cold blue eyes.

"Thank you. Just a spell of dizziness. I'm all right now."

Danielle took a few hesitant steps and the man was still with her.

"I can accompany you. It's no bother at all."

He was suave, confident. She quickened her pace.

"Really not. Really not."

As she hastened away Danielle could feel the man standing regretfully in the center of the sidewalk, his porcelain eyes following the movement of her hips.

The closer she came to where she was going the more slowly she walked. A sick feeling gripped her stomach, and her throat was dry. She hoped she would not be sick. This was not the freedom Patrice talked about but a sacrificial gesture on its altar. She wondered if she would be doing it had anyone but Patrice asked her. She was not sure. She remembered the time she lived in Saigon shortly after her father had been named an admiral of the fleet and how he had wrestled with his conscience over a case involving the death sentence. "When you condemn a man to death," he had said, "your own life begins to lose its value." The day after the execution he had said, "Yesterday a little bit of me died." Nevertheless, she thought that if he were still alive, he would approve what she was doing; but she was not sure. She had said nothing to Patrice. What was there to say when, practically speaking, she was the only one who could do it?

The church. The ancient blackened stones worn over the centuries by autumn rains and winter fog; drab, friendly stones caressed by the August sun. Inside, the lovely shock of cool air and the musty odor of petty sins confessed and still lingering. Doubt was a luxury now. Danielle walked briskly down the center aisle, turned left into a corridor, walked to the end of it and hesitated a moment before an oak door. Then she knocked.

"Come in."

She entered a small room that seemed even smaller because of the disorder in it and the dim light. Several straight-backed chairs, a table piled high with books and newspapers, more books helter-skelter on the floor in corners, a crucifix on the wall, the narrow window facing a wall of the church. The priest was sitting at a desk on one side of the room.

"Danielle! What a surprise!"

His black cassock rustled like a woman's skirt. The extended hand. A firm grip. Danielle sat beside the desk facing the priest. He had not changed much. His head was as bald and shiny as ever; the rimless glasses, the nose perhaps a little more pointed, the blue stubble around the chin, and the alert eyes. An intellectual wearing a soutane. He was a gentle man and Danielle had always liked him. Since she had stopped practicing Catholicism Danielle had wondered whether his intelligence did not rebel at the point where reason could go no farther and faith began. She had no faith. He was smiling, talking. She interrupted him.

"*Mon père*, I need your help."

"What is it?"

"I want you to give a friend the last sacraments."

"He is about to die?"

A fatherly expression, tender, encompassing. (Our Father, Who art in Heaven, hallowed . . .)

Danielle took a deep breath. "Yes, I'm going to kill him."

†

IN THE street outside the professor's house Patrice said to Lefort, "Now for the final check with Reboussin and Bourbon, then the Hotel de Ville."

He felt good cycling to the Tuileries. He would have liked to see Laval's face when the Vichy Chief of Government learned that Herriot was gone. Patrice could not suppress a spark of involuntary wonder at the wily Auvergnat's infinite flexibility. Having bet everything on his policy of collaboration and a German victory, the man who had begun his career as a socialist to become a fascist and whose name came out the same spelled backward was once again reversing his hand to cut his losses. Through Herriot he intended to convoke a National Assembly of pre-Vichy Senators and Deputies that would re-establish a Third Republic government. The new government, masterminded by Laval and headed by the eminently respectable Herriot, would receive the victorious Allies on liberated French soil. Having restored a parliamentary regime and prevented De Gaulle from taking power, Laval would discreetly fade out of the picture, knowing his subsequent return was already prepared. The Germans, though suspicious, were going along warily, persuaded by Laval that his plan to revive a parliament was an ultimate move against eventual revolution and a communist triumph. Patrice smiled as he recalled the flurry in the resistance leadership when it learned of Laval's plan. Patrice had said, "Without Herriot, Laval is helpless. Let's kidnap Herriot." Reboussin had objected: "What will we do with him when we have him?" But the others agreed it was better to have Herriot on their hands than in Laval's lap. He would be out of Laval's lap soon enough, Patrice thought.

Patrice and Lefort rolled through the Tuileries and stopped at a bench between the Louvre and the Carrousel. Reboussin and Bourbon were waiting. They rose. Both were tall, Reboussin thin and slightly stooped, Bourbon spare and erect. They looked like successful businessmen getting on in years. Both of them wore fedoras with upturned brims that rested flat on their heads, and Bourbon wore pearl-gray gloves despite the heat and carried a cane. Patrice's shirt was open and he wore no tie. He spoke to Reboussin.

"We're ready to deliver Herriot," he said.

"It's off."

"Off!" Patrice was stunned. "Why?"

"We just learned that Herriot won't go along with Laval, never intended to."

"But it's all set up. We can get him anyway."

Reboussin smiled. "What for?"

"If he's against Laval he's with us. It pays both ways."

"Too risky."

Patrice looked into Reboussin's eyes and knew it was futile to argue. The inner struggle for power was fierce enough, and Herriot was bigger and better known than all of them. They also knew Herriot would have American support over General de Gaulle to head a post-liberation government.

Turning to Lefort, Patrice said, "Better get to the Hotel de Ville and tell them it's off. Tell the professor too."

After Lefort left, Patrice said, "You win this round. You won't win the next one."

"Careful, Patrice," Reboussin said. "You ought to know that an insurrection is madness."

Precise and desiccated, he looked at Patrice with the funereal air of an undertaker regarding a corpse in the presence of the next of kin. Reboussin always wore the right expression for the right occasion and had the quality of speaking on one level while thinking on another, a quality developed over long years of political activity. Of all the leaders of the Paris resistance he was the most adroit.

"The Germans will crush us," he said. "If by some miracle they don't we will lose anyway: the communists will be the victors and Paris and the government will be theirs. That's the alternative if you insist on your insurrection. Suicide either way—cyanide or prussic acid." The hint of a smile crossed his lips at the faint play on words. "Unless of course you wait for London to call it."

Patrice had barely begun to answer when Bourbon interrupted.

"I tell you I will not allow it," he cried indignantly. His voice was harsh and strained, as if he were giving an order he was not sure would be obeyed. "As long as I'm military adviser to the National Council of the Resistance and responsible to that degree for its military decisions I will not permit an insurrection."

Bourbon—he had chosen that resistance name because of his royalist sympathies—was a career officer, about whom it was said in leftist resistance circles: when the army made him a colonel it brought a mountain of authority to a molehill of intelligence. Bourbon had a narrow, hairless face, glassy blue eyes and a severe mouth. He could not forget that he had fought in Morocco under Marshal Lyautey and that Lyautey had once offered him a cigar. Whenever a new officer of high rank arrived at his headquarters Lyautey called him into his office. Holding a box of cigarettes in one hand and a box of cigars in the other, the marshal would invariably say: "*Mon cher ami*, here are some cigarettes. I offer these to officers who know how to fight. And here are some cigars. I offer these to officers who know how to make those under them fight. Which will you have?" Bourbon had taken a cigar. Patrice looked at his obstinate face and thought of a line from a poem of Prévert's: "Those who are bald on the inside of the head."

"It's a scandal, a scandal!" Bourbon said, tapping his cane on the ground. "Paris will be liberated by the army, not by a mob. We don't want a revolution; we want to be rid of the Germans and then re-establish order."

Patrice did not want a revolution either. He appealed to Bourbon's patriotism with the plea that an insurrection was necessary for political and moral reasons, so that after the shame of the 1940 defeat, when Paris was abandoned without a fight, France could face the world with the shining words: Paris liberated herself.

"This time," Patrice said, "it's not an army in retreat led by a defeatist general and a demoralized government that is speaking for France. It's the resistance—us."

Reboussin countered that Paris could not liberate herself: the resistance lacked the men and arms. Just as Bourbon struck the wrong note for Patrice, Reboussin struck the right one. "Paris may be destroyed, a hundred thousand Parisians massacred! Look at what the Nazis have just done in Warsaw!" His words found their mark. Patrice envisioned ruined Warsaw, the rubble still smoking, its slaughtered patriots, their bodies already cold. The whole dismal tragedy of that premature uprising was a nightmare for the Paris insurrectionists.

As the argument developed, Reboussin and Bourbon played both ends against the middle. While Reboussin feared that an insurrection would end in the catastrophe of defeat, Bourbon was afraid of the much more terrifying possibility that it would result in the disaster of victory. The specter of communism haunted him and he was convinced that "as surely as smoke means fire" an insurrection meant a communist regime. Reboussin, on the contrary, did not believe there was a communist plot to take power. Such a plot had no chance of success and he knew the communist leaders knew it. Reboussin did believe, however, that an insurrection could be followed by a post-liberation communist landslide. So did Patrice. But they faced the danger in different ways.

"Paris wants an insurrection," Patrice said. "Even the cops, the most reactionary element in any city from Moscow to New York, have come out at great risk against the Germans. The real meaning of the strike is that the people are for any anti-German action, the more extreme the better. Good. The communists know this better than anyone. Now, it is fruitless to oppose the insurrection, because if we do the communists will split off from the rest of us and launch the insurrection themselves, carrying the people with them. That means we have to support the insurrection. The alternative is not whether there should or should not be an insurrection but whether we should let the communists take over the leadership of the uprising or hold onto the leadership ourselves."

"We'd become their instruments," Reboussin objected.

"Not if we could beat them at their own game. My idea is that we take the initiative and move into the most important key buildings before they do. We'll take the play out of their hands."

"Beware of them, Patrice," Bourbon said. "They're clever. They have fought well in the resistance. We cannot deny it. But they fought for themselves and for Russia first and then, because accident would have it so, for France."

"To be sure," Patrice said, and added ironically, "Your brand of anticommunism is both belated and premature. In 1940, of course. Five years from now, no doubt. But today it's an anachronism." He paused. "This is no time to say the correct policy for us is necessarily the opposite of theirs, not when they're our allies and certain of our purposes coincide—like beating the Germans."

"I am not a man of fashion," Bourbon said stiffly. "I do know that if nominally the communists are our allies, actually they are the antichrist. I face a problem of conscience. Yesterday I asked my confessor, 'Do I have the right to stop the communist leaders before it is too late? Do I have the right to shoot them?' 'My son,' he said, 'not only do you have the right; it is your solemn duty.'"

There was a moment of incredulous silence. Then Patrice tried to turn the matter into a joke. "Remember the old axiom about coalitions," he said. "'Never cut an ally's throat until he is no longer of any use.' We still need the communists."

Soon after, unable to swing them to his view, Patrice lost patience.

"Our task is to deliver Paris intact," Reboussin said. "There is only one danger. Anyone with political experience knows the only sensible policy is to avoid that danger."

"We don't all have your breadth of experience," Patrice said dryly.

It was a low blow and Patrice was immediately sorry he had struck it. A middle-of-the-road prewar deputy, Reboussin had supported Pétain in the confusion of the defeat, then had sunk into an obscurity as complete as it was deliberate. When the direction of the war was clear he had joined the resistance, certain that with his intelligence plus a few risks he would be a minister after the liberation, with good chances of the premiership in the following five years. A man of sound common sense, he believed that with the nation split between Vichy and the Gaullists, treason consisted in being on the losing side.

"Be realistic," Patrice said. "When the Americans get closer to Paris there'll be no holding back the resistance."

"What the resistance does depends on us."

"And the communists? What are you going to do about them?"

Reboussin's features relaxed as he composed his expression. "That's why we need you and everyone else we can get on our side. It won't be easy."

"It will be impossible. You can't stop the communists by outvoting them."

"We can stop them," Bourbon said, "if you and a few others don't play their game."

"You know I'm not playing their game."

Patrice noted their closed expressions and felt his own was no different, and he knew that none of them could change attitudes any more than they could change the color of their eyes. It was a matter of character. Each of them was blocked in his own mold and they neither wanted to nor could break out.

The argument dribbled off inconclusively, and Patrice pedaled away. Gray-stoned buildings fled past him. The air was a trembling pane of light behind which, white and brilliant under a blazing sky, Paris quivered in the summer heat. It was difficult to imagine an uprising—barricades, the metallic stutter of machine guns, corpses sprawled under the chestnut trees—in this sunlit patrician quarter. A handsome woman in a broad-brimmed hat cycled by, legs churning, skirt ballooning behind her, indefinably chic and Parisian in this summer without busses or automobiles. The streets were bright and empty, and Patrice heard only the whir of the spokes against the deep cushion of the city's silence. Low against the tall sky he saw the line of buildings rimming the left bank of the Seine. The light over the river, gossamer blue and transparent, pierced his heart like a pistol shot, and he thought, If Paris were destroyed . . . Would they send their planes and drop bombs on the Champs Élysées? Would Notre Dame fall under the explosives after all the centuries the cathedral had stood? Patrice saw the Eiffel Tower a mass of twisted metal lying flat across the Seine. He saw gutted buildings and razed quarters and the arcades of the rue de Rivoli from one moment to the next turned into mounds of dust and smoking piles of destroyed masonry. And at the top of the Champs Élysées he saw the Arch of Triumph flattened out and the entire city an ugly, meaningless shell. No, he would not believe it.

Alone before the responsibility of his decision, he wavered between exhilaration and panic. Against the hope of realizing his four-year-old dream of insurrection was the vision of shirt-sleeved Parisians facing German tanks with revolvers and muskets. It would be safer to do nothing—and perhaps wiser. But for good or for bad he felt the insurrection would come and that nothing, not the mind of any man or group of men, could stop it. He felt that even as the debate was being joined, events had already by-passed the moment of choice. They could argue all they wanted; it would do them no good. The insurrection was in the air like the smell and feel of a storm that a parched city prays for even though it may turn into a hurricane and bring disaster with relief.

Far off at the top of Montmartre the pastry-cake dome and towers of Sacré-Coeur gleamed white and Byzantine, shimmering on the horizon. Below, the city stretched vast and inert, without sound or movement, like a shackled giant prostrate before his destiny, waiting in the summer sun for death or freedom.

†

A HALF HOUR after Danielle entered the church she hurried into the street with the priest at her heels. The parched air enveloped her with its breathless heat, but she felt freer than in the obscure coolness of the church.

"I must go," she had said to end the discussion. "You can come with me or not as you choose."

The priest had come.

She was more resolute now. The priest's opposition had fortified her. What concerned the reverend father was the forms. Did he have a trial? Was he properly judged? What clawed at her conscience was the sheer fact: she would crook her finger and a human being, Adrien, would die, become an unheard echo in the vast unending silence of eternity.

The priest wanted a legal guarantee of Adrien's guilt when what she had to do was beyond legality. But he had made her think of her grandfather's story about the Commune: The revolution had been defeated, and the army once again ruled a sullen Paris. Tens of thousands of revolutionaries were being summarily executed. Near Père-Lachaise an officer stood over a pile of sixty or seventy corpses, Parisians who had just been shot as communards. With a contemptuous gesture at the bodies, the officer sneered, "I'll bet there aren't more than four or five innocent ones in the whole pile."

But trial or no trial, Adrien was not innocent. What she had to do was not an act of vengeance or even of justice: it was an elementary act of self-defense. Patrice's words last night: "One betrayal is merely a tragedy; one or two more and it will be a farce." He had given her a chance to step out and she knew she would do what he asked.

Danielle and the priest walked through the torpid streets. They sought the shade of chestnut trees, which stood at uniform distances like motionless sentinels. The priest's high black shoes squeaked at each step and the metal clips on his heels made sharply articulated clicks against the sidewalk. He kept talking with all the persuasiveness he could command. Danielle answered abruptly or not at all.

They crossed the noncommittal Seine, its metallic green waters sparkling in the sun. Down below on the quai, stretched inert like slabs of toast on a grill, lay a group of Bikini-clad sun bathers. Some boys were swimming off shore. Their cries seemed distant.

Danielle and the priest turned into a narrow street near the Invalides. Wooden shutters formed an even-rowed pattern on the walls of the time-worn buildings. The priest pleaded with Danielle. The street was neutral. He gesticulated, his emotion in the movement of his shoulders and arms. The ancient walls were indifferent. Danielle stopped before a building at the end of the street. They stood in front of a huge oak door, a door before which people had stood for two hundred years and more. It too was indifferent—as always.

"Is this it?"

"Yes."

The priest's shoulders heaved as though he were trying to put the weight of his body behind his words. "Danielle, for the last time—"

"We've been over it already. You can't go to the police. The Germans would kill me. I gave you a choice. You can leave now and he will die anyway—but without the final comforts of religion."

His face worked. Then he lifted his arms hopelessly. "I have no choice."

"Neither have I," Danielle said bitterly. "Remember, I have your word that you will simply perform your office and not interfere."

She preceded him up the stairs. Five flights. Up and around in the dark. On the fifth-floor landing Danielle paused, out of breath. The priest was breathing heavily too. They waited. Only the whispering sound of their lungs pulling in air and the gray filtered light from the small square of glass roof above the sixth floor. A flicker of light crossed the priest's bald head, and Danielle saw beads of sweat shining on his forehead. He took out a handkerchief and mopped himself. Danielle felt a sudden flood of gratitude. She was glad she was not alone.

"Thank you," she whispered.

He stared at her, the distress on his face mixed with surprise. Then she pressed the door bell. It did not ring. She remembered that there was no electricity in the entire city and knocked on the door. Silence. She hoped he would not be home. An instant later the sound of footsteps up to the door.

"Who is it?"

"Danielle."

The door swung open. A broad smile lighted Adrien's face. His hair was tousled; the collar of his white shirt was open, exposing his bronzed, hairless chest; he was very handsome.

"Late as usual, Danielle darling. You'll be late to your own funeral —I hope."

His face was dark and glowing from the sun. Danielle stepped over the portal. Just as he saw the priest she said, "I've brought someone with me, a friend."

"Fine," Adrien said quickly. "Come right in."

Danielle saw disappointment shadow his smile. When they were in the salon she saw he was not so gay, and she was pleased. Although the wooden shutters of the two casement windows were closed against the sun, the air in the long oblong room was stifling. Nevertheless Danielle shut the windows.

"Make yourself at home," Adrien said ironically. He looked at the priest, who was very grave, and gestured toward an armchair. "*Mon père.*"

The three of them sat down very formally. It was like the beginning of an awkward social visit. The priest sat on the edge of his chair; Danielle sat stiffly in hers; Adrien took out a cigarette, tapped it, then put it aside.

"Well," he said, "this seems to be a matter of some moment."

"It is," Danielle said, her voice strangely pitched and alive. "Why didn't you tell us you were arrested and released?"

The irony went out of Adrien's expression, which closed down over his face like a shutter across a window. It was impossible to tell what was behind it. Danielle's eyes did not waver from his face. This was no longer the man she had known.

"It's not true," he said.

"I suppose it's not true either that two men were arrested by the Gestapo yesterday afternoon in front of the metro La Motte-Piquet?"

"I don't understand why—"

"I know. You don't understand why this should concern you. It's funny that you're the only one who hasn't heard about it."

Danielle sensed that behind the curtain of frozen gravity Adrien had cast over his face he was thinking, thinking.

"Why should I have heard about it? I haven't seen anyone for two or three days."

"You saw Dunan yesterday morning."

At this the curtain dropped just below Adrien's eyes, which widened automatically, as if Danielle's words had pried them apart. The flash of intelligence. No need for the mind to turn and twist now.

"I haven't seen Dunan for four or five days. All we have to do is ask him."

"Dunan was one of the men arrested yesterday afternoon."

"No!"

"Anyway we don't have to ask him. He told us before he was arrested."

Danielle could see the panic gathering in Adrien's eyes. His face was frozen; only his eyes were alive.

"Adrien, why weren't you at La Motte-Piquet yesterday? You were supposed to be there."

Adrien stammered but did not manage to get anything said.

"You knew they would be arrested," Danielle said sadly.

Adrien looked at the priest and at Danielle, back and forth rapidly.

"It's not true," he protested. "How can I begin to deny anything so ridiculous!"

"You don't have to bother. You're not on trial. You've already been judged."

The priest, his hands folded on his lap, looked at Danielle, opened his mouth, then closed it again without saying anything. Hers is the power, he thought, and mine the compassion.

"What do you mean?" Adrien asked.

"We can't let the same thing happen again. There's only one way to be sure, not two."

Danielle took the revolver out of her bag and pointed it at Adrien. It felt like a toy pistol. A halfhearted smile made a halfhearted attempt to spread over Adrien's face, then faded.

"You can't mean it, Danielle. Why is the priest here?"

"Because I know your convictions and I wanted to do at least that much."

A sound came from Adrien's throat that was meant to be a laugh.

He could not quite manage the sneer and looked uncertainly at Danielle and the priest.

"*Mon père*, you're not going to stand by and let this happen. The crime will be on your soul too."

Adrien jumped out of his chair excitedly. Danielle rose nervously at the same time, pointing her revolver at him. The priest got up too.

"Don't try anything," Danielle said.

"Help me!" Adrien begged the priest. "Help me!"

"That's why I'm here," the priest said. He spoke with an effort. "You must resign yourself—"

"But she has no right to do this."

"It's not a matter of right, my son. She has the power to do it. There is nothing for you to do but resign yourself and appeal to a higher justice than that of man."

Adrien looked desperately about the room. The revolver was pointed steadily at him. Danielle was between him and the door. The windows and shutters were closed. Anyway they were on the fifth floor.

"We are all of us in a painful passage to our true life," the priest was saying, and it was as much the voice as the words that Adrien listened to. "Man's social justice is imperfect, barbaric. Men are not fit to judge each other, but, alas, they must. You have been judged, my son, in a land that is now but a waste of ignorance, where the spirit is dry and desolate and there is no pity but only hate and vexation. If it is vain to appeal for mercy and kindness in this poor savage world of men, there still is time to appeal to the judgment of eternity. Put yourself in the hands of God, Adrien, my son; put yourself in the hands of God, my child. He will not forsake thee."

The priest's voice was rich and it chanted, the accents rising and falling like the bittersweet notes of an ineffably sad song. It had a narcotic power, like the music of an incantation, and all the sweetness and compassion of infinite understanding seemed to be carried in its tone and rhythm. Suddenly Danielle felt that the priest was transformed. He was more than that intense man in a black cassock wearing squeaky shoes, an incarnation of something beyond this dim room where the three of them were playing out their grim little comedy. Danielle forced herself to resist the effect of the priest's words. These are the platitudes, she thought, that every prison chaplain in France has used with every condemned man since Christendom cared for the souls of the condemned, and who was more subject to such illusions than a condemned man, unless it was the priest himself? But Adrien fell under the spell and dropped to his knees in front of the priest with his hands clasped before him.

"The justice of God is a higher, an absolute justice," the priest intoned. "In the justice of man love is absent. But the justice of God *is* love. Give yourself up to love, my son. Give yourself up to God. Whatever your crimes may have been there is room in the all-encompassing love of God for mercy."

In the dim light of the shuttered room the priest spoke on, the voice soaring, the spirit singing, and all the while Adrien knelt before the priest, hands clasped, head bent, submissive, repentant, and Danielle stood in a far corner of the room, the revolver in her hand. The ritual words of the priest rang in the depths of cathedral silence, and the insulated room was plunged in its stillness, containing the voice and the scene. Faintly, through the closed windows, came the chanting cry of a junkman. *"Vieille ferraille, vieilles bouteilles*—old junk, old bottles." The chant faded and again the room was locked away in its silence under the counterpoint of the priest's litany. Then the priest's voice dropped to a murmur, and at last he was silent. In the quiet of the room, Adrien immobile at his feet, the priest made the sign of the cross and signed the cross over him again and again.

It was the moment to shoot. Danielle took two swift steps forward. But the priest was waving his arm above Adrien's crouched figure in the sign of the cross. Adrien was ready to die. It was the moment. But Danielle could not crook her finger. Not when he was on his knees with his back turned in a moment approaching beatitude. Her sensibility tricked her, telling her it would be cruel. It would have been cruel only to the moment; to wait was cruel to Adrien.

Then the moment passed; Adrien turned. It was too late. The priest's hand dropped; his eyes were closed, his head bowed. Adrien started to speak. She could not shoot him before he had his say. She stood with the gun in her hand, watching him closely, delaying, delaying to the very end. A look of terror took shape and came alive in Adrien's eyes. The oppressive silence. Finally his choked voice.

"You won't, Danielle. I didn't want to do it. They forced me. I won't do it again. I swear I won't."

He came toward her on his knees, his head and eyes up, the terror in his face.

Danielle made a tortured movement.

"Adrien, for the love of God! Don't die the way you've lived."

He got up on his feet slowly but his back was hunched like an old man's.

The priest turned away. Adrien came forward with halting steps.

"Stop! Don't come any closer!"

He stopped in mid-movement, paralyzed. They stared at each other, his mouth fallen open, her lips pressed together, both of them frozen in their attitudes like prehistoric beasts.

He seemed to feel she was going to shoot and with a last effort tried to reach her before the gun went off. She saw Adrien gather himself to lunge and that was the signal she was waiting for. She shut her eyes tight and yanked at the trigger. She did not hear the gun go off; she only felt it kick her arm back. Then she opened her eyes and saw Adrien looking at her across a curlicue of blue smoke, his mouth still a bit open but not frightened any more, a startled expression on his face.

I missed, Danielle thought. The bullet went wild.

Adrien seemed to be off balance and awkwardly took a step toward her, his hand coming up automatically as if to take the gun from her. She wondered why he walked like that, shut her eyes and again pulled the trigger. Again the kickback. Her breasts shuddered.

She opened her eyes. Through the smoke she saw Adrien standing stock-still, then slowly, involuntarily, his legs crumbled under him. Suddenly she was aware of the priest. All the while he had been in the line of fire. He was crouched on the floor, the grave expression replaced by one of fright. For Danielle it was as if an official photograph of the priest had been flipped over and an indiscreet one suddenly put in its place. It was incongruous and comic, and Danielle felt she was about to laugh, explode with laughter, really hold her sides with the pain of it because it was so unaccountably funny after all. But she stiffened her whole body, knowing she was on the edge of hysteria.

She felt another kick in her right arm and shoulder and this time heard the explosion. The gun had gone off as she fought against her impulse to laugh or cry, she no longer knew which. Then she heard Adrien's body hit the floor with a soft sound like that of a coat dropping, not much more.

The priest rose to his feet, the lines of his face taut with anguish. He came over to the center of the room where Adrien was lying and looked down at the inert heap.

Now it's over, Danielle thought. He's dead.

For the first time she was aware that the room was overpoweringly hot. She felt faint and trembly.

Just then the body moved. Adrien had fallen face down. He pushed himself around on his back. His white shirt was rumpled; in places it was drenched with sweat. Then Danielle saw the dark stain running down the white linen. It was very red.

Adrien looked up at the priest, and his eyes turned slowly toward Danielle. There was a peculiar look in his eyes, a helpless, puzzled look. The knowledge of his death seemed to be there, but it could have been the shock. He was no longer frightened and he did not seem to feel any pain. He kept looking at Danielle as though he wanted to say something but could not bring himself to say it. There was a question in his eyes and a deep wonder. The priest knelt down and lifted his head. Adrien looked slightly surprised, but the odd look never left his eyes, nor did his eyes leave Danielle's face. Finally, with great effort, he spoke.

"Forgive me, Danielle," he whispered. "Forgive me."

He looked up at her, his eyes wide-open and clear, with the look of a child. Danielle watched him, fascinated and bewildered, thinking, He's gone, he's finished. At that moment he slumped over awkwardly, almost slipping from the priest's arms. The priest gently put his head back on the floor and rose. Then something awful and mysterious happened to Adrien's face. The life went out of it. As Danielle watched, the nose and mouth took on a pinched look, and all the features became more prominent and marked, as if this difference in definition, stony and inhuman, would compensate for the spark that had defined it until now. The color changed too, becoming waxy and transparent. Adrien lay there like a castoff statue that a sculptor had failed to bring to life. He was no longer a person; he was an object.

Danielle knelt down and touched his hand. It was already cool. She touched his arm. It was still warm. She felt dredged, her throat was parched and she was wet through.

They said nothing; there was nothing to say. Danielle looked at the priest, but he looked away from her. He made the sign of the cross over the body and he thought, May God forgive her and may He forgive me too.

"We had better go," he said aloud.

Outside, the light was so bright it hurt their eyes. Nothing had changed. It was the same street with the same ancient walls on which the wooden shutters formed the same geometric pattern. It was reposing. What could have happened that was so important when the quiet dignity of the street remained untouched? Danielle and the priest parted on the corner. It was a silent parting, heavy with reproach.

After he was gone she felt terribly alone. She looked at her watch. Five o'clock. Patrice would be waiting for her. As she hurried toward the metro she thought despairingly that she had become a fanatic. She had killed a man, a man whose body she had once caressed in the gesture of love. Then she was capable of any act—murder, the irrevocable. In her heart she felt that what she had done could not be right, just as earlier she had known in her mind, and still knew, that she had to do it.

Danielle went quickly down the metro steps, holding the white bag against her hip so that it would not beat so hard at her with each step she took.

†

PATRICE looked at his watch. Five-fifteen. What could be keeping her? He lit another cigarette, went to the door of the bar and looked down the street. Nobody. The deserted Rue Montpensier languished in the sun, and the apathy of the street drifted into the bar. When Patrice sat down again at his corner table he puffed nervously at the cigarette. It was early for the apéritif hour, and apart from two elderly men he was the only customer there. From her perch on a stool beside the cash box the *patronne*, an overripe brunette in her early forties, gazed down on Patrice, shaking her head.

"She'll come, she'll come, young man. A little patience."

Patrice smiled wanly. Madame Jeanne was always making allusions to what she imagined were his romantic attachments. She had hinted once with exquisite discretion that he could see her outside the bar with results that would be equally agreeable for both of them. He had been gallant in his evasiveness.

"Patience. That's what you need," Madame Jeanne went on. "If you are patient enough she will come and she will go and she will give her favors to a few others and then she will come back again fresh as a rose. You won't even know what happened, she'll look so sweet and pure—if you're patient."

"It's our fate, Madame Jeanne, if we are patient or not."

"But wouldn't you rather be ignorant and have peace of mind?"

"I'd rather know and be miserable."

"Vanity. Some day you will be wiser and instead of knowledge you will seek ignorance. It is better."

"We don't have to seek ignorance. It's the natural state of man."

"Ah, la la," Madame Jeanne sighed. "My natural state is too often unnaturally disturbed."

She went back to reading the paper spread out on the bar before her. Patrice sipped his apéritif and smoked, smoked and sipped his apéritif, What could be keeping Danielle? He tried not to think about her and observed the two men standing at the bar. Neighborhood artisans, Patrice guessed. They looked like copies of each other, with their sad, drooping mustaches tinged with gray. One of them took a cigarette butt out of a white metal box filled with half-smoked butts. He lit it and took a puff.

"You have a good lunch?" the other asked, shaking saccharin into a black liquid that was called coffee.

"Not bad. A radish, a beet."

They stood there for a while, the one smoking, the other slowly drinking his ersatz coffee. At last the second one put down his empty cup and took out a thousand-franc note.

"Don't you have anything smaller?" Madame Jeanne asked. "There's been a run on small change the last two days."

"I know." He put the bill back in his pocket and took out a smaller one. "Nobody will accept a thousand-franc note any more. You all think the government is going to call them in. Now I ask you, can anyone in his right mind think the government will have time to anything but pack its bags?"

"That's why the people are nervous," Madame Jeanne said.

The man shrugged. "People who have a lot of money are always nervous. Look at us. Are we nervous?"

Madame Jeanne gave him his change. "Why should you be? You have nothing to lose."

"Except our chains."

At the door, the smoker turned around. "Personally," he said, "I'm a man of order. But to all that—" he made a vague gesture—"I prefer anarchy."

When they were gone Madame Jeanne looked at Patrice and shook her head. "I don't know what's gotten into them. It must be the American advance. They talk out loud as if the Germans were already gone. I can't blame them though. You heard what he had for lunch. A radish, a beet. And all the other restrictions. Imagine! Paris, the city of light, without electricity. You saw the latest about the metro. Next it will be the gas and water."

"What about the metro?" Patrice asked.

"It stops running tomorrow."

"For good?"

She smiled. "For good, for bad—it won't last long, if you ask me. They can stop the metro but they can't stop the Americans."

Patrice said nothing. He never said anything in public that might compromise him. It was one of the reasons he had survived.

"You heard about *Je Suis Partout* being banned?"

"No."

She laughed. "It was Laval. He read an allusion to himself in the last issue of the paper and banned it. "Listen. It's right beside the masthead." She folded the paper back to the first page and read, "Napoleon said of Talleyrand, his Minister of Foreign Affairs: 'It's *merde* in a silk stocking.' "

" 'We no longer have the silk stocking.' "

She laughed again, enjoying herself. There was a movement at the door. Madame Jeanne and Patrice turned. It was Danielle.

The drowsy afternoon atmosphere of the bar was suddenly gone. Patrice got up. One look at Danielle was enough. Her face was drawn, the lines about the mouth tight with anguish. It was a tense, haunting face, mobile, without repose, the depths bursting out on the strained surface. Her eyes were an astonishing blue, warm and darkly luminous. Over it all hovered a sensitized animal quality—the soul trembled naked on the lips and in the eyes.

Patrice stared at her with idiotic intensity as she crossed the room. Something seemed to burst and unfold within him. In that instant, seeing her face open and tormented, he grasped with the shock of sudden vision the extent of her resoluteness and the hard core of character that underlay her soft appearance. He also saw something of what the ordeal had done to Danielle and felt close to her, with the warm dark intimacy of a secret uncovered and shared. As he watched her come toward him, her lips tremulous in the oval face, his stomach dipped away and his heart flew out of him. In all the months that she had been working with him he had never seen this part of her, the dark-hued, shadowy depths beneath the sunny surface. He had an odd sensation of quivering excitement and complete paralysis, as though an electric current had sparked him with an intense shock and he was tinglingly alive but unable to move. The certainty that she had killed Adrien acted as an aphrodisiac, sending a perverse pang of sensuality shooting through him. His eyes filmed with desire. He was surprised at the violence of his emotion. His heart pounded. Can I care so much for her? he wondered. He was torn between an impulse to take her in his arms and the question that was formed on his lips; but he said nothing and made no gesture as she sank wearily into a chair, placing her white bag on the table. He sat down opposite her, leaning forward with his fists clenched, waiting for her to speak, still staring stupidly and intently, groping to penetrate the thoughts beneath her silence.

"I made a mess of it," she said.

Patrice frowned. The familiar anxiety was in his eyes. "He isn't dead?"

"Yes. But I did it so badly. It was ugly. You have no idea how ugly it was."

"I know." His relief was visible. "That's how it had to be."

"No. It didn't have to be as bad as that. It was my fault. I was a coward. I put off shooting him until I couldn't put it off any longer."

She would not tell him about the priest. That was her own affair.

"It was bad," she said, "bad. Not like—not like anything. He didn't have a chance. I feel like a murderer."

"It wasn't murder; it was an execution."

"But I was the executioner!"

She could still feel the shock, the vibration of her body and her breasts shuddering at the kickback of the gun when she crooked her finger on the trigger, and she still saw Adrien lying on the floor, stunned out of his terror and repentant, and the cherry-red stain on his white shirt. She could not explain it to anyone. She could not explain it to herself. But she felt the enormity of it. What depressed her was the monstrous simplicity of the act. The pressure of her finger on a bit of metal. It was as simple as that. And Adrien was dead, gone, nothing. Nothing! She tried to think of what "nothing" meant, to visualize it. It was beyond her. She only knew that all his warmth, his memories, his sensations and his laughter, all that was sweet and personal to him, were no more; and it was she who had put an end to it.

"If it were only a question of getting rid of a traitor there would be no problem," she said distractedly. "A traitor is a symbol, a word. You erase it. But *the* traitor is Adrien. He betrayed, yes, but there's so much more to it than that. When you kill him you kill everything—all the good with whatever is bad."

"He was in a position to compromise the entire leadership of the resistance."

"I know. I kept telling myself it was necessary. That didn't make it less horrible."

A pause. The tormented look in her eyes. She looked at his gaunt face, the deep-set brown eyes, sad for her and steady, the jutting forehead and clean line of the jaw. He was there—those two deep lines curving down the sides of his cheeks to the sensitive mouth—and she wanted to let go, weep, put her head on his shoulder and feel his arms tight about her and not think or do anything but just rest there. They looked across the table at each other. In his eyes there was the dark poignancy of his desire and the sadness for her. Danielle looked away. In the silence a fly buzzed noisily over their table, scooped down and hopped with nervous energy about Patrice's empty glass, then buzzed off, leaving a wake of silence. Her black hair was swept back on her head and fell to her shoulders, and the corners of her mouth turned down wistfully. He watched her and thought, I've never really seen her before. I've never really seen her.

"Take the revolver," she said. "It's in my bag. I don't want to touch it again."

He opened the bag under the table, making sure Madame Jeanne was not watching. Then he thrust the revolver into his pocket.

"I'm going to get rid of the bag, too," she said.

"It's very handsome."

"That's not important."

"You ought to have a cognac. It will do you good."

He ordered the drink, and Madame Jeanne brought it over.

"It's real cognac," she announced. "Maybe it's not VSOP or the same as the cognac before the war, but it's real, not like the eau de cologne I usually serve. It's for my special customers."

She smiled at Patrice and poured with a sure hand, stopping when another drop would have cascaded over the brink of the glass. Danielle took a sip, cupped the glass to warm the cognac with her palm, then drank the raw liquor in two quick gulps. It burned her throat, and its heat spread through her body and limbs. Her voice was low when she spoke. "I once loved him."

His surprise could not have been greater if she had slapped him. There was a great hollow in his stomach and the nausea rose in his throat. "You should have told me last night. I would have done the impossible to have made other arrangements."

Once the words had fallen, like lead on the weightless air, he realized the idiocy of his remark. Her remorse was bad enough without his re-proaches and idle words about "other arrangements" when both of them knew nothing else could have been safely done. She did not reply, simply gazed at him, the blue depths of her eyes feather soft and plead-ing. He made an effort to tear himself away from the sick feeling, as though it were a physical object from which he could be separated.

"I'm sorry," he said.

The fine line of her lips shaped her silent, melancholy answer. He simmered in his misery. The pain flared up, licked at the edges and recesses of his consciousness. She had been Adrien's mistress, and he had ordered her to execute him. How beautifully things work out, he thought bitterly, when you don't plan them. How could she have gone to bed with a man like Adrien? He closed his eyes to shut out the images he did not want to see and when he opened them he looked away from her. It occurred to him suddenly that he was jealous. It seemed incredible. Jealous because of what had happened probably before he had ever met Danielle, over a man already dead, killed by her own hand? No. He searched himself for the symptoms as a man after a bad fall might feel the parts of his body for broken bones. He could not deny his morbid thoughts and wretchedness. He had never suspected he felt so deeply about her, but he knew now that if ever there were a beginning between them there would never be an end.

"Patrice, what are you thinking?" she asked.

"Nothing."

"You look so . . . sad."

He forced a smile. "It will pass."

He was glad she had told him about Adrien and herself, but wished she had not. He also felt sad and happy at once, but more sad than happy.

"It's a long time," she said, hesitantly, "a very long time since I've been with him."

"Don't think of it any more," he said. "It will be better if you don't give it another thought."

"You don't think now I did wrong today, do you?"

"Of course not."

He thought, She is trying to erase the past with a confession and have me modify her sense of guilt with a word of comfort, and she doesn't even realize that not one woman in a thousand would be capable of doing what she did.

He reached across the table and took her hand. "Promise me one thing. Don't think any more of Adrien or what happened today."

"I'll try."

He squeezed her hand. "I think you're magnificent."

Her eyes brimmed with tears. Then he let her hand go and spoke in a brisk, businesslike tone. "You weren't followed?"

"No."

"Good. I have the latest report on the effectives in the Paris region. Tomorrow we'll finish the blueprint. See you in the office at the usual time. Now, take my bicycle. It'll save you some walking. Go home and get some sleep."

"What are you going to do?"

"I have to see Mignot and then the Dutchman about arms."

He paid for the drinks and they left. The bar was just coming to life for the evening, and cigarette smoke was beginning to fog the mirrors around the walls. Outside, the Rue Montpensier was silent and provincial in the dying light, the tops of the buildings jagged against the blushing sky. They went in opposite directions, Danielle leaving by the narrow stairs that led to the Rue de Richelieu between a dilapidated bookshop and the Bar de l'Entr'acte.

Patrice strolled toward the Comédie Française. He remembered Danielle's early attitude, her skepticism of the work and suspicion of him, and how he had fought her as she had fought him. He smiled. In those days they were supposed to form a tight little team. It had been more like a vendetta. Perhaps his skepticism had aroused hers. An admiral's daughter with her looks and clothes in the resistance! No wonder he had been skeptical of her despite the reports on her record. Women of her quality were rare in the resistance, and he could not believe what she was until she had proved it. He knew, however, that his attitude had been based on prejudice: he had extended his violent antimilitarism to Danielle. It was bigotry like bigotry of any other kind, and he was glad he had rid himself of it. He knew now that he loved her and wondered how it could have taken him so long to be aware of it. He had tried to close his eyes to her, but that had not been enough. Danielle had imposed herself; she had happened to him.

Suddenly Patrice realized that for the first time in weeks his thoughts were not concentrated on resistance problems and the insurrection. He thought of what he had done and how he had lived in the past weeks and months and it was as if he were thinking of a stranger. An hour ago the resistance defined the boundaries of his universe. Now there was Danielle. He knew that with the liberation close by his clandestine life would soon come to an end and he would have to pick up the fragments of his prewar existence. It was strange to think of returning to the pleasant uneventfulness of teaching philosophy. There would be Danielle, too. He thought then for the first time: Does she love me? His heart sank and the pain was back in it as he thought of her with Adrien. It passed. He recalled her face and the various talks they had had; he reconstructed how she had come around and how more recently they had worked together; and he was sure and uncertain and sure again that he would win her.

When he passed the theater and came out on the square he felt better than he ever remembered feeling. The evening air smelled good. It smells of Paris, he thought, and felt happy just to be alive.

†

PATRICE crossed the Place du Théâtre-Français. At his right the Avenue de l'Opéra stretched broad and stately up to the columns of the opera house and the monstrous green dome that crowned it. Across the square in front of the Café de la Régence, a haunt of actors and chess fanatics, Mignot and Gaudin were waiting for him. Standing together, they looked more like a seedy vaudeville team than like conspirators. Mignot was short and wiry, Gaudin tall and thick-set; they had good honest faces. Patrice smiled as he saw them. Who would believe, he thought, that the established order could be overturned by men like these? They were the undistinguished and undistinguishable people. No thunder of trumpets announced their passage, no lightning flashes of revolt flared about their heads. Nobody would have looked at them twice as they passed. But they were the soul of the resistance, the "terrorists" daily castigated by the German and Vichy press. That, Patrice decided, with some change in clothes, was what the sans-culottes in '89 and the communards in '71 must have looked like before they stormed the Bastille and took the Tuileries. Patrice loved them. Not as a brother or a friend; they were neither and much more. Sharing a common dream, they had lived at Patrice's side through a common nightmare. They saw Patrice as he approached.

"*Salut.*"

"We just got here too."

They chose a place on the terrace under the shallow arcade surrounded by gossiping groups of actors from the Comédie Française across the street, hangers-on and passers-by.

"Before we talk let's drink," Mignot said. "I'm so thirsty I could even drink water. *Garçon*!"

His rasping voice had the explosive, grating sound of a bag of nuts dropped from the seventh floor. He was a comic, a runt, a *titi* from the Parisian faubourgs. He had a wide mouth usually spread wider by a good-natured grin that uncovered uneven, yellow teeth. His nose was broad and flat, his eyes clever. While his body was squashed down, his face was aggressive in a Puckish, droll way; it was likable in its homeliness. He had a restless tongue and a violent sense of the ridiculous. As always, a cigarette butt with its blackened end unlighted dangled from the corner of his lips.

"What have you got that's good?" Mignot asked the waiter.

"Nothing."

"Nothing!"

Mignot looked quizzically at the waiter, an elderly man in a white jacket with a ruddy face and sparse gray hair.

"I'd take nothing," Mignot said, "but I'm thirsty."

The waiter shrugged. "I can give you tea if you order tea, but it won't be tea. It looks like tea, it smells like tea, but it doesn't taste like tea. Our tea is some kind of grass. So is everybody else's. If you like tea, don't order it."

"That's clear enough," said Patrice.

"Clarity is my strong point," the waiter said.

"I never drink tea anyway," said Mignot. "Do I look like a man who drinks tea?"

"No," said the waiter. "But I've been in the business for thirty years and I still can't tell what a customer wants when he sits down. Nobody can. Personally I like tea, and it makes me very unhappy."

"How's the beer?" Mignot asked.

"Order it at your own risk."

"White wine."

"A good choice."

"Beer," Patrice said.

The waiter turned toward Gaudin. Gaudin was a heavily built man in his early forties with the sour and harassed look of a man embittered by a lifetime of effort and failure. His nose dominated his face; it was heavy and despondent.

"Mineral water," he said.

"Mineral water," Mignot muttered. "Do you have a *chaude pisse* or are you a *pisse-froid*?"

"What kind?" the waiter asked.

"Anything but Vichy," Mignot said quickly. "It's flat and as old as a marshal of France."

"Your jokes are old and flat too," said Gaudin, adding, as if it were an afterthought, "like the breasts of your little friend." Then to the waiter, "Perrier."

"No Perrier. Badoit."

"Good."

The perfume of the late Paris afternoon, with its idle insouciance, was about them. The city sprawled gray and warm in the powder-blue light. Office and shop workers were hurrying home to their meager dinners, their joys, regrets and dreams. Without automobiles, Paris was like a town in the depths of the provinces. Pretty girls cycled by and Mignot watched the passing show with delight.

"Are they any closer?" Gaudin asked.

"Closer than yesterday," said Patrice.

"How much longer do you think it will be?"

Patrice shrugged. "The only thing that's sure is that we'll be in the streets before they get here. Openly."

"I made a small bet," Mignot said. "If they don't get here by Sunday I lose. I should have made it September first instead of August twentieth."

"You might as well pay off now," Gaudin said sourly. "First they crawl, then they fly. I would have bet a week or two ago that they wouldn't get here before Christmas."

"Whenever it is we've got to be ready," Patrice said. "You're probably our last hope for arms, Mignot. The Americans and British have refused to parachute any, and though I'll be seeing the Dutchman, I don't think he'll come through. That leaves you. Did you check the garage?"

Mignot was a mechanic. He worked in a garage occupied by the Germans in one of the obscure streets at the foot of Montmartre. The garage was jammed with Wehrmacht vehicles. Loaded on the back of one truck was a stack of arms—machine guns, rifles, grenades.

"I checked," Mignot said. "It looks good."

He lit the cigarette butt that hung from the corner of his mouth. His small, mottled-green eyes were shrewd as he puffed the butt to life, then let it die while he spoke, feeling it bob up and down with the movement of his lips.

"We can't do anything during the day, of course. Too many people around. But at night it's different. By ten o'clock the place is shut up tight. There's a guard on duty, but we don't have to worry about him after eleven. He's got a babe on the top floor of the building—one of the servants in the joint up there under the roof. The way she's stacked she'd do better swinging her can along the Boulevard Sebastopol. A factory job, but the latest model."

He held his gnarled, stubby hands a foot in front of his chest, his palms toward him and his fingers spread and cupped in a vain and astounded gesture of measurement.

"They stand up like two soldiers first class for a general. I still can't believe they're real. Anyway, the Fritz is up there with her and them by eleven. The garage is locked, but there's a simple way of getting in."

"Well, what is it?" Gaudin asked.

"The concierge's loge. It goes right into the garage."

"How do we get into the concierge's loge?"

"Simple. I knock on the door and say I forgot my tools. I have a job to do outside the garage early the next morning and I want to get them."

"Will she open up?"

"We're like that." Mignot thrust out his right hand, the index finger and thumb forming a circle. "I charmed her, the old cow."

"Are you covered?" Patrice asked.

"Like a wolf in sheep's clothing."

"Good. Three men ought to be enough to do it. I'll arrange for the false papers. It will be after curfew. That means we'll be members of the *Milice* for the night." He stopped abruptly.

Gaudin had the same thought at the same moment. "And the car?" he asked. "Where are we going to get a car?"

Their movement, which was in liaison with other resistance organizations, worked with an efficiency that had increased astonishingly since the first amateurish beginnings at underground activity years before. Things that in the early days had posed baffling problems were now dispatched like routine chores. They could forge any of the multitude of official papers needed to circulate in Paris or the provinces or to cross the line of demarcation between occupied and what was once unoccupied France. They had lines running into the agencies of local

Paris government and into some of the German military offices. They could send and receive messages to and from London, and when the moon was right they could get men out of the country and into England by airplane. But they had no money and they had no car. It was stupid. They looked at each other, frustrated.

"If we just stole a car that was parked in the street?" said Mignot, guessing what the others were thinking.

"We can't do that," said Patrice. "We're amateurs at it and we'd probably get caught. It would be idiotic to be arrested for anything so banal as common thievery."

"But without a car we can't do a thing," said Mignot.

"Maybe we can borrow a car," Gaudin suggested.

"And get the owner deported or shot if the car is spotted?" Patrice said.

"We're taking a small chance too," Gaudin replied sullenly.

"Anyway, we don't know anybody who would lend us a car."

They looked glum; then Mignot's face suddenly brightened.

"I just remembered an old pal. *Pierrot-le-pourri,* we used to call him." Mignot laughed. "What a sonofabitch that sonofabitch is. But we'll get a car out of him."

"How?" Gaudin asked impatiently.

"He's a car specialist. Once asked me to work for him. That was after he got back from Marseille and did a little time, too. We were kids together in the nineteenth."

"Where does that get us?" Patrice asked.

"About three weeks ago I ran into him near the garage. I'm in my working clothes, filthy; just did a grease job. Him, he's dressed like God, the Father. He looks me up and down and says, 'Still working for a living, eh?' 'Me,' I says, 'I don't change. And you?' Suddenly he lets the façade drop and he says, 'Listen, I got troubles. You look to me just jerk enough to be a terrorist. Right?' This time *I* ring up the façade. 'Good,' he says. 'I get it. Maybe we can make a deal. Trouble is that in the last four years I made too much money.' I look at him. 'For four years the Boches are a good investment,' I says, 'and you're a wise guy. Me, I'm a jerk because I'm in the resistance. Well, what are *you* worrying about?' 'Don't you read the papers?' he says. 'The Boches are washed up. I want to buy insurance and I'll pay the high price. Only, when the new government starts to ask me for explanations you tell them I helped the resistance.' So I says, 'We don't need anything.' And he says, 'If you do you can always find me at the *Boeuf qui boite* in the Rue Douai.' "

Gaudin was suspicious. "Suppose he made his proposition to sell you to the Gestapo if you fell for it?"

"Not a chance. I've known Pierrot since I was a kid. It's not his kind of work. He's a crook, but he's honest. We can trust him up to there." Mignot tapped his shoulder to show that Pierrot could be trusted up to the hilt.

"Sounds all right to me," Patrice said. "Are you with us, Gaudin?"

"If it's good enough for you it's good enough for me."

"Tell him we'll give him protection," Patrice said to Mignot. "But only if we get the car fast. We must have it tomorrow night."

Mignot nodded. They drank up and paid.

"The arrest yesterday," Patrice said. "It was settled this afternoon. Adrien is dead."

"Good," said Gaudin. "He was a bastard."

"And Danielle?" Mignot asked. "She's all right?"

"She's all right."

"Ah, there's a girl," Mignot said. "I knew she would do it." Lost in admiration, he added, "And what a smile! What eyes!"

Gaudin looked more melancholy than ever. He was thinking of his wife. Suzanne and her big black eyes, her warm, generous body, her breasts and buttocks and the smell of her hair on the pillow beside him. His Suzanne with whom he had not lived for a month now and whom he had been able to see only once or twice in that time, furtively, on street corners and in cafés. He had always loved her, he told himself, despite their differences. This summer separation—the first in their fifteen years of marriage—had awakened his passion, so long lost.

"Try to fix it up with Pierrot tonight," Patrice said to Mignot. "I've had a rough day. I'm going to see the Dutchman and then get to bed."

"I'm having dinner with my wife," said Gaudin.

"Just see that you get home before curfew," Patrice said casually. "No point in getting picked up by a German patrol for being out too late and shot in a couple of days as a hostage."

"We can get shot for better reasons than that," said Mignot.

"Well, see that you don't."

"*Oui, mon général.*"

They shook hands all around, and Patrice walked briskly toward the metro.

"A swell guy even if he is a professor," said Mignot, his stub of cigarette pasted to the corner of his lip. "And a tough customer."

Gaudin nodded absent-mindedly. He was thinking of Suzanne.

†

TWENTY minutes later Gaudin was waiting for Suzanne in a crowded and noisy bistro in the Rue Monsieur le Prince. The clatter of dishes echoed through the small room and died under the sound of a dozen shrill conversations. It was hot. Gaudin sat in the back of the room at a table covered like the others with a red-and-white checkered cloth. His elongated nose drooped like a flag on a windless day, and in the candlelight and racket he looked more despondent than ever. He was worried. How will Suzanne react? he kept asking himself. Suppose she refuses. What then? His nose drooped more and more with his reflections.

He wondered why, after such a happy start, their marriage had become so aimless, worn so thin and then suddenly fallen apart. It was a mystery to him. He only knew that what they had once had together they had no longer, and that changed everything. The emotion was dried up, he thought sadly. Yet, like a parched traveler who had no other recourse and in whom hope would not die, he would make still another effort to get water out of the dry well. Gaudin blinked his small brown eyes and felt the throb in his head; his blood pressure was always at its worst when he had to deal with Suzanne. Since they had agreed to go their separate ways the strain between them had magically disappeared and the jagged edges of discord had smoothed over. He had peace, but it was empty; yet the vacuum of calm was a relief. Life together had for so long verged on the unbearable that he was almost as pleased as he was resigned to give her the freedom she demanded. Their conflicts had eroded his feelings and, emotionally exhausted, he had wanted peace more than he had wanted her.

If they continued to live together, it was partly out of convenience and habit, partly because he did not, after all, want to give her up entirely; despite everything, a residue of affection remained. For a while they lived a pleasant paradox: their marriage, by mutual agreement, was finished, but not since their courtship had they lived in such easy harmony; the farther their lives went off in different directions the better they got along in their everyday dealings; the more they treated each other like strangers the friendlier they became. The paradox went further: since they had stopped sharing the same bed they had reached a degree of intimacy they had never before known. It was the intimacy of two people who had lived together for fifteen years and regulated all their long-standing quarrels; now that their passion was spent and their interests no longer clashed they were kind and honest with each other. Nevertheless their relations were cool, and Gaudin felt it keenly. Like two Englishmen meeting in a foreign land they felt intimate—at a distance. It's no life, Gaudin said to himself, thinking of what they had had before.

Vaguely Gaudin realized it was the resistance, in supplying him with a new focus for his life, that had given him the strength to break with Suzanne; and it was the resistance, or rather its imminent end, that was bringing him back to her. When he had been forced to hide from the Gestapo and had found himself suddenly alone her loss afflicted him and he suffered. At times it was as though he had dropped into a void and nothing had any meaning, or as though a door had closed, locking him in the dark. At other times his suffering took a physical form and it was like a gnawing hunger that became constantly more acute and unbearable. He felt that he had always loved Suzanne and could not live without her. He forgot all the troubles they had had, his fits of temper, her weeping jags, the days of silence weighted by his sullenness and her misery. The bad days and years evaporated in the light of a few ecstatic moments. As the realization came to him that soon the Germans would be chased from Paris and the resistance would come to an end, he felt with a sinking of the heart that he would be left with nothing if he no longer had Suzanne. And he wanted her now as never before. But as he leaned on the table with the red-and-white checkered cloth he found no words to express his feelings. His nerves were stretched as taut as the strings across the belly of a violin, and he thought, If only she makes it easy for me to speak to her.

Looking toward the door, he saw her as she entered the restaurant. The room was abruptly transformed and brightened by her presence, and he rose with a tentative smile on his lips. He was so absorbed he did not notice that men and women at different tables paused for a moment and stared at Suzanne. People always stared when she appeared. The women did so with cold appraising hostility, stripping back the qualities to bare the faults; the men stared at her differently. She was a handsome, coarse-fibered woman, and her strange, sensual face was set off with cool and startling effect by the upswept black hair that was plaited and coiled on the top of her head. Suzanne's face tended toward roundness, the nose was small but rather broad, which accentuated her sensuality. Her features were prominent, open and regular, the cheekbones high and pronounced, the wide mouth shaped by full lips. Because she was nearsighted she squinted and that gave her an intent, concentrated look. It was the fault that women criticized and men found irresistible. With her dark eyes narrowed and peering about, she appeared always to be seeking someone, something, and the shadow of desire seemed to hover on her face.

After searching around the dimly lit room for a moment she saw Gaudin standing at his table and started toward him, her heavy, tapering thighs outlined at each step against her thin skirt. Her firm, full body fitted snugly in a low-cut blue and white cotton dress that was nipped in at the waist below the swell of her breasts and molded her slightly domed stomach. When she reached Gaudin she offered him her cheek, and as he kissed her she pursed her lips at the empty air over his shoulder in the simulacrum of an embrace. They sat beside each other along the wall.

"When will this idiocy be over?" she sighed as she settled down. "I'm so tired of it all."

Her voice was throaty and warm, with full resonances, but she spoke petulantly. She was nervous, overwrought. All day long she had tried to decide whether to tell Gaudin she was going to leave him and now, without having made up her mind, she felt she would say nothing, not even hint at it to prepare him. She shrank from a scene, pitied and blamed him at once. He was a hindrance, but she knew he would suffer, and while she tried to justify herself, confusedly, under the surface of her thoughts, she felt she was doing wrong. It irritated her. She could not face him and looked away. At her attitude Gaudin's smile snuffed out.

"It will be finished very soon," he said.

He sounded apologetic, as though the war and occupation and all its inconveniences and privations were his fault and he had to answer for it to her. His nose dipped at an even more acute angle. What he feared happened: she cut his courage; he did not know how to tell her he loved her and wanted her back as they had been. The unshaped words caught in his throat, would not come to his lips.

"But then if it will be over so soon . . ." Her musky voice fluttered and she did not finish what she started to say. Suddenly her black eyes were moist. "I'm afraid," she said.

"Afraid?" The lines of his face relaxed almost to a smile. "There's nothing to be afraid of."

"I'm afraid," she repeated.

How could she expect him to understand? She glanced up at him quickly and their eyes held. Her eyes were dark and liquid, and he saw them as they had been one New Year's Eve that had remained with him down the years. They had come home well after midnight, just a little drunk from the champagne. He remembered the warmth of the room after the windswept streets and the coziness of being together after the noise and crowds, the music and gaiety. They had both been impatient to be alone that night. A cold white moon shone through the window, and by its light Gaudin had watched her eyes as though he were watching the creation of the world. It had been long, an *envoute-ment*, her warm skin smooth against him, satin and silk and alive with the silent communion, the senses seething. Her mouth was slightly open and the sounds that came from her parted lips were not words. He remembered that too; but it was her eyes—docile, then fierce— that he would never forget. All this he recalled in the instant their eyes held, and his face softened with a sweet nostalgia.

Seeing the puppy look come into his small brown eyes and the longing in them, she suddenly grasped what was in his heart. *Ah, no, no, not that*, she said to herself. We're not going to begin again! She turned away, distraught, wondering what he would do if he knew she was the mistress of a German and what Klaus would say if he knew her husband was a terrorist. It was all too much for her. Gaudin's humility made her feel heartless and cruel. The tangle of deceit in which she was twisted, with neither the guile nor the honesty to work herself free, oppressed and humiliated her. She was suddenly angry. She could not have said why.

"Your Americans!" she cried, speaking of the first thing that came to mind in her exasperation. "That's all you hear. As if they were any better than the Germans! And if they get here, *if* they get here, will anything be settled? Will it be any better than the mess we have now? *Pauvre France*! When I think that we may be ruled by the Americans, by the Americans—"

Her voice rose harshly and in it was all the contempt of her anger and wounded sense of superiority. Gaudin stared at her, too astonished to speak.

"One occupation replaced by another," she muttered. "And we hold our arms out to the young barbarians as if they were our saviors."

"What's the matter with you?" Gaudin finally gasped.

"But they won't get here," she went on, ignoring Gaudin. She was praying out loud. "At the last minute they'll be stopped."

"You must be the last one to think so," he exploded. "I never saw it to fail—" He stopped abruptly, scowling. A waiter was at the table offering them two menus. The man's voice floated cheerfully out of the smoke and chattering noise, and a flurry of laughter rippled over the group at an adjoining table.

"*Monsieur, dame?*" the waiter said.

Gaudin buried his head in the menu. It was beyond the outermost limits of his imagination to conceive that Suzanne meant what she said—Suzanne who was French and his wife and was so little interested in politics or even the war that she never opened a newspaper except to read a movie review or occasionally follow a crime. The conviction that she spoke out of perverseness only increased his fury. Bitterly he recalled her indifference to the horrors and humiliations of the Nazi occupation—the execution of hostages, the deportation of Jews, the Germanization of French life—and her unique concern about material comforts.

After they had ordered and put aside the menus they were silent for a while. Suzanne was sullen. Gaudin frowned and fought to master his anger. The dinner was not turning out at all the way he had hoped; it would be impossible now to speak to Suzanne as he had planned and that made him even angrier. Resentfully he compared her to Danielle. Suzanne was holding up her strange, sensual face to a small mirror, powdering her nose. She tried to give an impression of aloof dignity, but every gesture she made was an effort to camouflage her anguish. As she patted her nose with the powder puff her lips were compressed in a pout and there was a hurt look on her face. The thought that she might lose Klaus would not leave her; sitting there she felt an overpowering helplessness to do anything to save her own happiness, and in a sudden wave of confusion she could not grasp why anything so distant, impersonal and uncontrollable as the war should come between her and the man she loved. She could have wept and she could have screamed. Instead, without a word, without a sound, she sat there and with quick, nervous movements powdered her nose and tried to dominate her panic. Continents separated them. Gaudin writhed with frustration.

"I know one woman," he muttered reproachfully, "who doesn't sit around powdering her nose, saying there's no difference between the Americans and the Nazis."

"If she powdered her nose for a change it might improve her appearance. I've seen your communist women of the resistance."

"This one is an admiral's daughter, not a communist, one of the best-looking women—"

"What does she do? Blow up trains?"

In a cold, even voice Gaudin said, "Just a few hours ago she killed a man, a traitor." He blurted out what he knew about the plan to execute Adrien and how it was done, painting Danielle with heightened colors, to impress Suzanne.

Suzanne refused to be impressed. She shrugged her shoulders. "I still think it wouldn't do any harm if she powdered her nose."

Gaudin gritted his teeth and did not reply. They ate a thin soup and a tasteless vegetable diced with pitiful fragments of meat. Throughout the meal Gaudin tried to regain his composure. Few things enraged him so much as Suzanne's contemptuous references toward the resistance. It was the element of truth in her attitude that rasped his nerves. The weakness of the movement and the suspicion that there was something absurd as well as magnificent in pitting such feeble means against the German army made him sensitive to ridicule. It had always been a struggle for him to dominate his vanity, and often he had to tell himself fiercely that he would rather risk being ridiculous than stand by passively like most people and do nothing. Suzanne was sorry now that she had upset Gaudin; she had a faculty for doing or saying the wrong thing and regretting it once it was too late.

Their talk as they ate was desultory and trivial. Toward the end of the meal she asked about his printing plant. It was a small atelier, which he had closed after the Normandy landing in June to work full time for the resistance. He told her he would reopen the atelier as soon as the Germans were cleared out of Paris. At his words the thought of losing Klaus came back sharply and painfully to Suzanne. Her stomach seemed to drop away.

"What will happen to the Germans when the Americans get here?" she asked, trying to assume a casual tone.

"First there'll be an insurrection," he said with satisfaction. Enthusiastically he described the preparations for the uprising and the fighting mood of the resistance. Like most of the rank and file he knew little or nothing about the struggle in the leadership over the insurrection and said that every man and every group was ready and impatient for the signal to take arms in hand and rush into the streets to take Paris from the Germans. "If there's anything left of the Germans when *we're* through with them . . ."

She did not hear the rest of what he said and finished her meal in silence, scarcely eating another bite. All she could think of was that she had to see Klaus. They had to do something. It would be suicide to remain in Paris, to wait while the resistance and the Americans closed in on them. They would run away, go somewhere else, anywhere, but they had to leave Paris.

"Suzanne!"

He tried to reach over to her across the chasm, his voice vibrant. She was so far away, not at all in the room, not at all beside him. The way she looked at him. . . . They might be strangers. . . .

"Yes?" she said.

"Nothing."

It would have to wait for another time, perhaps the next time. He sighed. His round, sad face wore a melancholy, beaten expression. He looked at her with his puppy look and she saw nothing for thinking of Klaus, feeling cornered and frantic.

When they parted he pecked at the cheek she distractedly offered him, and the soft, cool sensation of her was on his lips as he left, dejected and alone.

†

THE Dutchman was late. Sitting on the terrace of the Mahieu opposite the Luxembourg Gardens, Patrice wondered if he ought to wait. In principle, no; it was dangerous. Experts in the art of conspiracy, the communists never waited a minute beyond the fixed hour of a meeting. Everybody did not have their discipline. Practically, Patrice had to know if the Dutchman could procure arms for him; and there was the code Lefort had handed him earlier that afternoon to pass on. If he missed the Dutchman now it would take him two days, maybe three, to find him again. The inconveniences of clandestinity: no telephones, no addresses and nothing but false names. He would wait.

As the minutes went by Patrice's impatience turned to anger. The Dutchman had the sense of responsibility of a gnat; he was never quite on time. Patrice drank the rest of his beer. In addition to the bad taste, it was warm. He scanned the square and its approaches, searching for the familiar figure of the tardy Dutchman. The square and the Luxembourg and the streets all around were touched by the soft sweet magic of the Paris evening. The light was clean, the way it is after the sun has set, and the air was only beginning to mist with the first delicate blue hues of twilight; two or three pink-tipped clouds hung suspended against the transparent sky. It was the quiet hour. Patrice sighed. He would never forget one September evening, his first in Paris, when, newly arrived from the north as a dazzled Sorbonne student, he had sat at a Latin Quarter café and watched the gray-blue, rose-tinted dusk settle around the city like a lover's embrace.

After waiting another ten minutes Patrice decided to leave. As he rose, however, he glanced across the square and saw a short fat man standing hesitantly beside the fountain in front of the Luxembourg. It was the Dutchman. He looked directly at Patrice without seeming to see him, then walked in the opposite direction toward Capoulade, the café across the street. Patrice strode toward the Dutchman and was talking angrily when he reached him.

"What's the matter? Don't you even remember where we were to meet?"

Apparently the Dutchman did not hear, for he kept on walking. Patrice grabbed his arm and swung him around. There was an intense look on the man's face, and his eyes worked as though he were trying to express something he could not put in words. Patrice dropped his arm.

"I beg your pardon," he said quite loud. "I thought you were someone else."

He turned to leave. On either side of him appeared two heavy-set, grim-faced men.

"*Pas de blagues*," the man on his right said in a heavy German accent. "No jokes."

For one shining moment of intense lassitude in the fading light of that peaceful square Patrice felt a flood of relief. The ball of fear lodged in his heart evaporated. He was caught and he felt free. In that moment every nerve slackened; the tension was cut and the fear that had constantly inhabited his body like a living thing, and that he had learned to live with as an invalid learns to live with a cancer, disappeared. The worst had happened. He was caught; and the moment was like a deliverance, for now it had happened and was no more to be dreaded. The next instant his torment gripped him again with redoubled intensity. He remembered the code that was in the inside pocket of his jacket.

"You win," Patrice heard himself say.

He tried to manage a smile, but his face felt frozen. The two men pushed him ahead of them toward a black Citroen parked at the curb alongside the Luxembourg. Patrice thought of the prison cell into which he would be thrown, of the interrogations, the torture when he refused to talk, the code in his pocket. . . . The Dutchman kept glancing at Patrice and away from him. He looked miserable. Patrice's mind worked, worked. . . . Once in the car it would be too late. . . .

"Come along," the man on his right said.

"Adrien. It was Adrien," the Dutchman said fiercely. His voice dropped and was plaintive as he added, "I thought if you saw me go toward Capoulade with them behind me you would realize—"

"Shut up!" snapped Patrice.

"Shut it!" the man on his left snarled at the same time.

It was stupid to be caught like this, Patrice thought, on the eve of the insurrection, days away from the end . . . Stupid . . . The evening air was sweet with the fragrance of a life he was walking away from forever. Two girls passed, books under their arms, their thoughtless laughter cascading strangely on the hushed air. They glanced with mischievous eyes at the four solemn men strolling across the square, and as they went by the wake of their gaiety washed abruptly away. Patrice looked beyond the chestnut trees lining the Luxembourg at the tall, endless sky, lofty and free, and his sensation of regret and nostalgia was so keen he stopped momentarily until he was pushed forward again.

They would find the code, he thought. His arrest would not be known until morning . . . No, it was too stupid . . . One chance before he got in the car . . . Two men and the chauffeur . . . One chance . . . As he bent to get in the car . . .

When they stopped at the curb where the car was parked the man on Patrice's right leaned down and opened the back door of the Citroen. At the same time he said to the chauffeur, "Avenue Foch." He pushed Patrice and growled in German, *"Schnell."* The Citroen was low-slung, and Patrice had to bend down to get into it. The man on his right was a full head shorter than he. In one sudden movement Patrice put his hands on the man's shoulders, pulling him forward, and snapped his forehead violently down on the bridge of the man's nose. He heard the sharp articulated sound of the nose cracking like a stick snapping in two and the man's howl of pain. Almost in the same movement he wheeled to his left, bringing up his right knee as he turned. It landed in the other man's stomach, a little high. The man grunted involuntarily as the air went out of him, and Patrice felt the sudden swift rush of hot breath on his cheek. Then he heard the chauffeur grappling frantically to open his door. He saw the door swing open and shoved the man hard against it. The man fell back off balance, his arms flying up, and slapped up against the door, slamming it shut. There was a baffled, pained look in his face as he slipped to the ground, his back and head blocking the door that the chauffeur kept trying to open. Patrice saw him reach awkwardly into his pocket for something and out of the corner of his eye saw the other Gestapo man bent over double with both hands clutching his nose. "Run!" he shouted to the Dutchman; then he broke away and sprinted across the square.

Patrice's long legs worked as fast as he could push them, but he felt he was going very slowly and strained to run faster. All the while he ran his thoughts raced ahead . . . The Luxembourg to the right and behind is a trap . . . If I run in I'll never get out . . . The Rue Soufflot ahead is too wide and straight . . . The Boulevard St. Michel to the left is full of cops and German soldiers . . . Only the Rue Gay-Lussac ahead and to the right . . . Then the first turn to the left . . .

He was halfway across the square when the first shots broke the silence. He heard a bullet zing by his ear with a vicious, terrifying sound of relentless, metallic speed. Then there were more shots, and out of nowhere people appeared, yelling as he flew past, "*À l'assassin! À l'assassin!*" His back felt electric with the bullets whizzing and singing all around him. Instinctively he ducked his head as he ran, and he kept thinking, I'm going to fall, I'm going to fall. But he kept charging ahead. He did not dare zigzag, thinking if he did they would catch him. It was better to risk getting shot. He was at the corner, into the Rue Gay-Lussac. He could hear them running and shouting behind him. His legs rose and fell, fast and faster. He turned the first corner. To the right, to the left, to the right, to the left. There was a greater distance between them now. He drew his breath in deep gasps. Pathetic how he had slowed up. He was at the Sorbonne. To the left into the empty square and to the right down the Rue Champollion. Downhill. Easier. His lungs burned. They were still behind him. How to get away? The metro. Cluny closed. Odéon. He raced across the Boulevard St. Michel into the Rue Racine, running more easily on his second wind. People stared at him as he fled by them, their mouths agape, an idiotic look in their eyes. The pack trailed him with the Gestapo man puffing in the lead and waving his empty revolver.

Patrice turned to the right into the Rue Monsieur le Prince and disappeared from sight. Across the street Gaudin, who had just left Suzanne, saw him and stopped in his tracks, startled. The pack turned the corner, pursuing Patrice, and Gaudin hastily continued on his way. Patrice dashed to the right again into a small street and plunged down a flight of stairs. His legs were heavy and with each step heavier; he gasped painfully in his efforts to breathe. One last bit of speed if it kills me, he thought. Get to the metro opening before they turn the corner and see me. He doubled around to the left, added another burst of speed. Only thirty meters, twenty, ten. He twisted into the metro opening, crouching as he started down the stairs and glancing up to see if they saw him. He thought not, but was uncertain. Hopping down the stairs three at a time, he ripped a metro ticket out of his pocket and thrust it under the controller's face. She punched it without even lifting her eyes to look at him and he hastened down another flight of stairs, then crossed to the far end of the platform near the steps leading to the tracks.

It seemed long as Patrice stood there, alert to the passageways and still trying to catch his breath, but in two or three minutes a train pulled in. It was crowded. He wedged himself beyond the middle door of the last car, feeling the people he pushed against move back. The doors closed slowly, but the train remained in the station. For perhaps a minute it did not move. Patrice tried the door. It was locked. He thought, The Germans have stopped the train, and tried the door again. Impossible. Trapped. A wave of despair swept over him, but his mind remained extraordinarily lucid. When they come around and open the doors, he thought, I'll shout, "Everybody out!" and in the confusion of the crowd on the platform I'll get away. He was trying to figure out where he would run when the train jerked, lurched forward, slowly got under way and rolled past the empty platform.

The danger past, Patrice's tension slackened. He shook violently and was scarcely able to stand, he felt so weak. To support his sagging body he leaned against one of the center poles of the car. His shirt was soaked through with sweat; his face was hot and it throbbed, and sweat coursed down his cheeks. He took out his handkerchief and wiped his face with it. As he looked around he was aware for the first time that a number of people were staring at him. When he wiped his forehead the place where he had struck the German on the nose was sore. He put his handkerchief back in his pocket and looked to the left. Patrice started; his heart leaped out of him; his hand gripped the center pole and he was tense again. Jammed against him was a German soldier. Patrice looked away; he wanted to move to another part of the car but he could not budge. Once again he took out his handkerchief and dabbed it at his face. He stiffened as he heard the soldier's voice in his left ear.

"*Heiss, nicht?*"

The tone was affable.

"Very hot," Patrice replied in German.

The soldier smiled gratefully. Patrice smiled in his turn. He could feel the hostility of the passengers around them and thought, There is nothing to fear; nobody knows.

The German looked like a good-natured Bavarian peasant type. His body was dumpy, his face round and red, and his eyes a pale watery blue. He asked if Patrice could help him and Patrice shrugged his shoulders, pretending he did not understand. The German fished a slip of paper out of his breast pocket and handed it to Patrice. Patrice read it and suppressed his laughter. The German beamed. Patrice chuckled, unable to contain himself. He looked at the icy faces around him.

"Maybe someone here can help this gentleman," he said.

He showed the slip of paper to two men standing beside him. Their faces broke into broad grins. The paper circulated rapidly. By the time the train stopped the hilarity was general. Scrawled on the paper in an untutored hand were the words: *Faites descendre ce con-là à l'Étoile.*

Still weak and shaky, Patrice was smiling as he got off the train and already beginning to feel himself again. He walked toward his refuge, the last in a long series of hide-outs that marked the lonely pattern of his underground existence over the past years. Home is where I lay me down, Patrice thought wearily.

When he arrived the Madam looked at him shrewdly with her bright little black eyes and acted very much the hostess. "What can we offer you tonight?" she asked. "A specialty of the house?"

"A drink and a good night's sleep," Patrice said.

"We can do better than that."

"Some other time."

"It's the amateur competition," the Madam said. "There are too many unfaithful wives in Paris and not enough virgins."

"I didn't know you were a moralist."

"Of course. It's good for business."

She left Patrice for a party of six that was coming through the door, prosperous-looking men with their wives. The women were flushed and looked around with embarrassed curiosity.

Patrice walked into the big room. It was crowded and noisy. The girls were young and they were all naked in different ways. Patrice went to the bar and ordered a cognac. He was joined by a pert little brunette wearing a string of beads. He ordered a cognac for her too, but she changed it to a lemonade, explaining that she never drank anything alcoholic.

"Doesn't this get monotonous?"

"Not as monotonous as being with the same man every night," she said.

"Even the one you want?"

"I don't want any of them. A man isn't worth the money you'd bet on a horse with a broken leg."

"Then you don't like it here."

"It's better than walking the streets. You don't get so tired and there's no overhead."

"Is there any in the streets?"

"Of course. What does a woman do when she takes a walk? She looks in shop windows. If business is good, the money burns your fingers, so you buy something. If business is bad, you have more time to shop, and you buy something to cheer yourself up. At the end of the month nothing is left. In a house you're off the streets and away from temptation. You don't wear out your shoes and kill your feet, and you can put a little aside for a rainy day."

"But the work?"

"Honest and professional," she said, not understanding him. "You want to try me?"

Patrice shook his head.

"Where's your intelligence?" she asked. "That's what I appeal to in a man."

Patrice looked at her from the string of beads down and back again. "With that body?"

She grinned. "If a man doesn't want it, he's not intelligent."

Patrice laughed, completely relaxed from the tension of the day. The girl sipped her lemonade.

"You look intelligent anyway," she said. "What do you think? Will Paris be an open city like Rome?"

"Is that the one everybody is asking?"

"That's all I hear."

"You worried?" Patrice asked.

"Who isn't?"

"Nobody knows what will happen. Maybe Paris will be liberated like Rome, maybe Paris will be another Warsaw."

"Never," she said. "Not another Warsaw."

"Why not?"

"Because everybody loves Paris, even the Boches. You can live anywhere, but it's only in Paris that you breathe. Why should they ruin it?"

"Suppose there's an uprising," Patrice said. "You don't think the Germans will admire the scenery."

She shook her head. "Somebody told me today that the resistance would force the Boches to blow Paris to hell and gone and shoot ten or twenty thousand Parisians. I don't believe it. We're not the Poles. We're too smart."

"I hope you're right," Patrice said.

He wished he could be sure. He thought now that if Paris were to vote on an insurrection, there would be no uprising. Most of the city would vote with Reboussin and the little brunette. They wanted to be liberated the easy way, which was understandable. But Patrice also thought that when the insurrection came the city would go along with the men who led it. He rose to go upstairs to bed.

"Well," the brunette said, thrusting her ripe body at him, "you taking me?"

He disentangled himself gently. "The way I like it you can't buy it."

She shrugged. "You'll never know what you missed."

The Madam led him up the stairs past the erotic frescoes.

"You can have the black room again, after all," she said.

In the corridor a door opened, and before it closed for them to pass Patrice saw two women sewing a French and an American flag.

"I didn't know I was in such a right-thinking establishment," he said. "Patriotism and morality. A fine combination."

"Sooner or later they'll be here," the Madam said. "The least we can do is give them a warm welcome."

"It won't hurt business, either."

"A woman alone has only one *Patrie*," the Madam said. "Money."

In the black room the atmosphere was completely unreal, and Patrice felt as if he were a boy again inhabiting a strange imaginary world and that his underground activity was a game that retarded grownups played with the seriousness of children. The game was a grandiose hide-and-seek, a more subtle and developed version of cops-and-robbers, and those who played it were so serious that if you played it badly they tortured and killed you. Patrice undressed quickly. He thought of Danielle and wanted the morning to come quickly. As soon as his head touched the pillow he was asleep.

†

MIGNOT was eating dinner, a good dinner. He was a little drunk, and *Pierrot-le-pourri* was mellow.

"Another shot of red?" asked Pierrot.

"Another shot of red," said Mignot.

Pierrot poured the wine and Mignot drank it.

"Ah, it's good," Mignot sighed. "It's a fine, delicate wine, a friendly, amiable wine. It has one of those perfumes . . ."

He sniffed in deeply with a hissing sound and made a grand and elegant gesture with his hands, flipping them over and around so that they finished stuck out in front of him, palms up, as if he were holding a large, invisible platter.

"Bouquet." Pierrot corrected him primly as a boy would repeat a lesson recently learned. "Not perfume. Bouquet. Like the odor of a flower, not a mixture of chemicals."

"If you wish, professor," Mignot said grandly. "Ah, it has a bouquet that makes you know why God gave us a nose. I ask you, Pierrot, what is food without wine? And now I will tell you. Love without a kiss. Do I make myself clear?"

"Perfectly. Without a kiss."

Pierrot poured more wine. Mignot held his glass up to the light.

"Look at it. What would we do without wine to push the blood around our bodies?" He turned his hand around and around, spilling a little wine. "It makes the palate happy. And what is happier than a happy palate unless it's—"

"But what is the name of the wine?" Pierrot interrupted.

"Who cares what name it goes by? It's the taste and the character that count. Like men, like you and me. What do I care if your name is Levy or Dupont as long as you're a pal!"

"Who said my name was Levy or Dupont?" Pierrot laughed and Mignot grinned happily.

"After the meat the salad," said Mignot. "And then the cheese and the dessert and the coffee and brandy. We are in France; let us eat and drink and then seek what follows."

Mignot had not eaten a meal like the one Pierrot was offering in years, if ever. It was the first time he had been in one of the better black-market restaurants. The restaurant was little more than a bistro, but it served better food than any of the famous places in the city. The well-known restaurants were too closely watched by the police to disregard the law.

"*Garçon!*" Mignot called.

The waiter came to the table.

"What do you have in the way of a salad?"

"Lettuce. It's a little tired."

"How tired can lettuce get?"

"This is exhausted."

"What else have you got?"

"Nothing."

"*Garçon!*" said Mignot sternly. He paused, then finished weakly, "I'll take the lettuce."

Mignot looked reproachfully across the table at Pierrot. "It's a funny thing," he said.

"What?"

"In all of Paris there is nothing but salad to eat, and this place has absolutely everything—cream, meat, butter, fish, sauces, everything—but it has no salad."

"That's because people come here for what they can't get anywhere else."

"That is understandable," said Mignot. But he looked unconvinced.

"No restaurant can be perfect these days," said Pierrot. "*C'est la guerre.*"

"This one doesn't do bad," said Mignot, mollified. "Not bad, not bad."

They drank a Moet-et-Chandon *brut* with the wild strawberries and fresh country cream. Mignot smacked his lips.

"Good, eh?" said Pierrot.

"Nothing is too good for the working class," said Mignot epigrammatically.

A cynical smile lighted Pierrot's face. He offered Mignot a cigar.

"Ah," said Mignot, taking the cigar and sniffing it. "Now you are beginning to overwhelm me."

They nipped off the ends of the cigars, and Pierrot lighted them.

Mignot settled back in his chair and contentedly puffed out the smoke into a shaft of daylight that cut across their table. There was a happy, petrified glaze in his eyes.

Pierrot clamped his teeth on his cigar, which stuck out of the corner of his mouth at a confident angle. He was a stocky man, with the features of a sly bulldog. His nose was small and pushed in, his chin jutted forward and his big ears stuck out of the sides of his head like jug handles. He was abnormally sensitive about his ears. The collar of his blue shirt was starched stiff as a board despite the heat, and in general his clothes, from the highly polished yellow shoes to the sparkling tiepin, were a triumph of the Place Pigalle manner. He was sharp. No chorus girl, *entraineuse* or unvarnished whore in Montmartre could fail to recognize at a glance what Pierrot was: a man of means, ready to empty his pockets with the same ease that he had filled them.

"If I understand you," he said, "all you want is a car, the big Citroen."

"That's right. But we must have it fast or it won't do us any good."

"How much time can you give me?"

"Tomorrow night."

Pierrot laughed. "You must take me for a magician. This has to be organized."

"How much time do you need?"

"Three or four days."

"Make it tomorrow night for a pal. It won't help us after that."

Pierrot thought for a while. He held the cigar delicately in his fingers to the center of his mouth, drew on it and blew the smoke up toward the ceiling.

"Let's see. This is Wednesday. That means Thursday night. Maybe it can be done."

"With all the papers?"

"Of course. What good is a car without papers if the car doesn't belong to you?"

Mignot grinned happily. "Good old Pierrot," he said.

"Naturally. The one time you really have to prove a thing is yours is when it ain't. That's why I'm always suspicious of a man who can prove black on white that something belongs to him." Pierrot sniffed. "It smells irregular."

The waiter had poured armagnac into big-bellied brandy glasses, and the aroma rose through the small opening of the glass as they drank.

"I can count on you afterward," said Pierrot. He said it more as an affirmation than a question. It was the last clause in the contract.

"You can count on us," said Mignot.

"Good. The car will be delivered tomorrow night."

He drank a little more of the armagnac, the taste suffusing his palate and remaining richly in his throat. Pierrot liked the warmth and ease it spread through his body and the turn it gave his head. It made him suddenly reflective, awakened an element normally dormant in him. He had a craving to understand things he heard all around him, but with which he felt only the vaguest relation. For some time now he had felt out of things, as though he were living in a universe that had little to do with the world of Paris. His curiosity was mixed with resentment.

"I see the cops are with you, Mignot," he said. "That's not good."

Mignot smiled uncomfortably. "Some of them aren't so bad."

"They're all alike," said Pierrot. "A good cop is a dead cop. What are they? Failures. When a man can't do anything else he becomes a cop. Then he spends his time trying to show he's as good as anybody else by bossing his betters around." He shook his head with unhappy wisdom. "The cops, are they men? No. Me," he went on, pointing his thumb at his chest, "I like a man, that's what I like. I don't care what he is—a pimp, a pansy, anything. But I like a man to be a man. He must have a heart." Pierrot thumped his chest twice. "A man."

He slouched back in his chair and looked at Mignot pensively for a moment. "Tell me, Mignot," he said. "Why do you do it?"

"Do what?"

"The resistance."

"I can't help myself. I'm a born hero."

"Seriously. I want to know. You risk your skin every day. If you're caught, r-r-r-r-mmmm—" he let his hand fall from a height onto the table, where it made a loud thud and jiggled the glasses of armagnac—"and where is my *mignon petit* Mignot? Finished! What for? What do you get out of it?"

"You take some risks too. What do you get out of it?"

"Dough, green stuff, money! It's worth the risk. I can have a meal like this one any time I want, twice a day if I feel like it. Any woman money can buy, and that means any woman in France or Navarre. I don't have to work in a factory, either. That's why I do it. So I can live the way I like to live."

"That's why I'm in the resistance. So I can live the way I want to."

"You're joking."

"No, I mean it. When the Fritz got here I felt they were crowding me, like I was being pushed into a corner. Maybe a part of that feeling was in my head, but it was real, anyway; that's the way I felt. I couldn't do what I wanted any more."

"I need freedom as much as you and I never missed it," said Pierrot.

"Then you must have had it," Mignot replied. "Freedom is like women—you don't miss it until you don't have it."

Pierrot grunted. "When the Germans get out you'll still have to slave away in a garage and get your fingernails black. What kind of freedom is that?"

"Some like brunettes; some like blondes. You need one thing to feel free; I need another. The work I do makes no difference. I like my job."

"You like to eat and drink too," said Pierrot. "And maybe you like blondes. You can't have the best blondes when you work in a garage."

Mignot thought for a while, toying with his brandy glass. "You know," he said, "if I had everything you talk about and the Boches were here I still wouldn't be happy. There'd still be something missing. It's like having a beautiful chicken on the plate in front of you. It's stuffed with *foie gras* and truffles and there's a sauce on it that makes you want to bow down and give thanks to God. Then you begin to eat, and it has no taste. You know what I mean. Just like a beautiful girl—" his hands curved through the air outlining her beauty—"a girl so beautiful you would poison your own sweet old grandmother just to spend an hour with her. One day you take her to bed, and paf! At the dramatic moment she has no temperament. Cold as a corpse. You feel as though you've been robbed. Afterward, nothing to say. You feel like crawling away, but you can't. There she is, draped across the sheets like a marble statue; heaven to look at, hell to hold. Enough to freeze your balls! Like a criminal, you wonder, What should I do with the body? Well, that's it. If the chicken has no taste and the girl has no passion, the better they look the worse you feel for having them. Give me the whole world but take away my freedom, and what have I got? The beautiful girl who gives me no desire to do the one thing I want to do. It's worse than having nothing. This way I feel cheated. No, I don't want to be a millionaire; I just want to be Mignot, working in a garage and living the way I like to live. The Germans couldn't buy me with all the blondes in Europe. I want to live in my Paris, not theirs."

"I never thought you'd turn out like this," said Pierrot, taking another drink. "You're a Goddamn patriot."

Mignot shook his head. "Patriotism has nothing to do with it," he protested. "I don't know how to tell you. It's hard to put your finger on." He tried to gather his mental forces behind the alcoholic haze clouding his brain. "If a sonofabitch raped your dame you'd want to get him. Right?"

Pierrot nodded his head vigorously.

"That's the way I feel about the Boches," said Mignot triumphantly. "Not so strong maybe, but that's the way I feel. It's humiliating to have the bastards here, running everything and shooting anybody who opens his trap. When you feel like that there's only one thing that makes you able to face yourself—fighting them."

Pierrot sucked hard on his cigar, which had almost gone out, and brought it back to life. "Me, I don't like them either," he said. "But I don't feel the way you do. I do business with them, but it's not to help them, it's to help me. You know what the difference is between you and me?" He waited for the question to sink in, his cigar poised in mid-air. "You're a communist. You have to get into a movement to get what you want. I do it alone, singlehanded, *Je les emmerde tous.* I'm an anarchist."

His gold cuff links sparkled in the candlelight as he lifted his brandy glass to his lips and put it down again.

"You're a good guy, Mignot. You oughtn't to be a communist. You don't think like a communist. You don't talk like a communist. But you act like one. You ought to be with me. Be an anarchist. Take what you can get; give nothing. No movement, no orders, no slogans. And tell them all to go to hell."

"Pierrot," said Mignot in a kindly tone, "the difference between us is that you're a sonofabitch and I can't let my pals down. But," he added, waving his cigar, "I'll say this: you're an honest sonofabitch."

Pierrot acknowledged the compliment with a grin that creased his smooth bulldog face. His big ears were red and felt hot. He floated in waves of alcoholic bliss. "Honesty pays and doesn't pay," he said. "A delicate question, very delicate. You know when I became an anarchist? When I was working in a café behind the bar, years ago. I was only a kid. Some of the older men came around to me and asked me to join the union. 'What for?' I says. 'We'll get you more dough.' 'I don't need you to get me more dough,' I says. What could they have got me? A few more sous a week. And it would have taken weeks, maybe months, and all along I would have been paying dues to the union. I had a better way of getting more money. I just dipped my hand in the cash box whenever nobody was looking. You see, you have to work for communism, but anarchism works for you."

Mignot laughed. "Some anarchist."

"And you, you're not a communist because you believe in it. You're one because your pals are."

Mignot shrugged. "I'm not much at politics. But I know who helps me get my *bifteck*."

"Is your mind in your stomach?"

"For such a question, yes. Like yours."

"That's all?" Pierrot asked, disappointed. He was certain there was something more, some secret Mignot had not disclosed, a key that would open locked doors. "That's all? And the ideology? What about the ideology?"

Mignot laughed. "Why bother your head over words? All I know is you can't be a sonofabitch. You can't let the boys down. That wouldn't be right. For the rest, this—" he pointed to his stomach— "understands better than this." He pointed to his head. "With the one you make mistakes. With the other there's no way of fooling yourself."

"I'll stick to anarchism," said Pierrot. "Any time you change your mind just let me know."

They drank up and puffed luxuriously on their cigars for a while in silence.

"What are you doing tonight?" Pierrot asked.

"Only one thing to do after such a meal," said Mignot. He spoke a little thickly. "Champagne and armagnac make me loving. It's a matter of finding a blonde, a pretty blonde, if possible. Anyway one with two thighs and all the rest. I love thighs."

Pierrot held up two fingers. "I know two blondes right here in the quarter. A couple of spare tires."

"Spare tires?"

"When the others blow up on you, there they are."

As the two men stepped out into the little Montmartre street, Mignot had an afterthought. "And the car?" he asked. "Will we be able to keep it?"

"If it runs, why not?"

Mignot slapped Pierrot on the back. "Good old Pierrot!" He laughed.

They walked down the street in the direction of two blondes whose tapering thighs met at the point of their desire. They did not stagger, nor were their steps completely steady.

†

SUZANNE peered about the shadowy room she had just curtained off from the fading light of the sky. This was what Klaus called home. The four absurdly papered walls and the bed, the stolid wardrobe whose cracked looking glass has mirrored their joy and the screen in the corner hiding the sink and bidet with prim but graceless delicacy. It was all the splendor they had known. Their oasis. A sordid Latin Quarter hotel room she had always imagined was just a point of passage leading to a flowered villa under a sun-kissed sky. This room, she thought bitterly, was all she had to remember.

Through the open window high above the Rue des Écoles the scented breath of the summer evening brushed past faded cotton drapes. Suzanne breathed the fragrant air and thought of wild roses in open spaces. She wanted to weep. Blinking back the tears, she glanced at the bed and saw that Klaus was already stretched naked on the gleaming sheets. He had been quick. His eyes were on her.

Once, long ago, she had known how to laugh easily, but time and disappointment had changed that. She did not know how or when her youth had left her; it was gone, like that gay poppy-red summer dress, so many years ago, like the Sunday outing at Fontainebleau where she had met Lucien Gaudin. All of it so dim and far away. She felt old and in a flash of panic was afraid her face betrayed her. All it betrayed in the muted light was her anguish.

"Klaus!" she called.

"I'm here, my darling."

She moved away from the window, her eyes somber, expression rapt, and her movements were automatic as she started to undress. When she bent to pull her dress over her head she thought, "Tonight I'll know how we stand," and a foreboding contracted her heart so sharply that she straightened up and stood rigid for a moment.

"What's the matter?" Klaus whispered from the bed.

"Nothing."

As the dress came over her head in one movement, her ripe breasts leaped free and trembled to rest. Despite the August heat Suzanne shivered. Then, glancing at Klaus, she saw the look on his face, watching her, and although the anguish was still there she thought no more. Her eyes filmed and she felt herself go soft to the marrow as always when Klaus was waiting for her and she knew she would soon be in his arms. She wriggled her buttocks free of her slip, which dropped to the floor, a puddle of white silk shining in the semidarkness. The next moment Suzanne slipped onto the bed beside Klaus.

She lay there, her firm, ample body incandescent against the dark. Shadows molded her breasts and thighs, wavering silently with the soft swell and fall of her domed navel. Klaus edged over to her, caressing the length of her body. He pressed her against him and she was pliant and warm. Huddled against him, she felt safe. Nothing existed any more but the two of them suspended in the dark and her warm sensations. After a while desire closed down on her mind, burying the last vestige of anxiety.

"*Chéri, chéri,*" she murmured.

For a long moment Suzanne was bathed in the lush, strangled sensation culminating desire. Then the pulsations ebbed, leaving her stilled, and they lay back on the rumpled sheets. Out of the well of sensuality her mind slowly rose to the surface. She was again aware of the languid weight of her limbs and of the even flow of the blood. When she reluctantly opened her eyes it was to the familiar anguish.

"Klaus."

He did not budge. Even his eyes remained closed to the ceiling.

"Klaus, what are we going to do?"

He opened his eyes and looked up at the ceiling, knowing what she was going to say, wondering vaguely how she was going to say it. It was the moment he dreaded now that the earlier, anticipated moment was gone. He was living moments, good and bad, moments without continuity. It was no life.

"Wait," he heard himself say.

"There isn't much longer to wait." Her voice was dull. "And when there's nothing more to wait for, what then?"

With varying degrees of despair she had been asking the same questions and getting the same answer for the past two weeks. But since her talk with Gaudin at dinner she felt a new urgency and a deeper despair. The atmosphere of Paris choked her. It was something Klaus could not sense. He was German, and the city locked him out of its councils and emotions. But she was French; the climate of Paris was all about her, inescapable. It blew in at the window of her apartment and seeped under the door. Wherever she went—in the streets, in the shops, in the homes of friends—it was present. But she knew that wherever he appeared, at that very moment it evaporated like laughter at a harsh word. She had seen it happen. Paris had created a void around the Germans, and they mistook the void for Paris. She was a Parisian herself and French and deep down too she wanted the Germans to be beaten. Yet she could not share the mounting joy of Paris since she identified herself with Klaus. The worst was that now she believed what the whole city believed: the German army could not stop the Americans; soon the Americans would liberate Paris. She had never thought of the war; now she thought of little else. Get away with Klaus. Get away. It was an obsession. She kept telling herself it made no difference that Klaus was not a Nazi or a soldier, that he was simply a functionary. He was a German. She could never think of the accident of Klaus's nationality without bitterness at the farce of frontiers. He had been born in Kehl, on the other side of the Rhine from Strasbourg. A few hundred yards to the west and he would have been French.

"All we can do is wait," Klaus said wearily.

He was an attractive man who looked somewhat younger than his forty-seven years, although the close-cropped hair around his temples was streaked with gray. His face was lean and his nose finely chiseled, but the long line of the jaw, which had a strong sweep, rounded disappointingly in a soft chin.

"They'll send you back to Germany when the Americans approach Paris," she said in a dull voice. "We'll never see each other again."

"They may put us in uniform. Every man will be needed."

"It comes to the same thing—worse. You'll be taken prisoner. We'll be separated, washed up."

"They may never get to Paris."

"Why fool ourselves any longer? They'll get here."

He was silent, his slender body stretched flat and immobile, like a corpse, on the distraught sheets. His inertia irritated her. He would lie there without moving until it was too late, until they came for him and led him away from her. She felt impotent. Her rage mounted suddenly and burst out on the silence.

"You can't just wait! Don't you see they'll get you? You've got to do something!"

"What?"

"Anything! What difference does it make? Do *some*thing!"

"It's easy to say. But what? What?"

She waited a moment, turned toward him and in a low, intense voice said, "Run away."

He turned his head and stared hard at her, and she could hear her heart beating in the dark silence.

"Run away!" he echoed scornfully. "I come under military law."

"Others have done it."

"And others have been shot for it."

The sweet smell of linden trees on the warm night air slipped past the drapes, and the poignant odor perfumed the room. They lay beside each other in the warmth, the sweetness and the silence, absorbed in their misery, the boundless night closing in and around them.

He did not want to lose Suzanne, but he could not run away with her. It was not physical fear; it was something else. He was terrified at the prospect of a future loosed from the past like a rudderless ship cut from its mooring. He was incapable of making a clean break. So he would temporize, unable to step out of a pattern of existence that was crumbling around him, knowing that failure to act meant to accept. He hated the role and always played it. At the same time he had convinced himself that it was not weakness of character that forced him to float along with events. It was what had happened that afternoon that held him in Paris. Feeling her stir beside him, he wondered if he should tell her. Out of the corner of his eye he saw her roll over on her side, propped on her elbow, facing him.

"Klaus, let me help you. It's for the both of us."

He turned toward her. For a moment she hesitated. Her coarse black hair fell loose to her shoulders and was a darker shadow behind the shadow of her face.

"Before the Americans get here the resistance is going to revolt. Paris will be a slaughterhouse. You'll all be massacred."

"Nonsense." He laughed at her panic. "What can a handful of terrorists do against the Wehrmacht? You can't fight tanks with slogans."

Her sense of local pride flared briefly. "Paris has had revolutions before. We have our traditions."

"And we have our cannons. How long do you think a revolutionary tradition can stand up to a few batteries of artillery?"

The tears glistened in her eyes. "The resistance will kill you, and if they don't the Americans will take you prisoner. I know it."

Her expression was plaintive, pleading. He reached over, cradled her in his arms and kissed her gently on her forehead, cheeks and eyes. She pulled herself free.

"You must listen to me," she said urgently. "Once the insurrection starts it will be too late to get out of Paris. You don't want to rot in a prison camp, do you?"

"You don't understand. I can't leave."

"Why not?"

"Where could we go? There isn't a place in France where I'd be safe. I have no papers, nothing."

Gaudin had once told her where resistants in flight sometimes hid. "I know a place. A house of assignation, a brothel. Nobody bothers about papers there."

"Impossible."

"Nothing could be easier. We'd go together."

He turned brusquely away from her. She wanted to make too many sacrifices for him. He would have to tell her about himself, and why he had to remain in Paris.

"Someday we'd have to get out of the brothel," he said. "What could we do then? I'd need papers. I'd need a job. We'd need money. We have nothing. And worst of all, we have no means of getting anything."

"We'd find a way. There must be some way."

He sat up suddenly on the edge of the bed, his back toward her. "There's no way," he said. "You don't know who I am, what I do. They'd track us down—your people or mine." He paused, facing the wall with his back still toward her, and in a voice that mirrored despair added, "I'm in the Gestapo."

"The Gestapo!" The shock was so complete that she stumbled on unthinkingly, "But the men of the Gestapo are monsters!"

There was no mirth in his short, harsh laugh. "You see we are not all beasts." And he added bitterly, "We are the exceptions who are worse than the brutes: we have consciences."

He reached over to the night table, took a cigarette and lit it, the match flaring his harrowed face, then burning out. In the new, intenser darkness he turned toward Suzanne and grasped her hand. "Don't leave me," he said, speaking quickly. "We'll get out together. I had it all arranged to go to Berlin, but everything went wrong today. Just give me the time to straighten out one affair and I promise we'll leave. You see, this afternoon something important slipped out of my hands, and I can't go back with that hanging over my head. It's an informer, a Frenchman in the resistance. He was very valuable and I should have taken better care of him. Of course, I had him watched. That was normal. He didn't want to work for us, so I had to force him. Oh, there was no torture. Threats were enough. They often are. But I couldn't trust him. You can't trust any of them. What could I do? I couldn't have my man stay right in his apartment. The resistance must have found out what he was doing, and this afternoon they got into his apartment and shot him."

Klaus saw Adrien as he had a few hours before, lying on his back in the middle of the salon, his lips blue and his body stiff, and he cursed himself for having let Adrien lead him on and for sending those rosy reports to Berlin saying that in two weeks he would probably be able to deliver the leadership of the French resistance. If he went back now they might throw him out of the Gestapo and put him in the army. Maybe the Russian front. He shuddered.

At the same time Suzanne recalled what Gaudin had told her at dinner about the girl in the resistance—what was her name? Danielle, yes, Danielle . . .

"I've got to find the murderer," he said. "We can't leave until I find him."

"What makes you think it's a man?"

"Why, I don't know. I—"

"We'll get out of Paris when you close this case?"

"Yes. This is all that's keeping us here."

"It was a woman," Suzanne said. "A woman. Don't ask me how I know. I can't tell you. Her name is Danielle, she's very beautiful and she's the daughter of an admiral."

"But—"

"Don't ask how I know. I beg you!"

After a long pause: "You're sure?"

"Certain. A member of her group told me. Trust me. I can't say any more."

He took her in his arms and kissed her, but she pushed him gently away.

"It won't be easy to find her in Paris," she said. "With only a first name to go by, probably a resistance name, it's going to take a long time to sort her out of the millions who live here."

"With some luck it may not take so very long."

Suzanne fell back on the bed. It was no good. She was sure she would never get away with Klaus, and she thought, in a few months I'll be thirty-five and in five years I'll be forty and then fifty, and all the years of my life I'll spend with a man I don't love and the one I want I will never be able to have. She felt old again and the tears burned her eyelids. They were hot and wet on her cheeks. Klaus held her ravaged face in his hands and tried to comfort her.

"It will work out. It will work out," he kept repeating. "The Americans aren't here yet."

She wept silently under his caresses, and all the while he cradled her like a child he kept repeating to himself, Danielle, beautiful, admiral's daughter . . . He would get her. First check in the morning the Navy Ministry at the Place de la Concorde . . . What an inhuman animal this beautiful Danielle must be to murder a man in cold blood . . . He kissed away a tear on Suzanne's warm cheek and thought how good and true she was. She wouldn't hurt a fly . . .

†

THAT night it rained. Jagged streaks of lightning cut across the sky and like cosmic flash bulbs cast weird flares over the blacked-out city. It was a heavy storm. The rain poured straight down and hit the asphalt with a loud, splashing noise. Peals of thunder rumbled overhead, and many people awoke during the night thinking as they came out of their sleep that it was the roar of cannon. Suzanne slept fitfully. Once, early in the morning, a shattering crack of thunder pulled her, wide-eyed and panic-stricken, out of a nightmare. Her nightmare was that the Americans had taken Paris; the thunder bounced her terror to the surface, and it was half an hour before Klaus quieted her and they went to sleep again.

It was still raining heavily when they arose and dressed. On the way out they crossed the chambermaid in the hall. She stopped and stared blankly at Suzanne as she always did. Suzanne swept past the squat, middle-aged woman, her head high and eyes averted, annoyed as she always was at the woman's insolence. It amazed Suzanne that Klaus, who was sensitive to the general hostility of the French, never seemed conscious of the immediate atmosphere around them. Perhaps, she thought, it was because when they were together the hostility was directed against her. They were afraid of him and showed contempt for her.

In the lobby the clerk gave her the same look she had just seen on the chambermaid's face. But when he took the key from Klaus his expression was neutral. Suzanne tried to tell herself she was being overly sensitive and imagining things; but she knew it was not true. They could not forgive her for sleeping with a German, she thought bitterly. She told herself she didn't care what they thought. She loved Klaus. That was all that counted. Yet the stares of the chambermaid and the clerk and their silent disapproval hurt her. She was stiff and self-conscious when she said good-by to Klaus. She felt a little angry with him, since she thought that the twinge of humiliation she suffered was his fault. More than ever she wanted deeply and desperately to get out of Paris. She did not care if she never saw the city again.

At home she stalked restlessly about the apartment. Its emptiness oppressed her. There was no doubt. She no longer belonged there. Nobody did. What had once been a home was now just three furnished rooms. Meaningless.

The morning passed slowly. Suzanne turned about ceaselessly with nervous energy, seeking something to do and not finding it. Wherever she turned she found herself up against the maddening blank wall that towered around her like the sheer sides of a prison enclosure. Without Klaus she could not get away and waiting for him was torture. The minutes crawled. But she could not hurry time with any of the usual distractions. The theaters and movie houses were closed; she was incapable of the effort reading demanded and she knew nobody in whom she could confide. In the absence of electricity she could not even turn on the radio or play the gramophone. It was impossible to raise so much as a curtain of sound, of sentimental nonsense, between herself and the reality she hated to face. All the normal resources—the emotion-deadeners and thought-killers—were closed. There was only one resource left—the last and real one: herself. And that was exhausted, empty as the apartment; it was precisely what she wanted to escape.

When the phone rang Suzanne sprang to answer it. She was tense and nervous, but managed to cover her disappointment that it was not Klaus. In her anguish it took a moment or two of stumbling before she remembered the caller whom she had not seen in a long time. She listened to him distractedly, and not until he had repeated his invitation did she realize that he was asking her to go to a reception with him that afternoon.

"Robert de Maurain is giving the party," he said. "You know him?"

"I know about him—like everyone else. I'd love to go."

It was a perfect solution, she thought as she hung up. She began looking through her closet for a dress to wear. At last she had something

to distract her from her morbid thoughts and something to do other
than wait.

†

Patrice rose early. He passed on the code from London during the
morning and learned that the Dutchman, as he suspected, had also
made good his escape the previous evening. Later, he went to his office
in the Rue Pernety at the far end of the fourteenth *arrondissement*.
The office was a starkly furnished three-room apartment in a grimy
tenement. Danielle was already there. She looked soft and dazzling in
a lemon-yellow cotton dress, and the moment Patrice saw her the
dreary room and its naked poverty fell beyond the edge of his consciousness.

"Are you all right?" he asked.

She managed a rueful smile. "Much better than yesterday."

"What did you do after you left me?"

"A lot of thinking. Then I slept. I did a lot of that too."

"It's the best thing you could have done."

"I know. I always try to sleep troubles off."

"I wish I could."

While they spoke Danielle brought out a large map of Paris and a
stack of documents. Patrice watched her and felt happy and at peace.
He asked for no deeper fulfillment. Although he wanted to talk about
a thousand things, he sat down beside her at the dining room table as
if it were any other day, and soon they were at work.

They deployed the scant resistance forces from sheets of paper listing underground units and their effectives to sheets of paper listing
strategically important buildings and installations. Patrice had been
given the lists together with a batch of reports. From this information
he had to draw up operational orders conforming with the two guiding directives of the resistance command. The directives contradicted
each other. One required enough effectives to defend the city's nerve
centers against German attack; the other required enough effectives to
launch an offensive and hold the streets. If there had been fewer critical
points to protect or more men to protect them, the directives would
have been consistent. As it was, both of them could not be implemented.
The list of gas works, electric powerhouses, reservoirs, telephone ex-
changes, railway yards, radio stations, newspaper plants, banks, government buildings, et cetera, covered page after page, and there were
no more than thirty thousand men of the resistance to hold them and

take the streets by force. These men, virtually unarmed, had the task of liberating Paris, and liberating it intact, so that when the uprising ended the city could return rapidly to normal life.

Patrice had been working on the blueprint for the past ten days. That afternoon, when it was ready, Colonel Rol, the commander in chief of the Paris insurrection, would approve it, then distribute it to the commanders of the four military sectors of the city. They in turn would make the necessary dispositions.

After working for several hours they finished the plan, and Patrice pushed back his chair and stretched.

"I can't think straight any more," he sighed. "My head's going around like a top."

His gaunt face was marked by the deep furrows on the inside of his flat cheeks. Lines of fatigue concentrated his expression. He was at that point of fatigue, despite what he had said, where his faculties were most acute. The fires burned brighter.

"How about the police?" Danielle asked. "There are twenty thousand of them, all on strike, and you haven't counted them in."

"Can't. Only a tenth or so are in the resistance. The rest followed the strike, but nobody can tell if they'll go along with the insurrection." He looked at her softly, his regard like a caress, and the intensity of her expression melted away too. "You must be exhausted," Patrice added.

"My father always warned me against getting involved with a chief of staff." She smiled.

"Well, we finished the job," he said. "I think that calls for a cup of tea."

It was their daily luxury. Patrice had never known how Danielle obtained so rare a thing as the stock of tea that was in the cupboard; but it was there with a diminishing mound of sugar. Danielle busied herself in the cubbyhole kitchen heating the water while Patrice prepared the dishes on a platter.

"You know," he said, "we've been working together now for half a year and yet we've never seen each other apart from work."

She smiled at him, her face smooth and soft. "I know. You've been rather forbidding."

"You haven't been very approachable yourself."

"Even lately?"

"No, not lately," he admitted.

"Well, this is apart from work," she said.

"What?"

"Tea things."

He looked at her to see if she meant it, and she laughed.

"Unfair," he said. "You caught me off balance."

"I don't know how else to catch you."

He smiled. "Where would you like to be taken, apart from work?"

"There's not much of a choice these days."

"Choose something anyway."

"Take me to a cocktail party," she said.

"I haven't been invited to one."

"I have. An old friend, Robert de Maurain. Will you take me?"

"When?"

"This afternoon. He gives one every Thursday afternoon."

Patrice hesitated. "There are things to be done—"

"They can wait."

"You're so forward," he said.

"Say yes."

"Yes."

Danielle laughed. "Thank you, sir," she said.

When the tea was made Patrice put it on the platter and carried it through the dining room into the salon. The salon was a bare room with only a battered old divan standing against a wall to relieve its nakedness. Patrice and Danielle sank down beside each other and drank their tea in silence. It revived them. They lighted cigarettes and watched the smoke drift off toward the brown-papered walls and disappear.

"There won't be many more days like this," Patrice said. "A week or so and we'll all be back where we started from four years ago."

"Not all of us. Some will be city councilors, some ministers—"

"Reboussin," Patrice said. "Well, politics is his business. We can't blame him. Some just wanted to resist; some wanted to get something out of resisting. If you don't wind up a prisoner or a corpse, the resistance isn't a bad way to make a career."

"And you?" she asked.

He sighed. "I'm going to take some adjusting. It won't be easy going back to a normal life and prewar occupations."

"You don't have to. Everybody says you have a brilliant political future. It's the first thing I was told when I came here to work with you."

"That's what Reboussin told me a dozen times. All I had to do, he said, was be more 'flexible' and he would do the rest. In politics the winds of doctrine are variable and if you don't bend with them you can't survive. I'm not the bending type."

It was the first time he had spoken to her of himself and he was saying exactly what she wanted to hear. She remembered why she had fought him in the beginning and why later she had come around. The remark about his brilliant postliberation political prospects had stuck with her. When she met him she had thought he was motivated, to the exclusion of everything else, by his personal ambition. Since his attraction for her was strong, her antagonism had been sharper. What she had been told about his integrity had made little impression. She had been told similar things about other resistance figures, only to be disabused. She was not the naïve golden girl she once had been. The resistance had cured her of that. Face values hid the reality underneath and they came to the surface with the debate on the insurrection. When Patrice argued for an uprising Danielle began to alter her opinion of him. Opportunism lay in the other direction. After that she came around to him fast. He had the qualities her father had taught her to admire: integrity and an aggressive policy.

She watched Patrice take a deep puff on his cigarette.

"Reboussin really worked on me," he said. "He finally got discouraged when I failed to bite."

"But you were tempted?"

"Very much," Patrice said ruefully, "and Reboussin knew it. But I knew that if I bit he'd reel me in, salt me away and serve me up between the soup and the meat."

"With a dry white wine."

"And a sauce that would raise cheers for the chef, while the poor fish served only to heighten its taste." Patrice ground out his cigarette. "Among other things the resistance has taught me that politics in France, or anywhere else probably, consists in manipulating for power while taking a mud bath. It's not for me."

"I'm glad," she said, loving him.

"I'm not. I wish I were different."

"You don't mean it."

He shrugged. "It's a case of sheer incompetence. There are so many pressures in politics that the shortest distance between two points isn't a straight line but a zigzag. I can't zigzag. I'm too damned Euclidean. If I weren't I might be able to do some good instead of having to hole up because life isn't patterned after my rules." He sighed. "I'll do for the resistance. It's a special case. But not for politics. Don't have the character. No surer way of losing your identity than by sinking yourself in a job you weren't meant for."

"What will you do?" she asked.

"Go back to teaching philosophy, I guess. I'm good at that and I used to like it." But he did not seem happy about it, and Danielle was distressed. After a pause he asked, "And you?"

"I haven't thought about it. Some job, something."

She looked lost, and his heart reached out to her. Sitting beside her on the divan, he made a movement and brushed against her, his arm warm against hers, the skin suddenly electric. Their eyes met and held. Then, without knowing it was going to happen, they were in each other's arms and all that existed was their lips and bodies crushed together. The smell of her hair, the perfume of her body, closed in on his senses with musky darkness. When he groped for the fastening of her dress she whispered, "No, not here, not like this."

"When?"

"Tomorrow night."

"Tonight."

"All right, tonight." She squeezed his arm. "At my house. I lo—"

He stopped her lips with a kiss. Her words sang in his ears and sang again, the touch of her in his hands warm and firm against him. He kissed her again, violently, and she rocked in his arms.

An instant later the doorbell rang, two short rings followed by a long one.

They had to wrench themselves back to the dull reality of the apartment. There was a wonder beyond wonder in Danielle's eyes, and their blue depths were endless. Patrice shook his head to bring himself back from the mystery of her. The bell rang again.

"I'll go," they said at once.

"No, I'll go," he said laughingly. "Don't go away."

As he reached the door the bell rang still again. Gaudin walked in.

"Thought you'd never open up," he said.

He was very excited. Healthy-looking pink spots colored his sallow cheeks, but his long nose remained defiantly sad. He walked quickly to the center of the dining room and stood by the table littered with the map of Paris and sheets of paper on which Patrice and Danielle had been working.

Danielle came in from the salon. She and Patrice waited for Gaudin to catch his breath, but kept glancing at each other all the while, their eyes restless on each other like the hands of children on a favorite toy.

"It's fixed," Gaudin said. He took a breath and said it again. "It's fixed."

"What?"

"The raid. Mignot fixed it. He was plastered, high as the moon. Pierrot is supplying the car. Tonight at nine in front of the Coupole in Montparnasse."

Patrice took it in. He was pleased and disappointed.

"It will have to be tomorrow night after all," he said to Danielle.

"What's this raid about?"

"Arms. You remember. We're taking the arms in Mignot's garage."

Danielle did not look reassured.

"I won't be able to take you to that cocktail party," Patrice said. "I'll have to set up the raid."

She looked disappointed. "I won't go if you don't. I wanted you to meet De Maurain."

"You go on ahead. I'll meet you there later."

They seemed strange to Gaudin. He had never seen them quite like this before, so much less businesslike than usual.

Patrice was gathering up the papers on the table and making a package of them. "Take this over to Rol," he said to Gaudin. "You'll save me a trip while I work on the raid."

"I have a message for you," Gaudin said, taking the package and handing Patrice an envelope. "Picked it up on the way over."

Patrice read the message, took a deep breath and looked from Danielle to Gaudin and back again. "It's coming fast now," he said and handed the message to them.

It carried the date and was headed "F.F.I.—Seine General Staff." The text read: "From the reception of this order, the F.F.I. of all sectors should consider themselves as permanently on the alert. The groups should be able to be mobilized in *one hour*. . . ." It was signed: "Chief of the General Staff, Dufresne."

The three of them looked at each other. They did not speak. But their hearts beat faster and the excitement that stirred them was in their eyes. After four years of struggle the climax was upon them. Gaudin broke the silence.

"This won't foul up the raid, will it?" he asked.

"I don't think so," Patrice said. "It means tomorrow's meeting will probably decide the insurrection one way or the other. That gives us a day, maybe two."

"Then we'll still be able to go to that party this afternoon," Danielle said.

"Of course. And we'll have the time to see each other tomorrow night too."

They laughed. They were delighted with each other and with the way events were developing. Gaudin looked at them, puzzled. It occurred to him that he had not seen Patrice laugh for a long time. Watching Danielle and her shining eyes, he thought of Suzanne and what she had been to him when her laughter had found its echo in his heart.

"Some tea?" Danielle asked. "You earned it with that message."

Gaudin shook his head. He wondered when he would see Suzanne's eyes bright again like Danielle's and eager with life and the joy of living.

†

ON HER way to De Maurain's party that afternoon, Danielle saw a patch of blue high overhead where a breeze was sweeping away the sullen clouds. She breathed in the sweet air. It smelled of rain on ripe blossoms and of wet streets in a late summer afternoon. Danielle smiled. Blue sky, my sky, she said to herself. Since Patrice had kissed her, she had changed worlds. As she cycled along the Seine, Paris was so beautiful she wanted to throw her arms around the city and hug it. Everything gave her happiness a sharper tang. Riding the bicycle was an effortless flight, and she felt good watching the arm of the river bend around the quai. She felt good too because Patrice would be joining her at the party and she would be seeing De Maurain again.

How a man like De Maurain and her father had ever become such close friends Danielle would never know. Perhaps, she thought, it was because they were so different. De Maurain, whose grandfather had made a fortune in construction materials, which was doubled by his father, had distinguished himself in more than half a century of virtually uninterrupted dissipation by entertaining everybody in Paris of any importance with unexampled charm and wit. His Thursdays—five to eight—were a Parisian institution.

Although De Maurain gave the impression of neglecting his affairs, he had handled them shrewdly; the business was as sound as the day it had been passed on to him and the fortune was as considerable. This did not keep some of his friends from trying to lead him away from what they called a "life of decadence." At such times De Maurain merely smiled. For purposes of morality, he claimed to be a Cartesian. Body and soul went their separate ways: the latter to his wife, the former to his mistresses. But when he was told he ought to have more consideration for the woman with whom God had joined him, De Maurain replied suavely, "True, she made my life a bed of roses. I sleep elsewhere to avoid the thorns."

"Elsewhere" was with Nicole, his current mistress, who was as devoted to him when he was with her as she was to a younger man when he was not. Until De Maurain retired Nicole to the relative privacy of her lavish little Montmartre apartment, she had displayed her superb body nightly and two afternoons a week on the stage of the Folies Bergère. In their less ardent moments, which were becoming more frequent, De Maurain affected to teach her "The First Principles of a Concubine," which he solemnly declared was the subject of a scholarly opus he was preparing. She was an apt pupil. "A concubine should never treat a lover as though he were her husband," he told her in a moment of tenderness. "A wife takes a husband for granted—it's invariably a case of mistaken identity."

"In an accent that was pure Belleville and belied her angelic face and innocent blue eyes, she shot back, "I never take a man for granted. I take him for what I can." Her vulgarity intrigued De Maurain as much as her beauty.

Danielle was the first guest to arrive at De Maurain's apartment on the Avenue Henri Martin. A white-jacketed butler led her into a high-ceilinged salon that was populated with Louis XV chairs and a profound silence. The austere room, with the luxurious appointments and grace, was her world, but she stepped back into the familiar frame with mixed feelings. She felt it was flaccid and effete beside the Paris she had come to know; but she also felt a deep pleasure and a sense of well-being she had never experienced in her new world. She sighed and looked up, and there was De Maurain.

"How is our revolutionary today?" he asked in his usual tone of negligent affability. "Ah, you're looking lovely."

He put out both his hands, which Danielle took, and kissed her affectionately on either cheek.

"If I had not known you since you were a child," he said as they sat down, "I should be kissing your hand or your lips. Kissing the cheeks of a girl as pretty as you, my dear, is a sign of age."

Her open smile greeted his wry one. Since De Maurain had reached the fifties a number of years ago, age had impressed him as one of nature's crueler jokes.

"The most tragic case I know," he said lightly, "is that of a man who is too old to change his habits and not young enough to pursue them."

A waiter appeared with two glasses of punch, and De Maurain offered Danielle a cigarette. He was a tall, angular man, straight-backed and square-shouldered, with sharp features and a haughty, slightly hooked nose. His face was youthful and unlined except when it crinkled into a smile, but his hair was quite gray. It added to his air of distinction.

"What have you been doing all these weeks?" he asked. "I missed you."

"The same thing," she smiled. "I'll spare you the morbid details."

"The resistance?"

"The resistance."

"Politics," De Maurain sighed. "*La politique* is a fickle woman who gives herself to the strongest."

"You sound as though she's just been unfaithful to you."

"If we aren't in her bed, she's in someone else's."

"Then give her up," Danielle said, "and we won't have any more arguments."

"Neither of those possibilities is very likely," De Maurain said with a smile.

They were very close and always had been. Danielle could not remember a time when she had not confided in De Maurain. He had been so much easier to talk to than her father.

"You know," she said suddenly, "I came here for a purpose today. I want you to meet someone I'm very proud of and tell me how you like him. His name is Patrice Vallois."

"He seems to mean a great deal to you."

"He does," Danielle said. "I'm in love with him."

De Maurain smiled. "I thought it would take more than the resistance to make you glow like this."

Danielle laughed and her color was high and she said, "I know you're going to like him."

"Not as much as you," De Maurain began, then added warmly, "but I'm sure I shall. When am I going to meet him?"

"In a little while. I asked him here."

"What's he like?"

But before Danielle could reply several people appeared at the archway of the salon. They came in gaily, the women wearing wide-brimmed hats and brightly colored dresses, and De Maurain rose to greet them.

In the next hour a steady stream of guests flowed into the salon, and bit by bit the tone of the room changed. Its air of cool austerity was quickly submerged by the crush of people that converged on the room. Chattering groups soon filled the salon from the walls covered with Gobelin tapestries to the casement windows overlooking the chestnut trees on the Avenue Henri Martin. The animated hum of conversation rose and fell over the Louis XV furniture.

Walking from group to group, De Maurain heard fragments of the talk and knew that all was well. "Impossible to get out of Paris. No trains, no gasoline . . ." "Did you like her dress?" "An absolute horror! I told her I *loved* it . . ." "Well, what does Laval want? Herriot can't make him President of the Republic." "You don't understand. If Herriot . . ." "The Gestapo and the SS want to fight to the last street, but the Army has decided to abandon Paris." "Oh, I do hope Paris will be declared an open city. What do you . . ." "But, my dear, her brassières were designed by an engineer from Polytéchnique . . ."

The party was in full swing. Suzanne, who had arrived half an hour before and been separated from her escort, drifted toward the far end of the salon and found herself standing beside Danielle. In the shadow of a picture hat Suzanne's handsome face wore a preoccupied expression. She looked around in her intent, nearsighted way, and her eyes met Danielle's. Danielle smiled at her and Suzanne returned the smile. A mousy little man, who had been presented to each of the women a few minutes earlier, introduced them. In the hubbub Danielle did not hear Suzanne's name.

"My luck isn't all bad," the man murmured wryly. "Here I am with the two most beautiful women in the room."

"Are you usually unlucky?" Danielle asked.

"I'm the editor of a collaborationist newspaper. What do you think?" The man shrugged. "Well, I had four good years," he added without conviction.

"Why did you do it?" Danielle asked.

He looked her right in the eye. "Because I thought they'd win," he said. "At least I wasn't fooled by any of the high-flown talk like some of my colleagues."

"Only by events."

"Four years ago we all had to face realities. I did it with a serviceable Rumanian proverb: 'The bowed head does not feel the edge of the sword.' "

"How are you going to face realities now?"

"By running away from them."

"Where?" Suzanne asked.

"To the east, madame, to the east."

Danielle glanced up at Suzanne's face. It was expressionless. She looked across the room and saw Patrice edging his way through the crowd toward her. She waved. Suzanne watched them greet each other and thought, "They're in love." It would have been hard to miss it. The mousy little man went off, and Danielle turned to Suzanne to introduce her to Patrice. Before she could speak he thrust out his hand to Suzanne.

"This is a happy surprise," he said. Turning to Danielle, he added, "I wasn't aware that you knew Gaudin's wife, Danielle."

"I didn't until a minute ago."

"Danielle!" Suzanne said almost at the same moment. "Are you . . ." She stopped short.

"Yes," Danielle said, and smiled. "I'm the girl who works with your husband."

"He's spoken of you. He admires you so much."

"So do we all," Patrice said.

Danielle looked pleased. A sudden crush of people pushed them toward a window. Two young girls close by laughed shrilly. Patrice saw nothing but Danielle's glowing face and twinkling blue eyes. Suzanne, her face clouded, looked from one to the other, struggling against a reticence she did not understand.

"I've been wanting to meet you," she said abruptly, and Danielle's dazzling smile met her somber look. "I'm worried about Lucien. You can help me."

"I?" Danielle's smile gave way to surprise.

"I must speak to someone about him. I have to be assured, the danger, being separated, all that." Suzanne plunged, her voice agitated and her hands working nervously. "You mustn't tell him. That would only make it worse. But I must see you. Tell me where you're staying, how I can reach you. I'll come whenever you say."

"Of course," Danielle said, now grave. "But you should have gone to Patrice. He would have been able to reassure you."

"It's better talking to a woman," Suzanne said, her eyes darting uncertainly from Patrice's look of concern to the gravity of Danielle's eyes.

"I understand." Danielle was already searching in her pocketbook for her appointment book. "Perhaps we can make it for tomorrow . . ."

She looked up, a tiny gold pencil poised in her fingers, the little leather-bound agenda flipped open to a naked white page.

"Danielle, you're neglecting me, and I won't permit it in my own house."

The three of them turned toward De Maurain, who stood at Danielle's side, accusing her with an expression of mock reproach.

"Lese majesty!" De Maurain pronounced in the tone of a judge.

"Not guilty, Your Highness," said Danielle, with a slight bow and a charming smile.

"Then we exact your immediate presence before the throne."

All submission: "Yes, Sire." Danielle turned toward Suzanne. "Do excuse me. I'll be back."

Still holding the open agenda and the gold pencil in her hand, she linked one arm into Patrice's and the other into De Maurain's, and moved away between them, the introduction and a flurry of conversation trailing behind.

Suzanne stood motionless. The salon, with its swarm of people buzzing around her, did not exist. There were just the three backs moving slowly away that she saw only indistinctly and her feeling of exasperation and relief. She liked Danielle. Very much. A deep astonishment bit into Suzanne's mind. What she had tried to do was ugly. She understood her reticence of a moment ago and why relief now dominated her frustration. Feeling faint, she sank into a chair and sat there for some time. There must be some other way for Klaus and me, she said to herself. But she could not think of any, and at the same time a question kept pounding in her tormented mind: How could I have tried to do it? Something writhed up inside her. She felt unclean. Abruptly, her tortured face averted, she started across the crowded room. She had to get out, had to be alone. At the archway of the salon a hand touched her shoulder. She turned, blind with tears that burned the rims of her eyes.

"Forgive me," Danielle said softly. "Shall we make it tomorrow?"

"No. I was foolish." Suzanne swallowed to keep her voice from breaking. "It won't be necessary."

Danielle's face was all softness and sympathy. "You may change your mind. Just in case you do, here's my address."

For a fraction of a second Suzanne hesitated before the slip of paper thrust out to her; then she took it—because there was nothing else she could do.

"Don't worry," Danielle said. "It will be over soon and he'll be back with you."

As Suzanne left, her escort forgotten, she crumpled the paper in her fist, the nails digging unfelt into her palm. She strode blindly out into the fragrant evening, turned a corner, and still her fist was clenched on the paper she could no longer feel and that all her heart and soul were concentrated on throwing away. She walked. With each step her resolution rose and fell. It would be abominable to use that address, abominable. She said to herself, Then open your hand and let the paper drop. Her hand remained closed. She was thinking that as long as she had the paper she had a choice. She would never make the choice, of course, never, never. But she would have it. And why have a choice if one is never to act on it? Why? Question and answer were deeper than reason, beyond thought, and Suzanne, certain she would never give up Danielle to the Gestapo, could not commit the simple act of opening her hand and dropping the temptation of that choice. If she knew with her head that the way to avoid an act she did not want to commit was to avoid the circumstance that made the act possible, a deeper impulsion surging dumbly in her blood made her feel mutely and beyond all the force of her will that she had to hold in her hand an alternative—any alternative—to disaster.

So Suzanne automatically made her way home through the streets of Paris, her ripe body swinging with easy animal grace at each step, her handsome face a brooding mask in the shadow of the big picture hat, and her right hand tightly clenched. All the way back, as always, men stared at her admiringly and women with envy.

†

It was late when Patrice and Danielle left De Maurain's. Side by side they cycled slowly under a thick arch of chestnut trees to the Trocadero, where Paris was spread out under the Eiffel Tower in the blue lace of twilight. They stood there a long while, watching the city melt in the violet dusk. Then they coasted downhill to the Seine and followed the quais along the left bank to the Latin Quarter. Patrice left his bicycle at a café and drove Danielle, straddled on the handlebars of her machine, to Montparnasse.

"I'm sure everything will be all right," she said, taking the bicycle from him.

"Of course."

"But you will be careful."

"I will."

"And you won't take any chances?"

"I won't."

"It's been a lovely afternoon. I'm so glad you came to the party."

"The ride was fine too."

"It was lovely."

"I wish it were tomorrow night."

"So do I," she said. "Another twenty-four hours."

"Ages."

"Make them pass quickly."

Her eyes were dark blue and wistful in the sweet night air, and the pressure of her hand in his was firm and warm. Then, without saying good night, she darted away.

Patrice found Gaudin and Mignot on the terrace of the Coupole, an oasis of humanity in a desert of unpopulated tables and chairs.

"What happened?" Patrice asked as he sat down. "Did everybody leave when they saw you arrive?"

"Can you blame them?" said Mignot, his cigarette butt dancing between his lips. "Look at Prince Cheerful, my gay companion."

Simultaneously they looked at Gaudin, whose face was so bleak it was comical. Gaudin sheepishly joined in their laughter. Patrice and Mignot were in rare form. They were unable to repress their excitement at the prospect of the raid. Gaudin fought against being infected with their enthusiasm.

"Well, where's the chariot?" Patrice asked.

"A little patience," said Mignot. "It's not due here for a while yet."

"I'll believe we're going to get it when I see it," Gaudin said.

"It'll come," said Mignot confidently. "Pierrot won't let me down now."

Gaudin grunted. Patrice grinned.

"Wait and see," Patrice said in English. "Translation—let's hope for the best."

A half hour later Pierrot still had not arrived. He was already twenty minutes late and night was falling. In another half hour the café would close. Their idle talk lapsed into silence. Patrice did his best to hide the disappointment he felt, and from time to time Gaudin looked ac-

cusingly at Mignot. Mignot, meanwhile, tried to keep up a pretense
of jauntiness under what he was beginning to regard as adversity. The
gaiety had gone out of him, and his humor was forced.

"Well," Gaudin said at last. "Are we going to see that car tonight
or after the city is liberated?"

"He'll come, he'll come," Mignot said, but the more he insisted the
clearer it was that he no longer believed it. "A man can be a little late.
It isn't as though he were driving here in his own car. This takes organization. Maybe he was held up a few minutes by something."

"A few minutes?" said Gaudin. "Wake up! He's a crook—okay.
But a *collabo* is a *collabo*. You'll never get anything good out of them.
After the liberation he'll probably come around for our help because
he showed good will."

"Okay, okay."

Mignot felt his prestige was tottering. There was nothing he could
do and he was ready to admit defeat. "To think that only yesterday
we were like brothers," he said.

He thought wistfully of the black-market meal and its aftermath,
of the blonde he had met through Pierrot. She was not as pretty as the
blonde Pierrot had taken and she had not even been a real blonde after
all, but she had virtues not visible to the naked eye that made up for
everything and more. Mignot sighed. Pierrot had promised him the
car, and now he had not come. This was treason. It sorely tried Mignot's
unquestioning faith in the word of his fellow men.

The three of them sat in moody silence as the waiter piled the tables
and chairs on the terrace against the front of the café. For ten or
fifteen minutes they sat in noble isolation in the middle of the sidewalk, three men gathered about a small round table facing empty
glasses and waiting for a gangster who had promised them a stolen car.
The longer they waited and thought about it the more unlikely it
seemed. Gaudin was angry; Patrice felt foolish; Mignot was miserable.
The waiter finally came up to them and stood by their table. Mignot
looked up at him. He hated to go even now.

"We're closing," the waiter said.

"Right away?" asked Mignot.

"Right away."

They paid and got up. Mignot went to the edge of the sidewalk and
looked down the Boulevard Montparnasse. It was empty.

"What's the use of looking for him?" Gaudin muttered. "He bitched
us up."

Their hands in their pockets, they strolled away. They had walked only a few feet and just gotten to the neighboring café, the Dôme, when a car shot out of the street opposite the Coupole, crossed the boulevard and screeched to a stop. The three men rushed to the edge of the sidewalk and started back to the car.

"It's him. He's come!" cried Mignot.

"Not even worth a look," said Gaudin. "Look, it's not a Citroen."

"No use," said Patrice. "It's a Delahaye."

Mignot saw that it could not be Pierrot and looked even sourer about it than Gaudin.

"I give up. I'm through," he said. "Let's get away from here."

They were at the corner when the Delahaye rolled up to them, stopped and blocked their path across the boulevard. A head with jug handle ears stuck out of the window and a voice sang out.

"Is this the way you keep a serious appointment, *mon petit* Mignot?" Pierrot asked. "If it was a dame you would have waited all night."

Mignot felt so good he could have kissed Pierrot.

"Not the latest model," said Pierrot, stepping out of the car, "but it's all yours."

The motor was still running.

"A Delahaye!" said Mignot, his eyes shining. "And all we ordered was a Citroen. *Sacré* Pierrot! What a pal!"

"Step right in, *messieurs*," said Pierrot. "Make yourselves at home."

He fished into his pocket, extracted a wallet fat with bank notes, took out some papers and handed them to Mignot, who was standing off and admiring the big black car.

"Here are the car papers," said Pierrot. "Everything's in order. The only thing I can't give you is the one-year guarantee."

"Never mind the guarantee," said Mignot. "Who knows where we'll all be a year from now?"

He slipped into the seat behind the wheel and stepped lightly on the accelerator. The motor hummed. He lifted his foot. The motor purred. He pressured the accelerator expertly, rousing the motor as he would a woman with caresses. The motor throbbed, then, at the release of his foot, whispered. He played with it for a moment, slowly graduating the sound of the motor in short snarls and gasps until for a split second the chassis quivered behind a mounting climactic whine. Suddenly Mignot stopped, and the motor murmured placidly. He could feel its power and speed at the soles of his feet, in the crook of his palm against the vibrating steering wheel. The sound of the motor was music; angels singing beyond the seventh sphere to the accompaniment of flutes and harps, skylarks and nightingales, would have sounded like sputtering harlots beside the sweet melody of that Delahaye motor. It was the first time Mignot had ever sat in a car he felt he could properly call his own—and it was a Delahaye, better than any car the Americans put out, he had always stoutly maintained, with a touch of chauvinism.

"Better than a fancy whore," he exclaimed, turning toward Pierrot.

"You said it," said Pierrot, slapping the fender. "This one will never screw you. You can have confidence."

Patrice got into the car beside Mignot. Gaudin sat on the back seat.

"How is it you're giving us a Delahaye and not a Citroen?" Gaudin asked.

"A little accident. Nothing much. You'll like this car better anyway." Pierrot waved the question away with a vague gesture. "So long," he said, and started walking off.

"What a question to ask," Mignot whispered over his shoulder. "Don't you have any tact? This is very delicate."

He called after Pierrot, and Pierrot returned to the car.

"Can we take you anywhere?"

"No, thanks." A candid grin spread over his bulldog face. "Being with you political people is too risky. When I get arrested I want it to be for what I do, not for who I'm with."

"Well," said Mignot, "you've been a Santa Claus."

"Nothing at all," said Pierrot modestly. "That's how it is when I feel I can have confidence in a man."

"You can have confidence."

Pierrot had an afterthought. "Be careful," he said. "Don't get yourself killed."

Mignot and Patrice laughed at his sudden concern.

"Aren't you going to tell us *merde* for good luck?" Mignot asked.

"*Merde,*" said Pierrot.

"Thanks."

Mignot threw in the clutch and the Delahaye leaped away. He turned the corner sharply, Patrice swaying against him, and they sped along the Boulevard Raspail. Five minutes later Mignot eased the car into a small garage on the edge of the thirteenth arrondissement near the Porte d'Ivry. A little Arab watchman led them into a dingy office separated from the garage by a glass partition. A naked electric bulb attached to a long wire dangled over a battered desk and threw a pale dirty yellow light over the room. The light fell feebly a few feet beyond the glass partition and then was overwhelmed by the darkness of the garage. Patrice and Gaudin sat down at the desk.

"Wait a minute," said Mignot.

He followed the Arab into the garage and checked the oil, water and tires of the Delahaye. Then he emptied two five-gallon cans of gas into the car's tank. When he returned to the office he was shaking his head sadly. "Such a beautiful car," he said. "It's a shame we have to use it to transport arms."

He drew a third chair up to the desk and sat down leaning his elbows on the desk's scarred surface. The silence was sepulchral. Acrid gas fumes and the oily metal smell of the garage filled the air. The dim light of the electric bulb fell flat on Mignot's face, making him look as if he had jaundice. For once no smile creased his face; the mischievous look was gone. Gaudin's face was half in the light, half in shadow. From where Mignot sat the chiaroscuro gave the illusion that Gaudin's nose did not exist; but from Patrice's angle it seemed even bigger than usual and just as melancholy. They looked at Patrice, his close-cropped hair circled by a halo of light from the bulb above and behind him, his eyes gleaming out of the dark shadow of his face. He opened the bottom drawer of the desk, took out three revolvers and passed them around. They checked the revolvers, the metal parts clicking with clean efficiency against the silence.

"I took care of everything this afternoon," Patrice explained. "All this was left here for us."

He took some papers, a long coil of rope and a big, single-blade pocketknife out of the desk and put it all in front of him. He gave sets of papers to Gaudin and to Mignot and put another set in his pocket.

"This makes all of us full-fledged fascists in good standing," he said. "We belong to the *Milice*. If we get stopped on the way these are the papers we'll show. Nothing else. On the way back we won't stop. Too dangerous. We shoot right through. Is that clear?"

Their heads nodded in unison, as if they were two intent schoolboys learning a lesson from their teacher.

"Drive at a good pace, but not too fast, Mignot," Patrice went on. "Say about seventy or seventy-five kilometers going and about eighty-five or ninety coming back."

"Unless we have trouble on the way back," said Mignot.

"Naturally. When we get there park the car right in front of the entrance so that we carry the arms the shortest possible distance in the street, and let the motor run. If the guard is there we'll put a gun in his face and tie him up with this." Patrice patted the rope. "There's enough here to tie up half a dozen people. The rest is for the concierge if she gives us any trouble. Ah, yes, I almost forgot." He took some rags out of the desk. "In case they're noisy."

"That part will be all right," said Mignot. "The guard will be up in the attic pounding beautiful's Maginot Line, and the concierge will behave."

"So much the better," said Patrice. "Gaudin, you'll stand guard outside. Hide in the entrance and watch the street. Don't do anything else. Don't even help us load the arms in the car. If a patrol comes along you'll warn us and we'll run. If possible, of course, we'll go in the car. If not, each of us is on his own. No heroics to save each other. Just split up and run." He paused. "The chances are there won't be any trouble. Now, do you have any questions?"

They had no questions.

"All right," said Patrice, "let's go over it all again and be sure there are no mistakes."

He repeated his instructions. After he finished Mignot removed the back seat of the car and the Arab put it away. The three of them climbed in up front. Then the Arab slid open the garage door, looked down the street and waved them off. The Delahaye rolled smoothly into the dark street.

They were tense and said little as they rode swiftly across the blacked-out city toward Montmartre. The streets lay before them in a pattern suddenly made strange and eerie by the darkness and their uncertainty of what awaited them in this maze of stone and shadow. All around, looming in the night sky, stood the buildings of Paris, brooding, enigmatic masses of shadow. Behind those shadows the city slept. Paris was deserted as a graveyard, a dead city swathed in a shroud of silence and night.

Mignot kept off the avenues as much as possible, guiding the Delahaye steadily through little-known streets, where German patrols were not likely to wander. He drove with the dims on, his eyes strained ahead at the racing darkness that swooped down at the feeble light of the onrushing car and sped beyond. They crossed the Seine at the tip of the Ile St. Louis and zigzagged through a labyrinth of small streets off the boulevards. Mignot turned so many corners that Gaudin became confused and thought they were lost.

"You still know the way?" he asked.

"Like my pocket."

It was when they crossed the line of the Grands Boulevards at the Rue du Faubourg Montmartre that they were stopped. There were four men in the patrol, all armed with tommy guns. One of the soldiers, the leader, looked tough. His face suddenly disappeared as a searchlight flared in his hand. The bright white beam streamed into the Delahaye and caught Patrice's pleasant, easy smile in the glare. Before the German had a chance to say anything Patrice thrust his false *Milice* papers under the man's nose.

"Heil Hitler," said Patrice. "*Milice française.*"

The German held the cone of light on Patrice's smile for a moment, then took the paper held out to him and pointed the searchlight at it. Mignot was holding down the clutch with the gear in first, ready to burst away at the first bad sign. Gaudin, squeezed between Mignot and Patrice, could do nothing and sat there frozen, feeling the blood beat in his temples. Patrice drew his revolver halfway out of his pocket. The German studied the paper for what seemed a long time.

"Hand over your papers," said Patrice to Mignot and Gaudin.

Patrice passed them to the German.

"We're all of the *Milice*," he said easily.

Silence. In an eternity of anguish time hung motionless on the beam of light. The German seemed unable to make up his mind. He drew off a few feet and consulted with the others. Three heartbeats ticked off endless minutes while the seconds crawled.

"We take off?" Mignot muttered.

"If they ask us to get out I'll shoot. Then you take off," Patrice whispered. "Now look confident. Smile."

Finally the German came back to the car. He returned all the papers to Patrice. "*Gut, gut,*" he said, and flipped up his right hand in a perfunctory salute.

"Heil Hitler," said Patrice, dropping the revolver back in his pocket and returning the salute.

Once again the darkness was rushing back at them and the sweet summer air was cool on their skin.

"Close," said Mignot.

"That Boche was lucky, too."

Gaudin said nothing. His nerves were taut, and he was thinking that the night was not yet ended. A couple of minutes later Mignot swung the car up on the sidewalk and parked in front of the entrance to the garage on the Rue de la Tour d'Auvergne.

The three of them got out. Mignot knocked on the door. They waited. Nobody answered. Mignot knocked again, louder this time. Still no response. He tried again and again without success. Finally he pounded on the door and shouted, "Ola, ola! Open up! It's me."

"Sshh," said Gaudin. "You'll wake up the whole street."

"I can't wake her up without making noise."

"Go ahead," said Patrice.

Mignot hammered on the door with both fists, crying, "Open up, open up!"

A man's voice boomed above them. "Quiet, *nom de Dieu*! It's an hour to sleep, not to break down doors. Get the hell outa here."

Two other male voices joined in the abuse and grumbled into the silence of the night. A window slammed shut

"I told you," said Gaudin.

But a light went on in the concierge's loge and they heard slippered feet shuffle toward the door.

"Who is it?" rasped an irritated voice.

"It's me," said Mignot. He was whispering now. "The mechanic. The little one."

"What do you want at this hour?"

It was the voice of an enemy, not at all suspicious, just angry. Awakening the concierge unexpectedly was an offense more villainous than deserting the ship, running up the white flag or serving the enemy. Mignot knew it. Getting up in the middle of the night to open the door was her job; like most concierges there was nothing in the wide world she hated so much.

"Be nice," Mignot wheedled. "I forgot my tools and I have a job to do early tomorrow on the other side of Paris. Open up."

Two bolts turned in two locks, one after the other, and the door squealed open. Mignot stepped in, with Patrice directly behind him, the coil of rope over his shoulder.

"Hurry up!" Gaudin whispered after them.

The concierge backed up when she saw the gun in Mignot's hand. She was a husky, square-faced Alsatian, who was always brushing her unkempt hair out of her eyes. She stammered unintelligibly and kept backing up.

"Nothing to get excited about," said Mignot. "We just came to get those arms in the garage. Nothing will happen to you if you just stay quiet."

"Where's the guard?" Patrice asked.

"Upstairs."

Her eyes turned up toward the ceiling. Suddenly she got over her surprise and started to shout at Mignot and wail. "You have no right to do this after I opened the door for you," she cried. "You're going to get me into trouble with the Germans and what will happen when—"

Unexpectedly a gruff, authoritative man's voice coming from the far end of the room cut her short in mid-sentence. "What's going on?" the voice bellowed.

They turned. The room was littered with spare parts, used wrapping paper, old tires, strips of metal, bric-a-brac, all strewn about in cataclysmic disorder. On the mantelpiece, dominating the chaos below, stood two enormous bronzes, mustached infantrymen of the First World War, wearing their greatcoats, leggings and old-fashioned helmets, rifles at right shoulder arms, marching proudly and heroically toward victory. Patrice's eyes and revolver swept to the right. A huge double bed stood against the wall. In it, sitting erect, was an irate man. Like the bronze *poilus*, a mustache bristled along the length of his upper lip, but unlike them, he was clad in a white nightgown with a lacy, embroidered edge. A tassled nightcap covered his forehead to the eyebrows and drooped over his ear like a limp cone. Hanging above his head in an elaborate gilt frame was a blown-up life-size photograph, tinted in thunderous pastels, of the man when he was twenty-five years younger. A stern, clear-eyed soldier in full regalia, his medal-bedecked chest thrust forward, stared courageously out of the frame at the confusion of the world and the room. He looked like Marshal Foch. Below, twenty-five years later, he looked like the concierge's husband. Patrice and Mignot stared at him. He stared back. The nightcap slipped over his eyes. Impatiently he pushed it back.

"What's going on here?" he thundered, ignoring the guns pointed at him.

Patrice repressed an impulse to laugh. The man deigned to notice the weapons.

"Your guns don't frighten me," he said. "I've faced worse."

Patrice thought he was about to start reminiscing about his war experiences. Instead he turned to his wife.

"Well, what is it?" he asked with an unruffled tone of authority.

Pushing wisps of hair out of her face, she told him, denouncing Mignot's treachery, protesting her innocence, bewailing what would happen to them. He listened awhile, then silenced her with a gesture.

"You can't let them take the arms," she cried. "The Germans will deport us."

"Silence!" he shouted.

It was 1918, he was once more a sergeant and he had to make a decision. He paused, looked at Patrice and Mignot, then turned to his wife. "Woman!" he cried, pushing the nightcap out of his eyes. "I did my duty. Let them do theirs."

Patrice grinned. Mignot laughed.

"That's it, Grandpa, tell her," said Mignot.

"I am not a grandpa," the man said with dignity; then to his wife, "Well, go ahead, give them the keys."

Still she hesitated. "We won't get in trouble?" she asked uncertainly.

"It's for the *Patrie*!" he cried impatiently. "And, besides, they covered me with a gun. What could I do? Anyway, it's that bastard of a guard who'll catch it. Ah, the Boche sonofabitch!" The man turned his head and spat in disgust. "A foot soldier who spends guard duty up in an attic riding between the thighs of that blonde filly! What does he think he is, a cavalry officer? Let him gallop and trot. This will teach him to keep his feet on the ground and his gun on his shoulder!"

He glared fiercely around the room and turned commandingly on his wife. Without another word she poked among the clothes lying across a chair and came up with the keys, which she handed to Mignot. Then, grumbling and still reluctant, she climbed into bed beside her husband.

Patrice and Mignot worked fast. First they carried out three cases of munitions; then they loaded a stack of potato-masher grenades in the trunk of the car. After that they packed eight light machine guns in the back and finally piled in more than a dozen rifles. Considering the poverty of the resistance in arms it was a magnificent haul.

As they were passing through the concierge's loge for the last time Mignot called out, "Thanks and good night."

The concierge's husband was still sitting up in bed. "What should we tell them?" he asked.

"Tell them it was me," said Mignot. "They'll never find me anyway."

"Aren't you going to tie us up to make it look real?"

Patrice hurriedly cut off a length of rope and threw it toward the bed. "Here. Tell them we tied you up and you wriggled loose. Just give us five minutes. We'll be safe in that time."

"I'd like to go with you," the man said. "If I were young again . . ."

There was a wistful look in his eyes, and when Patrice got to the door he turned back toward the disorder and the tassled head beyond, searching for a word the old man would like. "Thanks," he said. "You're a soldier."

The door was open and Patrice halfway out when he heard the man's voice, husky and cracked. "*Vive la France!*"

They raced back across the slumbering city, anxious to be swallowed up again in the safety of the garage. Mignot's eyes strained into the darkness as he guided the big car with a sure hand. But over the smooth hum of the motor they heard another sound. It was the steady, unremitting roar and rumble of tanks and trucks lumbering over the boulevards. They looked uneasily at each other.

"Sounds like a lot of tanks," Gaudin muttered.

"Retreating from Normandy," said Mignot, hunched over the steering wheel.

"Or sent in to hold the city," Patrice said. "We'll know tomorrow. Keep going. If anybody tries to stop us we'll lose them in the small streets."

But nobody tried to stop them. They crossed the boulevards and the Seine and shot through the blacked-out streets of the left bank right up to the garage without incident. After the arms were unloaded and hidden they ate sandwiches of black bread and an unlikely pâté that they regarded with suspicion and washed down with a raw red wine.

"If there's anything alive in the pâté," said Mignot, "this wine will kill it."

"Will kill them," said Patrice.

Mignot swallowed a mouthful of the food and took a long drink from a stained glass.

"Ouf," he said. "A mean, ugly little wine. All I can taste is the alcohol. Where's the grape?"

"They were badly brought up," said Gaudin. "All rain and no sun."

"The moldiness remains, the nobility is gone," said Patrice.

But they were hungry and thirsty and ate the sandwiches in great mouthfuls and drank the wine in huge draughts. It warmed and refreshed them. Not even the twinge of anxiety Patrice felt from time to time about the tanks they had heard moving in the city undercut his enthusiasm. He had the arms and with them the means to act independently. It was not much, but he thought it would be enough. With the raid on the garage he had achieved his preinsurrection goal.

They had to remain in the garage until the curfew lifted at six in the morning. Unable to sleep, they played cards for the balance of the night. Mignot never stopped joking. He won 247 francs. Even Gaudin wore a smile most of the night; once he burst into an asthmatic laugh, suffocating over one of Mignot's bland witticisms. And Gaudin lost more than half the amount that Mignot won.

†

THEY left the garage shortly after six. The sky was low and heavy, the city gray. For a while they walked together through deep, empty ravines that stretched endlessly between the steep buildings into the silence of the morning. Soon their ways parted.

"Now that I'm armed for the meeting this afternoon," Patrice said with a smile, "I'd better get some sleep."

"We all need sleep," said Mignot.

Patrice retrieved his bicycle at the café, where he had left it, and rode across the city to where a bed and rest awaited him. On the way he saw a flood of German convoys pouring through the central arteries of Paris in flight toward the east.

Later the sun came out and the day was hot and fine. By early afternoon thousands of strollers crowded the boulevards and the Champs Élysées; café terraces were packed; the population lined the sidewalks five and six deep: nobody wanted to miss the spectacle of the German retreat. With unsmiling faces and ironic eyes, Parisians watched sweating German military police, waving red and white disks, direct the avalanche of traffic rolling toward Germany. The vehicles were painted in black and green camouflage stripes and covered with much of the landscape of Normandy. The noise was oceanic. Churning through the city in a motley parade were Tiger tanks and horse-drawn wagons, limousines and green Paris busses, trucks and staff cars, half tracks and ambulances. The vehicles were jammed with grimy men whose bodies sagged from exhaustion. Their unshaven faces were powdered with dust. They looked stunned. The spectators betrayed neither sympathy nor antagonism. Like people at the wake of a distasteful old relative whose whims they have long suffered for the fortune they would now inherit, they prudently suppressed their joy.

The turmoil of retreat reached into quiet side streets. Service after German service moved out of requisitioned hotels and office buildings under the serene eyes of crowds of watchful Parisians. Clean-shaven garrison officers and neatly uniformed troops joined the procession on the boulevards toward home. Their trucks were piled high with trunks and rolled-up rugs, typewriters and refrigerators, cases of champagne and Louis XVI tables and chairs. Wags along the boulevards were saying, "They came, they saw, they were conquered."

Lefort, on his way to the meeting of resistance leaders, paused at the Place de l'Opéra and watched the retreat with the deepest pleasure. He did not hear the hawkers barking the prices of lollipops and candles. Nor did he hear the people around him, looking at the Kommandantur across the way, and asking, "Will they leave too? Will they leave too?" He closed his eyes for a moment, thinking of what this retreat meant, and, conscious of the opera house behind him and the imminent realization of his dreams, he heard the horns of *Götterdämmerung,* the siren voices of the *Walküre,* the trumpet of *Fidelio* . . .

"How do you get to the Champs Élysées?"

Lefort opened his eyes and saw a tall German major, bareheaded and erect in front of an open car. His face was yellow with a thin layer of dust that accentuated the lines of fatigue around his mouth and eyes. Lefort's arm came up automatically; it described an unwavering arc and wound up pointing down the Rue du 4 Septembre, the opposite direction from the Champs Élysées.

"Into that street and straight ahead," said Lefort. "Just keep going. You can't miss it."

The major saluted. Slowly, very slowly, his chauffeur turned around the square in a great circle and entered the Rue du 4 Septembre. Behind the major's car there followed a long line of trucks describing the same slow, graceful curve around the Place de l'Opéra. Lefort's eyes opened wide. This was a bigger joke than he had calculated. He counted the trucks. Ten . . . twenty . . . thirty-seven . . . He turned and walked quickly beyond the chattering tables of the Café de la Paix toward the Rue Royale. He was astonished at his lack of prudence. The trick of a child or a fool in the center of Paris. It was not the sort of risk a man in his position took merely to hold up a column of trucks for an hour or so. He thought that if he who was so cautious and lucid, who never committed an act or spoke a word without calculation, could spontaneously do anything so imprudent under the impact of the German flight, what then must be the effect of the Nazi departure on the city's millions?

Near the Madeleine a one-legged beggar was sitting on the sidewalk playing a nickel-plated accordion that sparkled in the sun. The beggar was squeezing out the same pathetically sweet air from *La Traviata* that Patrice had heard two days before. The frail melody rose weepily against the uproar of the German retreat like the innocent voice of a lost child. As Lefort walked past the beggar a truck screeched to a stop and a soldier dashed from it, brushing by Lefort. Suddenly a jangle of discordant accordion notes cut off the music in the middle of a phrase. Lefort turned. The soldier was tugging at the accordion, while the one-legged beggar held onto his instrument and tugged back. Seesawing between them, the accordian wheezed and squealed, gasped and moaned. Finally it gave a long one-note groan of despair as the German, yanking with all his strength, ripped it away. He squeezed the accordion noisily shut and held it against his hip. The beggar struggled up with one crutch, shouting, "Give it back! Give it back!" The German said nothing. He pushed the one-legged man off balance. Then, with the beggar sprawled on the sidewalk, the soldier ran to the truck and hopped into it, hugging the accordion. A moment later the truck was speeding up the boulevard, an anonymous part of the German retreat.

Rocking unsteadily, the beggar sat up. His left leg was thrust out stiffly, his right trouser leg pinned under the stump.

"*Salaud!*" he shouted. "You'll pay for this!"

The man tore into a burst of violent curses, then suddenly subsided, his first fury spent.

He had clear, angry blue eyes, straight blond hair, parted on the side, and a square face. His shirt sleeves were rolled up and showed thick-muscled arms. When he got up Lefort saw that despite the absence of a leg he was tall and powerfully built. The beggar shook with helpless anger.

"I'll get a dozen of them!" he cried. "A dozen!"

"Not so loud," whispered a woman in the crowd that had gathered. "They'll hear you."

"Let them hear me! Ah, the swine!"

He was still muttering, "I'll get a dozen of them, a round dozen," when Lefort left.

Along the Seine it was peaceful. History was a mile away in the turbulence of the boulevards. This was the turning point, Lefort thought. For the ones, freedom and an endless vision beyond horizons; for the others, the broken hope of conquest abandoned by the roadside as the bitter dust settled and the convoys rumbled home to the bare ruins of defeat.

The sun shone down on the placid green waters. The expanse of river, banks and quais was bathed in the clear light of the blue August sky. All around was the sleepy feel of just another lazy summer afternoon. Lefort felt his nerves unwind after the excitement of the boulevards. He strode along rapidly, his step vigorous. Twice he laughed aloud. He had seen the Germans fleeing. The impact of that single fact and his certainty that now nothing could stop the insurrection gave him a sense of unconquerable power. For four years he had led the life of a tracked criminal and today he had seen his trackers in flight. The summer smell of the sun filled his nose and throat, and he started across the Seine with the undivided mind of a man propelled by a destiny whose image he has seen and felt.

A ripple of laughter sang up to him from the river below. Lefort leaned over the stone parapet of the bridge. Strewn on the grassy bank were some women's clothes. Lefort shifted his gaze. One after the other three girls swam toward shore, their arms flashing wet in the sun. One after the other they reached the bank. As they hoisted themselves up Lefort was amazed to see their firm young breasts emerge naked from the water. They stood up and looked around, their panties pasted to their buttocks, their long-legged bodies dripping cool and bright in the sun. Nobody. Then one of the girls saw Lefort looking at them from the bridge. She laughed and turned her back, speaking quickly to the others, who glanced up at Lefort and turned away from him too. A moment later they were lying in the grass on their stomachs, drying themselves in the sun. The first one looked up at Lefort again, said something, and all three laughed and turned their heads up at Lefort. He hesitated, started down the embankment, hesitated again and looked at his watch. Just time to make the meeting. The boulevards and the fleeing legions of the German army were all so far away now. Lefort looked down at the three brown backs baking in the sun beside the sweep of river in the silence of the lazy afternoon, and the inviting sound of the girls' laughter stirred the depths of his desire. The embankment or the meeting? If it were only a question of the insurrection Lefort knew he would stay with the girls; his presence at the meeting would not tip the balance of decision. But he had to see Patrice to clinch a personal matter that might make all the difference for his future. Once the future was wrapped up in a neat little package . . . Lefort sighed, whipped out a handkerchief and wiped his brow. Vaguely he wondered why he always ran away from the warm and fleeting present, which could never be recaptured, into a seductive but remote future, which could never be reached. He recalled the look of the girls' breasts as they rose from the river. They were waiting for him, the three of them. An hour from now, somewhere, an apartment, a hotel room . . . But the future was even more enticing; an obsession deeper than any passion he had known in his twenty-five years of existence tormented him. He took a long last regretful look at the three girls and walked briskly toward the meeting.

†

LIKE everybody else who circulated in Paris that day, Reboussin saw the departure of the Germans. The sudden enemy movement came to him as a surprise, for there had been no prior hint of it, although rumors to which he gave no credence had been plentiful. It was clear, of course, from the Paris press and the Allied radio that the Germans were fighting a losing battle in Normandy; but the rigidly maintained Allied news blackout precluded any certain knowledge of the exact battle lines or the precise direction of the main Allied advance. The secret messages sent in code from London were even less informative on this score than the radio. So Reboussin, like millions of other Parisians, had his first indication that the occupation was coming to an end when he walked into the street that morning and saw the Germans leaving.

After a first virginal sensation of unmixed pleasure, Reboussin thought of the political implications of the event, and his delight gave way to concern. Politically, his aim was to keep the resistance in check until the Americans arrived and the city was safe from German reprisals and communist ambitions. The German flight, coming at the peak of the underground debate, was apt to cripple his efforts and give the insurrectionary drive of the resistance a new and irresistible propulsion. He set out for the meeting that afternoon with misgivings. The extremists would have some new and forceful arguments for their insurrection. There were rumors, possibly true, Reboussin now thought, of an agreement between the Kommandantur of Gross-Paris and the

American Command, that the city would be tactfully evacuated by the former and discreetly occupied by the latter. Laval and Herriot were still in Paris, so far as Reboussin knew, and there was the constant danger that they would convoke a National Assembly as provided by the constitution of the Third Republic and under the protection of the Americans take over the liberation government of France. The railroad and police strikes were successful. That very morning post office, telephone and telegraph workers had struck too. The Paris radio was off the air and no newspapers had appeared that morning. The city was crippled. The collaborators had fled. At times the distant sound of cannon could be heard in the center of the city. Only a few hours ago a thousand metro workers had demonstrated in front of the Hotel de Ville, crying for bread and singing the Marseillaise. All signs indicated that the people were ripe for violence. And now the Germans were fleeing, which proved they did not have the strength to hold Paris and were afraid to remain there.

These were powerful arguments which were not without their force, even on Reboussin—particularly the menace of the return of the old parliamentarians. But if the Germans were leaving Paris, they had not yet left. This was the moment of crisis. Warsaw all over again. The city was ahead of events: the people were ripe for an insurrection that the situation did not yet justify. Reboussin felt the wave of patriotic passion sweep over Paris like a hot southern wind blowing across the city. It coiled around, picked people up and tossed them into a vortex of emotion into which they in turn pulled friends, neighbors; old, young, cynics and even some collaborators suddenly and quite mysteriously became patriots. Reboussin fought against being carried away by this high wind of national passion. It was too soon, too soon, he thought. A premature act could still bring disaster to Paris.

†

AFTER sleeping soundly all morning Patrice cycled halfway to the intersection called Alesia, left his bicycle at a café and walked the rest of the way. Riviere, a resistance leader with whom Patrice had an appointment to go to the critical meeting, had not yet arrived. Patrice sat on a bench on the Avenue du Maine side of the Église St. Pierre, which was set back from the street and formed the most distinctive angle of the intersection, its single shaft of grimy stone thrust bleakly into the sky. Patrice removed his jacket and rolled up his sleeves; he wore no tie and his shirt was spread open, exposing his chest to the sun. Eyes closed and head tilted back to catch the sun flat on his face, Patrice relaxed contentedly.

Thinking of Riviere, Patrice smiled. A gnomelike little old man, Riviere was the *enfant terrible* of the resistance leaders and under his real name the most popular professor at the Sorbonne. In the Latin Quarter his iconoclasm was classic. "I have corrupted several generations of French youth," he often said. "Think of how many men and women must be grateful to me for the pleasures my ideas have procured them."

Considering some of his lectures, it was remarkable that through the years he had retained his professional chair. As Patrice luxuriated in the sun, he smilingly recalled the first words he had ever heard from Riviere's lips. He had walked into the Sorbonne lecture hall late, just as Riviere announced, "Virginity is not a virtue; it is a barrier to intercourse. I beg you to remember that society cannot exist without intercourse." It was the beginning of Riviere's famous lecture on incest, which Patrice was never to forget. The prejudice against incest, Riviere claimed, was illogical and even nefarious. Pretending indignation, he cried, "It is inadmissible that strange men deflower our young girls and unknown women seduce our boys."

Patrice still remembered vividly how the class had sat up, someone behind him whispering hoarsely, "There he goes again," as Riviere chopped and hacked at the moral structure society had arbitrarily built around the family and its sexual practices.

"Consider the irreparable damage that is often done," he said, "when a young girl is brutally introduced to what we may ironically call love by an individual who thinks, not of the girl's frailty and inexperience, but only of his own pleasure. This is criminal and another reason why sex, like charity, should begin at home. Who can better introduce a young girl to the mysteries of love and sex," he asked, "than her father, with his concern for his daughter's welfare and pleasure? Who is better fitted to teach a boy about sex with love, tenderness and experience than his mother? Who are more fit to live happily together as man and wife than brother and sister, with their similarity of background, upbringing and taste? Once they have learned the rudiments, intricacies and subtleties of sex at home," he declared, "it will be time for them to leave and fornicate abroad." He cited esoteric philosophers as authorities, delved into the history of the Egyptian royal family centuries before to prove that the fruit of incestuous relations was

often the healthiest, and turned up anthropological evidence that society did not always condemn incest but, on the contrary, sometimes
fostered it. He wound up by slyly suggesting, "Moreover, those who
consider what I say frivolous should bear in mind that there is probably nothing like incest that is so admirably calculated to keep the
family intact." Then, with no more transition than an "on the other
hand," Riviere maintained with equal force that the mixture of
strange bloods and races produced the best and most fascinating results. Intramarriage, he stated, led to sterile, repetitive patterns
and stultified human and intellectual growth, while intermarriage
resulted in a novel and vigorous progeny. One student objected that
it was difficult to tell whether one should have relations with one's
sister or take a Negro girl from the Congo as a mistress. "The two
possibilities," the professor had replied, "are not mutually exclusive.
I leave it to you to draw, with discretion of course, the obvious infer-
ence."

Patrice grinned as he recalled the amused incredulity of the class.
Riviere claimed he entertained outrageous ideas because outrageous
ideas entertained him, and there was no doubt that for an elderly and
respected professor of philosophy his views were singular. "I am an
intellectual sensualist," he insisted. "I like ideas that tickle my fancy."
Raised by the Jesuits, he had reacted violently against them and the
Church. "One's tastes should be catholic," he liked to say, "and one's
beliefs liberal." But as Patrice knew, he did not care if students left
his classes without a new idea in their heads; all his wiles were aimed
at developing enlightened minds; his concern was to give students the
taste and technique of taking ideas apart and putting them together
again. With his intellectual extravagance he goaded them to criticism,
convinced of the paradox that only a critical mind can be tolerant.
His formula, however, turned Voltaire inside out: "I disagree with
what you say and will defend to the death my right to say it." He
could be exasperatingly intolerant.

It was with such intellectual peculiarities that the professor, like an
embattled Heraclitus against the Eliatics, took the name of Riviere
and entered the resistance. "I have no choice," he had said to Patrice.
"If the Third Republic was ridiculous, Vichy and the Nazis are ab-
horrent." He had added, as an afterthought, "Individualism is a
plague exceeded only by conformity," and with characteristic individualism immediately tried to make the manifold and disparate ele-

ments of the resistance conform to his conception of what was best for it. His views coincided with those of a strong corps of nonpolitical militants. On the other hand, the Catholic faction treated him with unconcealed, if restrained, animosity, while the communists, recognizing his independence and unpredictability, tolerated but did not trust him.

Thinking lazily of all this, Patrice reflected that Riviere's idiosyncrasies and political ineptitude had alienated practically every resistance figure with whom he had dealt. Patrice yawned. He felt someone staring at him and opened his eyes. It was Riviere.

"Don't tell me how hot it is," Riviere said. "I know."

Patrice smiled. "It should be hotter where we're going."

"I know that too," Riviere said dryly. "The unity of the resistance is being welded in the heat of opposition."

He was an extraordinarily ugly man, with amazingly young, incandescent eyes. His head, topped by a flurry of disheveled gray hair, was enormous in relation to his slight, shrunken body; his back was stooped, his face wizened and his long nose pinched, sharp and hooked at the bridge. There was an expression of amused wickedness on his shriveled face, which was so bright and alive that he seemed, despite the face corrugated with wrinkles, like a very young man.

Patrice gathered his jacket under his arm, and they set out for the Porte de Vanves, where the meeting was to be held. For a while they walked in silence. Patrice broke it. "What do you think the risk is of Paris's being destroyed or at least badly damaged?"

Riviere shrugged. A strong supporter of the insurrection, he did not like the question. "It's a risk," he said. "Trouble is there's a risk either way—with or without an insurrection. If the Germans defend the city and the Allies besiege it who can predict what will happen? Our job is to make Paris untenable for the Germans. An insurrection will cut the risks, but we'll have to have the courage to take the first step. That won't be easy. To end the danger to the city we must first precipitate it. Everybody won't understand or agree. Some of our colleagues will want to sit on their hands."

"I imagine they'll come around," Patrice said.

Riviere smiled. "There are two ways of changing a man's mind—persuasion and force. Suppose we can't persuade them."

"What do you mean?"

"You're the military man in this affair," Riviere said.

Patrice thought of how Bourbon's confessor had said it was the colonel's duty to shoot communist leaders. "That isn't what you used to say at the Sorbonne," he said sharply.

"I'm not giving lectures on Plato's *Republic* any more. This is politics, not philosophy. At the Sorbonne we discussed abstract principles and chose the best. But politics is the art of imposing one's will on others. We must be practical. When diplomacy fails the sole recourse is war."

"We're already fighting one war," Patrice said.

"Two," Riviere replied. "One against our enemies and one against our friends. If we don't win the second we can't fight the first."

After a pause Riviere said, "We've got to impose our policy on our friends at all costs."

"At all costs?" said Patrice. "That goes a long way."

"Men like Bourbon, Sorel and Reboussin can no longer be coaxed or argued into changing their minds; they must be forced. You know the kind of men they are." Riviere's eyes glinted. "Bourbon is an army colonel and all his relatives are probably idiots too—a noble name encrusted on the skin of an ass. There are two things you can't do with him—separate him from an old idea or convince him of a new one. Apart from that he has an open mind. Sorel is a megalomaniac who believes he's Marx and Kropotkin rolled into one. He thinks stubbornness is strength, and if Bourbon is an ass he's a mule. Reboussin is a coward. The mere thought of an insurrection makes him want to pick up the phone and put in an emergency call for the police."

Only Reboussin was really important, Patrice was thinking, but all three would be at the meeting and each would have a vote.

"Against men like these," Riviere went on, "words are insufficient. We must go on to acts. What I am driving at is very simple. When the time comes we must have our insurrection whether these men and the others are for it or not—even at the price of an open split."

Riviere looked up sharply at Patrice to read his reaction. Patrice was one of a handful of men who had worked with the famous Max to unify the resistance. Patrice had been lucky. He had not gone to the ill-fated meeting at Calluire, near Lyon. Max had gone. Swallowed up in German prisons and concentration camps, he had not been heard from since and was assumed dead. With the loss of Max and the others, the existence of the National Council of the Resistance, representing in one underground governing body all the major anti-Nazi parties and movements in France, was as much the work of Patrice as it was of anybody else alive. Now Riviere was asking him to sabotage what he had struggled so long with so many others to achieve.

"Is that what you meant by 'at all costs'?"

Riviere nodded.

"I thought you meant something else." Patrice grinned. "It won't mean a split. You left out Bidault and Parodi. They'll go along. And the others will tail after them."

The two men walked through grubby streets filled with the bird-like cries of ragged children. Riviere was suddenly very gay. He told three Marius and Olive jokes in rapid succession, two quite funny. Then he whistled *Je suis seul ce soir*; if he had begun to skip Patrice would not have been more surprised.

"Of course," Riviere said as they approached the meeting place, "if we were really consequent in our reasoning we would do something else. You and I would call a meeting of resistance leaders. When they were gathered together we would divide them into two groups. We would choose them one by one. 'You, come over here with us. You, go over there against the wall.' After every man had been picked we would line up all the men in the group against the wall, stand off a short distance, and shoot them."

"Shoot half the leadership of the resistance arbitrarily?" Patrice said.

"A little more than half the leadership. And there would be nothing arbitrary about it."

"How would you choose them?"

"Nothing could be easier," said Riviere. "I would put up against the wall all those who wanted to become ministers."

He glanced up slyly at Patrice, a thin smile on his lips and laughter in his eyes. "You will tell me I'm impractical," he said, "and you're right. But isn't the project sublime?"

They walked into an ancient tenement and up three flights of rotting wooden stairs. Riviere was again whistling *Je suis seul ce soir*; he was a little flat.

"*Mon cher* Patrice," he said as they stood before the door of the apartment and he distastefully sniffed the fetid air, "I beg you to re-member that if we were meeting at the Hotel Matignon the atmos-phere would be more conducive to pleasant breathing and the attend-ants would be wearing frock coats with gold chains, but some of the men present would be no less fatuous than in this modest hide-out."

When the door opened Riviere murmured, "My dear minister," and waved Patrice on ahead of him.

†

A SCRAWNY woman wearing a soiled housedress and a frightened expression let them into the apartment.

"Hurry," she whispered. "It will begin soon."

But as Riviere went into the next room Lefort came out of it and grasped Patrice's arm. "Wanted to talk to you," he said. "I made a big decision about what I'm going to do when all this is over. It's the newspaper."

"*Le Saboteur*? But it's nothing, and you don't know anything about newspapers anyway."

Lefort grinned. "That's what they all told me. But finally they said, 'Good. If you want the paper take it.' I took it. Take and thou shalt receive; give and thou shalt want."

Patrice was interested. "What are you going to do with it now that you have it?" he asked.

"I have that all worked out," said Lefort. "It's only a resistance sheet now. Sometimes it appears, sometimes it doesn't. And we don't have many readers. But soon it will be one of the important papers in France, the biggest if we do things better than the others."

"Maybe," Patrice said.

"I don't blame you for being skeptical."

"How are you going to do it?"

"Let me tell you what I've done up to now. It may amuse you."

"Go ahead," said Patrice. "It's a long time since I've been amused."

"Well, the first thing I did was to buy two books one day when I was walking along the quai. One of them was called *The History of Journalism*."

Patrice smiled. "Very funny," he said. "Did the book teach you how to run a big Paris daily?"

"It did teach me something," said Lefort. "It said that in the days of the Romans when a politician wanted to get the ear of the people he went to the forum and made a speech. Today the forum to get the attention of forty million people is the newspapers. That taught me that newspapers are pretty important."

"Elementary. You should have known that without having to read a book."

"Seeing it in print gave the idea another dimension. If a newspaper were big enough it could be stronger than the government and the politicians who make it up."

"Maybe you *were* cut out to be a publisher," said Patrice.

Lefort grinned good-humoredly. "I bought another book too," he said. "*Journalism in Twenty Lessons.*"

Patrice laughed. "If you keep up at this rate nothing will stop you. You'll be the boy wonder of the French press."

"I also had a newspaperman friend take me on a visit to the *Pariser Zeitung*. I wanted to see the kind of thing I was getting myself into. It seemed complicated enough. All those machines. Anyway, I decided it shouldn't be too hard to start at the top with a fair chance of success. Here's my idea. In the resistance I'm an organizer and executive. It comes down to that, doesn't it? I'm doing the same thing with the newspaper and I'll learn as I go along with the best men in the business. To begin with I've hired seven men who know as much about editing a paper as anyone in France, and for the business and administrative side I have a former *Paris-Soir* man who should be able to keep the books nicely balanced. Practically all the other resistance sheets are going to become morning papers. We'll be one of the few evening papers. Not so serious maybe, but less competition and a bigger field. Everything is ready. All we have to do now is wait for the insurrection to break, take over the printing plant assigned to us and start the presses rolling."

Of course, Patrice thought. That was it. That was why Lefort favored the insurrection. It was the newspaper he wanted to get out of the resistance, and an insurrection would clinch the affair. No wonder political ambition failed to explain his position. Everything dovetailed now. Patrice knew that the resistance had worked out a plan to take over that part of the press—practically all of it—which had continued to publish during the occupation under German orders. Eliminating the venal press was part of the plan for the social and economic liberation of the country, the revolutionary aspect of the resistance. Once the insurrection exploded, not only would committees of liberation take over every aspect of government from the city of Paris down to the tiniest hamlet, but the press would be sequestered. The physical assets, buildings, machinery, paper stocks, equipment, would be turned over to those resistance groups now publishing clandestine sheets. To start them off the Provisional Government would advance three million francs to each group putting out a daily in Paris.

Lefort would be starting from scratch, but so would all the others. Why shouldn't he win the race for circulation, Patrice thought, if his editors did a better job than the others?

"There's the small matter of what building and presses we get," Lefort said lightly. "I have a weakness for the *Pariser Zeitung* place in the Rue Réaumur. Not merely because it's one of the best, although that doesn't make it less attractive. It's a matter of sentimentality too. The *Pariser Zeitung* has been so close to me for so long. And those are the only presses I've ever seen. It's just about fixed. But I'd like your support if you're consulted."

"I can't see any reason why I shouldn't give it to you," said Patrice.

After all, why not? Some group had to get the place. Why not Lefort's? His was as good as and better than most. Nevertheless, knowing Lefort always exercised his charm for a purpose and that the purpose normally determined the limits of his candor, Patrice wondered what he had left unsaid.

"Thanks." Lefort smiled. "That's good enough for me."

†

THEY walked into an ugly salon that was connected to the dining room and sat down. A dozen men, standing around or sitting elbow to elbow on straight-backed chairs, were cramped into the small space. Since the shutters were closed, the rooms were gloomy, and this absence of light in which the meeting was enveloped intensified the bitter and oppressive atmosphere of a showdown.

It was a socialist household. On the walls were three large photographs—Marx, Jaurès, Blum—hung, no doubt, in honor of the occasion. On the mantelpiece under Marx's bearded frown stood a small mischievous head of Voltaire, whose mercurial eyes flashed ironically into the intent faces of the resistance leaders.

Bourbon, erect and military even in a black business suit, stood by a window talking to Sorel, a rotund little socialist with a black, bristling mustache, whose small eyes peered shrewdly out of a pudgy face. Sorel was a pompous man with illusions of grandeur that puffed him up beyond his size. His ambition outstripped his ability, but his energetic persistence and confident ignorance of his mediocre talents had enabled him to go much farther than many another man of greater promise. He wore elevated shoes to gain an inch or two in stature, and his sparse hair was carefully plastered down in an almost successful effort to cover the bald spots. Bourbon loomed over him, and Sorel, with his hands behind his back, his body stiff and his chest stretched out almost as far as his stomach, seemed to be straining to match the colonel's effortless rigidity.

Near them stood Mazaud, a communist militant risen from the lower depths of the metallurgical industry to the heights of union leadership and a hard-earned niche in the upper ranks of the party hierarchy. He was a big, deep-chested man with thick, powerful arms and shoulders and a massive head. His face, with the square chin, heavy jowls and fleshy nose, was blunt and flat, like a rammer. When he spoke it was in a hoarse, abrasive voice with the tough accent of the Paris slum from which he came. He was vigorous and able, but communism circumscribed his world like the walls of a monastery that of a monk. Poverty, labor strife, party politics, Marxist theory were his school and marked the limits of his understanding, which, though narrow, was deep. He was sectarian and inflexible. If these limitations warped him as a human being, professionally they were qualities that multiplied his effectiveness. He was disliked and respected.

On the other side of the room Reboussin, remembering the socialist origins of Mussolini, Laval and Doriot and operating on the principle that no intelligent man in politics is beyond change or corruption, spoke earnestly with Laperche, trying to win his confidence. Laperche was a communist but as different from Mazaud as a starling from a hawk. A slender young intellectual with a sensitive face and huge liquid black eyes, Laperche looked more like a poet than a spoke in the party wheel. He was clever, relatively new to the party, ambitious and friendlier toward outsiders than were the old party war horses. Where Mazaud shouted, he spoke softly; where Mazaud turned an angry back, he made a gesture of compromise. They complemented each other—like a mallet and a chisel.

Patrice looked around the room and noted men and faces. The elite of the resistance. It showed. Professional socialists, communists, liberals, Catholics, labor leaders, politicians. Patrice ticked them off. The new professional, too—the professional man of the resistance, of which Patrice was one. Amateurs molded into professionals, idealists ground into realists, visionaries transformed into technicians. It was normal. Those who remained amateurs were left behind, those who made mistakes disappeared. The resistance was a tough school and only the fittest survived. But what happened to the survivors in the process? The clear motive blended into method and was blurred, the end into means and was forgotten; the dream became a blueprint and was dissipated; in the heat of combat the first fresh passion was forged into a cold instrument, a technique, and was spent. Only through the clandestine struggle for power could the dream be realized, but in the course of the struggle, through the necessities for its realization, the dream became shapeless, evaporated in the cold light of conflict, and the dreamers, wide-awake now, shrewd, subtle, energetic, ruthless, dreamed no dreams: they spoke with their lips, but their ideas, visibly, were behind their eyes. As good an elite as any, but an elite. It was the common anti-Nazi purpose and the risk that made them shine like armored knights striking out on milk-white steeds for God and glory. That fine romantic gleam was dazzling at a distance; close up, inside the magic circle, the luster tarnished. There were good people, excellent people, in this room, but leadership imposed temptations not easily withstood. They were struggling together and against each other toward a moment, close by, when power and position would be reshuffled; what some gained others would fail to get. More was at stake than Paris and French prestige.

They settled in their places. Bourbon's military report. Nothing new. The exact location of the Americans? Unknown. Speculation hedged with conditions.

The debate was engaged. Two estimates clashed: one, the Germans were abandoning Paris; two, the Germans were moving out administrative personnel, stripping off the fat to dig in and fight for the French capital.

"Digging in!" Mazaud cried scornfully. "Every Parisian who's looked out of his window today—every child—knows that the Germans have cut loose and are fleeing. Our job isn't to sit here and let them get away but to cut them to bits—"

"If the Americans are stopped on the Seine as long as the Russians were on the Vistula, we'll be the ones who are cut to bits."

Several men spoke at once; when the confusion became unscrambled Reboussin was advising caution. Patrice sensed a general restlessness as he spoke. The phrases sounded empty, as if Reboussin himself did not fully believe them.

". . . must not act prematurely . . . The situation requires a policy of progressive acts, graduated step by step, so that while controlling the strikes—"

"Control the strikes!" Mazaud cried impatiently. "The workers are striking spontaneously. They can't be stopped. Until now our policy *has* been progressive. We've done it step by step. But this is the moment for the last big step, the one we've got to take *now* for all the others to have any meaning. What the great masses of Parisians want is to fight. We ought to be leading them in that fight, not following them. We communists—"

A scattering of voices rose from all parts of the room and suddenly everybody was shouting and nobody could be heard. Mazaud's harsh voice rose stridently above the others, which were stilled as abruptly as they had come to life.

"The hour has come to unloose the insurrection on the Germans!" he shouted. "A few days ago it was too early; in a few days it will be too late. It's got to be now, *now*!"

"With what arms?" Bourbon cried.

"With whatever we've got and can get in doing it."

"Do you know how many we have?"

"A thousand."

"Eight hundred! And mostly revolvers! You don't unloose an insurrection in Paris with eight hundred arms!"

Laperche disagreed. "When the hour for an insurrection strikes, any and all risks must be faced; they're inescapable."

"The risk of having two or three hundred thousand innocent people massacred?" Reboussin demanded incredulously.

Mazaud leaped wrathfully to his feet and glared at Reboussin. "*All* the risks!" he snapped. "Those who don't dare to take risks wind up on the junk heap of history."

"And those who do end up in Père-Lachaise!" Reboussin shot back.

"The Communist party has prepared its posters and we are ready to slap them up on the walls of Paris." Mazaud looked around the room aggressively. "If you won't go along with us, we'll do it alone."

The room was silent as Mazaud sat down and his ultimatum sank in. A tense moment of indecision followed. Each faction waited uncertainly for the other to speak. But the extremists had stated their position, and none of the moderates wanted either to accept the ultimatum and with it the insurrection or to refuse it and thereby split the resistance irretrievably in two. In the dramatic silence of the gloomy room Patrice gazed up at Voltaire on the mantelpiece and Voltaire gazed down at Patrice. They exchanged disabused smiles.

Sorel was saying, "It is obviously impossible for this council to hold back a movement of revolt against the Nazis once it has been set in motion. The masses of people would refuse to stop no matter what we said, and it is inconceivable that we should separate ourselves from them."

"Then let's decide right now on the hour the insurrection will start," Patrice said.

"Not so fast," Reboussin interrupted. "The final decision will have to be made by a joint session of the Paris resistance committees, the National Council and the Delegation."

They agreed that the joint session would be held the following morning, and the meeting ended. No hard conclusion had been reached, but every man rose from his chair with the clear impression that the insurrection had been tacitly decided upon and would break out the next day.

Reboussin looked grave. He had the sensation of carrying a greater weight than he could bear: it seemed impossible to stop the uprising. He did not recognize this sensation as a crack in his will to fight. It flashed upon him and the next moment was gone. In that moment he had the feeling of being caught in something bigger than himself, something he could no longer control, and he saw an avalanche of events and forces sweeping Paris inexorably toward a communist-led insurrection.

On his way out he saw his own anguish reflected in Bourbon's eyes. The colonel was in a cold sweat. "Sorel is mad," he grumbled. "We can't go along with the communists. It's—"

Reboussin's face twitched nervously; Bourbon's opaque pigheadedness in the face of a lost cause exasperated him. Seeing Reboussin's expression of impatience, Bourbon stopped in mid-sentence, confused and uncertain.

"We've got to go along with them now," Reboussin muttered. "We can't let them isolate us."

Sorel passed them on his way out. The roly-poly little socialist was puffed up with self-importance, and his black mustache bristled fiercely in the middle of his round face.

"They're right," he said pompously as he went by. "I've always said that the success of an insurrection turned on the exact moment we broke it. The moment's come."

He was out of the door and calling over his shoulder, "My God, the work that has to be done by tomorrow morning."

Bourbon swore and Reboussin shrugged disdainfully.

"There's your signpost," Reboussin said quietly. "He's already forgotten that only twenty-four hours ago he was with us against the insurrection. One day and the communists have changed everything.

We'll have to go along with them. To do nothing now is political suicide."

"Is that worse than military suicide?" Bourbon asked glumly.

"We've got to stay alive politically." Reboussin's voice was suddenly agitated. He seemed not to have heard Bourbon. "They would like us to stay out, but we won't. Out, we're nothing; in, we can still give it the turn we want."

"And the Delegation?" Bourbon asked.

"The Delegation?" Reboussin blinked and stared at Bourbon, again aware of his existence. "That's what I'm going to see about right now."

He hastened over to the Delegation headquarters on the Avenue de Ségur, where he described the meeting of the National Council of the Resistance to De Gaulle's general delegate, Alexandre Parodi.

"Our view," Reboussin concluded, "is that the communists have pushed us into a corner and left us with little choice. A split must be avoided at all costs, namely at the cost of an insurrection—tomorrow! We can't delay any longer. Now, we have just about decided to go along, although as yet we've made no commitment. It's dangerous, criminally dangerous, but—" he lifted his hands in a gesture of helplessness—"we cannot abandon the resistance to the communists." He looked thoughtfully at Parodi. "It would be . . . awkward if the Delegation saw things differently from the Council and decided to stay out of the uprising . . ."

Reboussin left the sentence hanging in the air as if it were a question.

"I've just informed the members of the Delegation that we're in a state of alert," said Parodi. "I also sent a message to General Koenig in London; if we can't stop the extremists, we can at least try to speed up the Americans."

"Then you agree—"

"We all agree—the Council, the Delegation and London. London is worried by some of our dispatches. They're afraid of two opposite dangers: that the resistance may be replaced by the Third Republic parliamentarians and that the Provisional Government may be undermined by the communists. I've just learned that the Germans have arrested Laval and carted him and his ex-prisoner Herriot off toward Germany. That means the first danger no longer exists. As for the second, London's instructions are to appoint the new functionaries of the liberation government, avoiding, at the same time, all avoidable conflicts inside the resistance. That is precisely my point of view. Now the insurrection—" He rummaged around his desk, came up with a sheet of paper and handed it to Reboussin. "The copy of a cable sent to Koenig an hour ago."

Reboussin read the message hastily: ". . . situation paris very tense dash police post office railroads on strike with rising tendency general strike stop people in streets believe hear cannon and await hourly arrival allies stop all conditions preparatory insurrection realized stop local incidents . . . enough to cause gravest trouble with bloody reprisals for which germans seem to have taken decision and gathered means . . . paralysis public services colon no more gas hour and half electricity daily water lacking some neighborhoods food situation calamitous . . . atmosphere very heavy . . . consequently if military situation permits necessary you intervene with allies to demand rapid occupation paris stop if impossible urgent first you advise by cable policy we are to follow stop second warn population officially in clear and precise fashion by bbc in order to escape new warsaw . . ."

Reboussin's eyes came up from the cable. "But—"

"Of course," Parodi interrupted. "If we had known an hour ago what we know now we would have left London with no illusions as to what is going to happen tomorrow." He paused and smiled faintly. "Did you notice anything in the streets on your way over?"

Reboussin shook his head.

"You should have looked at the walls. They're covered with communist posters—freshly pasted up."

Reboussin was beyond surprise or indignation. "Already?" he asked dully.

Parodi nodded. "Already. It's a call for an insurrection signed by all the leading communists of the Paris region—Thorez, Duclos, Cachin . . ."

His voice trailed off. Into the silence of the office through an open window came the sound of a group of children playing in the street below. One was piping in a shrill, insistent voice, "It's not fair! It's not fair!" while the others laughed and shrieked. Parodi shut the window.

"Well," said Reboussin, "they're publicly committed now." He rubbed his chin. "There's no turning back for them any more."

"Nor for us," said Parodi. "We have no choice but the insurrection."

He did not seem displeased. Reboussin could still faintly hear the childish cry outside the window and the shouts and laughter that swirled about it, and for a moment he was seized with an infantile panic like that of a terrified child lost among indifferent strangers. But though he was very pale when he rose to go, his face was impassive.

†

AFTER the meeting Patrice walked toward the center of Paris with Riviere.

"For a leader of the resistance," he said, "Reboussin is as coy as a teaser. If he wants to keep his virginity, why does he get into bed?"

"To be a minister."

"Then let him pay an honest price."

Riviere shook his head. "He's reluctant as a virgin, but like most of the breed he's finally being forced to take the final step." The wizened professor was exultant. "Reboussin doesn't want to play in bed unless he's sure the Americans will arrive before his clothes are off. Bourbon doesn't even want to take that much of a chance. But neither of them can help themselves any more than a titillated adolescent girl who hates to take the risk but can't resist the temptation. They'll both be ravaged and won't enjoy a minute of it."

"They're stalling," Patrice observed. "But they can't stall any longer."

"Not a chance. If the Germans can't stop a couple of strikes, nobody is going to believe they can stop an insurrection."

Their paths soon parted, and Patrice continued alone through the torpid streets of the city. Many shopkeepers, fearing trouble, had closed their stores; the protective iron shutters dropped before the plate-glass windows glinted dully in the still air. As Patrice walked, the realization of the enormity of the event that he and the other resistance leaders were putting into motion slowly broke upon him. With the others he was to determine the fate of Paris. Patrice was seized with an intoxicating sense of power. He watched the people in the streets going about their business and wanted to grip each of them by the arm and tell them what was in the air, what was surely going to happen the very next day. Reality—this reality that he was going to transform tomorrow—took on a peculiar texture, an unreal tone; the outer world, bright and hot, was a pale phantom without flesh or pulse, and, gazing with private foresight at this unseeing creature, Patrice felt that he alone was sparked with life. The next day he would transmit that life to the city with the quickening current of the insurrection. His eyes lit up with these reflections and he strode along feeling a mounting exhilaration.

A wall—posters. Some words caught his eye. Patrice retraced his steps. The familiar, weather-stained French fascist and German posters were marred by long strips of colored paper pasted over them, but the fat, blood-red words of German warning, PENALTY OF DEATH, jumped out at Patrice. That was not what he had seen. Nor was it the half-obliterated sign showing a blond giant in working clothes before a swastika shaking hands with a handsome bereted workingman beneath the words: FRENCH AND GERMAN WORKERS—UNITE! There it was! It gleamed new-white and still wet in the afternoon sun.

FRENCHMEN, ARISE!

Three new posters were plastered over the walls, counterpointing one theme. The first, from the committee of communist and Catholic trade-union leaders, announced a general strike; the second, from the headquarters of the F.F.I. of the Paris region, proclaimed that "all sound Frenchmen and Frenchwomen" were mobilized; the third, signed by the leaders of the Communist party, called the people of Paris, "men and women, young and old," to insurrection.

"It's all there," Patrice said to himself as he hurried on. His mind raced ahead to catch up with the implications while he ticked off the points: General strike! Mobilization! Insurrection! With a shiver of excitement he realized that the resistance had at last burst out of the dark protectiveness of the underground and sprung full-born into the light of day. The posters were an open declaration of war. War itself had to follow. The extremists had taken an initiative against which there was no recall; when the governing bodies of the resistance met jointly the following morning they would be faced with an accomplished fact.

Patrice was elated. The time had come to precipitate the insurrection by executing his plan to take the Prefecture. He felt like a thief plotting to cut into the haul of a band of crooks. He was going to compound the communist felony; but his complicity, while furthering the crime, would frustrate the criminals. He knew that the moderates would no more agree to his plan than the communists; but he also knew that once it was under way all of them, moderates as well as extremists, would be forced to support it. He had the arms. All he needed was the help of one man—Marceau, his resistance contact in the police force. A telephone call would start the machinery rolling if Marceau agreed. He was sure that Marceau would agree. Thank God, he thought, that despite the strike of telephone workers, the automatic dial system within the city was working normally.

Patrice picked up his bicycle at the café where he had left it. He pedaled to the Régence. Mignot, Gaudin and Danielle were already there, sitting at a table under the arcade.

"Well?" Mignot asked before Patrice had even sat down.

"This is it."

"When?" Gaudin and Mignot asked together.

"Tomorrow morning."

"*Bon Dieu de bon Dieu!*" Mignot swore. "At last!" His exclamation was so loud that some people at the next table turned around. "*Garçon,*" he called.

When the waiter came Mignot ordered white wine for all of them. He could scarcely sit still. Danielle was flushed.

"Now we'll finish them off," said Gaudin. His eyes glittered and a blue vein stood out on his forehead. For once his insistently melancholy nose did not dominate his face. "What do we do?" he wanted to know.

"You'd better get over to the command post in the Rue Mazarine," said Patrice. "Pick up your brassards. All they say is 'F.F.I.' It's our uniform. Today we're terrorists—" he smiled—"tomorrow we're an army."

But they all knew that with or without brassards the Germans considered them guerrillas and had posted signs all over Paris warning them that if they were captured they would be treated as such.

"And after the brassards?" Mignot asked.

"Go to the garage. Load the arms in the Delahaye and paint the letters F.F.I. on the sides. Big! So people can see it. I want both of you to drive the car and the arms to the Prefecture of Police tomorrow morning at seven."

"Right up to the front gate?" Gaudin asked in astonishment. "On the Boulevard du Palais?"

"No, in the back. Beside Notre Dame."

"Oh." Gaudin seemed mollified but still unsure.

"Keep it to yourselves," said Patrice. "We're the ones who are going to set it off."

Although he spoke to them, his eyes were on Danielle. She vibrated to his words.

"Set what off?" Gaudin wanted to be sure he understood.

"The insurrection."

"Us!" Mignot was beside himself. *"Bon Dieu de bon Dieu!"*

He soared, unconscious of where he was—unaware of the terrace, people, chatter, street, pedestrians. He soared, dominating all that was real or imaginable, towering over Paris in the pure air of adventure.

"Curfew's at nine tonight," Patrice said. "Gaudin's all right. He lives close enough to the garage. But you won't have time to get home to Montmartre, Mignot. Where will you sleep?"

Descending reluctantly into reality, Mignot replied, "At the garage."

"Not very comfortable without a bed."

"Sleep at my house," Danielle said. "It's not too far from the garage."

Patrice stared at her in surprise. Had she forgotten about them? Danielle did not care if they knew about Patrice and her; she wanted them to know. And she was in such a tumult over Patrice's news of the insurrection. Mignot was a brother—no, more! She plunged.

"Do come. You have no place else to sleep and Patrice will be staying there tonight too." She added, "He can chaperon us."

They all laughed and Mignot agreed.

After they left Patrice took Danielle's hand and kissed it. "I love you," he said.

"You don't mind about Mignot?" She looked contrite. "He'll be at the other end of the house."

"I love you," he repeated.

A second tumult swirled up in her and was entangled with the first.

A bit later, when she was less agitated, she heard him say, "Tomorrow morning we'll go to the Prefecture together."

"It must have been exciting," she said, "when the Council decided on the insurrection."

"They decided nothing."

"Then—"

"I decided it myself—after the meeting."

"But—"

"Don't you see? They made up their minds today to make up their minds tomorrow. I'm going to jump the gun. I have some arms and through Marceau I'll get the police. Isn't it better that the police take the Prefecture than the communists?"

When she had thought a while she said, "But what if they don't make up their minds tomorrow after all?"

"They will. Those communist posters are up all over town. The insurrection has been declared before it's been decided."

"But they're just posters," she objected with a woman's common sense. "There's nothing irrevocable about them. It may be unlikely, but it's still possible that the decision will be delayed some days longer."

He smiled. "Not when they learn that we've taken the Prefecture."

She spelled it out slowly. "You want to be sure they don't make up their minds tomorrow to make up their minds the day after."

He grinned.

"If the resistance were an army, you'd be shot for mutiny."

"But the resistance is not an army. It's a conspiracy."

"And you're conspiring against it."

"For it."

"Well," she said, smiling, "as long as you conspire to carry the fight to the enemy I'm with you."

He had known his plan would appeal to her. Her face was soft in the shadow of the arcade and her dark blue eyes softer. Patrice pressed her hands. "I wish it were nine o'clock," he whispered.

"Hurry. I'll be waiting for you."

He paid and they sauntered to the edge of the sidewalk.

"Look!" he said. "It's like a ballet at the Opéra."

Thousands upon thousands of home-going Parisians were pedaling bicycles down the Avenue de l'Opéra, past the smart men's clothing shops and the Café de Paris and the travel agencies that had done no business since the defeat. Most of the cyclists were women and young girls. Their bright scarves and summer dresses were a wild splash of color that kept moving and changing pattern. The sun slanted across the buildings and the light was dusty gold and the shadows vaporous blue. At the end of the avenue, against the clean evening sky, stood the columned opera house. It was drenched in sunlight. Home-goers crowded the sidewalks too. The spokes of the bicycles glinted silver, turning brightly through the gold light and the blue shadows. At times an arm arched upward to buttress a picture hat; skirts ballooned like sails in a breeze; the faces of the girls were young and fresh, and there was something about them that made one know they were Parisiennes. In less than twenty-four hours, Patrice thought, this stage would be the scene of a popular uprising. It was hard to believe. His arm tightened around Danielle's waist. She looked up at him with shining eyes.

"I'm drunk," he murmured; then louder, "Drunk!"

She laughed. "You haven't been drinking."

"You don't drink the wine of Paris—you breathe it." He laughed and took a deep breath. "Look! It's Paris! And it's going to be ours again!"

She watched the blood of the city course through its heart and felt warm and fine and part of it. Patrice pulled her to him. While the cyclists rolled by he took her in his arms and kissed her.

†

EVER since Suzanne had obtained Danielle's address she had been torn between the temptation of giving her up to Klaus and the desire to forget that she had ever met her. Suzanne had no illusions about what would happen to Danielle if she fell into the hands of the Gestapo. Not that she associated any aspect of the German secret police with her lover, even though she now knew he was part of it.

She could see him in no other light than the one she personally knew. That Klaus's professional duties might transform him from the tender, considerate man she knew to the level of a Gestapo brute never occurred to her; or if it did she closed her mind and thought of something else. The key to her thinking was that Klaus could be no more than an underling caught in the machinery of an organization whose methods he was unable to change. She knew him to be humane and decent and the Gestapo to be brutal. She imagined that one could be swamped by the other and that Klaus would be helpless to stop it. So she had no illusions about what awaited Danielle if Klaus arrested her and she disappeared into the endless cells and corridors of the Gestapo prisons. At the same time Danielle was the key to Suzanne's happiness. If Danielle remained free, Suzanne could not leave Paris with Klaus. It was Danielle or them.

For a full day Suzanne struggled with the problem. She imagined that Danielle was arrested and saw her in a cell. Then she visualized the interrogation and the torture inflicted on the beautiful girl she had met in De Maurain's salon. She saw granite-faced Germans with bull whips in their thick hands push Klaus aside. Then she imagined them stripping Danielle and tying her hands to a beam overhead and lashing her back and buttocks with the long black whips that tapered down to a pencil point of knotted leather. She closed her eyes at this point in her imagination to shut out the picture of pain and humiliation. And when she opened them and the picture was gone she thought that as long as Danielle was free she and Klaus had to remain in Paris, and the longer they remained the smaller the chances were that they would ever get out together to live their lives as they desired.

The problem was all her own. She had nobody to turn to for help. She imagined that she would not tell Klaus what she knew, and saw the Americans advancing closer and closer to Paris. Then she envisioned the outbreak of the insurrection and saw barricades go up in the streets of Paris. She could hear the workers of the red belt surrounding Paris charge into the center of the city armed with rifles and pikes, tearing up the cobbles from the streets, breaking windows, plundering shops and apartments, killing or capturing Germans and summarily executing all prisoners. At this point she invariably imagined Klaus being captured, and then once again she closed her eyes to shut out the picture she could not bear to see. And she thought that it was in her power to save him, that nobody but she could save him and that if she kept what she knew to herself she was, by her silence, pronouncing the death sentence of the man she loved. Then the picture of Danielle came back to her and she saw her naked body, hands tied overhead to a beam, and the blows raining on her back and the red welts and bloody gashes and Danielle flinging her body crazily from side to side in an impossible effort to escape her tormenters.

But the thought of Klaus murdered by the Paris rabble was even more vivid, and after a tortured day and sleepless night she made up her mind to see Klaus in the hope that he had found some solution to their problem. As she left for his hotel in the Rue des Écoles she told herself that she could not tell him about Danielle, that she could never forgive herself if she bought her happiness at the expense of denouncing Danielle.

On the way, however, she still debated the question with herself. She was sensitive to the strange new atmosphere in the streets. When she had almost arrived at Klaus's hotel she saw a group of people reading posters freshly pasted up on the walls in front of the Cluny Museum. She went up to the edge of the crowd and, reading over their shoulders, was shocked to see the same signs that Patrice had seen on the other side of Paris. She stood there for a long while reading the signs calling for a general strike and for an insurrection. It seemed to her that the end of the world was about to come. The color ebbed from her face and the strength from her limbs. Once again she had that feeling of impotence, of being able to do nothing in the face of events that were cascading upon her like a series of overpowering waves. She looked dully about her and saw the satisfied smiles on the faces of those in the crowd.

"This is the end," she heard one man say.

"They have an agreement," another said. "The Germans are going to be out of the city by midnight tonight, and tomorrow the Americans are coming in."

She turned away and walked rapidly to the Rue des Écoles. "This is the end," she repeated to herself. She sobbed, momentarily unable to control herself, but kept walking toward the hotel. The sunny day and the contented look on the faces of the people in the streets taunted her, and she felt alone in her misery, isolated among hostile strangers. This feeling was intensified when she arrived at the hotel. The clerk at the desk, where she asked for Klaus, told her with a frigid smile that "Herr" Tellmann was out. She insisted that the man ring his room, and Klaus answered. When she looked accusingly at him the clerk merely shrugged and stared at her disdainfully. Going up to his room, Suzanne passed the chambermaid, who glared at her and muttered under her breath. She burst into Klaus's room in a state verging on hysteria.

"It's the end!" she cried. "All the Germans are leaving and the Americans will be here tomorrow."

Sobbing, she fell on the bed. Klaus, who had been telephoning when Suzanne crashed into the room, put down the receiver and sat on the bed beside her. He took her by the shoulders and lifted her to a sitting position.

"What kind of nonsense is this?" he asked. "We aren't leaving the city at all. We're just getting the administrative personnel out so that we'll be ready to fight for Paris."

"Fight for Paris?" She wiped her eyes, sat back and looked hard at him to try to fathom if he were serious. "But everybody is saying that the Germans and Americans have reached an agreement, that you will be out today and they will be in tomorrow."

"There's no agreement," Klaus said. "If there were, I'd know about it. Look! Do I look as though I'm about to get out?"

She looked around the room and saw that everything was normal. Nothing had been packed; there were no signs indicating a departure.

"But they'll be here soon," she said. "You saw the troops retreating from Normandy. If the Americans aren't here tomorrow they'll be here the day after. What about Danielle? Have you found her? Will we be able to leave?"

He looked away. "No luck. There isn't a trace."

"You haven't found out anything! The Gestapo that knows everything!"

"We know who she is all right. Danielle Tessier. But having her name is one thing, locating her is another. The police have a domicile for her, but she hasn't been there for two years."

"Then you have no hope of finding her."

"I think we'll find her, but . . ."

"But when? In six months?"

"We've only been working on it for two days. We're not miracle men."

"You'll never be able to do it before the Americans get here."

She was overwrought and rubbed her hands together nervously. She saw the signs on the wall of the Cluny again and the ironic faces of the Parisians as they watched the German convoys move out of the city. She saw the hotel clerk and his contemptuous smile when she appeared in the lobby of the hotel and she saw the insolent expression of the chambermaid and heard her angry muttering as she passed her on the staircase. Suzanne shrank up within herself. She was afraid and she was ashamed. Something was happening around her and to her that she did not understand, and she knew there was only one thing to do about it: leave Paris. She did not look at Klaus, but felt him sitting stolidly beside her.

"You, the famous Gestapo, have been working for two days to find this girl and you've gotten nowhere," she said angrily. "And in five minutes, all alone, I've learned more than you."

He grasped her arms and turned her toward him. She had never seen such a look in his eyes.

"You know?" he said. "Tell me. Hurry. There's no time to lose."

"You're right. Her name is Tessier."

Suzanne was surprised to hear her voice so firm. It sounded icy and she felt as though it belonged to someone else and was a voice over which she had no control. Klaus still held her arms in a tight grip. He shook her slightly and kept staring at her with that strange, new look in his eyes that she did not know and that frightened her.

"But where does she live?" he asked. "Where can we reach her?"

She told him the address in that same cold voice whose firmness surprised her, that voice that did not belong to her and over which she had no control. It was easy after all to recite the address. People gave out addresses dozens of times a day every day of the year. What harm could there be that she uttered this address to Klaus? The number and the name of the street. They looked at each other without a word, and although she braved his look, wondering what thought the depths of his silent blue eyes held, she hated herself as she might a stranger, the stranger whose voice she heard giving Klaus the address—and Danielle. At the same time she was thinking, it's Danielle or me. I've got to take care of my own life.

Klaus released her arms suddenly, got up and began pacing the room. She remained seated on the bed in the same position, frozen in the shell of a new personality that was unfamiliar and distasteful and that she could no longer cast off. She heard Klaus walking nervously up and down, but did not look up. She felt numb and her eyes were dull and there was only one thought in her mind—When are we going to leave?—but she did not, she could not, say it aloud. Deep down she felt it would have been obscene. But her silence did not help. Inside she felt unclean. Something within her was curling up into a small ball, turning about itself to become smaller and smaller, and that was herself, ashamed and shrinking away like a guilty child. She sat on the bed, rigid and expressionless, giving no sign of her anguish, unable to escape herself, while Klaus strode from the door to the window and back again. Finally he stopped in front of her.

"We'll get her tonight," he said. He rubbed his hands together excitedly. "With a little persuasion she should lead us to the top."

He dropped down to the bed beside Suzanne and grasped her hands. She let Klaus take them and without a word turned to him. Her eyes were naked, pleading.

"It will take another day," he said. "That's all. By tomorrow night we'll know everything she knows and we'll be able to act on it."

He was exultant. He held her limp hands tightly and shook them. "Don't you see what this means?" he cried.

She was beyond the reach of his excitement. Inside she felt shriveled up, and the naked look of self-humiliation was still in her eyes.

"You won't . . . hurt her?" Suzanne asked.

"Hurt her?" He seemed to realize for the first time what Suzanne was thinking. "My poor darling! Don't worry your little head about her. A few suggestions will make her talk. She'd be a very unimaginative girl if they didn't."

Suzanne was thinking, And then you'll hang her. But Klaus lifted Suzanne to her feet, threw his arms around her waist and kissed her. His face was bright with laughter.

"Darling," he said, "get ready to leave with me by the day after tomorrow. I'll make all the preparations. Just pack whatever you need, but don't take too much. A couple of bags. I'll phone you when I'm ready and send the car for you. Now smile for me."

He kept at her and finally she smiled and then he kissed the smile away.

"I'll never forget this," he said gravely, holding her close to him. "Not only did you save us; you saved me too. I would have been through if not for this."

She felt better when they left the hotel together. But she could not face the sneer on the face of the chambermaid as they went down the stairs, and though she turned away in the lobby her face burned under the clerk's look of contempt.

†

AFTER Patrice left Danielle he had a great deal to do. He rode his bicycle swiftly across the Tuileries and the Seine and went to his command post in a small street off the quai. The building was swarming with young men who were rushing up and down the stairs to and from the third floor office that had been set aside as one of the key points for the direction of the uprising. Patrice was amazed that they were so open about what they were doing, that they took no pains to disguise their haste and the place they were going. The security once observed was already a thing of the past, even though the occupation was as menacing a fact as ever.

Patrice took immediate measures to stop the general and open display of activity. Within five minutes he had gathered all the men into his office. They were bunched in very tightly. Patrice spoke briefly and to the point. "The Germans are still masters here," he concluded. "Take care. If one patrol passed and saw what was going on here we'd all be packed away to one of their prisons. Tomorrow will be plenty of time to make yourselves seen and heard."

He spent an hour getting information on the organization of the CP, giving instructions for various changes and making preparations for the next day. More time was spent talking to a variety of men about the jobs they would have to do. On the whole he found things in excellent shape. A team of thirty liaison men was attached to the CP, and many of them had motorcycles. The others would be on bicycles. They were young and they had a seemingly unquenchable enthusiasm. The longer Patrice remained there the more confident he became about the eventual success of the insurrection. The spirit was contagious. He knew that when he spoke to a man he was infecting him with his excitement at the same time that the man was feeding Patrice with his own enthusiasm. The eyes of the men there shone in a way that Patrice had never before observed anywhere. These men had the consciousness of their mission, and each of them knew he was part of a movement and an event that was bigger than any of them or all of them put together. And Patrice felt the same way about it as all the others did, and he understood them and they all understood each other. The communion of feeling was complete. They might just as well have been dependent on one central nervous system and one brain for all the difference that existed at that time between their thoughts and feelings.

None of them wanted to leave. Patrice, with the help of some of the local district leaders, was forced to tell them to get out and be ready early the next day for what they all knew was coming. As they were leaving, two boys who could not have been more than seventeen years old presented themselves to Patrice with shining but anxious eyes.

"We want to join up," one of them said. "We saw the signs for a general mobilization and here we are."

"How did you know we were here?" Patrice asked.

"I live on the fourth floor," the boy said, grinning and pointing at the ceiling.

Patrice turned the boys over to a short, swarthy man who was one of the neighborhood leaders.

"He'll take care of you," he said. "Be here early tomorrow."

When the office had been cleared Patrice made a number of phone calls. At last he reached Marceau.

"It's for tomorrow," Patrice said into the mouthpiece.

Even over the telephone line Patrice could sense the man's electric response.

"I want you to get two thousand cops rounded up tomorrow morning at seven o'clock around the Prefecture of Police. Can you do it?"

Patrice held his breath.

"It's not much time, but I'll do it. I'll be on the phone half the night."

"Tell them to bring whatever arms they have. Rifles, revolvers, anything. And all the ammunition they have, too."

"I'll tell them. Do you have any machine guns?"

"Some. Not enough to go around, but enough to make Fritz dance."

"Good. It'll be the first time I'll enjoy watching the bastards do a waltz."

Patrice dashed into a bistro and ate hastily. He was so keyed up he had no appetite. Events were snowballing and Patrice felt pressured. And there was Danielle, who by this time was waiting for him. Hours had gone by and he had not even had the time to think of her. His face softened. Hurriedly he paid his check and walked out into the soft evening. He looked at his watch and was astonished to see that it was almost nine o'clock. Curfew was at nine, he thought. The Germans were cracking down. It was the last curfew he would obey. He smiled grimly. But this one he would be delighted to observe. The last and the best. He hopped on his bicycle and sped across the city, his heart light, his eyes glowing. It was a magnificent world.

†

DANIELLE lived in a small villa on the southern outskirts of Paris. The villa, which was barely visible through a cluster of chestnut trees, was not very different from the other houses around it. It was set back inconspicuously behind a pretty garden, which was fenced off from a lonely, cobblestoned street that zigzagged capriciously between leafy trees and had the air of a village byway. A friend of Danielle's, having decided to wait out the occupation in the south of France, had lent it to her two years before. Though small, the house was attractive and tastefully furnished. Best of all Danielle liked the garden, where she spent hours of her free time lying in the sun and reading.

A five-month-old black French poodle called Napoleon, who belonged to a neighbor, was scampering around the garden, running in circles and jumping crazily at the fence when Klaus drove past the house. His black Citroen was followed by another. They turned the corner beyond a curve of the street and parked. Klaus spoke briefly to the two men who got out of the car with him. One was a wiry little man with close-set, crafty black eyes; the other was the husky fellow who had arrested and lost Patrice two days before.

"Now remember," Klaus said, "several people may be in the house, so let's get in quietly. You know what to do, Kurtz?"

The wiry little man nodded. He closed his dark jacket over a bulky object and hunched over so that nothing showed.

Klaus turned to the other man. "Do you suppose you can keep a prisoner from escaping tonight?" he asked. "That's fine, Hoelling. Maybe Hitler will pin a medal on you when you get back to Berlin."

Hoelling muttered under his breath. If he could get the bastard who had kicked him in the belly and gotten away, he was thinking, he'd break him into small pieces. He hated Klaus for his sarcasm and Kurtz, too, and everybody else he had seen in the past two days. The filthy French, he said to himself. Mongoloid, Latin bastards, all of them, as bad as the Jews and the Poles. His fists were clenched in anger.

Klaus looked at him distastefully, wondering why so much of the Gestapo was made up of men like Hoelling. "Ready?" he said.

They walked casually up the slope and around the curve of the deserted street. When they reached the gate of Danielle's house Napoleon stopped short and cocked his head alertly to one side. The three men stopped, too, and looked at the dog.

"Go ahead," Klaus said.

Kurtz opened the gate and stepped into the garden. As loudly as he could, Napoleon barked twice. Kurtz glared at the dog. Napoleon bristled. He barked again, defiantly, then relapsed into a low, menacing growl.

"Shut up!" Hoelling snapped.

The dog turned toward him briefly. He was newly and elegantly clipped, his head smartly coiffed with a pompon tuft, the sleek, shaved torso curving gracefully from a deep chest to a narrow waist and the black hair soft and fluffy on his legs and haunches. Kurtz was advancing down the garden path toward the house, his shoes crunching on the gravel. The dog wheeled around toward him and pointed, head high, stance rigid and the stub of a tail shooting straight out behind him. Huddled over the dark jacket he grasped about him, Kurtz moved stealthily forward. The dog suddenly broke out of his immobility and pranced playfully after him. Then his nose went down to the ground and he stole quietly along in the strange man's footsteps. Klaus and Hoelling started down the path not far behind Kurtz.

Inside the villa Danielle and Mignot were at the dining-room table finishing an after-dinner cigarette. The dishes had not yet been cleared away.

"It was a fine dinner," Mignot said formally.

Danielle impressed him so deeply that he stiffened up in her presence and was unnatural.

"Just a simple meal," Danielle said. "I'm sure you've had better."

"Yes, that's true," Mignot said ingenuously. "Only the other day with Pierrot."

She smiled, and Mignot wanted to go on and tell her the whole story. But he remembered how it had ended with the two girls in Pierrot's apartment and decided the story was not for Danielle.

"I'll help with the dishes," he said.

"Oh, no, you mustn't. You ought to be in bed. Think of how early you have to get up and all you have to do tomorrow."

He hated to leave because it was so pleasant just looking at her, and she wanted desperately for him to go because Patrice would be arriving in the next half hour.

"Don't worry about the dishes," she said. "They'll take five minutes to do and I have to wait up for Patrice anyway."

Reluctantly, Mignot said good night. He had hardly disappeared up the stairs when the doorbell rang. Patrice, she thought. He's early. Her heart leaped and pounded. She ran quickly to the mirror above the buffet, patted her hair, arranged her dress and put on some lipstick. It took her only a minute. The bell rang again.

"I'm coming," she cried.

After a last glance in the mirror she dashed out of the dining room, down the dark corridor and threw open the door. Her eager smile faded.

"Danielle Tessier?" Kurtz whispered urgently. He sounded frightened; his shoulders were hunched, his head bent—everything about him indicated a man in flight. "I must see you right away. Please. Quick."

He had a peculiar foreign accent, and the thought flashed through her head that he was an American aviator or an escaped prisoner being sent down the line.

"Come in," she said.

The dog slipped through the door before it closed and bounced ahead of them into the dining room. As she followed the three men down the hall Danielle thought it odd that the person who sent these men to her had not accompanied them. Suddenly, at the dining room door, she felt she had been trapped. It was too late. The frightened little man was now erect before her. A look of triumph was on his face and a stubby black sub-machine gun in his hands. The sawed-off muzzle pointed at her.

It had happened so fast that Danielle was too surprised to be frightened. Mignot, she thought. I must warn him. Then, with a wild look of despair, she thought that Patrice would walk into the trap. Klaus saw the look shoot across her face.

"Don't be frightened," he said quietly. "Come in and sit down."

She walked into the room saying, "It won't do you any good. There's nothing of value in the house. Not even silverware."

Hoelling snorted and Klaus smiled.

"We didn't come for that," Klaus said. "We came for you."

"Who are you?"

"The Gestapo."

"But what have I done?"

"You know that well enough."

Danielle tried to think but could not. Her mind was turning around full speed but, like a tire whirling in mid-air, found nothing to grip. Who had denounced her? How could Mignot get away? And Patrice? She looked at Hoelling. A block of concrete, insentient. Her heart sank. Never had a face accused her like that without expression or emotion.

"Is anybody else in the house?" Klaus asked.

She stared at him, thinking he looked more human than the other and trying to give the impression she was terrified. What could she say? She closed her eyes, clasped her hands on her breasts, raised her head and began to chant in a loud, fervent voice.

"Hail Mary, full of grace . . ."

All the time she prayed, her body transfixed, putting a fervor into the words she had not felt since she was a little girl, she thought, They're going to hit me, but Mignot will hear.

Aloud she intoned, ". . . Holy Mary, mother of God, pray for us sinners now and at the hour of our deaths."

When she opened her eyes nobody had moved. They were looking at her in silence and seemed to be at a momentary loss.

"Well, who else is here?" Klaus asked, breaking the spell.

"I don't know."

"We'll see," Klaus said coldly. He looked through her with pitiless eyes. "It's very unwise if you're covering up for anyone. Come along."

She led them up the stairs, certain that Mignot had heard nothing and was in bed.

"People come and go," she said. "I'm not the concierge."

There were three small bedrooms on the floor. She brought them to the door of Mignot's last and stopped. Then, with the sensation of a drowning man going down for the last time, she opened the door. Mignot was not there. The bed had not been touched. Feeling dizzy, she waited at the door with Klaus while Kurtz and Hoelling searched the room. She held her breath when they looked under the bed, shuddered when they opened the closet. She went to the window for air, thinking that Mignot must have dropped to the garden and gotten away. As they rummaged around the room, she glanced out of the half-open window. Suddenly Danielle was petrified. Mignot was out there in the dark, stretched flat on the narrow window ledge. For a moment Danielle could not move; then she turned and stood there defensively, blocking the window. She felt so weak and frightened that she swayed and sat down tentatively on the window sill. Glancing rapidly at the three men, she saw they had not noticed her spasm of nervousness. Hoelling wandered over and looked over her shoulder out of the window.

"There's still the top floor," Danielle said.

"Let's see it," said Klaus.

Danielle waited for Hoelling to move first. He became aware of it and glared at her.

"Move," he snapped. "And keep away from windows."

She walked to the door and turned around. Hoelling was leaning on the window sill and staring into the dark. His hands were inches away from Mignot. Danielle closed her eyes and held her breath. She waited for an unforgettable instant that hung endlessly in time. Then from a great distance she heard Klaus's voice, larded with sarcasm.

"Are you looking for fireflies?"

Hoelling wheeled around sullenly. "Thought I saw someone in the garden," he muttered.

When they returned to the dining room Klaus, who was disappointed to have found nobody else in the house, had them all sit down around the table.

"We'll wait with you until a little after curfew," he said to Kurtz. "Then you'll watch the place alone."

They waited in silence, and Danielle, feeling herself go from a bad crisis to a worse one, tried to think out a plan to warn Patrice. Her mind was barren. She strained to hear the garden gate open and Patrice's step on the gravel path. Nothing. The stillness of the room was eerie. After ten minutes of it Danielle felt she could not sit still another moment. But suddenly the silence was broken by a noise under the table. The three men jumped to their feet. Hoelling's chair tipped over and crashed to the floor. Danielle, the color drained from her face, stood up uncertainly. Pointing his tommy gun at the foot of the table, Kurtz barked: "Come out!" For a tense moment their eyes were fixed on the lower edges of the long tablecloth. Finally, Napoleon sauntered out. He looked around sleepily, shook himself and yawned.

Hoelling cursed; Klaus smiled self-consciously.

It was then that Danielle thought of a plan to warn Patrice.

"It's a neighbor's dog," she said. "He's always slipping in. I'd better put him out for the night."

Klaus nodded. "Go to the door with her," he said to Hoelling.

Danielle shooed the dog into the garden, looked out at the street beyond the gate and saw nothing but the dark mass of trees in the soft twilight. When she returned to the dining room she took a bottle of rum out of the buffet. Klaus refused a drink for himself and the others, and Danielle poured herself half a tumblerful. She drank it down in two fast gulps. It warmed and invigorated her. Then she sat down again. The minutes ticked off.

"Why don't we get this over with?" she asked impatiently. "The sooner we leave the sooner you'll question me and learn you're making a mistake."

"I'll decide when we leave," Klaus said.

He looked at his watch and began drumming on the table. There was a sound at the door. All of them sat up alertly.

"What was that?"

"Nothing," Danielle said casually. Feeling her heart race erratically, she was surprised at how calm she sounded. She got up. "It's the dog again. I'll chase him away."

"It didn't sound like the dog."

"It didn't sound like the dog under the table, either."

With an irritated gesture Klaus turned away from Danielle's mocking smile. This was getting out of hand. He no longer believed anyone would come and decided to stay just a bit longer to save face.

"Go to the door with her," he snapped, "and let her chase the damned dog away."

Kurtz was behind her; as they stepped into the corridor she heard the metallic click of the tommy gun's safety being released.

"That dog is always scratching at the door," she said in a tone one uses when speaking to the deaf. "We'll get rid of him in no time at all."

Afraid that Patrice might ring the bell, she hastened to the door, quickly yanked it ajar and leaned down. In the dim light she recognized Patrice's trousers. With a couple of rapid taps on the leg she edged him out of her line of vision, saying, "Go away, Napoleon. Go away. We don't want you here tonight. Go away." She rose and slammed the door. Holding onto the doorknob, she felt her legs had dissolved, as if nothing were there to keep her from collapsing; and yet she felt airy and light, as if nothing could bring her down. She could not believe the man behind her had not seen Patrice. So she leaned against the door and waited with closed eyes for him to pounce on her, toss her aside, throw open the door and start firing into the night. But nothing happened. Kurtz's gruff voice sounded almost sweet for the release it carried.

"Well, you're not going to stand there all night, are you?"

Ten minutes later Klaus and Hoelling led Danielle to the black Citroen, leaving Kurtz behind. As she left the house between the two men Danielle was seized with an overpowering sense of despair. She felt no joy for having saved Mignot and Patrice, nor was she afraid. She was too exhausted for fear. She felt only a deep futility. All her struggles all these years had been for nothing. Like so many others, she was being led away and she felt that, like the others, she would never return. Patrice was gone. She would never see him again and she was too spent for tears, too worn for regret to bite the ache into her heart. And the liberation for which she had struggled since the first day of the defeat, the liberation . . . Tomorrow they would be in the streets with arms in their hands . . . The liberation was not for her. She blinked and, repeating her father's words, said grimly to herself, Pity is for others, not for oneself.

†

WHEN Patrice arrived at Danielle's house he bumped his bicycle against the door. That was the noise Danielle and the three men had heard in the dining room. Patrice locked a chain around the front wheel of the bicycle and was about to knock on the door when he heard Danielle walking toward it. He assumed she was talking to Mignot and did not know he was there. Instead of knocking he stood there with a grin on his face, ready to take Danielle in his arms when the door opened. But the door merely slipped ajar and then Danielle frantically tapped his leg. He stood frozen for a moment after the door slammed shut, then carefully picked up the bicycle, tiptoed down the steps and hid among the bushes at the turn of the house. He waited there until Danielle left the house between Klaus and Hoelling, and his worst suspicions were confirmed.

For a few minutes he remained where he was, too stunned to think. He kept repeating to himself like a litany for the dead, They got her. My God, they got her. The nausea rose violently in his parched throat. Crouched in the bushes, he shook his head unbelievingly, trying to make sense out of what had happened. He could only repeat, They've got her. My God, they've got her. She's gone. He felt small, dull, weak and stupid. There was nothing he could do. He had seen her taken away and had not moved. He could not think and felt barren even of the most elementary emotion. His eyes were dry, though he wanted to weep. He might have had no heart, though it should have been breaking. He grabbed blindly at a shrub, ripped it furiously from its roots and hurled it at the ground. Behind him a twig snapped. Patrice leaped up and whirled around. His strong, lean hands lunged forward and closed around a man's throat. This one won't yell or get away, he thought fiercely. Then he saw the man's face pulling desperately away from him. "Mignot!" Patrice whispered, letting go.

Mignot wrenched back, gasping and holding his throat. "They nabbed Danielle," he said thickly.

"I know."

"What are we going to do?"

Patrice thought of De Maurain. "I'll see what can be done with a friend. Where are you going to spend the night?"

Mignot shrugged. "A whore house. There's one not far from here."

"Not the Sphinx. It's crawling with Germans."

"It won't be tonight. But I'm thinking of another. And you?"

"Don't know. I've got to see that friend first."

They left the garden stealthily, avoiding the path and the gate. Mignot sat on the rack over the back wheel of the bicycle, while Patrice pedaled through the dusk. When they got to the brothel Patrice went in with Mignot and phoned De Maurain.

"I must see you right away," he said. "It's about Danielle."

"Can't it wait until tomorrow?"

"She's been arrested by the Gestapo."

"Where are you?"

"The other side of Paris."

"I'll have a room prepared for you."

Patrice hurried off and Mignot called after him, "Seven in the morning at the Prefecture."

He no longer felt the lift and enthusiasm he had felt earlier in the evening. The fire was quenched. There was no place in his mind or heart for anything but Danielle. He rode steadily across the darkening city, through deserted streets and avenues, over the speechless Seine and under the chestnut trees that shadowed the right bank. Not a sound, not a soul, not a light. Paris was a cemetery, its buildings tombs. The city was dead. And in the morning—seven at the Prefecture—the dead would rise. But not Danielle. She was beyond resurrection. Patrice cut that train of thought. He pedaled uphill through the weird silence of the city. In the distance Patrice heard the dull boom and gathering rumble of an explosion that was swallowed up in the silence. Another explosion, and the silence, now ominous, closed over it like the sea over a depth charge. On the horizon he saw two enormous cones of pink and gray smoke rise majestically into the sky. They're blowing up dumps," he said to himself. Maybe the Americans will get here sooner than we thought. But he knew that even the next day would be too late. They would surely move Danielle out during the night if the city were going to fall.

De Maurain opened the door himself when Patrice rang, and led him to the study.

"Now tell me everything you know about this arrest," he said, "and we'll see what can be done."

When Patrice finished, De Maurain looked grave. "That's not much to go on," he said.

"That's all I know. That's all anybody knows except the Gestapo and whoever it was who gave Danielle away."

"We don't even know what she's accused of."

"The usual thing, I suppose. Terrorism."

"But we don't know. We can't be sure."

"Can you find out?"

"I can try."

"Can you find out where she's being held?"

"It won't be easy. Nothing is easy any more. We're living in anarchy. There's no government any more, no police, no authority. Just the naked power of the Wehrmacht and the Gestapo. The whole French cabinet is gone—fled or arrested and taken to the east, toward Germany. Even Laval has resigned; he's under arrest too. And right now in Vichy they're pressuring Pétain to get him to go to Germany. Everything is going to pieces, everything. One little push and the whole country will fall apart."

De Maurain was pacing back and forth, his urbanity gone. "Do you know what this means?" he said. "There's nobody to turn to. Paris is a vacuum. We're in a void while power changes hands. The old ones have gone and the new ones haven't arrived. There's nothing in Paris, nothing. We're in the jungle. Do you realize that if you died tonight there's be nobody to bury you. Even the undertakers are on strike. There's a dead man lying in his bed two floors below and nobody knows what to do about him. In this heat!" De Maurain mopped his face. "And upstairs a man was married this afternoon. 'If I don't do it today,' he said, 'God knows when I'll be able to. The town halls are closing one after the other, and for all I know the priests will be the next ones to strike.' Nothing. Nobody to turn to. Talk about a cataclysm. Now I know what the word means."

"There are still city officials who've been left behind to look after things," Patrice said.

De Maurain drew himself up. "I knew the rulers of France, not the caretakers of a graveyard."

He sank into a chair with his hands clasped on his lap. His long face was haggard in the jumpy candlelight; shadows shifted erratically across the hooked, aristocratic nose and gray hair, and now and again the worried blue eyes glinted in the flickering light.

"The twilight of the tin gods," De Maurain said with his familiar wry smile. But his voice was bitter. "It won't last long. But for a while, until the new rulers take over, there's nothing. Chaos. You see, I'm a string-puller. But the strings are no longer attached. The puppets are gone."

"The ministries are empty," said Patrice, "but how about the Hotel de Ville? The Prefecture?"

Only after he said it did Patrice realize that by morning when a string-puller would be phoning, he would be running the Prefecture, if all went well. And the Hotel de Ville, he wondered. Would the communists or some other resistance group be in charge there?

"The Hotel de Ville," De Maurain was saying. "They have no influence with the Germans. They're the puppets of puppets, or worse."

"And the Germans?"

"Yes, the Germans." De Maurain sighed. "I have few principles, but the Germans . . ." He sighed again and his hand, pointed at his stomach, turned a rapid circle of revulsion. "Funny, isn't it? In spite of everything I ever said, for four years I refused to recognize a state of war. I ignored it—as well as I could, that is. I wouldn't admit that we had lost and they had won. Always made my little deals through Vichy, never asked the Germans for a favor. Now in the last days I have to admit that they're the masters."

"And I thought you were a realist."

"I am. It was a question of self-respect. And after all, every realist is entitled to his blind spot."

"You can get the information about Danielle from the Germans?"

"There are one or two I know. If they're still in Paris."

"Are they big enough to—Do you think you can get her released?"

De Maurain shrugged. "We'll see about that tomorrow."

Alone in his room, where he rapidly undressed and blew out the candle, Patrice was depressed. If De Maurain had such small confidence of being able to help Danielle, there could be little hope. Precisely the elements in the situation that favored the success of the insurrection made it unlikely that De Maurain could do anything for Danielle. And there was nobody else to whom he could turn. Patrice slipped between the fresh, smooth sheets but could not relax. He lay in the soft bed and stared out of the window at the thick-foliaged chestnut trees on the Avenue Henri Martin. He could not resolve anything in his mind, and, depressed as he was, his emotions seemed to be suspended. Everything that should have made him joyful for the uncertain adventure into which he would be plunged by morning twisted at his heart, since it meant that Danielle could not be saved. From far away came the sound of an explosion and still another. The rumble was absorbed by the vast, soft night. Somewhere out there Danielle was a prisoner. Patrice gripped the sheets in anguish and frustration.

He heard a noise in the street below and went to the window. He could see nothing through the trees but heard the hoarse German voices clearly. A truck that had broken down. Back in bed, his eyes wide-open, Patrice listened to the soldiers repair the truck, heard the orders and the sound of tools clicking against metal and clanking on the sidewalk. After what seemed a long while the motor roared to life, and with the cries and laughter of the soldiers and a loud grinding of gears the truck rumbled away. Later, from the open bedroom window above, came the voluptuous sounds of a bride's conjugal bliss. Despite everything, Patrice thought grimly, the life of the city went on. Nothing, not even an insurrection, could stop that. It was hours before Patrice, completely exhausted, fell into a troubled sleep. Paris was dark and silent. The streets were empty. The city slept. In a few hours thirty thousand men would awake and try to take the future in their hands.

Part Two

The Insurrection

[AUGUST 19]

THE next day was Saturday. For the German garrison it began like any other day. A summer torpor hung over the inert streets. The boulevards dozed. Tanks stood at either end of the Champs Élysées like the poised claws of a nutcracker. One tank was anchored in the shadow of the Arch of Triumph, its gun pointed down the deserted avenue; the other faced it at the base of the obelisk. In between there was not a car, not a soul. No sound ruffled the silence; no movement broke the calm. A huge swastika flapped listlessly over the Navy Ministry on the Place de la Concorde. Here and there, with a great metallic clatter, isolated tanks lumbered along the broad central thoroughfares and turned about clumsily on squares like bull elephants with their trunks raised.

It does not take much to keep five or even ten million citizens in line. As a rule, the presence of a small armed force, plus a display of power, is enough. But the rule has exceptions. Despite the German tanks, the men of the resistance packed local command posts in apartments, enclosed courtyards and the backs of shops. For days the women had been sewing F.F.I. brassards, and now the men wore them like medals and waited with irrepressible excitement for orders to move.

Patrice woke up gritty-eyed and jumpy at six o'clock. He lay in bed a while, in a cold sweat, hating to face the day he had waited for so long. The insurrection turned on him and he had the sickish feeling that whatever happened would be bad. Overnight the shock of Danielle's loss had smashed his confidence. Her image leaped up insistently, and each time it did he tottered on the edge of nausea. Doubt ate into his will; he no longer knew what to do. Finally he got out of bed, wanting to hide, to see no one. "I'm losing my nerve," he muttered. "I'm losing my nerve."

He splashed his face with cold water and dressed hastily. Glancing in the mirror, he stopped short. The image he saw was that of a stranger. His grim, unshaven face stared unblinkingly at him, the lips tight, dark circles under the strained eyes. He turned away abruptly. In the dining room he found hot black coffee, soft white rolls, butter and jam. It was real coffee. Patrice could not remember when he had last seen such delicacies. But his throat was tight and dry, his stomach rocky. He gulped the coffee and left.

His bicycle was in the courtyard and he pedaled out into streets that had the clean young morning feel of a day just coming to life, with a sunny career before it. Nobody was about. Patrice was sorry now that he had set up the attack on the Prefecture. It would compromise the insurrection by starting it prematurely without the knowledge of its leaders. Reboussin was right after all, he thought. He was leading the resistance into a disaster on the Warsaw model. Once they moved into the Prefecture it would be too late to turn back. They did not really know how many German troops remained in Paris. At least two divisions, with the probability that two more could be sent in fast—and nobody knew how long it would take the Americans to reach Paris.

He had to do something, but what? Stop the attack on the Prefecture? He could do it. He had to gain time. The resistance leaders would not meet until eleven, so the insurrection could not begin before noon. The morning might give De Maurain the time to locate Danielle and perhaps to exert pressure to get her freed. Patrice did not even realize that his thoughts had swung from anxiety over the insurrection to concern about Danielle.

He rode along the quais through the silent city, nursing his newborn caution and beginning to feel that events had not yet overridden him. He could stop what he had put in motion; he could delay the uprising a few hours. Now that he had worked out a line of action he felt a little better. He breathed more easily and looked around. What he saw lifted his morale. Under a cloudless sky the Seine flowed placidly between serene rows of trees. The morning was innocent and could lead to no evil; the city was calm and could be rushed into no terror. It smelled and felt of summer. All was normal. Maybe Marceau's men would not even appear at the Prefecture! Patrice kept repeating to himself that, with the morning to work in, De Maurain would pull his strings, the puppets would be jerked to life, and Danielle would be set free. He gripped the handle bars and pedaled faster. He was finally going someplace where he had something to do. Was it too late? He cut off his thoughts. Stop the assault on the Prefecture, he said to himself. After that something else could be improvised.

It was exactly seven o'clock when Patrice sped past the front of the Prefecture, standing in gray, massive silence on the Ile de la Cité. He swerved around the corner, drove the length of the building along the Seine and stopped in the Parvis de Notre Dame. His heart sank : Marceau's men were there.

They swarmed over the square in front of the cathedral. There were so many they spilled over the lip of the square onto the quai. Thousands of them—three, maybe four thousand men were there. Most of them were in shirt sleeves. Many were armed. Revolvers, rifles, muskets . . . A few carried tommy guns in musette bags slung over their shoulders. Patrice stood motionless, thinking, It's a disaster. Marceau had taken his orders literally and done his job well, too well. They were out in the open. If a German patrol saw them . . . But something happened to Patrice as he watched them spread over the vast Parvis with its Gothic backdrop, looking as if they had just stepped out of a revolutionary print of the year 1789. At that moment Patrice felt they were fighting the same battle. The chills ran up and down his spine. Swept up into the scene despite himself, he suddenly saw everything differently. This was no normal summer morning. The rest of the city did not count. It was here in this square, before Notre Dame, that the heart of the city beat.

Patrice rode slowly around the Parvis. Everything about the men was shining and eager. No gathering of cops had ever been like this one, he thought. Grouped to smash a demonstration, they were tough and sullen. Now their role was reversed. They were supposed to keep order for the ruling authority, but they had gone over to the other side. Insurrectionists, they walked about with the elation of truant schoolboys. They were not like cops because they were no longer functioning as cops. When they stepped out of their uniforms they changed their identities. Patrice took it all in. He found Marceau trying to keep the men from going too close to the Prefecture.

Marceau greeted Patrice proudly. "We're ready to go," he said.

His lips were set in a thin line, his eyes leveled into Patrice's. He was tensed for the moment, the climactic moment that he felt his

whole life had led up to. Every line of his face and body, every gesture, cried out his will to act. This is how they all feel, Patrice thought.

Marceau's expression altered as he looked at Patrice. "What's the
matter?"

"Nothing."

"You look sick."

"I'm all right," Patrice snapped. He tried to get a grip on himself.

Marceau looked puzzled, then his face brightened. "We brought lad-
ders and rope in case we have to scale the walls. When do we move?"

Patrice looked around the square. All those men . . . So many with
arms . . .

"Is Mignot here?"

"Over at the quai."

Walking toward the quai Patrice said, "We'll have to wait for orders.
They should be here soon."

He could not make up his mind to send them in, nor could he decide
to call it off. He needed time to think. But there was no time. Here
were four thousand insurrectionists in the center of Paris. He could
not hold them here. If the Germans found them out, they would be
massacred. Should he send them away? Some were sure to be caught
crossing Paris. And yet if they went into the Prefecture they might
never get out alive. They might not even be able to break through the
guards at the gates. Whatever he decided he ran the most extreme
dangers.

Mignot and Gaudin were on the quai beside the Delahaye. The
letters "F.F.I." were boldly scrawled on the sides and roof of the car
in white paint. Dozens of cops surrounded the car, which was jammed
with arms. Mignot, a cigarette dangling from the corner of his lips,
was keeping them off good-naturedly. He grinned when he saw Patrice.

"When do we give these arms away?" he asked. "They're hot."

"When we get orders to move."

"I thought you had the orders."

"Not yet."

They waited. The square was noisy. A number of men came up to
Marceau and asked when they were going to move. Marceau put them
off. But he was getting nervous.

"What if the orders don't come?" he asked.

Patrice shrugged.

"We can't stay here all day," Marceau protested.

"I'll give them another ten minutes," Patrice said.

"What then?"

"I don't know. We'll see."

"You can't call it off now. You can't. You can tell them to do anything now and they'll do it. But if you send them away, you'll break their spirit."

Patrice said nothing. He looked around the square again and saw all those thousands of men waiting to be told to fight the Germans. It was all set up and he knew he could never do it again if he called it off now. Every minute he waited increased the danger that they would be discovered. He went over it again and again, the panic mounting. It was the first time he had ever been pinned in a situation where the lives of so many men depended upon his decision. He realized too that the fate of the city, the turn of the insurrection, depended on what he would do. He tried to think it out. Pressured and without the time to do it, he felt as if he were being torn apart. So much was at stake— the lives of these men, Paris, the liberation, Danielle too . . . It all came down to whether he told the men to move against the Prefecture or go home peacefully. He had been perfectly clear a few hours earlier about what had to be done. But he was clear no longer. Was it because Danielle had been captured? Was it to save her—if that was still possible—that he was holding up what he had planned and organized so meticulously, and what all these men had come to do? Measuring it that way, he knew only one decision was possible. But there was another way to measure it, and the thought that he might be leading a foolhardy attack to preordained defeat paralyzed him. If they were thrown back from the gates of the Prefecture with disastrous losses, it could mean that the insurrection would never again get under way.

Patrice gazed around the square, his mind whirling. What should he tell them to do? To go home? To follow him into the Prefecture? His thoughts were in a hopeless tangle. He couldn't straighten them out any more. The pressure was too great. There was not enough time. But he had to do something and he had to do it fast. He was suddenly afraid he was cracking. He was afraid to give the order to attack and afraid to tell them to go home. His tightly clenched hands were slippery wet; his shirt was drenched with sweat. He saw nothing around him any more. His eyes were glazed, and he was hunched over his racing thoughts, trying desperately to put them into some kind of order. But they would form no pattern. At last, knowing he had to speak whether he had come to a conclusion or not, Patrice balanced his twin fears and reached his decision by falling back on instinct, on what was deepest in him and had not been overwhelmed.

"All right," he said abruptly. "Let's distribute the arms."

Mignot opened the door of the Delahaye. The cops crushed around the car, and Mignot and Gaudin handed out arms and ammunition.

Patrice started across the Parvis toward the Prefecture. Marceau was behind him, and the men on the way, seeing that something was finally happening, were magnetized toward them and followed. Patrice stopped in front of Notre Dame.

"We're going into the Prefecture," he shouted. "I want a dozen men to go with me. The rest will follow if we get in. If we can't get in through the door, we'll climb over the walls. Are you with me?"

They were with him. Patrice picked out his men. Then he started across the street toward the Prefecture. He went to a huge door with Marceau and Mignot behind him. Patrice began pounding on the door. All the men flowed toward the Prefecture.

"Open up! Open up!" Patrice shouted.

The door slipped ajar and a Municipal Guard in full uniform with a frightened face peeked through.

"What do you want?"

"We want to come in."

"Who are you."

Patrice's foot slipped into the door. "We're the resistance!" he cried and shoved hard.

The color went out of the guard's face. He did not resist. The door swung back, its hinges squeaking. Patrice stepped into the huge courtyard of the Prefecture and saw the great empty space stretch before him up to the building. It flashed through his mind that the courtyard was covered by machine guns. But he moved forward. Behind him waves of cops flooded through the open door. Patrice dashed across the courtyard. The men swirled after him. There was no sound but their voices, no rifle or machine-gun fire, no resistance. A captain of the Guard, a captain of the Gendarmery, several Municipal Guards and gendarmes stood by, overwhelmed, neutral as the paving stones underfoot. A Black Maria stood at the far end of the courtyard. Patrice reached it, climbed on top of the motor and held up his arms. In a moment only the men, the sun and a strange silence filled the courtyard. Standing on top of the Black Maria Patrice felt a lightness and exhilaration, a joy and strength beyond imagination. He held his arms up as high as he could and began to shout. "In the name of the Provisional Government of the French Republic—" he had to take a breath—"I take possession of the Prefecture of Police."

He leaped to the ground and several hundred men crushed noisily about him. The rest of them had spread around the courtyard. They were a blind mob.

"Marceau!"

Marceau fought his way to Patrice's side.

"You know the building well?"

"Like my pocket."

"Pick me a good man who knows it as well."

Marceau did not hesitate. "Bailloux!" he shouted.

The call was relayed across the courtyard, and a moment later the circle around Patrice gave way to admit a big swarthy man in shirt sleeves with hairy arms and chest. Patrice sized him up.

"Can you run the show down here?"

"As well as anyone."

"Better!"

"All right, better."

"Good. Pick your men from that end of the courtyard and post them at all the doors. We took the Prefecture; now we've got to hold it."

Bailloux went to work and Patrice turned to Marceau.

"I'm going to post men upstairs at the windows to cover the approaches," he said. "Take thirty or forty men, divide them into four or five groups, put a man in charge of each group and have them arrest every police official in the building from the Prefect down." Marceau started to move and Patrice called out, "Take over the switchboard first—"

"And the teletype machines."

"Good. And stop all calls until you hear from me."

They went to it with crisp efficiency. At that moment there was a flurry of movement at the end of the courtyard. A stream of shouting men flowed toward the flagpole that stretched up from the cobbles high above the building. One of the men stepped forward, gripping a French flag. He was at the flagpole, working the ropes. Suddenly every man in the courtyard was aware of him. They fell silent, their eyes glazed on the strip of blue, white and red cloth. In short, rapid spurts it shot up into the blue Paris sky. The sun shone benignly on the flag as it rose above the roof tops and chimneys of Paris for the first time since the defeat four years before. At the top of the pole the tricolor unfurled in a gust of wind and flapped free and gay while the men below gazed up in choked silence. Then, uncertainly, one feeble voice began to sing into the silence; a second voice joined in, and an instant later the song rose from thousands of throats. *"Allons, enfants de la Patrie, le jour de gloire est arrivé . . . Aux armes, citoyens! Formez vos bataillons! Marchons, marchons . . ."* It was the most discordant Marseillaise and the truest they had ever heard.

Two hours later Patrice had done everything possible to prepare for a German attack. Thousands of sandbags, stacked in the cellar against a communist *putsch*, barricaded doors and protected snipers at windows. The Prefecture was long on men, short on weapons: it was defended by exactly seven machine guns. Patrice had sent some of the surplus cops to take possession of the police stations throughout the city, others to make announcements in the streets and mobilize Parisians into the fight. In a free moment he phoned De Maurain.

"Any news?"

"Nothing."

"Any hope?"

"Some. Can I call you later?"

"I'd better call you."

"She's not in Paris. I did learn that."

Patrice's heart dropped. "Could they have shipped her to Germany?"

"My man doesn't think so. She's probably somewhere in the suburbs."

"Will you have anything in an hour?"

"Not before two or three o'clock."

Patrice hung up feeling haggard and worn. But there was still some hope, he thought. De Maurain would track her down, and once he knew where she was . . . A burst of machine-gun fire ripped him out of his thoughts. He dashed into an office overlooking the Boulevard du Palais. Mignot and Gaudin were at the window. Below, a German truck was smashed against a shop front; prisoners, their hands locked behind their heads, were being led into the Prefecture.

Mignot turned to Patrice and grinned. "Good work," he said.

"Come with me."

They followed Patrice to his office and Patrice closed the door.

"We're going to be in trouble when the Germans hit us," he said. "We need help—on the outside. The more fighting there is around the

Prefecture, all over the city, the tougher it will be for them to concentrate on the building. I'm going to spread the word."

"What can we do?" Mignot asked.

"Start the street fighting—across the Seine at the Place St. Michel. It's as good a place as any to hit them."

Gaudin's eyes shone. "Suits me better than the Prefecture," he said.

"We've got rifles," said Mignot, "but we need some men with us."

"Get them at the command post. The entire resistance is mobilized. They're waiting for orders to go into the streets."

"Let's go," Mignot said.

He was at the door with Gaudin when Patrice called after them, "Hurry! Tell them the insurrection has begun!"

†

LATE in the morning the leaders of the resistance, gathered in an apartment off the Place Denfert-Rochereau, gave the color of unity to their council by voting unanimously for an insurrection. But Patrice's messenger was waiting outside the door, and they learned that their long-debated, momentous decision was meaningless: what the resistance leaders had decided to start was already happening. The communists were indignant; the play had been taken from them. Mazaud's smile drained off his face like water in dry dirt. The communist leader sped over to the Prefecture on his bicycle and shouted at Patrice that what he had done was intolerable. "You wanted an insurrection; I gave you one," Patrice replied blandly. But when Mazaud stormed out Patrice felt no sense of victory.

Throughout the city the insurrection swung into gear. Unobtrusively, men of the resistance set out to take control of ministries, *mairies*, industrial installations, banks, museums. Lefort hastened to the newspaper plant on the Rue Réaumur. Editors and typesetters had already turned the building into a fortress. Gigantic rolls of newsprint blocked the huge front door; an iron curtain barricaded the side entrance; the narrow back door was barred and guarded on the inside by a copy boy armed with a revolver. From the outside the building looked empty, like a department store on Sunday, but inside, a newspaper was being readied for publication. Lefort found he had been preceded by men who had a prior, and legal, claim to the premises: three representatives of the owners of the plant, who were installed in the publisher's office. Backed by a few editors and composing-room men, Lefort broke into the office, pointed a revolver at the three men and informed them that they were under arrest.

"Why?" they asked.

"You tried to take possession of this newspaper."

"For the owners."

"I'm the owner."

"Is this a revolution?"

Lefort smiled. "For you and me, yes. You lose the paper; I get it."

With varying degrees of politeness, such scenes, on a political level, were occurring in a large number of the city's public buildings when Mignot and Gaudin, having commandeered half a dozen F.F.I.s at their command post, set out to start the street fighting. Arriving at the quai next to the Place St. Michel, the small unit possessed two rifles, three revolvers (one dating from the Franco-Prussian War) and the unshakable conviction that armament, if they used what they had well, would not long be a problem. They deployed and waited. Above, up and down a long stretch of the left bank, heads appeared at hundreds of windows. The row of buildings extending along the Seine as far as the eye could see was like an endless Colosseum with spectators leaning on their balconies and window sills watching the gladiators below, anonymous specks on a city street transformed into an ancient arena. They all waited in silence. The figures below seemed indifferent, the spectators tense. Soon, through the silence, rose the sound of an approaching motor. All eyes were fixed on the point where the quai curved with the river. An open-topped truck appeared around the bend. In the back, standing up, were many German soldiers. They were young men with a look of youthful vigor. In that swift course into the arena nothing about them, not even their uniforms, gave them an appearance of the military. Their tunics were open, their heads bare. They were talking and laughing like any group of carefree youngsters who had never handled a gun. The sound of the motor grew louder. The Parisians leaned out of their windows and held their breath. The truck raced on, bearing its youthful cargo. Suddenly shots burst over the roar of the motor. They were followed instantaneously by a scream of brakes, the crash of the windshield splintering to bits and the terrified cries of the soldiers piled pell-mell against the cab of the truck. The truck swerved onto the sidewalk and jerked back violently as the driver tried to turn and flee. But the motor stalled. The driver worked frantically to start it. All the while bullets poured into the truck. Suddenly the driver fell limp over the steering wheel. A moment later the firing stopped. Mignot and the others rushed the truck, and the Germans who were still alive surrendered.

Then, from the entire length of the quai, from all the open windows glittering brilliantly in the sun, rose a wild shout of triumph. Small tricolor flags fluttered from violently waving arms as men, women and children leaned out of their windows and cheered. None of the spectators knew that the scene they were cheering was the opening skirmish of the insurrection; they did not even think of this incident that had unfolded below their windows as a movement of revolt. All they felt was that it expressed their deepest desires, that they had waited years to witness this precise scene, and now it had happened, so they shouted and cheered and waved their flags as if the millennium had come.

In an instant the spirit of a carnival swept the quai. Gaily chattering groups of people crowded doorways and corners; women dashed into the street bearing bottles of wine, which they held out by the neck to the thirsty F.F.I.s; spectators in the open windows above shouted encouragement and sang songs. The successful opening of a popular insurrection is an occasion for festivity. The Parisians of the St. Michel quarter celebrated.

Quickly, the F.F.I.s were armed with captured weapons; the prisoners were led away; the smashed truck was rolled down the embankment and the dead were laid out in a row along the river. Other skirmishes followed the first and were all of the same pattern. A truck approached. A voice called out, "Go ahead, boys! It's a Boche!" Everybody scurried for cover. Shots rang out, and when the smoke cleared the Parisians popped up at the windows, on the balconies, in the doorways and from around corners, and waved and cheered.

After one skirmish Mignot felt a tug at his trousers and, looking down, saw a neatly dressed four-year-old boy whose clear brown eyes were stained with tears.

"It's my mother," the boy whimpered. "My mother."

"Did you lose her?"

"She won't talk to me. She doesn't answer," the boy sobbed.

"Come on," said Mignot, taking the boy's hand. "We'll go see her together."

Still weeping, the boy led Mignot two doors down the street. They climbed two flights of stairs. A door on the landing was open. When he went inside the apartment Mignot found the boy's mother sprawled on her back, with her arms stretched out by the window where she had fallen. She was a young woman with straight, delicate features, and a bullet hole edged with blood stared darkly out of the center of her forehead. The boy, standing miserably just inside the door, looked up at Mignot with tear-stained, helpless eyes and whimpered.

"Why doesn't mamma get up?"

"She's very tired," Mignot said.

Holding his rifle in one hand, the wiry little mechanic tenderly lifted the weeping boy in his free arm and carried him to some neighbors.

Although most Parisians stayed out of the fighting, all sorts of people got into it. One-paw, the beggar, had not forgotten the accordion the German had stolen from him two days before. He was sitting in his furnished room in the Rue Monge when he heard the sound of rifle fire from the direction of the Place St. Michel. He listened for a moment, his thoughts interrupted, then heard a second volley cut short by the chatter of a machine gun. He hopped two steps across the room, grasped his crutches and swung his huge body out into the street. A few people stood at the doorway, talking in low tones and looking worried.

"Where are you going, One-paw?" an elderly man with a white mustache called after him.

One-paw did not answer. He swung along as fast as he could, his square jaw set in a hard line and his blue eyes cold and glittering.

"Come back!" the old man shouted. "Don't be a fool! You'll get shot!"

One-paw did not even turn his head. At the metro station Cardinal-Lemoine he came upon a crowd, grouped around a small Prefecture car, being harangued by two men. The men cried that an insurrection had started, that the police had taken the Prefecture for the resistance and that all Parisians should go to Notre Dame to fight the Boches and defend Paris. The men in the crowd looked at each other furtively but did not move.

One-paw spat in disgust and left. He was in a cold rage when he came to the bridge leading from the left bank to the Parvis de Notre Dame. The noon sun glittered on the windows of the Prefecture, and One-paw blinked as he looked at the building, dazzled by the glare. Halfway across the bridge he paused and drew a shaggy arm across his wet forehead. His shirt was open and his chest was wet with sweat; a dark stain marked his shirt under the armpits. He heard someone shout and turned to see a German tank facing the Prefecture. Its long gun jerked back; a puff of smoke floated out of the muzzle and, simultaneous with the concussion, a burst of machine-gun fire whistled over One-paw's head. Automatically, he went down flat, his crutches flying off in different directions. When he looked up the tank was retreating and bullets were whizzing all around. One-paw was suddenly aware that other men were near him. He saw a man a few yards away fall as if axed. Greatly puzzled, One-paw looked at him. The man lay there like a corpse. It seemed inexplicable. The idea that anyone could be shot dead in the streets of mid-town Paris only now began to take form.

The shooting stopped. One-paw got up, stooped over the body, then took the rifle lying near the dead man and said, "You won't need it any more." Three other corpses lay on the bridge.

One-paw turned back to the left bank. The streets were empty, as if a plague had swept all humanity from the city. The rifle slung across his back, One-paw swung along the Seine. A car with the letters F.F.I. scrawled all over it and packed with eight or nine shirt-sleeved men whizzed by him. A German car raced after it. Soldiers, sloped over the front mudguards, fired repeatedly at the fleeing resistance car, which fired back. One-paw leaped for protection behind a lamppost, thinking in the flash of excitement that this was like a scene from an American cowboy movie and he was part of it, right in the heart of Paris. He turned his head to watch as he reached the lamppost and grabbed it with both hands, holding the crutches in his armpits. One of the Germans was firing at him. Petrified, One-paw heard the sickening, ringing whoosh of the bullets as they zinged past him. Then *ping! ping!* two bullets sang ringingly in breathless succession smack into the lamppost, and One-paw yanked his tingling hands from the vibrating metallic pole as if it were a hot iron. His crutches clattered to the ground, and to keep from falling One-paw grasped the humming lamppost. It stopped singing when he grabbed it. The German car was now far down the quai, and swearing, One-paw reached down for his crutches. He saw then that the two bullets had punctured the lamppost with two neat holes exactly at the point where his right leg would have been if he had had a right leg. One-paw crossed himself. *"Bon Dieu!"* he said fervently, looking up at the sky. "Now I know why You took away that God-damned leg when You did. Help me knock off my twelve Boche bastards and I'll forgive and forget everything You did to me."

One-paw went through the narrow Rue de la Huchette. As he passed a brothel, a window blind on the first floor slipped open and a young woman with dyed blonde hair wearing a kimono peered out.

"Ola!" she called. "What's going on out there?"

One-paw turned his head but kept moving. "Come out and walk the streets, you lazy bitch, instead of waiting there to peddle your ass, and you'll find out."

Grinning savagely under her curses, One-paw heard the woman cry, "A leg's not all you're missing, you species of a miscarriage on crutches!"

At the Boulevard St. Michel One-paw spotted a lone German soldier walking away from him about a hundred and fifty yards off. One-paw looked around hastily. He saw nobody but an old woman dressed in black coming toward him. He leaned against the wall of a building to hold the rifle steady and brought the back of the soldier's head into the sights. One-paw squeezed the trigger. The explosion filled the air. Lowering the rifle, One-paw saw the German stretched motionless on the sidewalk. Still a good shot, One-paw thought. The elation rose in his chest and throat. He shouted, "Got him! Got the bastard!"

At the same moment the old lady in black was shaking a black-gloved finger under his nose, her voice shrill and insistent. "Shooting off a gun in the middle of Paris!" she cried. "Couldn't you wait until I passed, you scamp? You've made my ears ring!"

One-paw backed off and slung the rifle over his shoulder while she scolded him. He mumbled an apology with the confused feeling that he was not entirely in the wrong, but he did not know how to say it. Then he fled, swinging his big body rhythmically on his crutches. The German soldier, a rosy-cheeked boy in an ill-fitting uniform, was sprawled, face down, on the sidewalk, the back of his cranium smashed by the bullet.

†

A POLITICIAN without a policy is like a capitalist without capital—bankrupt. Reboussin had failed to block the insurrection. His policy was wrecked.

To get back into business the bankrupt capitalist seeks new capital, the defeated politician a new policy. An old hand at the game, Reboussin started his search quickly. After the meeting at which the resistance leaders decided on the insurrection he went off to be alone.

Walking toward his apartment, Reboussin felt the menace of the

Germans weighing on the city, and a sensation of impotence settled over him. Was there anything to be done? What goal should he pursue?

Reboussin's only resource was himself. Out of the rubble of his wrecked policy he had to create a new one. He felt that if he failed to invent a workable alternative to the communist line and a means of imposing it, he was abandoning the resistance and the city to the leftists. He knew that the Americans could not get to Paris for at least several days and was certain that if the Germans suppressed the insurrection they would be pitiless. But he was even more certain that if the communists led Paris out of the occupation, it would eventually mean the end, not only of his career, but of the life and institutions that had nourished him and all he loved. What could he do? It was too late to stop the insurrection—Reboussin stopped in his tracks. *Was it too late?*

He walked, faster now, so intent on his thoughts that he took no notice of the streets, of the rare people he passed or of the German patrols that roved the central arteries. He was no longer interested in the streets. He could not control them or turn the tide of battle. He was evolving a plan, turning it around and around, smoothing out awkward angles, analyzing, analyzing. This was his trade and he was a craftsman. The streets were for the insurrectionists. That was communist territory. But shooting off guns in the streets of a city was not the only way to win an insurrection. It was the crude way, the politics of the mob. The matter could certainly be handled with greater elegance.

Reboussin hurried along, thinking that Patrice had started the insurrection, that Patrice controlled the Prefecture of Police. It was the center, or one of the centers, of the insurrection. Reboussin frowned. He disliked Patrice. Not because their views clashed, although that contributed. He knew he would feel the same way about Patrice even if their ideas were identical. Reboussin disliked him because their ways of thought were so divergent. Patrice was alien. There were even some communists, Reboussin thought, some intelligent ones like Laperche, whom he liked and admired as men. However different their ideas, they were his kind. They thought and operated as he did. There was a hard common ground on which he could meet them. Their principles were recognizable, even though they started from different assumptions and fought for a different purpose. They were political. Patrice was not. He owed his position, Reboussin thought, not to a flair for politics, but to the special circumstances created by the resistance.

Reboussin wondered if he could trust Patrice and quickly decided he could not. He did not doubt Patrice's integrity. In fact, integrity defined Patrice for him. But how could he trust a man whose mind he did not understand? It was impossible. Why should Patrice jump the gun on the insurrection? He wasn't a communist, yet he supported the party's policy. In fact, he had out-Poped the Pope. Why? Reboussin found no satisfactory answer. But he thought he might need Patrice.

At his apartment Reboussin phoned F.F.I. headquarters, which had been established in the catacombs, deep under the Place Denfert-Rochereau. A staff officer told him the resistance had taken several public buildings in addition to the Prefecture and that there had been minor skirmishes in the suburbs, on the left bank and in Montmartre.

"Have the Germans reacted yet?"

"Not really. So far we've only seen some patrols and isolated groups."

"Any sign they're going to hit?"

"None. But we expect it any time now."

Reboussin hung up. He thought for a while. Patrice. How to reach him? The telephone. Thank God the telephone is working, Reboussin thought. He lifted the phone book on his knees and flipped pages. Then he dialed.

"I want to talk to Patrice."

"Who's calling?"

"Reboussin."

"Hold on."

Reboussin waited, relieved of the doubt he had suddenly had that the operator would not know who Patrice was, somehow pleased that the resistance held the Prefecture. An unrecognizably metallic voice came through the receiver.

"Patrice? . . . How is it going over there?"

"Not too bad."

"Got enough men?"

"More than enough."

"Arms?"

"That's another story."

"The Germans call on you yet?"

"They sent a tank around with a couple of bouquets."

"No more?"

"That's all. There are plenty of stragglers from Normandy who've been passing in front of the building in trucks. We stopped quite a few. Otherwise it's been quiet."

"Can I be of any help?"

"Can you get us any machine guns?"

"I'll try. Some rifles or revolvers are more likely—if I'm lucky."

"Thanks. You may be interested to know that Mazaud was furious at me for starting the insurrection. We yelled at each other like a couple of drunken cab drivers."

"Why?"

"He would have preferred that the communists take the Prefecture rather than the cops. Not that he said so."

Reboussin listened but said nothing. He thought it made little difference if the police or the communists were in the Prefecture; no matter who held what position he had no doubt that the only political group that could profit from the insurrection was the Communist party.

"I told him," Patrice was saying, "that an insurrection is a time for initiative."

Reboussin smiled. "You sound as if you've been reading a communist handbook, but I couldn't agree more." He was delighted to hear of the disagreement between Patrice and the communists. "I'd better get to work on those arms. Be over there later."

He called F.F.I. headquarters again and spoke to the same staff officer.

"The Prefecture needs arms."

"So do we."

"That bad?"

"Ha!"

"But they've got the men and they're empty-handed. The Germans may hit them any minute."

"That's how it is all over the city. We can't help them any more than we have. The arsenal's empty."

"What can they do?"

"There's only one way they or anybody else'll get arms today: by taking them from the Germans."

"They know that."

Reboussin hung up and successively phoned the headquarters of the four sectors of Paris. There were no arms. The slogan had already spread around the city: arm yourself from the enemy. Reboussin gave up.

Not long afterward Bourbon arrived. The colonel was distraught. His thin face was drawn, the lips tight over the severe mouth, and his glassy blue eyes strained.

"They've done it," he muttered. "God knows how we'll get out of it now."

Reboussin stared at him soberly. "They got us into this mess without God's help," he said. "We'll have to get out of it the same way."

"But the fight's started already. Haven't you been in the street? They're shooting. The fools have even occupied some public buildings as if they were an army and not guerrillas. They've strung up flags, so the Germans will know just where to go and flush them out." Bourbon paced feverishly, his tall body spare and tense. Abruptly he stopped in front of Reboussin, who was calmly seated, and pounded out his words. "We're committed. We have nothing to fight with and all we can do is fight."

"We can also try to stop the fight," Reboussin said quietly.

Bourbon looked oddly at Reboussin, who gazed back serenely.

"Stop the fight!" Bourbon finally gasped. "Are you mad? We're committed, I tell you. Even with communists in charge. The Germans are still the enemy. The battle is joined. My God, we can't split our own forces at a time like this. It would be treason." Bourbon paused, the shock wearing off, and finished weakly, "Besides, it takes two to stop a fight. The Germans would never agree."

"That remains to be seen. They must know Paris is lost to them one way or another. What good will it do to fight us if we make it attractive not to fight? Von Choltitz has the security of his garrison to think about and the very considerable fact that a large number of troops retreating from Normandy must still pass through Paris to get safely to the rear."

"The communists will never agree."

"Probably not." Reboussin smiled coldly. "But that may not be decisive. An insurrection is a time for all sorts of initiatives."

Bourbon stared at Reboussin with blank blue eyes. "I don't see it," he said.

"I don't either—yet. We'll have to see how things develop. At least we have something to work for, a door to open if opportunity knocks."

Bourbon shrugged, unconvinced. "I'm not a politician," he said. "All I know is that they have tanks. And we—we have a few muskets and our bare hands."

"I'm not a military man," Reboussin said, "but this much is clear: if you're bound to lose a battle on the battlefield, you can't do any worse across a table."

He led Bourbon to the door. "Let's keep this to ourselves," he said, "and keep in touch."

Bourbon sighed and said dourly, "When I think that we could have just coasted along until the Americans got here!"

†

His crutches beside him, One-paw leaned against the wall of the Prefecture next to the main gate on the Boulevard du Palais and waited, holding his rifle ready. Soon a German motorcyclist sped down the boulevard toward him. One-paw lifted the Mauser to his shoulder, aimed quickly, the rifle swinging around smoothly with the advance of the motorcycle, and pulled the trigger when the target was no more than forty yards away. The motorcycle twisted around sharply in front of the Prefecture gate and fell over on its side, throwing the driver several yards clear. The motor roared angrily for a moment as if wounded, then gasped and was silent. One-paw hopped into the middle of the boulevard. The wheels of the motorcycle were still turning when he passed it; the soldier was dead. One-paw picked up the German's helmet. There was a hole in it and a white slimy substance on the inner edge. Souvenir in hand, One-paw swung back to the Prefecture gate. Two men came out and dragged the corpse by the armpits into the courtyard of the Prefecture, while a third wheeled the motorcycle after them. One-paw followed them. A group of cops surrounded him. One offered him a bottle of red wine. One-paw was thirsty. He lifted the bottle to his lips and took a long drag. Never had wine tasted so good to him. He wiped his mouth with the back of his hand and breathed out heavily.

"By God," he said, "there's nothing like a shot of red to wash the dust out of your mouth." He patted the bottle and handed it back. "I like it when it scratches your throat as it slides down."

"He's a winetaster," one of the cops said.

"Every chance I get," said One-paw.

"What's anybody like you doing hopping around Paris on one leg and shooting up Germans?"

"They stole my accordion." One-paw's eyes circled the group around him cunningly. "And besides," he added, "there's *La Patrie*."

A cop took the German helmet from One-paw, and some of the men examined it.

"What's that?" a cop asked, pointing to the blob of white slime under the rim.

"His eye," said One-paw.

The cops stared at it for a moment with awe and disgust. Then one of them turned his back and retched.

†

ABOVE the courtyard in a spacious first-floor office Patrice studied reports flooding into police headquarters on teletype machines linking the Prefecture with all the police stations and *mairies* of Paris and the suburbs. The news was overwhelming. Throughout the city and the industrial suburbs the resistance was occupying one position after the other as if it were running a dress rehearsal of the insurrection on a split-second schedule. For hours there was not a single report of a skirmish, much less a battle, or of any German opposition to the occupation of public buildings. Patrice clutched the teletype reports and the scribbled notes of telephone messages, and his disbelief gradually faded as he read and reread the news. The Germans were stunned. The insurrection had raced off to a headlong start.

But Patrice was unimpressed. Thinking ahead, he knew that, like the Prefecture, each building occupied would have to be defended, and he failed to see the sense in taking what could not be held. The resistance was merely multiplying throughout Paris the number of targets the Germans would soon destroy. Each present victory was the build-up for a subsequent defeat. Yet there seemed to be nothing that he or anyone else in the resistance could do to stop this series of catastrophic victories. They had all dreamed for too many humiliating days stretched across the long years of the day when they would take their destiny in their own hands. Now that the moment was upon them they had cast away their old cunning and grasped whatever was in reach without considering the consequences. Patrice knew from his own experience in attacking the Prefecture what demon of irrepressible exultation was sweeping them up and thrusting them into the crucible of the insurrection. But enthusiasm was not an emotion that thrived under withering gunfire; and in any case, something more would be needed to hold what was being taken against the inevitable German assault. That something more the resistance did not have. Alone, it could not beat the Germans. It did not have the strength. For that reason, and because its unity was largely a fiction, the resistance had no real insurrectionary plan. Various resistance groups, including the one at the Prefecture, were acting independently of the established central control. Operations were not co-ordinated; they aimed at no single decisive purpose and could not, therefore, except by a most unlikely accident, lead to a decision. A neat, clean-cut insurrection, Patrice thought, was the Latin-American brand, with a compact, armed force occupying the presidential palace, arresting the president and proclaiming a new regime. This one was unorthodox—and would be a mess. With no possibility of following the classical policy and destroying or neutralizing the enemy force, the resistance was enthusiastically occupying territory, taking buildings. After that, since the resistance was impotent to carry the fight to the Germans, it could only wait until the Nazis reacted and destroyed them or the Americans arrived to snatch them out of the grave they were now so industriously digging for themselves. The prospects were not promising.

Nevertheless, as the picture slowly came into focus out of the blur of a thousand piecemeal reports, it looked much better than could have been expected. The two other police forces in Paris—the gendarmes and the Republican Guards—had gone over to the resistance following the arrest of their Vichyite officers during the night. Having raised the French flag and sung the Marseillaise in their caserns that morning, the gendarmes and Republican Guards had gone about their regular business of guarding certain government buildings, the Bank of France, prisons and various industrial installations with such admirable discretion that the Germans were not even aware of their change of allegiance. The resistance, for its part, had occupied the *mairies,* ministries and other strategically situated buildings in Paris and the suburbs with a minimum of political conflict between its various elements. During these first hours the communists had come out in no better position than the other groups; for the most part, the communists had not gone after political objectives. It was now clear, Patrice thought, that the right wing of the resistance had been wrong about communist intentions: the communists had no revolutionary master plan for the insurrection.

Throughout the morning and into the tropical heat of the early afternoon an unending stream of men flowed in and out of Patrice's office, seeking orders, demanding decisions, delivering reports. Couriers and liaison agents trooped in and out; Marceau and Bailloux dashed through for constant conferences; the telephone rang incessantly. After half a day of unrelenting pressure Patrice, unshaven and hollow-eyed, was functioning on his nerves. He kept wiping the sweat from his forehead with the back of his hand; his shirt clung damply to his body. On top of his physical discomfort he was worried, and his anxiety sapped his energy as much as the heat and the unending deluge of work that poured over him. He was worried about the German attack, when it would come, how powerful it would be and what he could do to defend the Prefecture and the men in it at the point of crisis. Deep down he was also worried about Danielle. Through the agitation engulfing him, his anguish sprang repeatedly to the surface. Every few minutes he looked at his watch. Finally, at two o'clock, he phoned De Maurain. The butler told him De Maurain would not be back for an hour. Patrice left the Prefecture phone number.

Between two other phone calls he scribbled an order that was sent out on the teletype circuit. The order read: USE ALL MEANS TO PERSUADE THE POPULATION TO GO HOME. TELL THEM THE LIBERATION IS NOW TAKING PLACE. But he had little hope that the order would be effective. Knowing Parisians, he was sure their curiosity would be stronger than their fear.

Shortly afterward Reboussin came in.

"Did you get anything?"

"Not even a water pistol," Reboussin said dourly, " 'Get your arms from the Germans,' they told me."

"What do they think we've been doing?" Patrice suddenly noticed that Reboussin was pale and jittery. "What's the matter?"

"Nothing. Your boys are trigger-happy. They fired a few rounds at me before I managed to get in."

"No harm." Patrice smiled grimly. "Let's hope their aim is better when the Germans come."

"Let's hope so," Reboussin said dryly.

"How does it look outside?"

"Quiet, except here and there at intersections. They have some tanks prowling the boulevards and a few motorized patrols roving the streets, but no more than that so far."

"Can't understand it. What are they waiting for?"

"They won't wait much longer."

"Of course not. Well, we're as ready for them as we'll ever be."

Reboussin looked Patrice directly in the eyes. "It's going to be murderous when they hit the Prefecture," he said with an air and tone that combined both candor and urgency. "Let's work together, Patrice.

We've got to. You won the fight for the insurrection. Now that it's begun, we're fighting the same battle. Let's forget the past and all our differences. Only one thing counts now: beating the Germans, if we can, and coming out whole." Reboussin paused, then said very quietly, "I'm an old hand at politics, Patrice, a very old hand. I know how to accept facts no matter what they add up to and go on from there. Will you take my hand on it?"

Patrice was astonished. He hesitated, then, without a word, crossed the room to Reboussin and grasped his hand.

"We can use you here," Patrice said. He felt good; this was more than he had expected, much more. Although he could not like Reboussin, he felt that he almost did, not having suspected him capable of such a gesture. "There's plenty of work—Wait a minute." He pressed a buzzer and an F.F.I. appeared. "Clear out the office next to mine," Patrice told him. "Reboussin here and I are going to be working together until the Germans are cleared out of Paris."

Reboussin smiled; Patrice wiped the sweat from his forehead and grinned. They shook hands again. Then Reboussin followed the F.F.I. to the office adjoining Patrice's and sat down at the desk. Its surface was shiny and inviolate. Not a scrap of paper, not a blotter. On one corner of the desk stood a telephone connected with the Prefecture switchboard; on another corner there was a direct phone. Reboussin looked at it, recognized his private line to the outside world. He looked up at the F.F.I. who was hovering at the door. "This will do," he said crisply.

†

THE interoffice telephone on Patrice's desk rang shortly before three o'clock. It was Bailloux, the dark, stocky cop Patrice had appointed as his lieutenant soon after the Prefecture had been taken. Bailloux had worked out well. He was in charge of the first floor overlooking the approaches on the Boulevard du Palais. Businesslike, vigorous, competent, he stalked about the floor from one sandbagged window to the next, overseeing every detail and exuding confidence. He had natural authority; the men obeyed him without question and they liked him.

"The Boches are moving," he barked into the phone. "They're going to hit us in another minute!"

"I'll be right there!" Patrice cried.

A few seconds later Patrice was at Bailloux' side, looking over a pile of sandbags down the Boulevard du Palais. Bailloux' thick, hairy arms were sticking out of his rolled-up shirt sleeves and the swarthy face was pearled with sweat.

"Here they come," he whispered.

The Germans were still quite a way off, but, standing at the window, Patrice felt naked and fragile, as if he were in the path of a racing locomotive and could not move; a chill of terror skated up his spine. To the left, three trucks packed with helmeted infantrymen had drawn up to the middle of the bridge. To the right, scores of soldiers crouched over their rifles, held in front of them, and advanced down the boulevard, dashing from doorway to doorway. Several huge tanks lumbered noisily forward and quickly rolled out of sight around the corner of the Prefecture.

"They're going to hit us on the other side!" Patrice cried.

"On this side too," Bailloux muttered.

"Who's in charge in the courtyard?"

"Marceau."

"I'm going to give him a hand."

Bailloux clutched Patrice's arm. "Wait!" he cried. "We may need you here."

At that moment a tremendous burst of firing poured from all the windows of the Prefecture facing the Seine and the boulevard. The shattering noise of a thousand explosions splintered the air as the whining bullets flooded over the advancing Germans to the right and to the left. Bailloux shouted in excitement, but the noise was so great that Patrice, standing beside him, could not hear a word. Then the deafening clatter of firearms subsided as suddenly as it had begun, and a cry from hundreds of throats rose from the Prefecture.

"Look!" Bailloux shouted.

The three trucks on the left had been stopped in the middle of the bridge and the foremost truck had just burst into flame. The flames leaped high out of the motor, making a soughing noise that could be heard fifty yards away. Another concentrated flood of bullets poured over the bridge. The Germans abandoned their trucks and retreated. One of the infantrymen panicked under the downpour of bullets and, throwing his rifle away, leaped upon the railing of the bridge and jumped into the Seine. As he floated through the air, the shouts from the Prefecture redoubled. Quickly a dozen F.F.I.s rushed to the bridge. Dashing past the burning truck, they worked the other two around to block the bridge and form a barricade.

On the right the Germans were backing away too, leaving a dozen dead sprawled on the sidewalk.

Patrice patted Bailloux on the arm, said, "We beat back the first wave," and with a bouncy feeling of exhilaration started for his office to find out if De Maurain had called. In the corridor a wild-eyed young cop suddenly sprinted up to him, grabbed him by the arm with one hand a waved a revolver in his face with the other.

"Hurry! Hurry!" the man panted.

Patrice snatched the revolver; the cop caught his breath.

"Tanks are breaking into the courtyard! The men are running away!"

At the first words Patrice broke away and raced for the stairs. He saw Reboussin step out of his office and yelled, "In the courtyard!" Patrice took the stairs three at a jump, hearing the dull boom of a cannon as he charged down headlong. He burst into the sunlit courtyard and instantly took in the appalling confusion. At the far end of the courtyard the huge main door, consisting of two ponderous wooden elements, was smashed. The left-hand element was ripped from its upper hinge and lay back in the courtyard, its tremendous weight having torn it loose from the lower hinge. Through the gap Patrice saw a Tiger tank. Its big gun was lowered on the Prefecture. With a spasm of terror, Patrice felt he was looking directly down the gun's muzzle. He started to walk toward the center of the courtyard when the Tiger fired. The shell swooshed overhead and crashed into the building. But though the breach was open, the enemy had not poured through; there was not a German in the courtyard. Several hundred cops, however, had turned into a scrabbling mob. Fighting to get away, they were bottlenecked at the metro opening in the courtyard.

As Patrice moved toward the mass of fleeing cops, he noted that most of the men with arms had remained at their posts. Marceau was at the edge of the crowd trying to stop the panic. It seemed hopeless. The men pushed, shouted and ripped at each other to get away, but succeeded only in jamming the way of escape. The broken door, the tank with its cannon and machine guns pointing at them, the terrifying noise of rifles and automatic weapons, the smell of gunpowder, combined to infect them with a spiraling and uncontrollable terror. All about them they heard the quick, deadly sounds of lead and jagged fragments of steel being propelled against them at an inhuman velocity. It was too much. They wanted to preserve the flesh intact; in the sounds whizzing and humming and whistling around they heard the metal flying to rip at their bodies. They stampeded.

Marceau shouted, his face purple with fury. He pulled at one man, then another. They shook him off and clawed at those in front.

"Cowards!" Marceau shouted. "Come back and fight!"

He might as well not have been there. The blind, bellowing stampede swirled around him. Patrice reached Marceau's side, the revolver still in his hand. It was impossible to push his way in front of the crowd jammed at the mouth of the metro entrance. He ran to the side of the opening. The men were crushed against each other, tugging and shoving. Just in front of Patrice a broad-shouldered cop suddenly bawled hysterically, "Let me through! Let me through!" He drew back and threw his powerful body into the mob, ramming them again and again with such wild force that the group swayed and shuddered with each thrust. Patrice made a stab at holding the man back, but the cop threw him off and pounded into the crowd again.

"Stop it! Get back!" Patrice roared.

They did not even hear him. Then, bellowing curses to get their attention, Patrice swung the hysterical cop around and smashed the muzzle of the revolver into the side of the cop's head. The blow opened a gash and stunned the man. His eyes glazed drunkenly and he staggered back. A dozen men saw the blow and came to their senses. They went to work with Patrice and Marceau, tugging at the edge of the crowd, shouting sense. Bit by bit the men stopped struggling. A gap opened near Patrice and he forged his way toward the front. On the way he hit another man with the revolver. This time most of those still fighting to get away saw the blow. It cooled them off. Just as Patrice worked his way in front of them the men stopped struggling and were silent. Some looked uneasy and ashamed; others were sullen. A deep savage fear still crouched in their midst. Only about a hundred men remained. They kept looking at the far end of the courtyard, where the armed cops were still firing. They heard the irregular metallic rattle of two machine guns from Prefecture windows and the boom of guns from the tanks outside. They strained to get away but did not move; their eyes were on Patrice; he was all that stood between them and the cool dark safety of the metro. Patrice waved a little circle with his revolver.

"I'm going to shoot the first man who tries to get by me."

Sullenly, they watched him standing there with his jaw stuck out. He meant what he said. They had already seen him use the revolver as a club.

"Get back into the Prefecture."

They did not move.

"Get back!" Patrice repeated.

"What for?" one of the men cried. "We have nothing to fight with. Should we go back and be slaughtered like pigs when the Germans get in?"

Menacingly the crowd muttered its approval. A machine gun coughed overhead; there was an answering stutter from a tank outside, then small explosions of rifle fire and the boom of a German gun.

"You'll get arms," Patrice snapped. "And if you don't, you'll be sent to take your place somewhere else where there are arms. But you're not going to run away like rabbits."

"If we stay, we'll get shot like rabbits."

"You bunch of bastards! You knew what you were getting into. You all had firecrackers between your buttocks! You jumped in to take the Prefecture as if you were afraid it was going to run away. Well, you got it; now you're going to keep it! None of you will get past me alive. And I'm staying to the end if I have to stay alone!"

They said nothing. None of them looked at Patrice. They were afraid of him and ashamed of themselves. It was Patrice's last remark that hit them hardest, because it was absurd and true, and Patrice had rapped it into their skulls with every syllable.

The firing was now sporadic. Unsupported by infantry on that side of the Prefecture, the tanks withdrew.

Behind the crowd, Reboussin climbed on a pile of straw stacked against a courtyard wall. He raised his arms. "Listen!" he cried.

They turned.

"Listen! The police discredited themselves during the occupation. They worked for Vichy and the Nazis; they arrested patriots. Only five days ago the people of Paris hated you. In the past you have fought against the people. But today you are fighting with them. You all know the strike has made you popular. The insurrection will make you unforgettable!"

Patrice had cowered, then shamed them; Reboussin gave them back their pride. When he finished speaking they filed into the Prefecture, leaving only those with arms in the courtyard. Patrice placed two guards at the head of the metro entrance and supervised a group of men who laboriously pushed the battered door back in place. Then he went back into the building with Reboussin.

"If they had had fifty determined men under a good officer they could have swamped us," Reboussin said. "They were just feeling us out. We've got to get reinforcements and arms."

"Try F.F.I. headquarters. I'll send out a teletype call to the police stations."

"I already tried headquarters. They have no arms."

"They may have gotten some by now from the Germans. The men have been getting weapons all day everywhere, from German depots, garages, trucks, fights, all over. We have twenty machine guns more than we started out with ourselves."

"I'll put on the pressure."

"Ask for men. They'll be more likely to send over men with arms than just deliver the arms to us."

Back in his office Patrice wrote out a call to all policemen with arms to come immediately to the Prefecture in civilian clothes. He had it sent out on the teletype circuit. It was three-thirty. Patrice rang the switchboard.

"Did anybody named De Maurain phone me?"

"Yes, half an hour ago."

Patrice hung up. He dialed De Maurain's number on the direct phone. His stomach was in knots. De Maurain's voice floated over the wire.

"Patrice Vallois. Any news?"

"What I expected. Nothing—nothing we can do anything about." De Maurain sounded as miserable as Patrice felt. "The Gestapo has her, all right, but nobody knows where. Probably somewhere in or near Paris. Trouble is the Germans are in a frightful uproar. The administrative services have moved out and only the garrison and some divisional elements remain. Nobody knows where or how to reach anybody. The Gestapo has moved out of the Rue des Saussaies and the Avenue Foch. Only a few of the brutes have been left behind. God knows where they took Danielle."

Patrice said nothing, trying to master his disappointment; then: "Any hope of getting the name of the Gestapo man in charge?"

"I have that. A Klaus Tellmann. My man tried to get him all morning, without success. That's what he told me, anyway. This afternoon he wouldn't go to the phone to speak to me. I went to see him. He wouldn't see me. You know why. Now that the resistance has acted up, anything I might have done for Danielle this morning is no longer possible."

"I know. I was afraid of that."

There was a long silence.

"Come and see me when this is all over, De Maurain said at last. His voice was resigned. "I really mean that. Danielle is a great deal to have in common."

"I will—but later, a lot later."

Patrice hung up. The switchboard phone was buzzing, buzzing. Reboussin appeared at the door. There were two other men behind him. Wearily, Patrice lifted the receiver, spoke mechanically into the mouthpiece. There was no hope, no hope at all.

†

DANIELLE was in a villa on the height of St. Cloud overlooking Paris. The villa was tucked away behind a deep lawn edged with poplars and set off spaciously from the suburban homes around it. The room in which she spent the night was sumptuous. The walls were lined with light-blue satin and the furniture, elegant and discreet, was authentic Louis XV. Gaily draped casement windows opened on a balcony that ran the length of the room. Beyond the balcony, almost within reach, it seemed, stood the Eiffel Tower. It was cloaked that morning in a sparkling blue heat haze. Danielle looked at it sadly.

The night had been a torment. Why had they put her in such a room? What would they do to her? She huddled in bed, curled up on herself, her eyes wide-open. All the stories she had ever heard about Nazi brutality came back to her. It was like having nightmares while wide-awake.

At the moment of her arrest and immediately after she had felt neither fear nor courage. The shock had stupefied her. Torn brutally from one universe and plunged into another, she had been incapable of any reaction. Now she was afraid. For a while she gave in to panic and was almost sick. She had no inkling why the Gestapo had arrested her, no suspicion of who had denounced her, no idea what they knew. But she decided that if she was not to break, there was only one thing to do: deny everything. She would go in knowing nothing, and if they tortured her there would be no struggle between her suffering and her will. When there is nothing to tell the will has no reason to resist. Torture becomes meaningless. At some point they would be convinced she knew nothing. She was extraordinarily lucid on one point: if she admitted the slightest connection with the resistance, they had the means to get the rest out of her.

Tossing in bed, she imagined the questions they might ask and planned her answers. Then, exhausted, she tried to think of nothing, to sleep. But images kept floating up out of the darkness like the hallucinations of a madman. She tossed all night, dozed off toward dawn, but almost immediately leaped awake, shuddering. She rose and washed. By morning, waiting, just waiting, was itself a torment.

She could not know that the delay was an accident. Klaus had wanted to start her interrogation immediately, but when they arrived at the villa a message awaited him to report to headquarters at the Hotel Majestic. Conferences held him there until a late hour, and he had to return to the Majestic early the following morning to finish up. At ten o'clock he phoned Suzanne.

"Everything worked out fine, darling. We have her."

"Is she all right?"

"Of course. She spent the night in a magnificent villa. Suzanne, you're sure she's the woman we want?"

"Certain. But you're not going to hurt her. Promise me you won't."

"That's very unlikely. There are plenty of ways of getting a woman to talk without hurting her. I'll phone this evening and let you know about leaving Paris."

"I'll be here. Klaus, there was shooting this morning not far from here and during the night, too. They're not in Paris, are they? The resistance—"

He laughed. "Of course not. I'm at the Majestic. If anything had happened we'd be the first to know about it. Don't be afraid. I'll phone tonight."

It was noon before he returned to St. Cloud. He went directly to Danielle's room. Three young men in civilian clothes followed him in. Danielle was on her feet, tense, facing them.

"Sit down, please," Klaus said, indicating a divan.

He made himself comfortable in an armchair, facing her. She glanced at the three young men, who stood behind Klaus and stared at her curiously.

"Now," Klaus said, "I don't want to waste my time and I certainly don't want to waste yours." He smiled. "I want you to tell me all about your friends in the resistance—" he nodded his head backward toward the three young men—"without any persuasion."

"You're making a mistake. Believe me. I never was in the resistance. I don't know anyone who is or ever was."

"I'm sorry you're taking this line, really sorry. It's going to be unpleasant." Klaus was no longer smiling. "There's no point in denying what we know. It's not going to help you. Suppose I refresh your memory—Adrien, for example. You knew a man named Adrien Lemonnier, didn't you?"

Danielle felt the hot flush mount and burn her cheeks. She had not imagined that they would have connected her with Adrien. How did they know? How much did they know?

"I see you knew him."

"I know him very well. We were close friends before the war. But I haven't seen him for a long time, and anyway I don't believe Adrien is the sort who would be in the resistance."

"But he was the sort. He was in the resistance and you worked with him. You also saw him rather recently. Four days ago, to be exact. In the afternoon."

"No, I would remember that. I haven't seen him in months. I can't remember when I saw him last."

"You don't *know* him—you *knew* him." Klaus jumped up, stood over Danielle and shouted. "You knew him so well you shot him! You killed him on orders! You walked into his apartment with a revolver and shot him in cold blood!"

The color was dredged out of Danielle's face. She looked at Klaus, but her eyes wavered. She thought he was going to strike her and she was braced for the blow. Now it's coming, she thought. But she also thought he didn't know about the priest. Then she had one last flare of unthinking courage. Suddenly she stood up.

"Why are you standing?" he cried.

"Because it's less humiliating to strike a woman when she's on her feet than when she's sitting down."

"Sit down," he shouted savagely.

Klaus shook with anger but drew back, controlling himself with effort. He sat down again after Danielle, realizing how tough-fibered she was. Until that moment he had not been entirely sure that Danielle was the girl he wanted. She seemed to be gentle, much too soft to shoot a man even in a wave of passion, let alone for political reasons. Now it was easier to believe she had done it. She was intelligent—that was obvious; but she had made a mistake in that display of courage and contempt. She was well-bred, too, and that had made him think she would be quick to crack. He no longer thought so. He knew he had an extraordinary girl before him and that nothing would be easy, and he was truly sorry. Klaus was a weak man and he did not like being in a position that required the exercise of strength. He was ill-equipped either to give or take brutality, but the weapon was in his hand, and he felt obligated to use it for his own survival. He determined that any kind of preliminary violence would be more than justified in the hope that it would preclude the subsequent indecencies. But he already feared that nothing would be accomplished until he had been forced to go the limit. It was too bad. It was particularly unlucky for her. Klaus knew that under any other circumstances, with him as an interrogator, Danielle would have had little to worry about. He would never force it to the end. He was one of the "good ones." But his career was involved. He understood Suzanne's concern about the girl. Then he stiffened and stopped thinking of Suzanne because it softened him. When he spoke his voice was so hard that for the first time since Klaus had come in Danielle was deeply frightened.

"You're not going to leave this room," he said icily, "until you've made a full confession."

He said nothing more for a moment, letting his remark sink in. He just looked at her, hard, and she could not meet his eyes. She felt herself shrinking up inside. She knew she was lying and that the best she could do was brazen it out. She felt dry and empty. It was all twisted up. She was right and he had put her in the wrong. She could not attack him and she had no means of defending herself.

"It's warm, isn't it?" Klaus remarked suddenly.

Silence.

"When I ask a question I expect an answer," he said sharply.

"Yes, very warm."

Klaus smiled coldly. "I imagine you'd be more comfortable with your clothes off," he said speculatively.

Her face reddened slowly and deeply. She sat, tight and small, as small as she could, and said nothing, hearing herself breathe.

"Call in the others," Klaus said to the men behind him.

The door opened. Two other young men came in. Danielle did not look at them.

"Now, what do you think?" Klaus asked with forced joviality. "Should we let her be comfortable and interview her with her clothes off?"

The men grinned.

"You see," Klaus said. "It's your beauty that makes them so thoughtful. Frankly, I'll be disappointed if you don't tell me now about your career in the resistance, and they'll be disappointed if you do. You're going to tell us about it sooner or later. Why not now?"

She looked at him, the anguish in her eyes. "Because I have nothing to tell you—nothing, really nothing."

There was conviction in her voice, the conviction of her anguish, born of fear, nourished with despair. Klaus stared through her. He was sure she had done it, every minute he was with her he was surer. If she would only talk. The thought flashed through his mind of Suzanne being in the same situation as Danielle. What would he do? How would he feel? His expression never changed; his eyes did not flicker. Danielle must see that he would not soften. She must realize that she would be forced to tell them what she knew.

"Take her clothes off," he said quietly.

As they came to her, she said quickly, "I'll do it myself."

She did not want them to touch her. Slowly she bent down to take off her shoes.

"You can leave your shoes on."

Her eyes darted up at Klaus and away.

"Your country has a great tradition. We Germans have learned a few things in the cradle of civilization. Come on! Come on!"

She slipped her dress over her head.

"The rest too."

Danielle took off the rest.

"Remain standing, please. With your hands at your sides."

She looked straight ahead, her head high, but saw nothing, felt nothing. She was numb. It was as if she were no longer herself.

"Walk around the room."

She walked. It lasted three or four minutes, minutes that had no relation to time. Her legs were stiff; they moved mechanically, propelled by a puppet, jarring at each step. She walked blindly in the obscene silence, the room a whirl of pale-blue satin and faceless faces. One of the men stepped toward her and she swayed away from him, stumbling in a panic of revulsion and trying at the same time in that grotesque moment to retain a last fragment of dignity when that was the one veil, despite everything, they had not yet been able to strip from her naked body.

"No, not now," she heard Klaus say from a great distance, and the man backed away obediently.

"All right, stop."

She stopped.

"Look at me."

She looked at Klaus. He was a blur; she did not see him at all.

"Are you going to talk?"

"I have nothing to say. I didn't even know Adrien was dead. Would I go through this if I could get out of it by saying anything that went through my head?"

Klaus turned to the five young men. "Go out and wait at the door."

They left with a regret they made no effort to hide.

"I'm going to speak to you with complete candor," Klaus said to Danielle when they were alone. "Sit down—to me you're just a prisoner, but to them you're a woman and a very beautiful one. None of your charms—none of your physical charms, that is—have escaped them. When they come back, they're going to want to know them—more intimately. And they will—unless you talk."

She shook her head. "I tell you I was never in the resistance. I can't say any more than that. There's nothing more to say. I don't know anything about Adrien."

"I know you do," Klaus said tranquilly. "I'm going to give you one more chance. I'm going to tell you what we're going to do if you don't talk." He watched her closely as she sat rigidly opposite him, her face a tormented mask. "You will struggle when they come in for you. All the women always do. But it won't help. Two of the men will hold your arms! You'll kick of course. But two of the others will grab your legs. They'll throw you on the edge of the bed and hold you there with your legs apart. The fifth man—well, he will do as he wishes. After two or three of them have passed over you it won't be necessary to hold you any more. It never is. . . ."

She sat perfectly still, white-faced, feeling nothing but an overpowering impotence. She sensed her heart beating, heard the regular intake of her breath, knew her body was warm and that her hands and feet were icy, and for all the rest she was dead.

Klaus watched her, catlike, through half-closed eyes. He saw her eyes glaze, the color leave her already pale face and a mask of hopeless passivity fall over it. She said nothing, did not move or look at him, and this in itself was a sign to him of how his words had lashed her spirit. He saw how she tried to suppress her anguish by not moving a muscle, but the set of her body, unnaturally poised, the blind incommunicativeness of her face and her slightly quickened breathing told him all he wanted to know. He was pleased that his words had cut so deep. He was pleased more out of weakness than strength. He thought that just a bit more would carry her beyond the breaking point and spare him the necessity of following through. He hated this kind of interrogation, hated the torture involved. It was probably the reason he had more success than most others in getting what he wanted through a knowing use of threat. So he hopefully observed the expression on Danielle's face and, pursuing his advantage, said a few other things as though they were the most natural things in the world. It penetrated her state of shock. She flushed. Instinctively she turned away. Seeing the effect, Klaus went even further.

"If you aren't ready to confess by then," Klaus continued impersonally, "and I think you will be, then we'll have to go on to more old-fashioned methods. They're painful. We have a specialist who will keep you suffering but alive for quite a while. You have no idea how intensely alive you can feel when you really suffer. The only escape will be to die. But you can't die just because you want to. Get one thing straight: there's no escape. Either you'll talk or you'll go through it all to the very end. Ah, yes, the end. We have some small distractions for our soldiers, you know. Among others, mobile brothels. They follow the troops in the field behind the front. I saw one once camouflaged on the edge of a clearing. A few women take on a battalion at a time. A thousand men. They line up outside the shack. It's a very long line and they all wait most patiently for a very long time. The first few men on the line already have their pants unbuttoned. There's no time to waste with so many to be serviced. And they crack jokes at each one who comes out buttoning up his pants. That's the end. When you recover from your experience with our specialist there's a cubicle with a bed and a washstand waiting for you somewhere behind the eastern front."

A long silence. A hush as deeply soft and puffy as cotton enveloped the room. Danielle still sat motionless; but now her shoulders sloped and her head was bowed, and Klaus could not see her face seared by the dark-blue, tormented eyes. She was beyond thinking of dignity; the horror had burned itself into her numbed mind. Klaus rose, took out a cigarette and lit it. The blue smoke floated through the stillness toward the pale-blue satin walls. He was delighted and relieved, and it was all he could do not to show his feelings. He knew she was at the point of cracking.

"Think about it," Klaus said matter-of-factly. "No woman can go through this kind of thing without breaking."

Danielle did not lift her head.

"I'd rather you confessed before than after . . ."

Danielle did not move, but he saw her hands were clenched and the knuckles white.

"The result will be the same. You can still avoid everything." He looked at his watch. "Remember! A full confession with names and addresses and I'll free you. The matter of Adrien Lemonnier will be forgotten. It's not too late. I'll give you ten minutes to think it over."

As he was saying these last words there was a light tap on the door and one of the young men opened it.

"Telephone. Von Choltitz's headquarters."

"I'm coming—think hard. You have ten minutes."

Klaus hurried to the telephone, muttered his name. "Can't it wait? . . . But there's something here that's urgent . . . I see . . . Yes, yes. I'll be there."

Klaus bit his lip nervously as he hung up. Then Suzanne had been right, after all. But how long could an insurrection stand up against the garrison? A matter of hours? A day or two? The fools, they would be crushed, and nobody would be any better off. He could not understand why anyone should butt his head against a wall, why any group should fight a force palpably stronger, why a woman like Danielle should stake everything against the impossible. It made no sense. And he had been taught the French were a reasonable people. No, there was something about them he did not understand. In Danielle's place he knew what he would do. He had no admiration for her. Should he let them begin? After watching her walk around the room naked they were like five tomcats. No, he had to be there. If she wanted to talk they wouldn't let her until they had all had a turn or two. He went back into Danielle's room. She looked up defenselessly.

"You'll have a little more time to consider your position. I'll be back later this afternoon. If you don't talk then, I can promise you the most memorable night you will ever spend."

Her lifeless eyes followed him to the door.

"My clothes," she said without conviction. "They've taken my clothes."

"You won't need them. They might keep you from thinking lucidly."

For a long time after Klaus left, Danielle did not move. Then she went to the bed and lay under the covers, curled up the way she used to when she was a little girl and was unhappy because her mother had scolded her or because she had broken a favorite doll. The bright summer sun streamed through the casement windows and flooded the room. Beyond the windows Paris was spread out in the valley, where the narrow, glittering band of the Seine twisted in huge arcs among the red-roofed buildings. Just out of reach, the Eiffel Tower stretched its familiar iron frame into the soft blue belly of the Paris sky. Danielle huddled in bed in a childlike, atavistic ball, dry-eyed and numb, finding no protection, no defense, no hope.

†

LIKE Patrice, some of the resistance leaders were beset with grave doubts about the course the uprising would take. Having committed themselves to the insurrection in the morning, they began asking the military experts if they had acted wisely in the afternoon. The answer was no. The underground head of the British Intelligence Service for northern France was consulted, rather late for the weight of his opinion to alter the balance of a decision already being tested on the scale of history. He told them simply and concisely that Paris was now at the mercy of the Germans.

"You jumped off too soon," he said. "All the bridges across the Seine are down except those in Paris. Several German divisions are still retreating west of the city and will have to cross the river here. You can't possibly face them; you can't even beat the garrison. And the Americans can't get here to save you before Wednesday—if then. By that time you may be annihilated. . . . I'm in direct radio contact with Eisenhower's headquarters. I've already sent a message urging them to hurry. If you wish, I'll send another specifying it's you who are asking for help."

The worried resistance leaders agreed. But it was Saturday, and Wednesday, even if the Americans could reach Paris that quickly, was four long days off. They held a meeting and agreed that the situation was hopeless. What to do? Since the resistance was too weak to wage a successful battle behind fixed positions, the insurrection had to take a guerrilla form. The Prefecture, now the heart of the insurrection, was indefensible; it would have to be abandoned.

Bourbon was sent to transmit the order. The silver-haired colonel arrived during one of the sharp clashes that had been flaring up sporadically all afternoon. Small groups of infantry moved in against the Prefecture; isolated tanks nosed through the small streets around the building and poked against its walls. Each move was tentative, like a fighter feeling out an opponent. After a brief skirmish the Germans withdrew. Having waited for the fighting to stop, Bourbon crossed the boulevard, headed for the main gate. But he heard the sound of an approaching motor and dashed back for cover.

When he turned, he saw a one-legged man with a rifle slung across his shoulder leaping on crutches with amazing agility to the center of the boulevard. A German truck charged upon the lone man, who had stopped directly in its path. Leaning on his crutches, One-paw swung his rifle to his shoulder. "Get out of the way!" Bourbon shouted. "You'll be run down!"

One-paw did not seem to hear him. For the past hour he had been playing at the same curious game. Firing earlier from the cover of a doorway, he had seen men beside him tumble to the sidewalk, victims of Germans shooting from the cabs of passing trucks. He suddenly realized it was less dangerous to fire at the trucks head-on, since the Germans could not shoot straight ahead with the windshield in their way; nor was it likely that he would fail to stop the vehicle when all he had to do was hit the center of the driver's side of the windshield without shifting aim. What it took was the guts to stand up, nakedly exposed, in the middle of the boulevard with a truck roaring down at you and armed men in it. One-paw was the only man there with the nerve or the conviction or the insensitivity, or all three, to do it. Watching him, Bourbon was certain he would be killed. He kept shouting, "Get out of the way! Save yourself!" All the while the truck raced toward One-paw with a grinding roar. He stood frozen on his crutches, the rifle motionless at his shoulder, a tattered image of a crippled France. When the truck was a bare seventy-five yards away, the shot exploded and a second one followed almost immediately. The truck came straight on for a second or two, then swerved, bounced up on the sidewalk and rammed against a wall with a terrifying crash of breaking glass and crumpling metal. The next moment a dozen men from the Prefecture swarmed around the smoking vehicle, taking shocked prisoners in tow. The chauffeur was dead, a bullet through his neck and the steering wheel jammed into his crushed stomach.

Bourbon did not wait. He went through the main gate and was led to Patrice's office, where he was surprised to find Reboussin with Patrice. He told them about the meeting and the strategic decisions that had been taken.

"As for the Prefecture," he concluded, "we all agreed it should be evacuated."

"We're not leaving," Patrice replied calmly. "We took it; we're holding it."

"But you can't let your men be massacred."

"You can't fight an insurrection by running away, either. This isn't 1940. We're going to fight, not run."

Bourbon turned helplessly to Reboussin. "Talk sense to him," he said. "There isn't much time."

"But I agree with Patrice," Reboussin answered slowly. Bourbon stared at him, disbelief scrawled over his smooth, hairless face. "Evacuating the building would be difficult at best. Besides, it would be deadly for morale. These men are proud of the fight they're putting up. If they were ordered to leave now, without any pressure from the Germans, they wouldn't understand. It might be impossible to get them to continue the fight anywhere else. Remember, they're not soldiers, but insurrectionists. My feeling is we ought to stay as long as we can."

"You've changed quite a bit in the last few hours," Bourbon said harshly.

"The situation has changed; we can't remain behind events."

"They're leading you by the nose."

"To stay here isn't good, but it's better than leaving."

For a moment Reboussin and Patrice thought Bourbon would explode. His face reddened; he glared at Reboussin, took a deep breath, opened his small mouth as if he were going to let out a bellow of fury, and then closed it again. He stood in the middle of the room, stiff and straight and speechless with anger, his pale-blue eyes darting from one to the other, while they waited for the outburst to break over them. Then, without a word, Bourbon wheeled and strode out of the room. Reboussin frowned and said, "We can't let him leave like that." He caught up to Bourbon on the stairway.

"Don't lose your head," Reboussin said, holding the colonel by the arm. "I have more reasons than I mentioned for not wanting the Prefecture evacuated."

Bourbon turned his stubborn face toward Reboussin; the expression was closed, like a shutter before a shop front, his pale-blue eyes were distant, distrustful. "What, for example?"

Reboussin spoke urgently. "Patrice wants to stay here out of desperation. If he leaves, his policy collapses. He's spoken to me of his ideas. He's making the mistake of trying to fight the communists— and the Germans, too, at the same time—with the communists' own insurrectionary methods. I'm staying here to stop the insurrection. Keep cool; we have to work together—now more than ever. Don't you see that with a purely guerrilla action we can't hope to talk with the Germans. But as long as we hold the Prefecture we're not just roving armed bands, and they may deal with us."

"Small hope of that," Bourbon muttered.

"Agreed. But I'm ready to stay here and risk my life for that small chance. The other way there's no possibility of a deal." Bourbon wavered; the anger was gone from his face. "The odds against us are enormous," Reboussin added, "but they're the only ones we've got to play."

"All right, if you want it that way. It's your funeral, not mine."

They shook hands and Reboussin returned to Patrice's office. Marceau was there. Reboussin sensed a change of atmosphere; there was a strange expression on Patrice's drawn face.

Patrice said, "Marceau has just been telling me the prison here is jammed with German prisoners. He doesn't know where to put any others we capture." Patrice's tired eyes gleamed feverishly. "I say we ought to contact the Germans and offer an exchange of prisoners."

Reboussin's instinct was to leap at the idea. Instead he glanced from Patrice to Marceau and back again, his shrewd eyes screwed up, taking in Marceau's relaxed figure slouched wearily in a chair and Patrice, standing at his desk, tautly waiting.

"The Germans probably won't want to deal with us," Reboussin finally said. "We're still terrorists so far as they're concerned."

"Let's try it. It won't hurt if they say no, and it might work. How will we go about it? Direct contact is impossible. A neutral intermediary. The Swiss, maybe."

"Sweden," said Reboussin. "Nordling, the Swedish Consul, has been doing quite a job during the past week. He's gotten the Germans to release many prisoners in the Paris area. He'd be the perfect intermediary."

"Good," said Patrice. "Why don't you handle it? You're the diplomat."

"If you want me to. How many prisoners do we have?"

"I'll go down and count them," said Marceau.

After Marceau left Patrice said, "There must be more prisoners around the city. I'll get the figures. And a list of our people who've been taken in the past few days. I can give you one to begin with: Danielle Tessier."

"Danielle arrested? I didn't know."

"Last night." Patrice looked haggard. "Well, let me know how it goes."

Reboussin went to the Swedish Legation and Patrice worked at the Prefecture, and the afternoon slowly edged its way through the heat of the day toward evening. As the hours slipped by and the skirmishes continued, Patrice wondered why the German attack did not come. He expected it all the time. The men were at their posts, augmented by twenty F.F.I.s armed with light machine guns who had been sent over after Reboussin's urgent request earlier in the afternoon. In periods of calm they heard the sound of rifle fire from other parts of the city. The air was heavy. The sky had turned a viscous gray.

Patrice sat in his office, hoping and not daring to hope. In the past couple of hours, with less to do, he had not stopped thinking of Daneille. He paced the floor, sat down and got up again. When people came for orders he gave them curtly. He was close to exhaustion. Every few minutes he stepped down the hall to see if Reboussin had returned. The long twilight, weighted with storm clouds, and the hot, damp, storm-scented air were unbearable. Patrice felt he could wait no longer, when the door opened and Reboussin stepped in.

"Do they agree?"

Reboussin nodded. "They agree, but we don't."

"Why not?"

"Their terms are impossible."

"What are they?"

"Ten of theirs for one of ours."

Patrice looked steadily at Reboussin, then slowly went to his desk and dropped into a chair. His face was drained; his hands trembled. He felt so weak he could not stand. The spring was out of him, the tension gone, and the weariness flowed over him in enervating ripples. What could they be doing to her? he wondered. Whatever they wanted to know, he hoped she would tell them. It could do no harm now. But she would not be sure of that, and in any case he knew her too well to have any illusions. She wouldn't talk unless they forced her. He tried not to think beyond that, because beyond that he had the feeling he was going crazy.

"I guess we'll have to write it off," Patrice heard himself say.

He didn't mean it. He knew the German terms were unacceptable, but still he didn't mean it. He would exchange a hundred Germans for Danielle. A thousand. But there were realities. It didn't matter how he felt. He couldn't transgress them.

Later the rain came down. It fell straight and hard, with a heavy splashing sound out of the darkening sky. Flashes of lightning illuminated the city with a lurid blue light, and rolling claps of thunder burst overhead. The fighting stopped. With the downpour and the failing light the men of the resistance faded away from the streets and disappeared into their homes.

Thrown back into the machinery of the Prefecture's defense, Patrice had the impression that he was living in a tiny world with a split personality. The men with arms were proud and confident. They had fought all day against a stronger enemy. They had inflicted casualties, captured prisoners and booty, and their losses had been slight. Having survived the first day, they were sure of the next. The handful of leaders, upon whom rested responsibility for the defense of the Prefecture, were worried and depressed. They knew what the men with arms did not know—the Prefecture was indefensible.

Marceau phoned his wife and said good-by to her in an emotion-choked voice. "It will all be over when the Germans hit us," he said. "I'll probably never see you again."

They said nothing to the men. But the climate on the top level seeped down and infected the other levels. Munitions ran low. The men sensed that something was wrong. Then Patrice sent out an order that no man was to fire except in self-defense. A rumor raced through the building, followed by a deep feeling of uneasiness. The word "Warsaw" was on many lips. In the course of half an hour the two personalities merged and became the one created by the leaders.

Patrice sent out repeated calls for armed men to come to their aid. But no armed men came. Riviere and Sorel appeared out of the rain, bearing cheerful news about the rest of Paris. But when Reboussin described the situation as he saw it Sorel's chubby face lost its radiance, and the fat little socialist's fervor was soon as dampened as his rain-soaked clothes. Riviere, impish, shriveled, professorial through everything, would not let his high spirits be quelled. Incurably optimistic, he insisted that all was well.

"We're in complete control of forty-three out of the eighty quarters of Paris," he said. "That's more than half the city. We have armed patrols roving most of the principal arteries leading in and out of

Paris, shooting and killing Germans when they meet them, stopping German traffic, destroying or capturing their trucks and men. The Nazis have gone out of business. Where are they? It's very simple, messieurs. They're afraid of us. They think there are thousands of us here armed to the teeth and they won't dare attack."

Patrice knew that part of what Riviere said was true. They held more than half the city. The Germans had drawn back into half a dozen strong points. But what did it mean? Not what Riviere thought. They could strike out at will and destroy any position the resistance held. But the resistance lacked the strength to reduce a single German strong point. No decision favorable to the resistance was conceivable without outside help. That was far off. Meanwhile, less than five hundred men remained in the Prefecture out of the thousands who had occupied it in the morning. Half were without arms; of the others, many had only a revolver. With all the booty taken during the day and the twenty reinforcements sent in with light machine guns, there were barely more than fifty automatic weapons in the Prefecture. It was not enough. If the German command sent over a battalion of infantry, preceded by five tanks, to smash in the doors and neutralize the fire from the windows, all the courage in the world would not help; the building would fall in a matter of hours.

Patrice drew up a plan to evacuate the Prefecture, should the Germans swamp the building, through the metro in the courtyard. The men were not told of the plan. But they did not have to be told. They saw the unarmed men being led out one by one. Two hundred and fifty men remained behind. They waited in an uneasy silence as dusk and the rain fell over the gray city.

The atmosphere in the first-floor offices was that of a death watch. Slumped in a deep leather armchair, Patrice tried to get some sleep. But despite his exhaustion he was too wrought up to relax. He felt he was floating through a bad dream. Life was too divorced from its normal routine; it had become too acute, too overpowering; having achieved its essence, it seemed unreal. He measured the moment against that other one when he had set off to see Danielle the previous night. That was only twenty-four hours ago. In so short a time everything was gone, all of it gone. Patrice stared at the wall of his office with sleepless eyes, feeling the pain probe at him, accepting it as part of himself, since it was all that was left him of Danielle.

Outside, the rain pattered down on the city in revolt. It seemed peaceful. But somewhere beyond the line of buildings that cut off mid-town Paris from the view of those at the Prefecture were the German strong points and the headquarters of the Commander in Chief of Gross-Paris. Whatever General von Choltitz was planning to do, the men at the Prefecture would know about it soon enough. Meanwhile, all they could do was wait with their private thoughts and brace themselves for the blow.

Part Three

The Truce

[AUGUST 19-21]

AT THE St. Cloud villa Danielle huddled dumbly under the covers a long time after Klaus left. The sun-laden air filtered into the room and saturated it with the sleepy torpor of the summer afternoon. But Danielle was insensitive to it all. The day passed in a dreamlike daze. Chills swept over her naked body, and she shivered, then trembled feverishly when heat waves followed the chills. Outside, the sun, just as on other days, rose to its peak, held it, then began its slow descent across the sky. But Danielle was unaware of the lengthening shadows, unconscious of the fading light.

Late in the afternoon the door of her room opened and she turned toward it with a start, thinking they were coming for her now. Under the covers her body was rigid. Two of the young men came in, bearing a tray of food and a pitcher of water. They placed the tray and water on a table near the door and looked at her expectantly. She did not move.

"It's your dinner," one of them said.

Danielle did not answer.

"We're not going to serve it in bed. If you're hungry, come and get it."

They grinned, waiting for her to get out of bed.

"I'm not hungry."

"We'll take it away."

"Take it away then."

"You ought to eat something. You'll need it for later on."

They laughed, and Danielle turned toward the wall.

"Come on, have a little."

She heard one of them walk toward the bed, and her throat was suddenly dry with fear.

"Better not," the one at the table said. "There's not much longer to wait."

Danielle sensed the man at the bed, leaning over her.

"You don't want it?" he asked so close to her ear she could feel his breath.

She shook her head.

"All right. But later you'll be sorry."

She heard them pick up the tray and leave the room. It was the first time she had heard them speak, and as they went out she realized they were not German but French. Then something inside her welled up and burst. She began to weep, pressing her face into the pillow to muffle the deep, rending sobs. It was a long time before she regained control of herself; but she felt no better for having cried. She had never felt so childlike and weak, so incapable of doing anything to help herself. There was a bitter, sickish taste in her mouth and a void inside her that was like nothing she had ever felt before. It was as if she were a stranger to herself, as if she did not belong to the body she inhabited. She sensed the presence of her body, smooth and warm, from which there was no escape. She knew it would cause her grief, feeling that that was not what mattered, but that through it they would get at what did matter; and she was afraid. More deeply, she became aware that nothing about herself was any longer familiar, and she wondered, in a traumatic daze, What has become of me? It was a sensation that was worse than the terrible one of being alone that had afflicted her all day. She was lost, lost to herself, as she had been that day so long ago when she shot Adrien. Somehow the familiar self she knew so well had split away from whatever she was without it, broken its thread with the past. And she was left lying in an isolated villa with no identity, with only her body and a terror of the pain and humiliation it would bring upon her.

No thought of the insurrection crossed her mind; it was as far behind her now as her childhood. Nor did she think of Patrice, or even for a long while, of Klaus and when he would return, although that was the key to what would happen to her. An hour or two after they brought her dinner and took it away it occurred to her that they were waiting for nightfall to begin her torment. She looked miserably out of the window and watched the sky change color as the dusk slowly rose up out of the horizon and settled over the Eiffel Tower. Then the rain poured out of the gray sky, splashing against the windows and filming the grounds with a melancholy gray veil. She thought of Klaus now, felt more isolated than ever within the walls of the storm, and dreaded his return.

But Klaus was having his own problems. When he drove to General von Choltitz's headquarters he expected to get away in a couple of hours. He was certain Danielle would talk and that her information would lead to high places. Having handled other French women in similar circumstances, Klaus knew that a moment came to the most resolute when the spirit broke under rape and the systematic obscenities beyond it. When the break came it was complete, and the only problem was to control concomitant hysteria.

He thought about this when he arrived at the Hotel Meurice, calculating how long it would take for Danielle to break and how he would organize his dragnet around the resistance figures she led him to. But he had not been in the headquarters ten minutes before he realized that something incalculably more important than he had estimated was going on. There was an air of crisis in the building that was translated by funereal faces, a rare, energetic rushing around and gloomy whispered conversations in the corridors. Klaus reported to a starchy colonel. The colonel looked personally offended when Klaus walked in.

"What!" he exclaimed. "You're not in uniform! Every German in Paris must be in uniform! That's been an order for three days."

"It doesn't help the Gestapo to have its agents in uniform, colonel."

"But you're in the front lines now."

"Is it that bad?"

The colonel unbent and said grimly. "It's an insurrection. That's always bad." He thrust his arm out and slowly clenched his fist. "We'll squash them."

"How long will it take?"

The colonel shrugged. "I don't know the general's plans yet. A day, maybe two. —But, about your uniform, I'm only telling you for your own good."

"I'll have to go to my hotel to get it."

The colonel shook his head. "You should have moved over here days ago. I'll give you transportation and some men. If you work fast you can be back in thirty minutes. They won't be calling you for another hour."

Five minutes later Klaus stepped into a small truck in front of the hotel. He sat in the cab beside the driver. Two armed men were sloped over the front mudguards and two others stood in the back with tommy guns. The truck sped down the Rue de Rivoli, turned into the Tuileries, crossed the Seine and followed the quais. Klaus had a queer feeling at the base of his spine: the city was terrifying. The buildings towered over the speeding truck and each one seemed to menace it. The enemy was there unseen; there were thousands, tens of thousands, of them. At any point a trap could be sprung and they would be snapped into it like rats. Klaus began watching the streets carefully, wondering what lurked behind each corner. They were approaching the Place St. Michel when a volley of shots exploded around the truck. Klaus ducked below the window line and the driver hunched low over the wheel. "Faster!" Klaus shouted, and the driver's foot pressed flat on the floor. The truck shot ahead. The soldiers on the mudguards and in the rear were returning the fire. In a moment the truck swerved into the Boulevard St. Michel on two wheels. A few seconds later they stopped in front of Klaus's hotel, and Klaus jumped out.

"Nobody hit?" he called out. "Good. You three stay down here and keep your eyes open. You two come up with me."

The two soldiers helped him throw his belongings into two valises. In ten minutes everything was packed and they were back in the truck. The blowzy chambermaid stood at the entrance of the hotel watching them with an ironic smile. Klaus turned away, irritated.

"Don't take the quai," he said to the driver.

"Not if I can help it."

Five minutes later, after being fired at again on the Boulevard St. Germain, they were safely back at the Meurice. Klaus was assigned to a small room on the top floor and changed into a uniform. He had already been delayed longer than he had expected, but he told himself that by evening he would be back in the St. Cloud villa. He waited impatiently to be called for the conference that was keeping him from the important work at hand.

†

WAITING was not easy. The men in the Prefecture gripped their rifles or revolvers and stared into the hazy blue dusk enveloping the building; but they saw nothing, heard nothing. Nerves snapped like dry twigs. Quarrels flared over trivialities and as suddenly died, leaving the acrid smell of resentment in the air. A sense of hopelessness embittered them, and there were mutterings against their leaders for having led them into an impasse. The Prefecture could not be held and it could not be abandoned. They would be slaughtered. A feeling of doom settled over them like a shroud over a corpse.

With Marceau and Bailloux, Patrice circulated among the men, but they were unable to lighten the climate of disaster. In a corridor Marceau and Bailloux crossed paths.

"We're cooked," Marceau said grimly. He shook his head. "I'd never have thought when the flag went up this morning that the day would end like this."

"We may still be able to get out through the metro when they crack the building."

"Look at where the metro entrance is and where the Boches will be coming in. By the time we start to move it will be too late."

After a moment's silence Bailloux said, "You're lucky. You were able to phone your wife and say good-by. I can't even do that. We have no phone." His thick, hairy arms hanging limply at his sides, Bailloux added wistfully, "It's funny, but ever since I've known it was bad that's the only thing I've been sorry about: we never did have a telephone."

Shortly after nine o'clock sounds of orders being shouted and of iron-shod boots on the asphalt floated out of the twilight. Then the streets were quiet again. The storm had slackened, and a fine, warm rain was falling. Some of the men leaned far out of the windows on the first floor but saw no Germans. One of the F.F.I. reinforcements, a brawny communist metalworker, grumbled, "This is a hell of a time for them to start work; they ought to be unionized."

Two men managed a forced laugh, and a voice piped up, "Why don't you tell them to strike for better hours?"

"Tell them to go home," another voice chimed in. "We only fight between nine and five."

There was some laughter, brief and uncomfortable. Then silence.

"Hear it! They're coming!"

Each man held his breath and felt his heart pound. They heard the metallic churning of a tank. It appeared, rumbling slowly down the boulevard. A volley of rifle fire rang out. Marceau shouted, "Hold your fire! Wait for the Boches!" But no infantry followed the tank, which lumbered around the side of the building. The boulevard remained empty under the soft drizzle.

The tank, meanwhile, continued down the length of the Prefecture along the Seine. As it moved, its treads clanking inhumanly on the asphalt, a cop leaned out of one of the last windows on the first floor holding a wine bottle filled with gasoline, on which was pasted a strip of chemically treated paper. The bottle had been prepared in the Prefecture laboratory. When the tank was beneath the cop, he dropped the bottle. It fell behind the turret and broke. The gasoline spread over the tank's hot steel shell, coming into contact with the chemical on the paper. Suddenly a ring of fire sizzled around the tank. The next instant there sounded, deep and intact, the hollow thump of combustion. With a whooshing roar a stream of flame spurted into the air, like water gushing from a power hose, spraying at its peak. The turret never opened; no cry penetrated the flaming steel trap. Standing back from the intense heat, the men in the Prefecture windows watched while the tank blazed away like a gigantic cigarette lighter.

A few minutes later Patrice learned the Germans were massing on two sides of the Prefecture. He made certain the men were alerted, then settled down to wait out the last few moments alone. He checked his revolver, the one with which Danielle had killed Adrien, and filled his pocket with bullets. When the attack came he would take his stand with the men. He had no hope of getting out alive and was beyond caring. But what of the others, he thought, who would die too because of the decision he had taken? There was still time to evacuate the building through the metro. Patrice drove the thought from his mind. He had to be as hard with the men who were his responsibility as with himself. It was not easy. He knew that Bourbon was right. From a military point of view his stand at the Prefecture was untenable. As with the Prefecture, so with all of Paris. From a military point of view the entire insurrection was untenable. But military operations were only part of a larger picture. That was where Bourbon was wrong. The insurrection was a means to a political end: the recapturing of France's prestige by demonstrating before the world that Frenchmen would fight for their freedom. Paradoxically, that end could now be achieved in defeat as in victory. The important thing was that the resistance act; they could not stand by passively while the Americans fought and died for the liberation of Paris. The Prefecture would be a bloody standard, flaming and tragic, for Paris, and Paris would be a fighting symbol for all of France. Ideally, of course, the insurrection should have been co-ordinated with the Allied advance. But the communists had refused to wait, while Reboussin had wanted to wait too long—and Patrice had been caught in the middle.

He had chosen as wisely as he could, with the bitter knowledge that in politics there were no ideal choices. He still thought he was right. True, the shock of Danielle's arrest had opened his eyes to the military limitations of the resistance. Nevertheless, apart from the major reason of prestige, the insurrection had to be supported to prevent the communists from capturing it and rising after the liberation as France's leading political force.

Scattered firing interrupted Patrice's thoughts. Then his door burst open and Sorel rushed in. Patrice sprang up. The revolver was in his hand. He felt calm, but thought, This is it, the last act. He was striding toward the door before he looked up and saw the extraordinary expression on Sorel's face. The little socialist's eyes glistened with tears; his round face was radiant. He flung his arms around Patrice's shoulders. Tear streamed down his cheeks as he embraced Patrice.

"We're saved!" he cried. "The Germans have asked for a truce!"

"Impossible!"

"It's true! It's true!" Sorel was gleeful. "I got the message myself from the Swedish Consul."

"Nordling? But why did he call *you*?"

"He didn't. I took the message. 'The Germans—General von Choltitz—have a proposition for you,' he said. Then he told me what it was."

"It's a trick. Why should they propose a truce when they can take the Prefecture?"

"I don't know. But if they can take the building, why should they want to play tricks?"

Patrice was pacing back and forth, thinking out loud. "Maybe they're not as strong as we think. Maybe they think we're a lot stronger than we are. Who can tell? But you can't turn an insurrection on and off like tap water. Suppose it is a trick and we order the men to hold their fire and then the Boches use the truce to spring a surprise. The insurrection would be wiped out. But if we refuse the truce all we can lose is the Prefecture. I don't like it. It smells to high heaven of a trap."

"But we can't say no to them at this point. We ought to negotiate at least, find out what they're after, what we can get out of it. We ought to do anything to gain time."

"But gaining time means a truce. What else did Nordling say? There must have been conditions."

"Yes, there are. Von Choltitz agrees to talk with us if our attacks stop. On their side, the Germans won't attack any buildings we hold. And finally he will grant us a short truce, which can be used to examine the situation calmly and may then be extended." Patrice said nothing and Sorel added, "Let's get the others in and talk it over."

When he went to Reboussin's office, Patrice found Bourbon there too.

"Just arrived," Bourbon said self-consciously. "Reboussin thought I could be of some use and phoned."

They looked uncomfortable, and it occurred to Patrice that perhaps the initiative for a truce did not come from the Germans. He told them about Nordling's call; their reactions were identical: the German offer spelled salvation.

"That's what worries me," Patrice said dryly. "Why should Von Choltitz let us hold the Prefecture when he can take it?" Patrice turned to Reboussin. "The more I think of it the less likely it seems that the offer of a truce originated with the Germans. It sounds to me as if they were giving their answer to a proposal."

"A proposal? But who could have made it?"

"You've been in contact with Nordling. Did he give any indication that the Germans were thinking along these lines?"

"No." Reboussin thought for a moment under Patrice's steady gaze. "But Nordling did hint that he was working on Von Choltitz not to destroy the Prefecture. He told me he warned Von Choltitz that if German guns were turned on the Prefecture, Notre Dame would not escape. The initiative may have come from Nordling."

Reboussin's impassive face told Patrice nothing. As the three of them walked to Patrice's office, where Sorel and Riviere were waiting, Reboussin said, "In any case, it doesn't matter how the truce talk started; the important thing is that the Germans are making the offer."

Riviere lined up with Patrice. "It's the same old question that's being posed," the wizened little professor said. "The question of the insurrection. Only this time it's being posed in the middle of the insurrection. Should we fight or stop fighting? That's it, isn't it? The Germans are on your side," he went on, speaking to Reboussin. "They want to stop the fight as quickly and inexpensively as they can. Of course! Their mission is to keep their lines of communication open to the east, and a truce will help them. Our job is to tie up Paris so that no German troops can get through. We can't agree to a truce."

Reboussin, Sorel and Bourbon started talking at once. The telephone rang through the clamor of voices. Patrice lifted the receiver.

"He's here," he said, and handed the phone to Reboussin.

Reboussin barked his name into the mouthpiece. Nobody paid any attention to him. Bourbon was speaking forcefully, with sharp, hard gestures. The grim lines on Reboussin's face relaxed.

"Yes, Monsieur Nordling," he said quickly.

The others heard it. They turned. Bourbon stopped in mid-sentence. The metallic voice coming through the receiver penetrated the sudden silence; they strained for the words. Their eyes were on Reboussin's face. It was calm, concentrated.

"I understand . . . Yes, of course . . . I'll call as soon as I have an answer."

Reboussin hung up and nobody said a word. They just looked at him.

"Another proposition from Von Choltitz," he said. "He agrees to the exchange of prisoners on a one-to-one basis provided we accept a truce and maintain it."

"That changes nothing," said Riviere.

Sorel exploded. "And the lives of our comrades!" he cried.

Reboussin was watching Patrice, whose tense face, marked deeply with the lines of exhaustion, did not reveal the struggle that had suddenly erupted within him and shaken his conviction like a willow swept by a hurricane. But Reboussin saw a certain hesitation, an absence of decisiveness. A tormented look shot into Patrice's eyes as he grappled with himself. He nervously rubbed the stubbly growth on his unshaven chin. He was faced with a choice of betrayals and no time to make up his mind.

"We've got to come to a decision. Nordling says he must have an answer immediately."

"The answer is no," Riviere said sharply.

"I say yes," Bourbon said sternly.

"Yes," Sorel echoed.

They turned to Patrice, knowing the decision was really his, since he controlled the Prefecture and the men in it like a local war lord, Chinese fashion. Patrice hesitated. It was not like him. He remembered how, earlier that day, he had hesitated too in front of the Prefecture before deciding to take it. Something strange was happening to him that he did not understand. In all the years he had been in the resistance he had always been clear and sure. Decisions had been simple because questions reduced themselves to simple elements and something practical had to be done about them immediately. But now he seemed unable to draw upon the resources he had always felt were inexhaustible. Although he stood there without changing expression, inside him, in the brief seconds he had to make his choice, a struggle whose violence the men looking at him could never have imagined was taking place. All the certainties of the past few months flooded through his mind and with them were mixed his doubts of the last twenty-four hours. At the first shock of the truce offer he had reacted with a deep and sure instinct, and had expressed it to Sorel. Now he wavered. The same pattern that had formed that morning when he wanted to delay the insurrection to help free Danielle was reappearing. If they agreed to a truce, the prisoners would be exchanged and Danielle could be saved. If the truce was rejected, Danielle would be lost. He thought of her and of the insurrection and of the truce and what it might mean. Above all, the idea that had been haunting him all day infiltrated and dominated his thoughts. From a military point of view, the insurrection was untenable. Under the pressure of the event, this thought became much more important than it ever had been. Whatever reasons of policy, whatever political reasons there may have been for the uprising, this thought that it would end in a military disaster took hold of Patrice's mind and he could not shake it off. At the same time the thought of Danielle combined with it to weaken his resolve. He thought that if he voted to continue the insurrection, he ran the risk of making two mistakes: it might result in a catastrophe for the resistance as well as in the loss of Danielle. But the roots of his convictions were still spread firmly around the policy of fighting the Germans at every point, and he thought that if he decided for the truce it would be a betrayal of all he had fought for and most deeply believed in. What would his comrades think of him? He didn't care—or did he? The ideas raced through his head and canceled each other out. No single thought dominated and reduced the others to zero. For a moment it occurred to him that the thing to do was to fall back on his instinct, as he had done in the case of the Prefecture. But that is not something that can be commanded. His will failed him because he did not know what he wanted to do. He blinked and strained and his head hurt at the nape of the neck and upward, and then he noticed that they were watching him, impatient. He took a deep breath, still not entirely sure of what he was going to say. Then he heard his own voice breaking the silence.

"I've changed my mind," he said. "I vote for the truce. We've got to save our people if we can."

Riviere looked stunned. "What's happened to you?" he said. "You can't mean it."

Reboussin was already at the phone.

"Yes, let's get on with it," Patrice said. "But you must insist on one thing. The truce holds only if we get every prisoner we name, as well as all the hostages. Every single one with no exceptions. Otherwise the truce is off."

Reboussin relayed the message to Nordling. Shortly after, the Swedish Consul called back. It was 9:50 P.M. Von Choltitz, he said, wanted the truce to begin in five minutes and to last until 10:50 P.M. If the truce is observed, the prisoners will be exchanged and the truce extended. Reboussin specified that the exchange of prisoners was to take place in front of the Prefecture before midnight. Patrice then gave the order that nobody in the building was to fire unless he was fired on first. A few minutes after ten Nordling was on the phone again. To exactly how much of Paris did the truce apply? Reboussin replied he could only answer for the Prefecture, but that by morning the word would go around the city. In the event of any violations, Reboussin added, he hoped General von Choltitz would distinguish between isolated irresponsible acts and a planned attack.

Fifteen minutes before the deadline, Nordling called once more. Von Choltitz was satisfied with the way the truce was maintained and proposed that it be extended through the night. German troops would deliver the French prisoners to the Prefecture gate on the Boulevard du Palais under a white flag and the exchange would take place within an hour.

"Well, you have your truce now," Riviere said. "You'd better get on your bicycles and get around to headquarters. The men who think they're running the insurrection ought to know that you've pulled down the curtain on their show."

After some protest Patrice bowed to their insistence that he report to F.F.I. headquarters. He hated to leave before the prisoners arrived, but once it was decided, he hastened away, hoping to get back that night, perhaps to see Danielle. He could not yet believe she would be freed and that he would see her again. But now there was hope where before there had been none. It altered him. The spark of hope caught at some deep, hidden place and set everything in motion again. His eyes, ringed by dark circles of fatigue, were no longer somber. If his gaunt face was marked by deep lines, it was no longer grim. He left the Prefecture a different man from the one he had been that morning. He had begun the day as the instrument by which the insurrection had sprung to life; he was finishing it as the instrument by which it was laid to rest. But what did it matter? By turning the edge of the sword he might save Danielle. He thought now that the rest did not count, though it troubled hiim. Life was a personal matter. If what was closest to the heart died, the rest would wither away. And if Danielle were not released? If, in shutting the door on the insurrection, he were not opening it for Danielle? The choice was made, he thought. Whatever happened, it was worth it.

After Patrice left, Reboussin went to his office, where Bourbon joined him. They looked at each other and grinned.

"I never would have believed it could have been done," Bourbon said.

"We owe it all to our good friend Patrice," Reboussin said modestly. He chuckled, then became serious. "Think of it! He might have bargained for the Ministry of the Interior, and he just changed his mind!" Reboussin looked odd and added, "What is France coming to with leaders like that?"

So far as Reboussin was concerned, Patrice had committed the ultimate blunder: he had sold out and not asked to be paid off.

On the quai the German tank burned steadily. The flames threw a bright, dancing light on a corner of the Prefecture and reached across the rain-shining pavement of the Parvis like a huge medieval torch to underlight the ghostly Gothic form of Notre Dame. The cathedral stretched high above the feeble illumination of the burning tank, a shadowy mass looming in the night sky.

†

KLAUS had not waited long before he was called down to confer with two officers on General von Choltitz' staff. The conference was unpleasant. Klaus was unable to give precise answers to any of the questions they asked. There were three key questions: Who were the leaders of the Paris resistance? How many men in the Paris area belonged to the resistance? How were they armed? Klaus did not know and the officers did not hide their annoyance.

"I see the Gestapo knows as little as we," one of them observed sourly. "We may as well adjourn. This is getting us nowhere." They rose. "Don't leave the hotel, Tellmann," the officer added. "We may need you later on."

"But I have work to do," Klaus protested, "important work that may lead to the information you're after."

"What is it?"

Klaus explained. The officers looked unconvinced.

"It's a little late for that sort of thing," one of them said. "Even if she belongs to the resistance and confesses to the murder—and neither is certain—I can't see that it will lead to what we want. Knowing where resistance leaders live won't do any good anyway; they would hardly be sleeping in their beds tonight."

Klaus argued, but the officers were adamant. Disappointed and angry, Klaus went to his room and toyed with the idea of disobeying his orders. The Gestapo was independent of the Wehrmacht, but these were extraordinary circumstances. If the girl's confession turned out to be uninteresting after all and they really needed him while he was away, there would be more trouble for him when he got back to Germany. He had enough as it was. Finally he decided to remain.

Pacing the floor, he considered the possibility of letting the men in the villa go ahead without him. It was dangerous, since none of them was really responsible. They'd probably gag her, he thought, just to be sure she couldn't talk if she wanted to. He shook his head. No, he reflected bitterly, musicians never play as they should when the conductor is away.

He was called down three times for brief conferences and after each one he climbed up the steps to his room. The general situation had become a matter of indifference to him; he was concerned now only with his own problem. Having moved into the Meurice, he was tied down to the military; his freedom was limited. And Suzanne? He had given her up, given her up without even having thought of it. The problem was solved. Time, events had taken care of it. He had solved his problem by not facing it. Evasion was paying dividends: a note was due and it had been wiped off the books. He was an indecisive man, and now that it was too late he began to pose the problem that no longer existed. A sense of guilt plagued him; for a moment the tiny voice of conscience became a roar. But he knew, below the surface of his thinking, that he lacked the courage to run away with Suzanne or take her with him when he returned to Germany. The material impediments were too great. His thoughts went back again to his professional predicament and how his superiors in Berlin would react to the Adrien affair. If only the Tessier girl knew what he hoped she knew. They wouldn't keep him here all night. There was still time.

The hours passed. Surly and impatient, Klaus waited in his room. The light began to fade. Rain fell. At last the phone rang again. Klaus pounced at it. Yes, he would be down immediately. On the way he rehearsed a new plea to get away. He walked into a spacious salon. Three officers, one a general. The general, sitting at a desk, had a ruddy complexion and small eyes set close together in a jowly face.

"Herr Tellmann," he said amiably, "I believe you have a prisoner named Danielle Tessier."

Klaus nodded. At last they were interested. The general scarcely paused.

"Where is she?"

"In a villa in St. Cloud."

"I want you to get her here immediately and turn her over to the captain here as soon as she arrives. You can use my phone."

The general pushed his phone toward Klaus. Klaus looked over it without moving.

"Why?"

The general sat back, locking his fingers behind his head, and, still amiable, though his small eyes had hardened, said, "Because we're going to release her."

When Klaus found his voice he stammered, "But she's my prisoner!" His voice grated harshly. "She's a terrorist! A killer! She murdered our most valuable informer!"

"Has she confessed?"

The general's fingers were still laced behind his head. His nonchalance infuriated Klaus.

"Not yet, but she will when I interrogate her."

"Haven't you interrogated her yet?"

"Yes, but—"

"But she denied knowing anything about the murder?" the general asked with quiet irony. He unlocked his fingers and leaned forward, his arms on the desk. "Maybe she didn't kill your informer."

"I think she did. With a little persuasion she'll change her story."

"No doubt," the general said dryly. "What makes you think she did it?"

Klaus hesitated. "An informer," he said, realizing how hollow it sounded. "A completely trustworthy report."

The general threw up his hands. "A denunciation! You base a murder charge on a single denunciation and want to hold the girl with no more evidence than that! It's not enough for me. I want you to turn her over to the captain immediately. There's no more time to be lost."

Klaus darted one quick, frantic look at the captain and the other officer, who were regarding him with blankly unsympathetic eyes. The general was now anything but amiable.

"But why do you want to release her?" Klaus asked desperately.

"We've negotiated a truce with the insurrectionists and an exchange of prisoners, including the girl, is one of the conditions." The general fixed Klaus, standing white-faced before him, with a cold stare. "We can crush these terrorists if we want to, but it would be a nuisance and that's not what we're here for. Our objective is to keep Paris clear so our troops in Normandy can retreat through the city without being impeded. We can do that more efficiently by signing a truce than by suppressing a revolt, and we're certainly not going to risk a snag because of one dead informer and a girl who may or may not have killed him."

Klaus wavered irresolutely. "I have to answer for the informer and the girl to my superiors in Berlin," he said. "If you want the girl you'll have to put your order in writing."

The general's small eyes became smaller; his fleshy jowls quivered. Standing his ground, Klaus stared back. The officers watched without stirring. Without a word the general picked up a pen and began to scrawl on a sheet of white paper, the scratch of the pen curdling the creamy-thick silence. He signed his name, wrote under it, "for Von Choltitz," and pushed the paper toward Klaus with one hand and the phone toward him with the other.

Klaus read the general's scrawl slowly while the three officers watched. When he finished he looked up and met their gaze. For another instant he hesitated. Then he shrugged helplessly and reached for the phone. But he still had a reservation and was thinking fast under pressure. Above all, he needed time—just what the general was not giving him. He heard the receiver being lifted at the other end of the wire.

"Prepare to move the prisoner," he heard himself say, thinking all the while of what he could do to hold onto Danielle. One possibility, of course, he thought, was simply to move her directly to Germany. "I'll be there in a quarter of an hour and I want her ready to go when I arrive."

He saluted the general, who stared at him blankly. The other officers had the same neutral expression on their faces. Klaus left, wondering if it might not be the better part of wisdom to give Danielle up to the army. But his failure, or what he regarded as his failure, gnawed at him. Whatever he decided—to hold or release Danielle—he ran immense risks. He did not want to run afoul of the army, but his career was with the Gestapo. He thought that he still had a fifteen-minute ride to St. Cloud to make up his mind and wished he could be sure what his chiefs would be inclined to do—shoot him or decorate him—if he refused to give up Danielle.

†

A FEW minutes after Klaus's telephone call the door of Danielle's room opened and three of the young men walked in, the last one carrying her clothes.

"Get up!"

Slowly slipping from under the covers, Danielle stood trembling by the bed. The rising contour of her breasts was outlined in the light coming from the window behind her.

"Come here and get dressed."

Her clothes were thrown on a chair, and as she turned, startled at the command, she saw them. Was it an obscene joke? She hesitated. Would they grab her as she went toward them?

"Come on!"

She went to the chair; they made no move but just watched her. Quickly she picked up her clothes in trembling hands and dressed. Then she straightened up and faced them. She felt stronger now, protected; the familiar blue cotton dress that caressed her skin comfortingly did more than cover the nakedness of her body; putting it on was like settling back into her old self.

"Come along."

They led her to a Citroen parked in the driveway, and she sank into the low-slung back seat between two of them. Then they waited. Presently a car swept into the grounds. Klaus stepped out of it, went into the villa and came out with another man. The two of them went to the Citroen in which Danielle was huddled and sat in the front, the man with Klaus in the driver's seat. The motor snapped alive. A moment later the car purred down and around a twisting hill, spurted across a bridge, through the Porte de St. Cloud, and sped through the darkened streets of the sixteenth *arrondissement*. Not a word was spoken. Danielle was so relieved to be dressed and out of the villa that at first she did not think of where they were taking her. Any change was for the good. Speeding through Paris, she wondered what had happened that day. She looked at the streets rushing by. There was no sign of an uprising. She thought that maybe it had not begun yet after all. And the Prefecture, Patrice . . . He would have had to go home from her house last night after curfew. If he had been picked up by a patrol, the Prefecture plan might not have been carried out.

The Citroen rolled on through the blacked-out city, hugging the edge of the Bois de Boulogne. It was when Danielle became aware that they were at the Bois that she began to wonder where they were taking her. They were going to shoot her, she thought. They always did it in the Bois de Boulogne or the Bois de Vincennes. She felt sad and wondered if she would be frightened when the car stopped and she had to get out. Then she thought that they might be taking her to Germany. It would not be to a villa with a soft bed, but to a concentration camp. The sweet fresh shell of summer rain saturated the night air. It was good to be alive. Hunched in the back seat of the Citroen, speeding through the night, Danielle found herself hoping wildly, passionately, that she was being driven to Germany and a concentration camp.

†

PATRICE waited with a small group of men headed by Reboussin near the entrance to the Prefecture on the Boulevard du Palais. He breathed in the fresh, wet summer night air and took hope, but hardly dared express it. In the past hour he had been busy racing from one headquarters to another on the left bank in search of Mazaud, Laperche, Colonel Rol or one of the other communist leaders. But they were even more active than he. At each point he missed them. At each point he also left word of the truce. Before long, Patrice knew, the communists would be looking for him. His search had one virtue: the hour had fled quickly, bringing him to this strange nighttime rendezvous between resistance leaders and German officers.

The men on the Boulevard du Palais waited quietly but impatiently, staring into the darkness toward the right bank. They kept looking at their watches and when they said a few words it was invariably about the time. It went slowly now for Patrice. The Germans were late.

"They should have been here half an hour ago," Reboussin muttered to Patrice. "I don't like it."

"You don't suppose—"

"You know how punctilious they usually are. I'm just beginning to wonder if they'll show."

For another quarter of an hour Patrice paced back and forth in a torment, the minutes dragging interminably, as if they were chained to each other. Then somebody called, "They're coming!"

A convoy of two trucks and two armored vehicles led by a staff car flying a white flag, rolled slowly up to where the resistance group was waiting. As Patrice stood in the background, Reboussin approached the staff car and spoke with the German officer in charge. Their negotiations were swift, but to Patrice the minutes dragged more and more. He stared at the trucks, thinking that Danielle couldn't be in there with the others, then convinced himself that she must be there. He strode over to Reboussin.

"Is everything all right?"

"We're all straightened out," Reboussin replied.

At last chains clanked out of iron rings and the back flaps of the trucks went down with a loud noise. In the street a German officer flashed a pin point of light on a sheet of paper. Beside him, Reboussin held a sheet of paper too. He raised it toward the pin point of light gleaming from the officer's hand. The officer called a name. There was no answer. He called it again, louder. An answering cry came from the truck.

"Come down!"

A prisoner jumped to the ground. There was a dead hush on the truck. The officer and Reboussin checked the name on their sheets of paper. Then an F.F.I. standing beside Reboussin said to the prisoner, "You're free. Go into the Prefecture." The prisoner's face lighted up in the dark and the next instant he was gone, happily swallowed up behind the walls of the Prefecture.

The officer called out another name, a third and a fourth. Each time a name was called Patrice's excitement intensified. The trucks quickly emptied. When the last prisoner jumped to the ground Danielle's name still had not been called. Under the toll of French names shouted into the night Patrice's elation turned to despair. As the last prisoner went by, Patrice was at Reboussin's side. The Germans were already leaving.

"What about Danielle?" he demanded. "Her name was on the list. It hasn't even been called."

Reboussin gestured toward the officer who had already climbed into the staff car."The colonel told me at the outset that she was not arrested by the military like the others."

"What difference does it make who arrested her? She's a prisoner of war and on the terms of the truce must be exchanged."

"They agree, but they claim they haven't been able to locate her."

Patrice's face was grim as death. His eyes penetrated Reboussin. "She's in Paris, isn't she?"

"They don't know. They're working on it, the colonel said. After all, they didn't have much time to round up the prisoners."

Patrice turned away without another word. It had failed, he thought. His entire maneuver has failed. He walked despondently back into the Prefecture.

†

PATRICE stopped uncertainly on the first-floor landing. The corridor was illuminated by candles, which cast fluttering shadows upon the walls. In the faint light he made out the stooped figure of Riviere rushing by. Riviere saw Patrice and turned back to him. Patrice was startled by his bitter expression.

"What's the matter?"

"Everything!" Riviere spat out. "I don't understand you, or maybe I do. This morning Reboussin and Bourbon were anathema; tonight they're your sleeping companions. How do you add that up?"

"You wouldn't understand."

A disabused expression settled over Riviere's wrinkled old face and his brows arched over the lively young eyes. "Maybe I will," he observed dryly, "when I see what post is confided to you in the liberation government."

He turned and left Patrice standing there. His shaft had hit its mark. It irritated the hurt that already stabbed at Patrice's heart. The hurt twisted inside him, sharp and sickening, as he realized how high his hopes had been that he would see Danielle walk back from the dead and into his arms. All the emotions of that violently charged day suddenly cascaded upon him in a torrent. Disappointment shook his certainty in himself. Doubts showered over him. The balance of his judgment was unhinged. Desperately, he groped for something firm and steady to hold onto. But without Danielle there was nothing. He tried to shake himself out of it. He had a job to do, he told himself, and finally, with an effort, got a grip on himself.

When he walked into his office a few minutes later he found Riviere, Bourbon, Sorel and Lefort there. Lefort, his hair disheveled, tie awry, had come to the Prefecture an hour before. He was frustrated. The four pages of the first issue of his newspaper were set in type, but he could not give the order for the presses to roll. As part of the curious and paradoxical policy decided upon that afternoon—to revolt but to revolt discreetly—publication of resistance newspapers had been prohibited. He had come to do some lobbying and fallen upon the truce.

"The prisoner exchange is completed," Patrice said. "Reboussin will be up any minute now."

He went dispiritedly to a far corner of the room, where Lefort joined him.

"I hear you switched," Lefort said. "What's up?"

Looking at Lefort's clear eyes and untroubled face, Patrice felt they lived in different worlds, stemmed from different species; Lefort seemed empty and fatuous.

"I'd rather not talk about it," Patrice said sourly.

Reboussin came in at that moment, catching everyone's attention by saying as he entered, "It's done. The prisoners have been exchanged." He was in a mood that for him bordered on exuberance. His eyes swept the room and, seeing Patrice, he spoke solemnly, with that knack he had which led cynics to say of him that he was always sincere whether he meant what he said or not, "Tonight, Patrice, you have proved yourself bigger than any of us." Reboussin paused and Patrice, feeling his cheeks go scarlet, shifted his eyes. "You've proved yourself to be a statesman," Reboussin added.

Patrice's face burned. For a long time he did not hear a word of what was said. Praise from Reboussin was the last thing he had expected or wanted. It clogged his throat. But there was nothing he could say. And yet Reboussin's words were like an ax aimed at the arch of his faith. Nothing was so calculated to bring arch and all the rest toppling down. Patrice sat perfectly still in his crisis of self-confidence, willing nothing, and yet his doubts hacked away, cutting and chipping at the heart of what he had always believed he was. He did not realize that he was not himself, and had he known, he could have done nothing about it. In the past twenty-four hours everything had changed. Suddenly he realized why. It was not simply that Danielle had been snatched away from him. The insurrection had begun. Time itself had changed, racing with events and the abruptly altered minds and characters of men. It filtered through his mind that though years of erosion might not have changed him, the concentrated shock of the insurrection could. Reboussin's tone of voice as he had called him a statesman came back to him, the word "statesman" chopping with relentless regularity at his consciousness until he shook his head to throw it off. But nothing he could do was really any good. Now that the arch of faith had split, the entire structure of his emotions seemed to crumble. He watched the ruins tumble, helpless to stop it. He was hurt and disappointed. Nothing had worked out.He could not bear to think of Danielle. It was too painful. As for his vote on the truce, he knew his motive was not base and he also knew that some of the men in this room thought differently. But the motive was less important than the fact. Without wanting to, he had changed sides. Events had overwhelmed him. The thought did not help matters. When, finally, he looked up, Riviere was speaking.

"It's done," he was saying. "But if we have a truce, let's use it. For a few hours we had an insurrection; we were told to fight it with discretion—by hiding from those we were supposed to drive out of Paris. Now we have a form of suspended peace. If it's conceivable to fight a passive uprising, it's reasonable to wage an aggressive truce."

Pleased with the formula, Riviere looked sardonically from one to the other, his brows arched inquisitively for their reaction. Lefort smiled indulgently; Bourbon frowned; Sorel looked puzzled behind knit brows.

"What do you suggest we do?" Reboussin asked.

"Occupy the Hotel de Ville!"

Riviere said it as though he were exploding a bomb, and in a way he was; then he paused to see if they would blow up. Varying expressions of surprise come over their faces, but they were stunned rather than quickened.

"The first objective of any self-respecting insurrectionist," Riviere went on, "is the seat of government. Historically, every Paris insurrection tried to take the Hotel de Ville, and every successful one confirmed its victory there. We would do well in this case," he concluded, his voice edged with irony, "to follow in the footsteps of our illustrious predecessors. I may be a man of the left, a progressive, but what could be more conservative than to follow the examples of the past?"

Irritated by Riviere's professorial manner, Bourbon blurted, "We're not here to learn the history of Parisian insurrections."

"No," Riviere snapped. "We're here to make it."

"Why not?" Reboussin said suddenly. "After all, why not?" They looked at him in surprise. "The Germans don't know which buildings we hold and which are under Vichy control."

Lefort picked up the thread. "What's more," he added, "there's little chance that the Germans will intervene with the truce on. They'll never know whether we took it a few hours ago or a few hours from now."

"And any agreement we negotiate during the truce," Reboussin said, "will be on the basis of the buildings we hold."

"I don't like it," Bourbon said.

"Think of the symbolic value!" Riviere said, exasperated with the colonel's stubbornness. "We already hold police headquarters, the index of physical control over a city. If we also occupy the administrative nerve center from which Paris is governed, it will appear that the city is ours."

Reboussin added a more persuasive argument. "It's better that we hold the Hotel de Ville," he said, "than that Vichy does, or, for that matter, some element of the resistance that is less responsible than we are."

It was a point to which Bourbon was sensitive. He nodded agreement. Reviere, who was less concerned with the political ramifications of what group occupied the Hotel de Ville than he was simply with its being occupied, muttered under his breath, "Ah, la, la! He understands quickly, provided you explain for a long time."

The discussion went from the agreement in principle to the question of how and when the Hotel de Ville would be occupied. Bourbon suggested that Reboussin should lead the operation, since the building was more a political than a military objective. The others agreed.

"It's delicate," Riviere said. "In an important sense, whoever occupies the Hotel de Ville thereby seizes political power; and the communists are being left out. I don't care as long as we take the building. But how will they react?"

"The devil with them," Bourbon said. "For all we know they're planning to seize the building themselves."

"That wouldn't make things any simpler after we took it," said Lefort.

"Theoretically the Parisian Committee of Liberation should occupy the Hotel de Ville," Reboussin said. "We all know that two of its three members are communists. Nevertheless, I would have no objection to inviting them to take office in the building after we have occupied it. The important thing is that if the communists take it, the building and the victory will be theirs and they will create such an atmosphere that nobody will be able to prevent them from doing exactly as they please; we would be their hostages. The atmosphere will be quite different if we take it. And they can't cause much trouble if we ask the Committee of Liberation to sit in the building, as we are obliged to do in any case."

"Good," said Riviere. "But let's make the occupation as democratic as possible. Some cops, some F.F.I.s, some Delegation guards, even some women, perhaps, so that the people of Paris are represented. Nobody will be able to make much of a case against an occupation like that."

"I'll go along," Patrice said.

"I'll be going too," said Riviere.

Bourbon was given the job of organizing the operation. The others prepared for sleep. Patrice's office was carpeted, and they lay down around the room. Blankets had been brought from another part of the building and were distributed. The men folded their jackets and used them as pillows. When Patrice stretched out on the carpet he suddenly realized how exhausted he was. He asked for no greater luxury than the oblivion of sleep. An instant after he lay down he was asleep.

†

PATRICE felt himself being shaken and heard the words "Wake up!" They seemed far away and unreal, and he resisted. Then, quite involuntarily, he rose to the surface and opened his eyes. Bourbon was kneeling over him. "Ah, at last," he said, and was gone.

He twisted up on his elbow, his body feeling strangely stiff, and looked around. The cool, gray light of the dawn filtered through the high windows into the room, revealing the huddled mound of a sleeper here and there. In the half light Patrice saw Riviere put on his jacket and Sorel get up, yawn and stretch. Beyond Sorel, outlined against the window, was the silhouette of a half-dressed man that looked like a music-hall caricature but was vaguely familiar. With a malicious smile, Patrice recognized Reboussin. At the intimate morning hour the astute politician, his dignity down, was caught in *flagrante delicto* —with his pants off. His spindly legs, encased in high socks held up by garters, stuck out of shorts that dangled from his needle-thin waist like a listless flag at half-mast. He put on his shirt and, balanced on one foot, held his trousers delicately in front of him. At this point Patrice recalled the photographs of Reboussin on the front pages of the prewar Paris press and imagined others, posed like this, or *à la Na-poléon,* in the newspapers after the liberation. He watched the spindly legs and ill-fitting shorts disappear as Reboussin stepped primly into his trousers and public personality.

Patrice stood up at the same time as Riviere.

"Let's go," said Riviere. "We're having breakfast before we leave."

Reboussin, however, asked them to wait for him. "My tie is gone," he complained. "It's really exasperating not to be able to find the only tie you possess."

"It's unimportant," Riviere said. "Think of what the Germans would put around your neck at this hour if they could."

"At this hour and before breakfast that's not funny."

"It's the finest compliment I could pay you."

"I've still got to find that tie," Reboussin said grudgingly. He searched on the floor, under the desk, by the window.

"What difference does it make?" Patrice asked impatiently.

Reboussin straightened up. "All the difference in the world," he said sharply. "There are certain proprieties one observes in politics when that is one's calling."

"*Nom de Dieu!*" Riviere swore. "This isn't politics; it's an insurrection!"

"I will not take possession of the Hotel de Ville," Reboussin cried, "without wearing a tie! It would be undignified." He looked at them stiffly, as proud in his formalism as he was absurd, and stubbornly aware of both.

Patrice and Riviere stared at Reboussin openmouthed. Then Riviere laughed and said, "Very well. I bow to tradition, if that's what it is."

He and Patrice helped look for the lost tie, but they could not find it. Finally they borrowed Lefort's, which was handsome and appropriate—a blue tie with small red and white polka dots.

They breakfasted in a large room on canned sardines and bread, which they washed down with red wine. Reboussin, sporting Lefort's tie, was much more cheerful.

"A dry white with the sardines would be better," he murmured, "but considering the circumstances . . ." and he finished off the raw wine in a gulp.

Bourbon briefed them and they left. The Hotel de Ville borders the right bank of the Seine, a short five-minute walk from the Prefecture. Just before six o'clock Reboussin, Sorel, Riviere and Patrice met a detachment of almost a hundred men on the Parvis de Notre Dame, which was still wet and shiny from the rain. The morning sky was clear, the air was fresh. They walked quietly through empty streets, crossed a bridge and were in front of the slumbering Hotel de Ville. Stealthily approaching the door Bourbon had indicated, Reboussin cautiously tried it. It was locked. Riviere swore and Reboussin, nervous now, hesitated, not knowing what to do. After a hasty conference they tried another door. It opened. Just inside were the Gardes Mobiles. The two groups faced each other uncertainly, but without discussion the Gardes Mobiles went over to the resistance.

Led by Reboussin and Sorel, they were barely inside the building when they ran into their main resistance contact man in the high-vaulted corridor leading to the heart of the building. He showed them the way to the office of the Prefect of the Seine and rushed off to wake up the Prefect. Reboussin directed Sorel to post the men at key points around the building. This was quickly done and Sorel rejoined the others in the Prefect's office.

It was a huge, impressive room. Beneath its four immense windows stretched all of Paris, with a long arm of the Seine, straddled by rows of bridges, swinging through the city. A gigantic chandelier hung from the carved, gilt ceiling; rich tapestries adorned the walls, which were paneled with gilt wood; museum pieces were artfully placed about the room—chairs, tables, desks and divans from the most aristocratic periods of the kings of France.

More than a dozen men had surged into the splendid setting. Most of the men were in shirt sleeves and were armed. They were unwashed, unshaven, unkempt. Despite Reboussin's tie, it looked as if the rabble spawned by the Paris gutter had poured into the last refuge of a dying government, the sanctum santorum from which Paris was ruled.

Seeing a bust of Pétain on the mantelpiece, Sorel cried, "Throw it out! It doesn't belong here."

A young F.F.I. with a rifle slung over his shoulder carried the bust to a window and held it poised beyond the ledge when the Prefect burst into the room. The Prefect glared at the young man. Looking over his shoulder at the Prefect, the F.F.I. let go of the bust. The crash rose like a snicker. Nobody said a word.

The Prefect strode behind his desk, turned and faced them. "Who are you?"

"That should be obvious," said Reboussin.

The Prefect sat down.

"Comrades, sit down," said Riviere. "This is our office."

"You may ruin everything I'm trying to do," the Prefect snapped. "The Germans threaten to destroy Paris. I'm working to save the city from—"

"A Frenchman doesn't save Paris by working *with* the Germans but *against* them!" Sorel interrupted. "You can't save Paris on your knees and you haven't been off them in four years."

"You're making a mistake—"

"Enough!" Reboussin cut in. "There's only one way to treat the men of treason. *Monsieur le Préfet,* you're under arrest."

The Prefect rose slowly, as if he were very tired. He leaned on the desk, his face suddenly haggard. "May I pack a bag?" he asked.

Quivering with rage, Sorel sprang to his feet. "Did your police allow our men to pack a bag before you turned them over to the Gestapo to be tortured?"

The Prefect's face was gray. "You're being unjust," he said.

"Unjust!" Riviere sneered. "For four years you persecuted us; now it's our turn to persecute you."

The Prefect was led away, and Reboussin took a few men to another part of the building to arrest the mayor of Paris. Patrice went to a window and gazed at the line of bridges braceleting the arm of the Seine. The green waters sparkled in the sun, flowing past Notre Dame toward the Eiffel Tower. Patrice felt heavyhearted. The taking of the Hotel de Ville had given him neither joy nor even satisfaction. Freedom, he thought, was a good cause and he would never renounce it; but the cause, like all causes, led to scenes like the one he had just witnessed. The men of the resistance were only too human. Sooner or later a man's purity, if he had it to begin with, was tainted. The lust for power, the lust for profit, the lust to persecute—when the lust was there, when a man itched with lust, and the arms of opportunity were open wide, few could resist. Vichyites and collaborators would pay now for having bought the wrong article cheaply when it was costly to buy the right one. The accounting was at hand; the books would be balanced. But what saddened Patrice was the thought that between the crime and the punishment men could not resist imposing the inhuman element: humiliation. He had no taste for vengeance, no taste for vengeance at all. What he wanted was Danielle.

He stood at the window a long while, looking over the city in the powder-blue morning light. The nightmare he had struggled through the previous day was still so close he felt he had but to reach out and he would touch it; instead, Paris lay newborn at his fingertips and the terror was wiped clean. The moment of impossible choices was gone. He no longer was forced to decide if an insurrection should be started and if it should be stopped; he no longer had to say if men would live or die; he no longer had to measure the value of the things he could not help believing against the freedom of the woman he loved. The truce had turned the edge of the revolt, and Patrice felt as if a loaded gun had been removed from the nape of his neck. But the ache of Danielle's loss was more acute than ever. Without her he felt as if the ground had been cut out from under him and he was clinging to fragments in a void. There was still a chance, he thought, as long as the truce lasted, to put pressure on the Germans to get her released. If only she were in Paris! She had to be, he told himself fiercely. No matter what he was told, he had to assume she was here where he could help her. He would talk to Reboussin. Reboussin would talk to Nordling. Nordling would talk to the Germans. Something could still be done and he would do it.

The morning mist hung over the waters of the Seine and girdled the waist of the Eiffel Tower. Above, the sky was blue and the sun bright. It would be a fine day. Patrice did not care. He clenched his fist and turned away from the city rising serenely out of the low mist into the caressing sunshine.

†

PARIS awoke late on Sunday to familiar and reassuring morning noises rising from the peaceful streets. The storm of the previous evening had passed like the signs of battle. Shutters opened and rooms were drenched with sunlight pouring out of a sky bleached pale blue by the heat. It was a magnificent summer Sunday and many Parisians thought the war had left the city in its wake. Sunday strollers, in much of the city, saw nothing out of the ordinary—not a uniform, not a military vehicle, not a tank or patrol—nothing to break the illusion of a city at peace.

Patrice knew better. The truce could not last unless nurtured, and even then it had small chance of surviving. He lingered a while at the Hotel de Ville, then left for the Prefecture. Something had to be done and Patrice thought he knew what it was. As he dashed into the Prefecture he met Lefort leaving it.

"What's new?" Patrice asked.

The tieless, unshaven Lefort smiled at the tieless, unshaven Patrice.

"Reboussin's back," he said. "He left Sorel in command at the Hotel de Ville."

"I know that," Patrice said impatiently.

"Sorel's the general," Lefort went on imperturbably, "and what a general he'll make! Reboussin is the diplomat. He's going to nurse your truce along as if he were Talleyrand at the Congress of Vienna."

"That's fine. We need a Talleyrand—anyone who'll turn a defeat into a victory." Patrice made a gesture of impatience. "It's futile to argue about it. Is there anything new on the truce?"

"Zero."

Lefort stopped Patrice as he turned to go. "How about getting some newspapers published?" Lefort asked. "Nobody knows what's going on. I'll bet half of Paris doesn't even know it was hit by an insurrection yesterday. A little shooting here and there, a building or two occupied by the resistance—that's all yesterday's events meant to most of our good citizens. People don't know that history is happening to them until they read it in the papers."

"Parisians don't believe it then," Patrice said, hurrying toward the staircase.

"Patrice!" Lefort called out. "It means recruits."

He turned away, swearing under his breath, just as a wiry little man with roguish eyes set in a Puckish face brushed past him. Mignot, his eternal cigarette butt in the corner of his lips, caught up to Patrice on the stairs.

"Just the man I wanted to see," Patrice exclaimed.

"What's the word on Danielle?" Mignot asked eagerly.

Patrice shook his head. "Nothing since she's been taken."

Mignot looked as crestfallen as Patrice. They stopped on the first-floor landing, and Mignot told Patrice what he had done the previous day.

"What are you doing now?" Patrice asked.

"I came to see if you needed me here."

"Let's find a place where we can talk."

They found an empty office, where Patrice told Mignot about the truce and outlined the situation.

"We can annoy the Germans, as you know, but we can't beat them," Patrice said. "The truce can't last. When it's broken the Germans will slaughter us. We have only one hope." Patrice gazed steadily into Mignot's intent face. "That's where you come in."

"Me?"

Patrice nodded. "The Americans don't know what's happening here. Nobody outside of Paris knows. Damn few people in the city know. Somebody has got to get to the American High Command and urge them to hurry troops here. It's our one chance."

Mignot's stub of a cigarette hung motionless from the side of his mouth.

"You know how to get things done, Mignot. That's why I thought of you," Patrice went on. "Do you think you can get through the lines?"

"I'll talk my way through."

"Not easy."

Mignot's eyes twinkled. "I'll slip through disguised as a breath of hot air."

Patrice laughed. "I knew you'd go. —It will be dangerous," he added, serious again. "Here's my plan. A doctor I know will drive you to the front. When the Germans stop him he'll say he's going to see a patient —an emergency case. You're the doctor's assistant. If that doesn't get you through, you're on your own. Get through however you can."

"I'll get through," Mignot said.

"Remember what it means and you'll make it." Patrice looked at Mignot silently for a moment. "You're just plain Mignot now; but when you get on the road you're going to be the key man of the insurrection. Everything will hinge on your mission. If you get through, Paris can be saved; if you don't, well . . ."

Mignot nodded. "When do I take off?"

"As soon as I can get the doctor here. Wait. Meanwhile I'll prepare credentials in English and a note for the American commander."

Patrice went to his office. Reboussin was there.

"I was looking for you," Reboussin said. "A lot has happened. I'm just back from seeing Nordling at the Swedish Consulate with a group of others."

"Just a minute until I make a phone call."

Patrice dialed the doctor's number. A woman's voice said the doctor was out.

"Tell him it's urgent, to call Patrice at the Préfecture. Turbigo 92-00. It's about the trip he offered to go on yesterday."

Hanging up the receiver, Patrice turned to Reboussin. "I still haven't seen the communists. As you know, I left word. They'll be on our necks any minute. Now, before you get to what's happened at the Swedish Consulate, I want to know what's happened to Danielle."

Patrice's aggressiveness took Reboussin off balance. "I don't know," Reboussin said. "We didn't get around to it."

"Well, we've got to get around to it—now, right away. I tell you the Germans doublecrossed us. They're holding her back deliberately. How long do you think the truce will last? Once it's ended we might as well forget her. We'll never see her again."

"I know how you feel, Patrice," Reboussin said quietly. "I know how close—"

"Put pressure on them!" Patrice cried. "Make them act fast. You're our best negotiator. You know how to do it. We can only ask for her while the truce is on. Once it's over she's through."

"It may last longer than you think."

"Will you do what I ask you to do? Will you get on it right now?"

"You can depend on me."

They looked silently at each other, and Patrice seemed to be weighing Reboussin's dependability. "I'm sure I can," Patrice said.

"But as I've been trying to tell you," Reboussin said, "the situation could take a better turn than you expect. Nordling told us that Von Choltitz wants a general armistice and will ruthlessly suppress the insurrection and bomb the city if we refuse. The Germans obviously don't want to fight and won't unless we force them to. We agreed that the truce will be announced today to the population by armed F.F.I.s wearing arm bands. They'll do it in police cars mounted with loudspeakers, and each of the cars will be followed by an auto filled with German officers. It means Von Choltitz recognizes us as a regular army. We wrote the announcement ourselves."

Reboussin handed Patrice a sheet of yellow paper. Patrice read:

> Because of the promise made by the German Command not to attack public buildings occupied by French patriots and to treat prisoners in conformity with the laws of war, the Provisional Government of the Republic, the National Council of Resistance and the Parisian Committee of Liberation ask you to suspend fire against the Germans until the promised evacuation of Paris.

"The communists won't buy it," Patrice said.

Reboussin shrugged. "We'll face that when it comes."

†

THE communists did not buy it, and Patrice and Reboussin had to face that fact even sooner than they had anticipated.

Mazaud was accompanied by two other communist leaders when he charged into Patrice's office in a state of high fury. They clustered around Patrice's desk at the far end of the room, all of them standing, and Mazaud opened the talk by shouting and shaking his fist at Patrice and Reboussin. His shirt open at the neck, his face drawn and very pale, his eyes deep-set and tired, his lips tight, Patrice faced Mazaud. He looked, and indeed felt, cornered. Mazaud pounded away at them. He stood there, deep-chested, broad-backed and indignant. The veins stood out on his forehead, and his clenched fists made the veins stand out on his thick forearms, bare below the rolled-up shirt sleeves. When Mazaud stopped shouting the room became so suddenly quiet that the tension redoubled.

"We had no alternative," Patrice said quietly. "We had to accept the truce or be slaughtered."

"You should have evacuated the Prefecture!" Mazaud cried. "Since when do you abandon an insurrection because one building is untenable?"

"We didn't abandon it," Reboussin said. "We insured the insurrection with the truce, which permits us to hold what we've taken. It's a victory. The Germans admit it."

"As long as the Germans are here," Mazaud shouted, "we've won no victory!" His face was red and he shook his fist. "You have nothing to be proud of. You don't start an insurrection and then stop it like a parliamentary debate. You're breaking its back! Men have been hanged for less!"

"It had to be done," Patrice insisted stubbornly. "We had no choice."

"You had a choice of fighting the Germans or fighting us," Mazaud cried. "Yesterday you took the Prefecture without orders or letting anybody know. Today you run up the white flag. What's happened to you in twenty-four hours? You're not fighting an insurrection. You're conducting a political campaign! Every one of your acts is directed against us. It won't work. There's not going to be a truce. You've capitulated on one front to fight on another. We're going to fight on both."

Mazaud turned abruptly and, followed by the other two communists, strode from the room. Reboussin ran after them. Wearily, Patrice sank into the chair at his desk. It had happened just as he had known it would happen. The truce was condemned. The communists would kill it. The only question was when. Would it survive the day? Not if the communists could help it. What chance then did he have to do anything for Danielle? He needed at least twenty-four hours, probably forty-eight. Patrice sat there, hunched over his thoughts, his sunken, anguished eyes staring out of the dark frame of his unshaven face. He had not budged when Reboussin returned half an hour later.

"Impossible to do a thing with them," Reboussin snapped as soon as he walked into the office. He was irritated after a futile session, during which he was showered with insults and from which he had emerged with no more for his pains than a thorough drenching. "Talk about closed minds—theirs are hermetically sealed."

He sat down glumly opposite Patrice. They looked at each other, each depressed for his own reasons, then looked unhappily way.

"I could have told you that before you took off after them," Patrice muttered.

Reboussin shrugged. "I know," he said.

"How long do you think we can hold them off?"

"We won't be able to end the truce until we have a full-fledged meeting and we won't be able to get the members of the various committees together until at least tomorrow."

"But the communists will probably keep right on fighting."

"That won't end the truce. Not as long as the Germans want it— and they want it. It doesn't make any difference how much shooting there is, we're bound to have a truce—for what it's worth—for another day and a half anyway."

"That might be time enough to get Danielle sprung."

"I'm going to see about that right now," Reboussin said.

†

IT WAS a bad day for Patrice. After thinking he had saved Danielle the previous evening, he realized he had lost her. He also knew he had lost what he had won in the resistance. But winning his reputation as a resistance leader had taken four years, and losing it had taken only the time to say, "I've changed my mind. I vote for the truce."

It was a bitter thought, and Patrice put it out of his mind. It was much harder to put Danielle out of mind, but circumstances helped. Discussions, conferences, arguments, compromises and renewed discussions followed each other all day. The work absorbed Patrice's energies and left him frustrated. It was a day of heartbreaking confusion.

When the truce was announced early in the afternoon, Parisians thought the shooting was over, and spontaneous celebrations broke out throughout the city; French flags sang from windows and balconies;

in outlying quarters men and women danced to the music of accordions as if it were Bastille Day.

But not for long.

No sooner was the truce announced than the fighting, if ever it had stopped, began all over again. The Germans did not attack any public buildings; to this extent they observed the truce. Instead, they concentrated their fire on the streets. Meanwhile, with unity imperative, the resistance was split. Mazaud kept his word: the communists, as well as other resistance groups, continued to fight, and contradictory directives flowed into the streets. First came the command "Cease fire!" Then came the order "Hit them wherever you find them!" The resistance had turned into a two-headed monster. One shouted, "Let the Germans evacuate the city!" The other screamed, "Not one Boche must leave the Paris region alive!" One part of the resistance fought on; the other held its fire. As the confusion rose to terrifying proportions, street skirmishes increased, and the position of the resistance degenerated hourly.

Through it all, large numbers of Parisians, presented with a hot and sunny August Sunday, proceeded to put it to use with customary insouciance. They could not leave the city, but the Seine, with its scattered strips of grassy bank, was at their feet. By midday bathers lounged on the river's edge, splashed in the tepid waters and floated under the cloudless sky on pneumatic mattresses. Here and there men in shirt sleeves, protected from the sun by tricornered hats made of old newspapers, dangled lines into the philosophical old river in a tireless effort to catch the world's cleverest fish. The sporadic crackle of firearms seemed to offend no one.

†

PATRICE worked on in the Prefecture, which was under strict orders not to fire unless attacked. In the middle of the afternoon Reboussin came in to see him. As soon as Patrice saw his solemn face he knew the news was bad.

"Let's have it straight," Patrice said.

"It's not conclusive," Reboussin replied, "but it doesn't look exactly promising for Danielle. I had a call from Nordling's office. The Germans are trying to locate her, but they haven't been able to, not yet. My impression is that they're telling the truth."

"What makes you think so?"

"For one thing, I can't figure out any reason why they shouldn't. For another, they forwarded this information on their own initiative, before they had word of our pressure to do something about it. Whatever we think of them, there is a difference between the German army and the Gestapo. I very much doubt that the army is doublecrossing us on a matter like this one. All Danielle is to them is a name on a list. But they were supposed to produce her and they haven't, and now they're trying to tell us in their punctilious German way that it isn't their fault. It probably isn't."

Patrice looked haggard. "We can't assume that, not yet, not as a working principle."

"You needn't worry about that," Reboussin hastened to assure Patrice. "I'll be making things hum between here and the Swedish Consulate and between the Swedish Consulate and the Meurice. But between you and me, I just wanted to say what I really think."

Patrice said nothing.

"We ought to know something by tonight," Reboussin said. "If she's within reaching distance, the army ought to find her, and if they find her, she'll be delivered to us."

Reboussin was whistling in the dark for Patrice's benefit, but Patrice scarcely heard him.

"Where do you suppose she is?" Patrice said, more to himself than to Reboussin. "Where in the world do you suppose she can be?"

†

KLAUS was convinced that Danielle had murdered Adrien, but, paradoxically, that was not enough to convince him to hold onto her. Klaus was no fanatic. God, country, the human condition, even the Gestapo, were essentially matters of indifference to him. Like most men, he was not one to linger over the principles of his behavior. But he resolutely, if unconsciously, operated on the principle that a man's highest cause was his own interest. It was of his own interest that Klaus thought deeply and intensely on his ride from the Meurice to the villa in St. Cloud to pick up Danielle.

Klaus did not like, any more than any other man, to be caught in the middle between the Wehrmacht and the Gestapo. He did not doubt that with the agreement to exchange prisoners a condition of the truce and the truce an instrument of German policy, it made more sense to release Danielle than to hold her. He had kind rather than cruel instincts, and although Danielle had caused him incalculable difficulties, he bore no animosity toward her. In fact, he rather liked her, though his sense of sympathy for Danielle never came to the surface of his thoughts. His feelings were indeed such that as a matter of simple sentiment he would have been happy to release Danielle and see her go off a free woman. But Klaus was not involved in any matter of simple sentiment and he was working for the German secret police, not for the German army. He quickly decided that his Gestapo superiors in Berlin were more likely to be pleased with him if he held Danielle than if he let her go.

The decisive solution was to ship Danielle straight off to Germany. That was what Klaus instantly decided to do. But Klaus was far from a decisive man. He had no sooner made his decision than he began having second thoughts. He was a man for whom complicated problems defied simple solutions. Before long he had found a way to hedge his decision. He would send Danielle to Germany, he thought, but first he would wait for the truce situation to be clarified. There was no point in taking inordinate risks. Danielle had already caused him trouble enough. If the army insisted that her release was essential to German policy in Paris, then he would have her on hand to turn over. Meanwhile, the army knew she was at the Gestapo villa in St. Cloud. To be certain that the army did not simply remove Danielle without bothering to get prior approval, he would transfer her to a place of safekeeping. He knew of just the place—on the Boulevard Suchet at the edge of the Bois de Boulogne.

Minutes after he arrived at the villa in St. Cloud the arrangements were made for Danielle to be moved into the villa on the Boulevard Suchet. The move was made without a hitch. Klaus did not bother to go back to the Meurice that night. He decided, in view of events, to forego the Wehrmacht's hospitality.

That night he slept badly. He was worried. When he awoke Sunday morning from a fitful sleep he was still worried. What measures, he wondered, would the army take against him? He felt they could do nothing, but they had an insurrection to hold as a weapon over his head. He felt that anything was possible and spent a large part of the morning trying to figure out as many eventualities as he could and what he would do if he were faced with any of them. Regretfully, he had to admit to himself that it no longer made sense to press Danielle for information. With the insurrection on, information about her fellow terrorists could lead to little of any value to the Gestapo or the army. But that situation would change once the insurrection was crushed. Immediately after lunch he went to see his prisoner.

Danielle had been put in a tiny room on the top floor. It had obviously been intended to serve as a maid's room and barely had space for a narrow, iron bed, a bureau and straight-backed chair. The window, high above a garden enclosed by a stone wall, was barred. In a corner of the room was a sink with running water.

"I trust you have everything you need here," Klaus said with heavy irony as he stepped into the room. He gave the impression of being in a genial mood. "You must really forgive us if we keep a couple of men outside your door. They're placed there for your convenience—and ours."

Danielle was standing beside the bed. She looked paler and sleeker than she had a day before. Her eyes were calm and grave. She had had time to think about her predicament and had decided that the Gestapo knew less about her than they pretended, or they would have gone through with their threats of the previous day. Overnight she had decided to take a more aggressive stand. It might work, she thought, and if it did not, she would still be no worse off than if she tried nothing.

"Don't you think the joke has become a little stale?" she asked. Then she mustered an edge of indignation as Klaus stared at her, seemingly stunned. "How long is this comedy going to continue?" she demanded.

She did not like the way Klaus smiled as he sat on the chair.

"You told me yesterday, he said, "that you were not a terrorist. Is that right?"

Danielle nodded. "That's right."

"You also said you knew nobody in the resistance. That's correct, isn't it?"

"It is."

"Did you know that an insurrection broke out yesterday in Paris?"

Her heart leaped. "You ought to know that I haven't exactly been reading the papers or listening to the radio since you arrested me."

"Well, an insurrection did break out in the morning."

Danielle tried to keep the emotion hidden behind her eyes as she realized that since the revolt broke in the morning, Patrice must have started it according to plan at the Prefecture.

"And last night there was some question of an exchange of prisoners."

Again her heart leaped. She was going to be exchanged. She would be free. This time she felt she must have given herself away, but Klaus gave no sign that he had seen any reaction. She was glad of that, because an instant after her hopes had risen they sank. It's a trick, she thought. An exchange is inconceivable.

Klaus was looking at her tranquilly. "Your name was on the list submitted to the Wehrmacht," he said, just as she knew he would. He waited a moment, but Danielle said nothing. "Well, aren't you pleased?" Klaus demanded. "Your friends haven't forgotten you. They think so much of you that they put you on their list. Only one thing puzzles me." He paused and looked at her again with an expression of pitying amusement. "If you were never in the resistance and you know nobody in the resistance, how does it happen that the resistance puts your name high on its list of prisoners to be exchanged?"

"It can't be true," Danielle protested. "It's impossible. I know nobody in the resistance and nobody in the resistance knows me."

Klaus rose from the chair while Danielle was speaking. He was at the door as she finished. He shook his head sadly. "This is no trick, believe me," he said. "Your name was on the list. You mustn't blame them, of course. They were trying to help you. But I think you ought to have a better answer than the one I just heard when we have our next chat. It won't be as brief as this one."

Without waiting for her to answer, Klaus stepped out and shut the door. That will give her something to think about, he thought. But his smile faded as he set out for the Meurice to learn just how important the army felt the truce to be and just how important his prisoner was considered in the army's scheme of things. His tactic, he thought, must be delay. He was sure that the truce could not last. If he could only hold onto Danielle another day or two, he felt certain that the army would not care how long he held her. He thought he knew just how to handle that general now. He would refer him to Berlin. By the time a reply came through, the truce would be broken.

†

It was late in the afternoon before the doctor who was to transport Mignot to the front phoned Patrice. He drove to the Prefecture immediately, full of enthusiasm and excuses.

"If I had only known," he said as Patrice introduced him to Mignot. "I would have gotten a replacement and been here earlier. It was just a delivery, a slow one."

"Well, now you've got a whole city to deliver," Mignot said, and grinned. "But we'll have to speed this one up."

The doctor smiled good-humoredly. He was an energetic, youngish-looking man in his early fifties, still trim despite a thickening waistline and graying hair. He wore large, horn-rimmed glasses.

Patrice, sober and unsmiling, handed Mignot his credentials and a letter addressed to the General Commanding the Allied Armies in France, appealing for troops. "You're our ambassador," he told Mignot. "After you get through the lines go right to the American commander. Explain what's happening in Paris. If anything goes wrong, tell him you want to see Leclerc. Leclerc will know what to do. But hurry. Every hour counts."

Patrice waved them off.

"Which way?" Mignot asked as they settled into the doctor's Peugeot.

He suddenly realized he had no idea where the front was.

"Leave that to me," the doctor said, stepping on the accelerator. "A colleague of mine drove to Neauphle-le-Château last night to see a patient and found the town liberated by the Americans. We'll get to them by the same route he did."

They said nothing as the little car darted through the sun-filled gorges of Paris, but they swelled with pride and excitement, each feeling through speechless communion what the other thought—the destiny of Paris lay in their hands.

They arrived quickly at the Porte d'Orléans, where they were stopped by a detachment of F.F.I.s holding the gate of the city. After showing their papers they were allowed to continue. They sped through the southern suburbs, then turned right, taking the road to Versailles. Not a car was in sight. For miles the thin strip of road unraveled desolate before them, winding between flat fields and dusty, deserted towns. The farther they advanced the more they feared the Germans would be suspicious and not let them approach the front.

Just beyond Buc they came upon a long column of German tractors hauling big guns that was stopped on the side of the road. Some German officers were gathered near the lead tractor. The doctor accelerated, but, looking behind through the mirror, he saw it had been unnecessary. The officers had not even noticed them.

At Versailles the doctor drove into a garage in a narrow street near the château. It was a clandestine depot of the resistance. He filled the tank with gasoline and drove off.

Leaving Versailles, the car was stopped by a German road block. The doctor's papers were legitimate enough for the officer who examined them and he waved the doctor on. Going into Saint-Cyr, they went through the same routine at another road block.

The gashed, disemboweled buildings of Saint-Cyr standing stark against the tender sky had no effect on Mignot or the doctor; riding through the ruins of the bombed-out town, they were much closer to the Americans, and for all the trouble they had met they might have been out for a peacetime Sunday spin without the hindrance of peacetime Sunday traffic. It began to look, Mignot thought, as if they would slip by the Germans with the ease of a couple of haloed angels flying past the hosts of winged concierges guarding the gates of paradise. And if what the doctor's colleague had said were true, there was no front in this sector; they would just drive smack into the arms of the Americans. Mignot lit a fresh cigarette and grinned happily at the doctor; the doctor, glancing at Mignot from behind his shell-rimmed glasses, grinned back.

Beyond Saint-Cyr, however, the air of Sunday tranquility evaporated. They saw no more civilians. German infantrymen, rivulets of dusty sweat running down their sunburned faces, trudged along the side of the road. They did not even glance at the little Peugeot as it scooted past them. Farther on, traffic was dense, with a convoy of trucks and a few tanks grinding slowly ahead in a long line. The Peugeot weaved in and out and finally shot through the choking dust into the clear.

Mignot heaved a sigh. "Funny," he said. "Back a way there's peace. Move up a little and you're in the middle of a war."

"Doesn't look so good any more," the doctor said. "The front must be up ahead."

A minute later the Peugeot rolled to a stop before a road block guarded by two tanks and a dozen infantrymen. A major, obviously astonished to see a civilian car, came up to the Peugeot.

The doctor pulled out his papers. "I'm a doctor," he announced in fluent German. "It's urgent that I get through for an emergency case."

The major smiled patronizingly, not even looking at the papers. "All the roads in this sector are cut or mined and the bridges are blown," he said. "You'll have to go back."

The major's attitude admitted no discussion and the doctor turned around. He swore as only a graduate of the Paris School of Medicine can swear, and Mignot, his face drooping as dismally as the cigarette butt dangling from his lips, looked as if he had just heard himself condemned to celibacy for life.

"Twenty-four hours ago there was nothing here," the doctor grumbled. "Now the Germans have an organized line of defense that probably covers the whole sector."

"Maybe I can walk through," Mignot offered without much conviction.

"And maybe you'll walk right into their arms."

They turned off to the left on a road that doubled back toward the west, but presently they were stopped by a barricade of trees flung across the road. The doctor stepped into a house by the road to see the officer in command. He was a pleasant young lieutenant who looked bored as he listened to the doctor's story.

"If you want to risk it, go ahead," he said, with a weary smile. "It's no affair of mine. But watch out for the mines. Stick to the middle of the road and keep your eyes open. A bit ahead is our advance post. After that you'll be in no man's land."

The doctor raced back to the car. Some soldiers pulled aside the trees, and the Peugeot spurted ahead.

"We made it!" the doctor chortled exultantly.

"What did you do?" Mignot laughed. "Feed him hypnotic pills?"

"Didn't have to. He was just a nice kid. There are probably not more than half a dozen like him in the whole army. —Well, we're only eight kilometers from Neauphle-le-Château and the Americans."

They were excited now and impatient, and they leaned forward in their seats, the doctor hunched over the steering wheel, as if that would get them there faster. He kept the Peugeot in the dead center of the road and nursed the bouncing little car along as fast as it would go. Just before a turn in the road a soldier, waving his rifle like a red flag, signaled them to stop. It was the advance post. It consisted of a private and noncom dug in between two birch trees and hidden behind a rock. They must have been the loneliest men in the German army.

The doctor spun out his explanation once again, remaining behind the wheel, with the motor running. The private, a squat middle-aged man with a hopelessly anonymous face, shrugged indifferently; so far as he was concerned the doctor could go where he pleased. But the noncom stepped in. He was much younger than the private, a big choleric man with a ruddy, heavy-featured face and vapid blue eyes like windowpanes opening on a void. At the small outpost he was authority. He spoke gruffly to the doctor, making imperious gestures that he turn back.

"What's he saying?" Mignot demanded impatiently.

"He says his orders are to let nobody pass."

Mignot was indignant. "But his boss, the lieutenant, said it was okay. Tell him."

"I told him. He won't budge."

Once again the doctor turned his shell-rimmed glasses on the light-blue windowpanes. He had the uneasy sensation that he was gazing on the arid landscape of the noncom's mind. The doctor's insistence stirred the noncom's choler. The hulking soldier shouted, waved his arms and shook his rifle at the doctor. Standing under the impersonal sky on the desolate country road so far from home, the noncom poured over the doctor's head his long-hoarded bitterness at living in a hole and being shot at. For a moment the doctor toyed with the idea of scooting ahead and forcing his way through. But he could not assume that both the Germans were such bad marksmen as that.

Frustrated and discouraged, he turned the car around. Neither he nor Mignot spoke for a long time. Mignot soon recovered his sense of detachment and thought that the lieutenant, who had permitted them to cross the lines, was unquestionably intelligent, while the noncom, who had stopped them, was obviously stupid; nevertheless, the lieutenant had been wrong and the noncom right. It was, of course, all a matter of chance, he told himself; neither had known what he was doing.

They drove in a northerly direction until shortly before nine o'clock, the hour of curfew, when they slipped into a village where they knew nobody and had no information about the local resistance organizations. They decided to seek out the village gendarmes, since many of them were sympathetic to the resistance. The streets were deserted, but finally they came upon an old woman who told them there were no gendarmes in the village and that the mayor was the only official around; he was at his farm, a couple of kilometers away. Most incumbent mayors were Vichyites, so they questioned the old woman discreetly on the mayor's views.

"He's certainly not for Pétain," she said.

It was after nine when they arrived at the mayor's farm. The mayor, a fat man with a highly polished bald head and a small black mustache, listened to the doctor's story about the emergency case beyond the lines and appeared to believe it.

"I'll leave my car here," the doctor said, "if you can get us a guide to cross the fields.' '

"It's out of the question tonight," the mayor said in a rich peasant accent that smelled of black upturned earth. "The German lines are just outside the door. There's a Boche every few meters as far as you can see from the roof of the house." He shook his head and sighed. "Liberty is a fine thing, but who can afford to be liberated? The battle is going to be right on our doorstep. Those who have fled have had their houses pillaged by the Boches. Those who remain are forbidden to work in the fields. The crop will be lost. They're no good, these Boches. They're the SS. They've taken everything they could find that's on wheels—autos, motorcycles, even wagons. Next they'll be after our wheelbarrows. Ah, we'll be glad when the Americans get here, but if we're still in our skins that's all we'll have to be thankful for."

"And for being free," the doctor said.

"And for being free," the mayor echoed, mopping his glistening bald head.

What a pig, Mignot was thinking. He prefers to risk his life by staying here rather than take a chance on losing his sheets and silverware. He regarded the perspiring mayor with a neutral expression. He did not trust him and saw that the doctor did not either.

Clearly, they could go no farther that night. The mayor insisted that the doctor sleep at his farm; since there was but one spare bed, he took Mignot to the house of a neighbor. The door was opened by a handsome, full-breasted peasant woman in her late thirties, who had been in bed when they called; all she wore was a faded cotton robe, and her light brown hair was done up for the night in two long braids that twisted down her shoulders and rested on the swell of her breasts. One look was enough for Mignot; all thought of his mission was submerged by the new mission he set himself. After the mayor explained why they had come he left, and the woman led Mignot into the house.

"You must be hungry," she said, showing him to the kitchen.

"Thirsty, too," Mignot said as he sat down at the table in the middle of the room.

She smiled at him, crinkly little wrinkles forming around her fine gray eyes, which were breath-takingly light against a face bronzed copper-dark by the sun and the wind in the fields. He felt at home and communicated his sense of ease to her. He felt hungry, too, and ate the good, coarse homemade bread and slabs of cheese she served in big mouthfuls. She lit a candle against the deepening night and, plunking a bottle of red wine on the table, sat by him just inside the circle of light.

"To drink," she said, uncorking the bottle, "we have *pinard*."

She rolled the "r" deliciously.

Looking at her curiously, Mignot said, "But you're not French."

"I'm Russian," she replied.

"Ah, the Russians!" Mignot cried, picking up her accent and rolling the "r" on the tip of his tongue. "For them my blood boils like hot borsch."

She laughed. "You are a funny one," she said simply; then added, "It's the first time I have laughed in such a long time."

"Why?"

She shrugged. "Life is not always for laughter," she murmured. "I was married to a good man, but for four years he is a prisoner."

"Tonight is for laughter," Mignot said. "Don't think of the four years."

"It is lonely here without a man. To you I can say this. You are a stranger and I will never see you again."

"Tonight a man is in the house and you are not alone." Mignot lifted his glass. "Let us drink. To laughter."

She smiled a slow smile, her gray eyes veiled with the obsession of her loneliness and desire, a desire too deep and tormenting for Mignot to understand, and she drank with him.

"You see," he said. "A jokester."

"Who?"

He pointed to the wine. "A comic. It laughs as it slips down your throat."

"It's not the wine. It's you, the comic. I wish I were like you."

"I wish I were you."

Looking pleased, she asked why.

"Because then I'd be able to have me."

She laughed unaffectedly and said, "You are not serious. You mean nothing you say."

"But you understand what I mean."

"Yes," she said in a choked voice.

"And I understand what you mean."

They drained their glasses. Her cheeks burned as she set the glass down again. The gesture tugged her robe free at the bosom. But she was so agitated that she was unaware of it until, glancing up, she caught the direction of Mignot's eyes. Then, with a quick gesture, she drew the robe so tightly that her ripe breast was outlined against the thin cotton.

"No harm," Mignot said.

Her cheeks bloomed, the color blending with her deep bronze, and Mignot saw she was pleased that he desired her.

"You had better get to bed," she said. "It is late."

She lighted the way up the stairs and, his mouth dry, he followed the swaying movement of her hips with yearning intensity. Inside the door of a bedroom, she set down the candle, turned to him and started to say something. But he was already moving toward her and then she was sitting on the bed, struggling a bit, quivering, and he was close and hard beside her.

"But so quickly," she gasped. "I am ashamed."

"You must not be. It's what we want." Then he added disarmingly, "And besides, we will never see each other again."

Her halfhearted resistance subsided. Mignot slipped his hand into her robe and cupped her heavy breast. He heard her sigh a deep, contented sigh and felt her tremble, and working himself out of his clothes and her out of her robe, he lay beside her and felt her crush her urgent body against his own. There was a roaring in his ears. Her sighs now were half moans, and she hugged him tightly, desperately, seeking his mouth with her warm, biting lips. He sank into the pleasure and the sensation without thought, like a rock into the sea, and was swallowed up in the sweet, woman's smell of her arms and breasts and the warmth and pressure of her thighs.

†

MIGNOT had the sensation of rocking from side to side, as if he were in a small boat tossing on a swollen sea. He made an effort to stop the movement and, struggling, opened his eyes. The woman, standing by the bed in her faded robe, stopped shaking him.

"Your friend is waiting for you," she said.

His eyes fuzzy with sleep, Mignot squinted up at her, warmly aware of the compact, swelling roll of her body under the cotton robe. He remembered the whispers and cries, the naked avowals and the prolonged cataclysm of pleasure. Then he recalled the mission, shook the web of sensuality from his mind and was wide awake.

"Tell him I'll only be a minute," he said. "The time to put on my pants."

When Mignot was dressed she was back again, standing just inside the door, soft-eyed and silent. He came up to her and kissed her on the forehead, holding her close to him.

"It was good," he said. "Are you pleased?"

She smiled. Her face was smooth, and her gray eyes serene and marvelously light gazing out of the dark bronze frame of her cheeks.

They kissed, this time on the lips, simply and without passion, but her body was warm and alive against him. It brought back to him the turbulent night and, remembering the violent secret of her, he wanted to stay. But she slipped out of his embrace and looked away with a veiled expression. He knew her desire was the same as his and that nothing could be done about it. Then he was following her down the stairs, and a moment later they were no longer alone. They said good-by like strangers before the doctor, who was impatient to get started, and she thanked him with her eyes. As the car lurched forward he waved to her, but she did not wave back. She stood by the house in the clean light of the early morning and seemed to express everything that needed to be expressed. It was only after they had left the village that Mignot realized he did not know her name.

†

THE Peugeot crawled forward, and Mignot and the doctor quickly agreed it was pointlessly dangerous to try to cross the lines in that region; they decided to move southeast to the Dourdan-Étampes area, where the doctor had numerous contacts with the local resistance. They understood now that their best chance of getting through the German lines was a trustworthy local guide. Once their decision was reached, the car picked up speed. It raced along deserted secondary roads and through the empty streets of sleeping villages. At one point they lost their way and stopped at a crossroad to check the signs. Suddenly a dozen German infantrymen appeared out of the landscape and surrounded the car. One of the soldiers threw his bicycle across the hood, while a giant of an officer rushed at the car, swearing and pointing in the direction the Peugeot faced. Ahead of them Mignot saw two civilian cars creeping forward; on the roof of each car a German soldier lay prone, aiming an automatic weapon at some near-by target.

"Do you want to get killed?" the officer shouted. "The Americans are over there and you're running right into the line of fire. Turn around! Back where you came from! *Nach Paris!*"

The doctor turned around and drove off. He looked ruefully at Mignot. "Too bad," he muttered. "If that Boche hadn't tried to save our lives, we would have stumbled on the Americans."

"Who would have known that was the front?" Mignot said. "It was just wide-open country, with nothing in sight but fields and trees and the sky."

Later in the morning they drove back through the ruins of Saint-Cyr and through Villacoublay, stopped at a clinic, where they saw the head surgeon, a liaison agent of the resistance. The surgeon told them they had come at the right moment: only the previous evening an F.F.I. named Laurent had established contact with the Americans near the village of La Ferté-Alais.

The surgeon took off his white smock, put on a jacket and, getting into the Peugeot with Mignot and the doctor, guided them to a flour mill outside Corbeil where Laurent worked. Laurent, a stocky man whose pleasant face and eyelashes were dusted with a fine layer of flour, listened attentively as the doctor told him about Mignot's mission.

"I'll take you through myself," Laurent said to Mignot. "Not the doctor. No point to that. Just you. We'll ride through in my jalopy like farm workers going to work the fields."

Directed by Laurent, the doctor drove them through a labyrinth of small roads to a shack on the edge of a swamp. Seven or eight young men were lounging in front of the shack, beside which stood a small battered truck of ancient vintage. The truck consisted of a weather-beaten cab high over the motor and a floor of boards behind. Its tires were worn smooth and, with the fenders stripped from the chassis, looked naked.

"This is our little *maquis*," Laurent said, striding to the truck. "Come on," he called to Mignot. "Let's go."

Mignot climbed into the cab beside Laurent, and the ancient motor rasped to life. Looking forlorn, the doctor waved as the truck chugged off, jerking spasmodically; then, catching its stride, it bounced over the bumpy road until the shack, the Peugeot and the men around it were out of sight.

What would have been impossible for the doctor and Mignot, or for anyone who did not know the country, was simple for Laurent. He avoided forward German posts by taking back roads and by-passing villages and hamlets. After twisting back on his own route and circling the area for half an hour. Laurent eased the truck onto a cratered dirt path and jogged grindingly over it for ten minutes in first. He stopped at a farm, where the path opened into a negotiable dirt road.

"We'll find out how we stand here," he muttered, and disappeared into the building.

A few minutes later he returned, looking pleased.

"The last of the advance elements are up ahead a bit," he said, getting into the driver's seat. "Seven men camouflaged in a haystack, and the Americans in the valley a few hundred meters beyond them. Here, have a cigarette. Look relaxed. We're going to breeze right past them."

The truck strained up a slight incline, picking up speed with intolerable slowness. Mignot looked behind and saw only a screen of dust. At the top of the incline the road leveled off and they went somewhat faster. Then they came to a turn and saw a fertile valley spread out below them.

"There they are to the left," Laurent said very low.

A few German soldiers, almost completely hidden from the road by a stack of hay, were gaping at them but gave no sign that they should stop. The truck was on a downgrade now, already past the Germans. Half a minute later the truck jerked to a stop and Mignot leaped out into a group of American GIs. He stared at them delightedly, with a broad foolish grin pasted across his face, and was barely able to resist a deep compulsion to throw his arms about these men in the strange uniform and embrace them. They gazed back at him curiously.

"*Bon Dieu!*" he cried in French. "It's good to see you! We were beginning to wonder in Paris if you were really alive."

He went up to a tall, loose-limbed sergeant, touched his arm, then patted him on the shoulder.

"You're alive all right," Mignot grinned at his uncomprehending audience. He was as close to sheer ecstacy as he ever would be outside a woman's arms.

"The man's nuts," the sergeant said.

A few grunts of agreement came from the circle around the grinning Mignot. He finally realized they didn't understand him and, inspired by the transcendent moment, gave enthusiastic utterance to the first English word that came to mind.

"Good-by!" he cried. "Good-by!"

"Hell, we ain't goin' nowhere," the sergeant said.

He was smiling now and so were the others. Mignot just grinned and grinned, his eyes shining with delight.

"Christ, lookit how happy the poor bastard is to see us," one of the GIs remarked.

"Don't start gettin' proud now 'cause a dumb frog hasn't sense enough to run in another direction when he sees you ugly bastards," the sergeant said. "The guy's nuts, I tell you."

He gazed speculatively at Mignot as the wiry little Frenchman gesticulated and kept repeating the word, "*Officier, officier.*" Finally the sergeant came to a decision.

"All right, men, break it up," he said. "I'm gonna take this boy to see the lootenant. Maybe he talks Kentucky."

The sergeant motioned Mignot to follow him. Laurent called out that he was returning to Corbeil by another road, and Mignot waved good-by and shouted his thanks.

As soon as he saw the lieutenant Mignot handed him the credentials Patrice had typed up in English on Prefecture stationary. The lieutenant, a slender, boyish fellow with rosy cheeks, slick blond hair and a nervous manner, looked up from the credentials and spoke to Mignot in a slow drawl. Mignot visibly had no notion of what the lieutenant was saying.

"No compris, eh?" the lieutenant said.

Mignot looked at him dumbly, while the sergeant stared at the officer with a touch of disdain.

Noting the sergeant's look, the lieutenant snapped at him. "You can hot-ass it back to the platoon now, sergeant. We won't need you any moah."

He watched the sergeant's retreating back with unexpressed thoughts.

"Collins!" he shouted.

A Pfc appeared as if he had sprung out of the ground.

"Take this man back to division," the lieutenant said. "See that he gets to G-2 in a hurry."

The lieutenant handed back Mignot's credentials and managed a grudging smile. Then he turned back to the Pfc and snapped, "And don't goof off like the last time!"

With a sense of elation, Mignot followed the Pfc to a jeep. He was on his way up the line. It was as simple as that. His mission, he felt, was as good as accomplished—if only the truce would hold until the Americans arrived. An edge of nervousness cut his elation.

"Hurry!" he said, with gestures to the driver.

The Pfc shifted into first, and the jeep bounced up onto the road and scooted off toward division.

Mignot did not know it, but he still had quite a way to go before what he knew would reach the ear of an American general named Dwight Eisenhower. It was with the Supreme Commander of Allied Forces in Europe that the decision rested to send or not to send troops to Paris.

†

ALL DAY Sunday until late in the evening Patrice waited anxiously but vainly for word about Danielle. He waited for word about her all through Monday morning, too. None came. By early afternoon he was desperate. In the past twenty-four hours the confusion that had been sown in the resistance by conflicting policies on the truce had lessened. A meeting had been called for the afternoon. It was the first general meeting of resistance leaders since the truce and was bound to be decisive for policy on the insurrection. Patrice had no doubt that the meeting would officially kill the truce, and every time he thought of it his stomach churned sickeningly. When Reboussin appeared in his office shortly before they were to leave for the meeting, Patrice was prepared for the worst.

"Still no news?" he asked before Reboussin had a chance to speak.

"Worse than that," said Reboussin. "I've heard from them. All they say is that the prisoner 'is not locatable in the Paris region.' "

Patrice swore obscenely.

After a silence, Reboussin said, "It's time we left for the meeting," and Patrice rose to go. "If the truce survives this meeting—"

Patrice interrupted. "There's a bigger question. Will the resistance survive?"

"If we give up the truce, we'll be handing that decision over to the Germans."

Patrice did not answer. Morosely, the two men left the Prefecture and started toward the meeting place. They had walked only a short distance when One-paw, a Mauser slapping rhythmically against his hip, crossed their path. The one-legged man recognized Patrice, who had been pointed out to him as the leader of the Prefecture insurrectionists. Without stopping, One-paw growled, "You can do what you like, I'm shooting every German I can put a bullet into." He had heard the truce announced the previous day near his furnished room in the Rue Monge. It had infuriated him. Just when the Boches were beaten, he had thought, they were letting them go. The next moment his mutiny had found its voice. "The hell with the truce!" he had cried. "It ain't even patriotic."

One-paw passed Patrice and Reboussin and moved along the left bank of the Seine on his crutches, dark stains of sweat circling his armpits and perspiration sparkling on his forehead. Ahead of him he saw a man beside a lamppost leaning intently over a fishing line. At that moment a volley of shots cracked the placid afternoon silence and whistled past the one-legged man's ear. One-paw dodged into a doorway, but the man who was fishing did not even turn his head. Holding the rod motionless in one hand, he stepped to the far side of the lamppost, reached around it with his free hand, to which he shifted the still-motionless rod and, withdrawn behind the questionable safety of the lamppost, continued to concentrate on the line dangling into the impenetrable green waters of the Seine. One-paw swore under his breath. "The bastard has got to catch a fish," he thought, "even if he catches some lead with it."

Presently he slipped out of the doorway, swung along to the next corner, turned it and stopped. At the end of the street two German officers, their backs turned, were conversing and smoking cigars. One-paw swung his rifle to position. The shots burst out sharp and quick. Over the sights One-paw saw the officers sprawled on the sidewalk. He leaped toward them. Both were dead. One-paw looked around furtively. Nobody was in sight. A cigar, smoking evenly, lay near one of the bodies. One-paw picked it up and clamped his teeth on the wet end. Quickly he moved away.

He was suddenly exuberant. Seven Boches, he thought. Another five and he would have his count. All was well. The weather was fine; he enjoyed the execution of his self-imposed challenge; he had enough to eat and plenty to drink; wherever he went people admired him; he was, after a fashion, a hero; and he was smoking a really excellent cigar. If he had put it in perspective, One-paw would surely have told himself that these were the most beautiful days he had ever lived or was ever likely to live. He could hardly have desired anything more. The death at his hands of twelve Germans of any age, identity unknown, in the sunlit streets of Paris was One-paw's bid for sublimity. For the music he had produced on it, his stolen accordion was a costly instrument.

That the truce was in a state of most unstable equilibrium was not One-paw's concern, and had it been, he would have tripped over the balance. That was what the communists did later that afternoon. At that time Patrice and Reboussin gathered with the other leaders of the resistance in a small left-bank apartment. The salon, with its worn Louis XVI chairs, was tiny, and the men, many standing, were crushed into the small space for the critical session. When the communists arrived they were so incensed at "the betrayal of the insurrection" that they refused to shake hands with moderate leaders.

The meeting was violent. Quickly, despite the heat, the windows were closed to keep the cries of embittered voices inside the room. The debate went on and on until a decision had to be reached. Neither side had given ground, but the resistance leaders, exhausted by the pressures of the past two days and worn down by the tropical heat, had reached such a point of depleted physical resources that they were ready for any workable agreement. Parodi found the compromise. Although he was worried about the possibility of a catastrophe, he knew that a large part of the resistance demanded that the insurrection continue, and that no matter what the leaders said these elements could not be held back. The truce had to be disclaimed or the resistance would be split and the insurrection would go on anyway. In addition, a political specter haunted De Gaulle's general delegate to metropolitan France—the specter of AMGOT, the American Military Government. To escape the imposition of American rule and give its own direction to France's destiny the resistance had to be firmly entrenched in power and unified when Allied troops arrived. At the same time, Parodi wanted to gain time against the crushing military superiority of the Germans. He agreed to end the truce on condition that the new call to the population to fight would not be given before the following day at four o'clock. The communists agreed, and a proclamation was unanimously voted. It read:

PARISIANS . . .

THE STRUGGLE CONTINUES. IT MUST BE PURSUED UNTIL THE ENEMY IS CHASED FROM THE PARIS REGION.

MORE THAN EVER, ALL IN THE FIGHT!

CUT DOWN THE TREES, DIG ANTI-TANK DITCHES, RAISE THE
BARRICADES!
A CONQUERING PEOPLE WILL RECEIVE THE ALLIES.

The unity of the resistance was restored. The menace to the city
was greater than ever. When Patrice left the meeting he was worried
and harassed. The consequences of the decision were unpredictable.
There was much to do, people to see, conferences to attend, and on his
way back to the Prefecture Patrice unhappily felt that everything
that was important to him was slipping from his grasp. No more than
three days ago he had had an assignation with Danielle. It was a love
affair that was fated to die before it even bloomed. Only forty-eight
hours ago the entire insurrection, like a giant pyramid turned upside
down, rested precariously on his decision. He had undone everything
with one word, by agreeing to the truce. He knew that that act had
convinced many of his comrades that he had betrayed the insurrection. It was the ultimate and unredeemable sin. Patrice knew how they
felt because he felt the same way. But how could he convince them
that he had not betrayed? He himself was no longer entirely sure, if he
ever had been, of the balance of factors that had led so swiftly to his
decision. Would he have reached the same decision if he had thought
the Prefecture and the insurrection itself defensible, not completely
hopeless? He did not think so. But he did not think, either, that he
would have reached the same decision if Danielle had never been taken
prisoner. That was the heart of the matter and he had no illusions as
to what it meant. Nor did he have any illusions that in war or politics
love could be an excuse for betrayal. In 1944 that was absurd—even in
Paris. His friends, if he still had any, might regretfully say that he
had cracked, and Patrice knew how close to cracking he had been. It
was no crime, he thought, and his anger rose to a slow boil. But he told
himself again, as he had a thousand times since that moment of decision, that he did not regret what he had chosen to do. At the same time,
he had a harrowing realization that a man's entire life could be shat-
tered by what he did in one compelling instant.

He realized suddenly and acutely that Danielle was irretrievably
gone, that nothing he could do would bring her back, and the pain of
it was like a dagger thrust in his heart. He told himself that he must
phone De Maurain as soon as he got to the Prefecture and tell him the
news. Then, Patrice thought, he must concentrate on his work and not
think of Danielle. Thinking of her could not help now. But he thought

of her for a while anyway, of her quick, searching look and of how firm yet gentle she could be. He thought that she was a woman, with a woman's beauty and a woman's infinite, irrational rightness for a man, and again the pain hit him.

Presently, however, his thoughts swung back to the insurrection. It was not surprising, he thought, that the control he had exercised at the outset had gone back to those from whom he had usurped it. His power at the Prefecture was still considerable, but now once again the political balance among the parties that formed the resistance determined military decisions. Patrice knew, however, that he might still be the factor, through Mignot, to alter the course of the uprising and propel it to victory. He was now certain that the Americans, and only the Americans, could save Paris.

He was less sure, on the other hand, that his policy to force the insurrection by taking the Prefecture had been correct. The occupation of the Prefecture had thus far in a large sense defined the character of the insurrection; it was also what made it vulnerable. The insurrection—any insurrection—in his opinion, stood or fell on a policy of action; for that reason, deep down, he had reservations about the truce. But the Prefecture could not be held against the superior German force and therefore should never have been taken. It was a mistake that the communists, more experienced in the theory and practice of insurrections, had not made. Their policy was guerrilla warfare. They struck and dispersed. The quicksilver policy—when the enemy reached out, he could grab nothing; it slipped between his fingers.

Patrice saw now that because of the division among the resistance leaders and what he had done there were really two insurrections in Paris: the one at the Prefecture and the one in the streets. In a sense there were thirty or forty, for despite the resistance command structure, control over the uprising in the streets was negligible. Liaison was uncertain; every strong man with initiative ruled his fief of square blocks. The result was a concentrated dose of anarchy.

By far the most depressing part of the picture for Patrice was its hopelessness. The disproportion of forces was too great, the menace to the Prefecture too immediate. The following afternoon the resistance would invite the fatal attack when it proclaimed the end of the truce.

Tormented with the loss of Danielle and depressed by his reflections about the insurrection, Patrice arrived at the Prefecture. One question persistently returned to his mind, the one really important question: Had Mignot reached the Americans and persuaded them to march on Paris? The fate of the city and of the resistance hung on the answer.

†

MIGNOT set off in the jeep with the Pfc late in the afternoon and arrived before long in the village where divisional headquarters had been established. The G-2 was a hard-bitten young major. After listening to Mignot through an interpreter for a few minutes, he sat back, tilting his chair on two legs.

"This isn't our baby," he said. "It's for Army."

He called in a lieutenant, typed a note and handed it to the officer. "He's from the resistance in Paris," he said, nodding at Mignot. "Take him to Army G-3, Lieutenant Colonel Powell, with this message. I'll phone ahead."

"Aye, aye, sir," the lieutenant said blithely.

He did not conceal his delight at getting away from division for a few hours. The major stopped him at the door.

"You deliver your package, lieutenant, and you return to division," the major said.

"Of course," the lieutenant said, looking serious.

The major grunted. Mignot sensed that they were not much concerned about Paris. It made little difference. The interpreter had told Mignot he was on his way to Army headquarters. That was good enough.

The jeep driver this time was a corporal. Mignot sat beside him and the lieutenant sat behind. They rode swiftly over country roads in the blue summer dusk, and Mignot breathed the heady air of success. He remembered the ride through Paris with Patrice and Gaudin the night they had raided the garage for arms. It had been good, he thought, but nothing at all compared to this.

They passed long convoys moving up to the front. Tanks and half tracks, trucks loaded with troops and matériel rumbled in an interminable line past Mignot's admiring eyes. He glanced at the corporal and lieutenant, but they seemed to notice nothing. Mignot swelled with pride. This was the power that *he* was bringing to Paris; these were the men, with their tanks and guns, who would turn the faltering insurrection into the liberation of his city. He breathed deeply of the sweet country air and rehearsed what he would say to the Army authorities.

Night had fallen when they reached Courville, headquarters of the U.S. Third Army. Mignot was taken directly to Lieutenant Colonel Powell, showed him his credentials and Patrice's letter, then described the situation in Paris, emphasizing the urgent need of aid. When Mignot finished, the colonel, displaying a thorough knowledge of the resistance, questioned him in great detail. At one-thirty the colonel decided the news was important enough to warrant awakening General George Patton so that the commander of the Third Army could take whatever action he thought necessary.

A few minutes later Mignot was brought before Patton. Through an interpreter the burly American general listened attentively to the wiry little Frenchman. As he spoke, Mignot had the feeling that this was the pay-off; this was the man who could give the order that would save everything. Mignot spoke better than he ever had in his life; his simple words carried the impact of truth, and, reading Patton's ruddy face, he saw that the general was catching their full force.

The room was deathly still when Mignot stopped talking. Patton seemed deep in thought. Then he sighed and shook his head. "It can't be done," he said. "Our plans have been made, orders given. These operations are too vast to be modified in the middle of our advance across Europe." He shook his head again. "No, it's too late. Paris is an incident, a detail. . . ."

The words fell upon Mignot like the blow of an ax. Paris a detail? Paris was the world. Couldn't the Americans understand that? He was too stunned to speak. He listened in a daze as Patton explained that the American objective was Berlin and the destruction of the German army. The Americans were by-passing Paris; it did not constitute a military objective and therefore its immediate capture had no strategic value. On the contrary, the liberation of Paris would be a burden; men, machines, gasoline would have to be diverted from supplying the front to run food into the city for its immense population. It was too bad, since a question of humanity and sentiment was involved, but that had to be balanced against the bigger question of the war as a whole. The resistance should not have launched the insurrection without orders from Allied headquarters. Under the circumstances the Third Army could do nothing.

Through his disappointment Mignot understood that Patton's decision was categorical and that nothing he could say would alter it. The affair was too big; the machinery was in motion; masses of men and machines were plunging after an objective—a quick, sweeping victory—and Paris had not been included in the plan. He felt, listening to Patton, that there was no more chance of changing the direction of any part of the Allied war machine than there was of repairing a faulty piston with a motor roaring at full speed. Then he remembered Patrice's instructions.

"If your plans can't be changed," he said. "I'll have to get back to Paris. But first, I'd like to see General Leclerc."

"I don't know where Leclerc is," Patton replied. "His division isn't part of my army." After a moment's thought he added, "Wait a minute. I'll make a phone call."

Patton strode out. A few minutes later he was back.

"If you're not too tired," he said, "you can leave right now for a long ride. You know the town of Laval?"

"Hope it's prettier than the politician of the same name."

Patton smiled. "It is. Army Group is there now. I'll give you a fast car, a good driver and a major for a chaperon, and you'll be there first thing in the morning. You'll see General Sibert when you arrive; he's General Bradley's chief of staff. Sibert will take care of you. Now, how about one for the road?"

The general uncorked a bottle of champagne. The pop of the cork was loud, but to Mignot it sounded hollow; he had heard the sound on more festive occasions. They clicked glasses.

"To victory," the general said.

"And Paris."

The wine was cold and dry. It was edged with a slightly fruity flavor and Mignot liked it. But as he drank he was thinking that victory was going to sound as hollow as the pop of the cork if Paris went under. What kind of a victory would it be for Parisians if Paris were destroyed? His farewell to Patton was reserved. Mignot was morosely aware that he had failed.

Shortly afterward he sat with an American major in the back of a staff car that sped through the soft August moonlight toward Army Group. It was an unhappy drive for Mignot. He had visions of a new Warsaw in Paris, and all along the moonlit road the specter of the city's destruction hovered over him.

†

THE specters that haunted Klaus were of a different kind, but to him, too, they held out the prospect of destruction. Sunday had been a bad day. Monday was worse. On Sunday he had waged his battle with the general, pitting the Gestapo against the Wehrmacht. The battle had continued, on and off, all day. "I will only give my prisoner up on the authority of my superiors in Berlin," he had insisted. Late in the evening he knew he had won—at least for the time being. But by Monday noon the victory seemed hollow. It was the truce that upset him. If it lasted too long, his temporary victory would be turned into a permanent defeat. This constant, gnawing fear was aggravated by the disquieting gossip at headquarters. Why should Von Choltitz deal with the terrorists when he could exterminate them? The explanation that his mission was to keep Paris open for the troops retreating from Normandy worried Klaus. It seemed to mean that once the troops passed east of Paris, the French capital would be abandoned. Staff officers assured him he was wrong. All the bridges over the Seine except those in Paris were down, and everything the Germans had to the west had to pass through Paris. Two to four fully equipped combat divisions would be coming through in the next few days. They would reinforce the garrison and crush the uprising; then they would make a stand in front of Paris. There was some hope in this, Klaus felt, but he was also concerned about the speed of the American advances. He knew the Americans were driving to encircle Paris and not to attack it head on; and he realized that if the maneuver were successful, the garrison would have to flee precipitately or be doomed. That meant him. It would be a disaster in more ways than one.

During the morning Klaus navigated between the Meurice, where he slept, and the Boulevard Suchet, where he had too little time to busy himself with Danielle. Holding onto her was a matter of prime importance, but doing anything about her for the time being was only of secondary concern. He was at the Meurice in the early afternoon when he thought of Suzanne. I'm going to have to leave without her, he told himself. I ought to see her and tell her. But he lacked the courage to do it. Nonetheless, Klaus kept toying with the idea, though he knew he would never go through with it, when quite suddenly another idea shot into his mind. "Of course," he said aloud, "Why didn't I think of it before?" The next instant he had the telephone receiver in his hand and was jangling at the instrument to get the operator's attention.

The telephone had hardly begun ringing when Suzanne lifted the receiver off the hook. It was Klaus. She had done well to wait, then, she thought. Her throat was thick with emotion. The phone call Saturday night when he had told her to be patient and the strange, guilty sound of his voice had frightened her. Patience! The one thing she had no capacity for. Then the silence all day Sunday. She had been mad to think he had left Paris. She gripped the receiver and crouched over his voice, feeling protective and warm and wildly happy.

"Let's make it the Concorde bridge," he said. "I'm at the Meurice, but you won't be able to get through. We've closed off the Rue de Rivoli and the Tuileries."

"I'll be there right away."

She was alive again as she hung up the receiver, and the dead hours of hopeless waiting disappeared behind her in the empty apartment when she slammed the door and hurried into the street.

From far off the dull sound of an explosion floated lazily through the air followed by the quick crackle of machine-gun fire. Suzanne waited a moment in the doorway until the sounds faded into the silence of the city. The old man who lived next door, his eternal cigar clamped in his teeth, was parading his manicured black poodle at the end of a bright yellow leash. He nodded to her as she passed. At the corner a boy was hawking newspapers. He kept looking around furtively and shouting, "*L'Huma, Franc-Tireur, Combat!*" Suzanne was startled. She stared at the flaming headlines.

PARIS FIGHTS, PARIS LIBERATES SELF

INSURRECTION BRINGS
REPUBLIC TO PARIS

DEATH TO THE BOCHES AND TRAITORS
PARISIANS! RISE AND FIGHT

Suzanne shuddered as she read the last headlines in the Communist party paper. Then she fled. Turning into the quai on the left bank, she ran into a housewife carrying tomatoes in a net bag. She hastened on, passing two old-maidish women dressed in black and wearing white gloves, seemingly on their way to Mass. Suzanne could not understand how people could go about in this normal fashion doing normal things when the times were so abnormal. For the past two days she had not eaten or slept; she had been incapable of doing anything. Every bridge she passed was guarded, some by ragged F.F.I.s, others by German soldiers. Between the bridges sun worshipers, indifferent to machine guns and history, floated across the placid green waters of

over his head, corsair fashion, with the end trailing down his back. This was the frontier beyond which, along the Avenue de l'Opéra, German-occupied Paris began. Patrice cycled along the boulevards to the Madeleine, down the Rue Royale and up the Champs Élysées. He saw only a rare civilian. The sweeping vistas were lined with shuttered shops. It was a dead city spored with the maggots of helmeted figures along its lifeless body; tanks towered here and there like monstrous black insects. Every few blocks Patrice was stopped by a barrier of German troops, frisked and questioned; but each time he was allowed to pass.

He rode into the liberated quarters and circled the city, returning to the Prefecture down the Boulevard St. Michel. The liberated part of Paris impressed him even more deeply than the empty, mechanized horror of the occupied zone: so much of it seemed completely normal. Men sat in the cafés; women were at the windows; children played in the streets. More clearly than ever Patrice realized that only a fraction of the city had been touched by the uprising; only a handful of the population was committed to the battle; and fewer than a dozen men had precipitated Paris, with its millions, into this moment of its destiny. The enormity of what so few could determine for so many staggered him. For the first time he grasped the full consequences of his decision to take the Prefecture. He wished now that he had worked to cut the risks by co-ordinating the uprising with the Allied advance. Coasting down the Boulevard St. Michel, Patrice thought wryly that it was a little late to learn that lesson; he would never have another chance to use it. Nor would he ever forgive himself if the Americans arrived too late.

At the Place St. Michel there were two barricades, one blocking the mouth of the Rue de la Huchette and the other on the terrace of Perigourdine, the fashionable restaurant on the corner of the quai. Patrice approached the Perigourdine breastwork and saw above the green flower boxes that topped it a familiar face.

"Gaudin!" he cried.

They shook hands.

"What happened to Mignot?" Gaudin asked. "He disappeared."

Patrice told him. He was amazed at the change in Gaudin. Gaudin's face was open and bright, the lines horizontal instead of vertical.

"Mignot's lucky," Gaudin said, "but so are we all. Look at me! They chased me long enough; now I'm giving it back to them." He smiled happily, his heavy, despondent nose so ludicrously incongruous that Patrice laughed. "You know what I've been thinking?" Gaudin said. "I've been thinking that if I die this minute they can never take these last days away from me. Every minute I think there's this much more, this much more. We're men again and they can never take that away from us no matter what happens."

"It's the first time I've seen you really happy, Gaudin."

"Happiest week of my life. But I'll be happier tonight. I've been sleeping in a hotel across the way. Tonight I say *merde* to the Germans and their Gestapo. I'm going to sleep at home—with my wife."

A shadow crossed Gaudin's face and Patrice's too as he thought of Danielle. Suzanne will come around, Gaudin was thinking. He smiled again and they shook hands.

Back at the Prefecture Patrice found Reboussin in his office.

"It's magnificent and terrifying," Patrice said. "We hold most of the city, all right—at least seventy of the eighty quarters. Most places you wouldn't know anything was happening, it looks so normal. But they're still here. They're swarming over the boulevards, the Concorde, the Champs Élysées. Those tanks! If they ever mass them against us with the infantry behind . . ."

"We could hold out three hours, maybe four," Reboussin said. "Ammunition is very short."

"We hold the city," Patrice said bitterly, "and they hold us."

"They mined the Chamber of Deputies—several tons of dynamite. I have two reports that they're mining the bridges."

A haggard look settled with familiarity over Patrice's face. He missed Danielle, feeling his need for her with a deep, quiet desperation.

"If the Americans . . ."

Patrice stopped in mid-sentence. Listening intently, he looked unseeingly at Reboussin, who was frozen rigid like a pointer, listening too. The sound grew louder, unmistakable.

"A Stuka!" Patrice cried. "He's leading the pack in!"

They dashed for the window, leaned out, gazing up at the heavy gray sky. A plane appeared behind Notre Dame, flying low toward the Prefecture. On the Parvis in front of the cathedral a crowd gathered; all heads were bent back and all eyes were on the small plane.

"It's an American!" someone shouted.

Incredulous silence for a moment, then someone else cried, "He's right! It's an *Amerlo*!" A tremor of excitement ran through the crowd. The plane flew in closer, hovered over the Parvis, dipped to about five hundred feet, tipped a wing and began to circle the square. They all saw the tricolor painted under the wing.

"It's a Frenchman!" they cried. "It's a Frenchman!"

They could make out two men in the plane and they waved wildly at them; the aviators waved back. Then one of them held out his hand and something flew out of it. The object was picked up by the wind and swept higher; then, turning and fluttering, it floated white and hesitant on the air and began to settle toward the earth, twisting down, floating up, dipping suddenly at the whim of the breeze. The plane had already left, but the crowd had eyes only for the bit of paper, which it followed with upturned heads as the paper slowly weaved and tumbled down. It was carried from the center of the Parvis toward the Prefecture and the crowd below trailed after it, impatient for the paper to end its long fall. At last, in a final swoop, it fell beside the Prefecture and was snatched up by one of the Prefecture F.F.I.s. He read it; then, without a word, dashed around the corner through the protesting and curious crowd and into the Prefecture. He ran to Patrice's office, banged on the door and without waiting for an answer, burst in. Before Patrice or Reboussin could say a word the F.F.I. stretched out the paper.

"This was just dropped by a French plane," he gasped.

Patrice grabbed the paper. It was a United States Army message form. A few words were scribbled on it: "To F.F.I. Prefecture of Police Paris: Hold tight. We're coming. General Leclerc."

A cry of triumph burst from Patrice. He threw the paper in the air and his arms around the F.F.I. Reboussin picked up the paper and read the message. He grinned for the first time since the truce ended.

"We've won," he said.

"Now we can change the password," Patrice said exultantly, "from *On les aura* to *On les a*—We got 'em!"

They laughed, Patrice with abandon, Reboussin in a contained way. They were so delighted that they liked each other. It wasn't until quite a while later that Patrice had the sobering thought that he might be sharing his joy with Danielle and wasn't.

†

ONE hour after the message from Leclerc was dropped, Klaus phoned Patrice. From the first word Patrice knew who it was.

"I wasn't able to get away until now," Klaus said, "or I would have called earlier."

"That's all right," Patrice said with a casualness he was far from feeling.

From the instant of recognition Patrice was thinking to himself, "This time I'm going to hold on. This time whoever it is who belongs to that voice is not going to get away." But the next words Patrice heard were unexpected and chilling.

"It may be too late," Klaus said.

"What do you mean?"

"Danielle is being moved out."

"When?"

"Tonight or early tomorrow. I won't know until later in the day for sure."

"What's the transport?"

"Automobile. There are no trains."

"Good," said Patrice. "Do you know the route they're going to take?"

"Suppose you miss her. Will the deal still be the same for me?"

"Don't worry about that. We haven't missed her yet, have we?"

"No, of course not. If we could see each other—"

"Come right over. I'll be here."

"In a neutral place," Klaus said.

Patrice had been sure his proposition would not work, but he was disappointed anyway. "Where?" he asked.

"The Place des Pyramides, by the statue of Joan of Arc."

"We can find a place more neutral than that," Patrice objected dryly.

"Where do you suggest?"

Patrice had thought that one out long before and decided on a place that was open, minimizing the possibility of a trap snapping shut on him. "Across the Seine from Joan of Arc," he said. "How about the corner of the Rue de Beaune and the quai?"

"All right," Klaus said, and then he played his last and what he considered his best trump card. "I'll see you there at seven-thirty to-night. If I'm a few minutes late, don't worry. Wait for me. I'll be there."

Patrice was stunned. "Seven-thirty! It's out of the question. It'll be too late."

"I told you it may be too late," Klaus said tranquilly.

"But it's not too late now. You said she may be moved out tonight."

"I can't make it any earlier. I'll have a time making it at seven-thirty."

"But what if Danielle is moved out of Paris by then?"

"Oh, I don't think she'll be moved out quite as early as that. Under the circumstances they would hardly move before nightfall and probably not before ten or so."

Patrice was exasperated by the man's serene tone of voice, but there was little he could say to force an earlier appointment. "You're cutting it pretty fine," he said.

"It's not by choice. If I can do better than seven-thirty, I'll phone you and advance the hour. But I won't be able to phone you again until four at the earliest. And if you haven't heard from me by five, it means I can't get away until seven-thirty."

"Good," said Patrice, although he did not think so. "I'll be here between four and five. If I don't hear from you then, I'll see you at seven-thirty on the corner of the Rue de Beaune and the quai. Will you be in uniform?"

"Yes. How will I know you?"

"You'll know me. I'll be in shirt sleeves."

"One other thing," Klaus said. "Come alone. If you're not alone, you won't see me."

When Patrice put the receiver back in its cradle he was torn between exultation and anguish. Danielle was in Paris, close by. But she would not be there for long and he would not know for many hours what, if anything, could be done about it.

Klaus was pleased. He felt that his tactic had worked to perfection.

†

STANDING at a window of her apartment, Suzanne watched the sun sweep over chimney tops and the shining wet street below, wiping out the vast shadow before it in one broad movement, like a cosmic eraser pushed by an unseen hand. Suzanne turned away from the window, paced the room for a moment, then stretched out on a divan with a book, which she did not open. She wore an expression of the most intense misery. Ever since Monday, when she had spoken to Klaus in the Tuileries, Suzanne had been waiting for him to phone. The bitter hours and days had crawled with their burden of hope and despair to other hours and other days that crawled even more slowly, the burden becoming heavier as time passed.

On both Tuesday and Wednesday she left the apartment just once, each time at this hour of the afternoon. From the Rue Clovis, where she lived, she had walked what now seemed to her almost a romantic pilgrimage along the path she always had taken to see Klaus. She passed in front of his hotel on the Rue des Écoles and, circling the quarter, returned to her apartment. The walk, with its memories, was painful and sweet. Longing for Klaus, she had looked into the entryway of the hotel the previous day and seen the harridan of a chambermaid, who had stared at her with such open hatred that it frightened her. But that was part of the past; knowing it was finished, Suzanne shrugged it off.

It was the future that concerned her. She put aside the book and stared at a crack on the unpainted ceiling. The future was Klaus— anywhere. She saw no more than that. If she could have her life with Klaus and the integrity of emotions he breathed into her aching senses, then she would make any sacrifice, live under any conditions, without money or possibilities, in misery, in flight, anything. But it was beyond her imagination to conceive what such an existence would be like or what it might do to them, and she was beyond caring. She would not go back to the mediocrity of her marriage, to its swamp of small lies and boredom, to living with a man whose touch repelled her. Whatever her existence with Klaus might be, it would at least have the grace of sincerity and the warmth of her love. She had made her choice. The alternative to Klaus was—nothing. She told herself fiercely that she would rather die than go back to living with Gaudin; for the first time in her life she thought of suicide.

She stared moodily at the ceiling. Her head was set off beautifully by the mass of luxuriant black hair, plaited and coiled in an upsweep, and her handsome face, because of the nearsighted eyes, had its characteristic intense expression. For a long while she lay on the divan caressing her thoughts of disaster. It suffused her with a warm, sentimental pleasure. How unhappy Klaus would be! The tears welled up. Blinking them back, she dipped quickly down to reality and was engulfed again.

None of that would be necessary, she told herself. She looked around the room, and her eyes fell upon two valises in a corner. Her bags had been packed for so long now; one word—Come!—and the next instant she would be out of this apartment forever without a regret.

For two days she had waited for that word, watching like the rest of the city for the arrival of troops; but, unlike the rest of the city, the troops she yearned to see were the German divisions Klaus had told her were marching toward Paris. For the past three mornings she had awakened with choked anguish and hope to learn, on peering into the street, that nothing had changed.

The spirit in the streets, with their barricades and fanatical intensity of emotion, appalled her, but it was not, in her own opinion, for lack of patriotism. Patriotism was a word she never used; the idea was alien. She was unpolitical and deeply, though thoughtlessly, French. If anyone had asked her, she would have replied that of course she wanted France to win the war. What a question! But she wanted, passionately, to see the Germans hold Paris—until she could get away with Klaus. She was beginning to despair, however, that the German divisions would ever get to Paris, just as the rest of the city was beginning to despair of the arrival of the Americans.

She rose abruptly and went to the phone, debating whether to call Klaus. He had told her not to. But, after all, why not? At that moment the telephone rang.

"Hello."

Her heart was still pounding, but she could have wept on hearing Gaudin's voice.

"I just have a minute, Suzanne. It's almost over."

"I know," she said dully.

"Leclerc is on his way to Paris. Isn't it wonderful?"

"Wonderful."

"Is everything all right?"

"Fine."

"No . . . visits?"

"None."

"I think it's safe now, don't you?"

She hesitated. "I guess so."

"I've been on the barricades all these days, darling, but tonight I'll be home. . . ."

Her throat thickened.

"Suzanne . . ."

"Yes, I heard you. I heard you."

He thought her emotion was the same as his. "Things will be different now, my darling," he said. "We'll talk about it tonight. I have so much to tell you."

When she put down the receiver she looked around the room in a mounting panic. The suitcases stood soberly in the corner. She couldn't take much more of this, she told herself. It had to be now. Quickly, in jerky movements, she dialed the Meurice.

"Monsieur Tellmann."

"It was a long while before Klaus's voice broke the silence.

"I must see you." Her voice was barely controlled. "It can't wait."

"Impossible. I can't get out and you can't get in."

"There must be some way."

"None." His voice was strained, but the note was final.

"Klaus!" She sounded a heartbroken cry for help. "I can't stay here any more. My husband is coming home tonight. He just called. I've got to get away. You promised . . ."

"Don't you understand, Suzanne? It's too late. I can't do anything." His voice was harsh, pitched on the taut upper register of anguish. "We're locked in. It's like a besieged fortress. Even if I could get out, we'd never be able to run through the resistance lines—and there's no transportation. I tried—"

"But the troops!" she cried. "They're still coming! They'll be here!"

"Yes, of course. They're coming down from the north. They'll be here soon. We've got to wait."

Wait, she said to herself angrily, putting back the receiver. He had said it too glibly. She didn't believe him, yet she needed faith more than ever and had to believe. The bags stood in the corner. Her face clouded. What to do? She opened her purse and counted the money in it. Not much, but enough. The apartment stifled her. She had to get out where she could think.

Nervously, she strode into the bedroom, glanced into a full-length mirror and patted the dark, high crown of her hair into place. A dab of lipstick and her mouth bloomed out of a smoothly pallid, frowning face. She was looking her best, for when she smiled, flashing small, even white teeth, her mouth was too wide, and the strangely seductive effect created by her nearsighted eyes was lost. Recognizing how handsome she looked, she held the frown, admiring her exotic image in the mirror. A snug skirt outlined her hips and domed stomach, and her firm breasts pointed free and dark against the white silk blouse. In a moment, however, the pleasure she had looking at herself was dissipated. She slipped into the gray jacket of her suit and went into the street.

Automatically, she took the same route she had taken on previous days. She walked quickly looking neither to the right nor left, and turned into the Rue des Écoles. As she walked her thoughts began to clear. Whatever she did it had to be done immediately. She would move to a hotel, anything, rather than face a showdown with Gaudin. And Klaus? If the German troops did not arrive . . . Her mind blurred at the possibility. If Klaus were captured or killed . . . She walked through a nightmare in the wake of the supposition and was not even aware that she had just passed in front of the hotel where she had spent so many lost hours in Klaus's arms.

Suddenly she was aware of a hand grasping her shoulder. She turned, her dark eyes half closed, and looked nearsightedly into the contorted face of the chambermaid. The woman's hand slipped down and held onto Suzanne's arm. Suzanne wrenched free.

"What do you want?" she cried indignantly.

The woman grabbed her again. Suzanne backed away, frightened, the woman hanging on, ferretlike, unshakable, her red face frozen in an expression of stubborn, brutal hatred. Terrified, Suzanne struggled violently for one intense moment and tore her arm free. The next instant another hand gripped her other arm. She turned and saw the hotel clerk. His thin lips, pressed tight together, were bloodless, and there was a wild look in his eyes. The woman held Suzanne's other arm again.

"Let me go! Let go!"

It made no sense; she wanted to shout for the police but didn't. She pulled and twisted, throwing herself from one side to the other, trying to break away and run, but she was not strong enough. Then other hands grabbed her arms. She writhed in their grip, working her hips and stomach and legs, unable to budge the upper part of her body. A crowd swarmed around her. Helpless, she stopped struggling and looked frantically into the sea of strange faces. They were her people; they would help her. A confusion of voices roared over her, through which the chambermaid's voice stabbed sharp and strident.

"The slut, the dirty slut! We've got her now!"

"What's she done? What's she done?"

The woman's piercing cry and the staccato questions jabbed in swift counterpoint, interlaced and mounted with each repetition to a new and wilder pitch of fury.

"The slut, the bitch! Let's give it to her!"

"But who is she? What's she done?"

"She's been whoring with the Boches! Opening her thighs for them while we—"

The questions stormed down together. "How do you know? You're sure? But is it true?"

"It's true!" the clerk shouted. "Right in the hotel here!"

"I ought to know!" the chambermaid cried. "I made the bed!"

"You're hurting me! Let go! Let go!"

The tears fogged Suzanne's nearsighted eyes. She wrenched against the hands that gripped her, writhing, her stomach rolling. The hands only gripped her more tightly.

"Let go! You're hurting! Let go!"

"You see, she doesn't deny it."

"A Boche every night, the slut!"

"Over here! Over here! Bring her here!"

"Take her clothes off! Strip her!"

"No, no! Her hair! Clip it off! Shave her!"

She was being pushed. The crowd broke in front of her, opened out, then swirled back in around her and shuffled sluggishly in her wake. She tried to hold back, but they pushed and pulled her forward. She stumbled, but they held her up. The buttons on her jacket tore and the gray suit flapped open. Her breasts bounced in the white silk blouse with each movement. She felt something brush her hair, something tug at the coils. A strand worked loose, and the crowd, moving forward all the time, let out a cry. Hands plucked at her hair as they pushed her on. Her hair, loosened and disarrayed, cascaded over her shoulders and down her back. The cries and taunts redoubled.

"Let me go! Let me go!" she sobbed, but they pushed and half carried her forward.

The chambermaid, her eyes shining out of a red, distorted face, still held onto Suzanne's arm. "The bitch!" she kept screaming. "Ah, the slut! She has it coming to her!"

They were at the entrance of a shop. Suzanne made a last effort to hold back, but they shoved her on while the crowd shouted, "Bring her out! We want to see her hair-do!" She was forced down into a chair and held there by a dozen pairs of hands. A hand swept up her thick, rich mass of black hair and held it high over her head. Something cold skated up the back of her neck to her scalp; she heard the quick, dry clicking sound of the clippers. Then she looked up and in the huge mirror before her she saw the fuzzed image of a tormented

face that was inhumanly ugly. She did not recognize the face but she
knew it was her own.

†

"Give us a song," Gaudin said. "Go on, it'll help pass the time."

He laughed happily as a short, middle-aged man with a bristly two-
day growth of beard leaned his rifle against the barricade on the terrace of the restaurant Perigourdine and cleared his throat. It had been
quiet all day at the Place St. Michel. The Germans seemed to have
changed their itinerary. A dozen men, armed and wearing F.F.I. brassards, looked expectantly at the singer. Leaning against the piled-up
sandbags topped by the restaurant's green flower boxes and a large
portrait of Hitler, the unshaven little man began to sing in a rasping,
lugubrious baritone.

> *Cocu, cocu,*
> *Tout le monde sera cocu.*
> *Et tout le long de la semaine*
> *Tous les cocus se promenent*
> *Et moi, comme les autres.*
> *J'en ferai cocu bien d'autres.*
> *Cocu, cocu.*
> *Tout le monde sera cocu.*

"There's a song for all of us," one of the men said.

"Speak for yourself. Leave us out of it."

A swelling roar came from a short way up the Boulevard St. Michel.
It had begun with the song; now it was quite loud. They looked at
each other, listening and trying to guess its cause.

"I'll run up and have a look," one of them said.

A few minutes later he was back.

"Well, what was it?" Gaudin asked.

The man shrugged. "Nothing important. They shaved off a woman's
hair for horizontal collaboration and they're showing her off around
the quarter."

"Good!" Gaudin said. "It'll teach the bitch."

"Nobody'll go to bed with that one for a while."

"She'll do all right. Who cares what they got on their heads."

"How will she get around until it grows back?"

"Turban. You need an X-ray machine to tell what they got under
them."

"If all the women in France who slept with Germans had their hair shaved off and wore turbans, we'd think we were in Turkey."

Some of the men laughed.

"It's bad enough; thank God it isn't as bad as that," Gaudin said. "Let's forget about her! Come on, more music!"

"First a little gasoline," the baritone said.

They passed him a bottle of red wine and, holding it to his lips, he pointed the bottom of the bottle toward the sky while his Adam's apple bobbed up and down. When he lowered the bottle he exhaled, making a whispering sound, and passed the bottle to the others. Then he wiped his mouth with the back of his arm, cleared his throat and, working a catch into his voice, succeeded in passing from the lugubrious to the lachrymose. His alcoholic baritone floated across the sunlit square.

> *Et tout le long de la semain-e*
> *Tous les cocus se promen-ent.*

Gaudin glowed; he was delighted with the song. But that was not strange. Everything delighted him now.

†

PATRICE lost no time, after his talk with Klaus, in getting over to the Rue de Beaune. He felt that he had chosen well. If it turned out after all that the man was not a soldier but a Gestapo agent, he would not have an easy time setting his ambush here. Patrice noted all the approaches to the spot where he had set the appointment, then went to a bookstore in a near-by street. It was a resistance command post. In the back of the shop Patrice shook hands with a thin, bespectacled young man who kept tossing back his long blond hair, which constantly fell across his forehead and over his eyes. Patrice had already spoken to him over the phone two days before, when he had originally made his plans.

"He finally agreed to meet me in your quarter," Patrice said. "It's for tonight, probably at seven-thirty."

The young man brought out a map of the quarter. "Where will it be?"

Patrice pointed to the corner of the Rue de Beaune and the quai.

"Good," the young man said. "We'll do just what you asked. This is the one bad house along there. The concierge is unfriendly. But the concierges in the other buildings are with us, and three of our people live in apartments overlooking the corner. If anybody so much as comes around to look the place over between now and tonight, you'll know about it. I'm going over there now myself and I'll get them on the lookout." He added with a smile, "All I can spare in the way of men are some RDH."

Patrice smiled back. "No, thanks," he said.

With victory in sight, hordes of zealous but inept recruits had flowed into resistance ranks, and among the aristocracy of the resistance—those who had been in it for the longest time—these impassioned but late arrivals were dubbed the RDH—*Résistants de la Dernière Heure.* The Resistants of the Last Hour were the indispensable resource on which the resistance had depended, but nobody had forseen that in the last days of open fighting they would change the character of the resistance. It was no longer an exclusive club operating underground. Heroism, as usual, was being watered down by the prospect of success.

"You can't take a chance on seeing him all alone," the young man said. "What are you going to do?"

"It's pretty much set," Patrice said. "I've made arrangements to get armed men from Bourbon."

"You're lucky. He's a hard man to get anything out of."

"I'll check with you here tonight," Patrice said and left.

He hurried to Bourbon's headquarters in the Rue Soufflot. The stiff-backed army colonel was in an expansive mood.

"I've got some news for you," he announced with a grandiose wave of his hands. "Leclerc is driving on Paris! He may be here in a few hours. Tomorrow at the latest!"

"I know," Patrice said.

"Well, then, cheer up, old man, cheer up! We've got them just the way they had us. I haven't felt so good since the Riff."

Patrice had always known that Bourbon was insufferable in defeat, but had not realized he was intolerable in victory. Bourbon strode about his office with a thoroughly repulsive air of arrogant and contemptuous superiority. Patrice saw that the colonel was treating him as if he were a fool and a line of Courteline's came to his mind: "To pass for an idiot in the eyes of an imbecile is a choice tidbit for the gourmet."

"I've come about the matter we discussed over the phone the other day. I need five or six men armed with tommy guns for tonight."

"A bagatelle," the colonel said airily and, sitting at his desk, wrote out an order and handed it to Patrice. "They'll take care of you. You know where it is—at the café where we used to meet."

Patrice read the order hastily, nodded, and was out of the door with the barest excuse of a farewell. He was walking down the Boulevard St. Michel to iron out the last details of his plan at the café when a sound floated up to him from lower down on the boulevard. He looked but saw nothing. As he hurried on, the sound took on volume, swelled and became a roar. He recognized it now. Excited by the pulsing voice of a mob, he rushed to meet it.

Suddenly the crowd swept out of the Rue des Écoles onto the boulevard. It was hundreds strong and fanned out into the middle of the road, centering on something Patrice could not see. They marched raggedly toward him, shouting and hooting, scrambling around in an enormous arc, turning toward the thing in the center. Then Patrice saw *it*. The horror was so grandiose it staggered him. At first he thought that thing, driven like an animal by the mob, was a man; but in a flash he knew he was wrong. The jacket of its suit flapped open and Patrice saw the protruding breasts jutting into a white silk blouse, showing dark at the nipples, bobbing up and down at each step. The woman's head, clipped to the skull, was obscenely naked. Her face was the hallucination of a madman, corpselike, the bones projecting skeletally into the tight, chalky skin, the demented eyes blind and inhuman.

The woman came on as the taunting mob danced around her with vicious hilarity. The women tormented her more than the men, shouting coarser insults and plucking at her. One little woman, wriggling with excitement in her tight silk dress, gasped, "Oh, I'd die if they did it to me."

Patrice could no longer tell whether the mob was driving the woman forward or whether she was trying to flee. The woman dragged on, her mouth open, panting, with the pack on her heels. She was revolting and pitiable, like a leper. What does she feel? Patrice wondered.

"No, no!" the woman sobbed. "No, no!"

It sickened and revolted Patrice. Then they were upon him, the mocking cries and turmoil sweeping over him like icy waves. The next moment they were beyond him. Patrice shuddered and walked away from it, hearing over and over again the woman's heart-wrenching, "No, no! No, no!" This was what an insurrection could mean. It struck him with stunning force. This was not what he or the resistance had fought for, yet this was part of what had been born of their struggle. He was neither soft-headed nor subject to romantic illusions. He was a man who held strong views. But he had never contracted the disease of the age, that ultimate barbarism of wanting to humiliate and banish to outer darkness all those who disagreed. The steady flame of faith he had so long kindled in the purity of the resistance had blown out. He saw how radically it had changed in the past few days and understood that it was no longer a bright vision or dazzling dream. It had grown up and achieved the imperfections of reality. As he walked away from the violence of the mob, Patrice knew that soon the resistance would be dead. Victory was killing it. With no occupation to resist, there could be no resistance. Patrice's heresy bit into his mind. He knew now what had been wrong with his thinking. Neither the insurrection nor the resistance were ends in themselves. They were instruments that men had created to forge their liberation, and when instruments have served their purpose they should be tossed on the rubbish heap. Suddenly Patrice felt as if he had taken the first long step toward his own liberation. He felt that he was no longer the slave of a doctrine, that he was no longer being shackled by unbreakable political imperatives, that at last he could think for himself, act like himself, be himself. He felt better about the resistance than he had since the insurrection had begun. He also felt that it was in the process of rapidly becoming part of his past.

He arrived at the café still deeply involved in his thoughts. The café was closed, but there was a back entrance where Patrice knew he would be admitted. He walked toward it casually, noted an old man sitting across the way in front of a closed grocery store and nodded to him. The old man nodded back. He was the lookout. Inside the café were the men and the arms that Patrice needed for the night. Once again he put his mind to the problem of liberating Danielle.

†

THE bigger news is, the fewer words it takes to tell. The agony of Jesus can be compressed into two words, "Christ crucified," the end of a world war into, "Slaughter ended," or, happily, "We win." The significance of such words is out of all proportion to their number.

On Thursday morning nobody in all of Paris thought that Allied troops would reach the city very quickly. Then, shortly after noon, Leclerc's message was dropped in front of Notre Dame, and three stunning words raced through the city: *Leclerc is coming!* Leaping from barricade to barricade, from quarter to quarter, those words transformed Paris in the course of the afternoon. Parisians poured into streets that for days had been as desolate as parched river beds. The

Germans, their patrols, vehicles and tanks, had disappeared from most of the city. But the people flooded their neighborhoods, looking as if they had all just heard some colossally funny joke and were still thinking of it. They circulated through the liberated quarters with that deep need at climactic historical moments to be in contact with other human beings and share their emotions. Rumors swept through the crowds.

"They're only ten kilometers away."

"They're coming by the Porte d'Orléans."

"No, by the Porte de Versailles."

"By both."

"There's heavy fighting along the way."

"No opposition at all."

By seven o'clock, when the special edition of the evening paper *Défense de la France* hit the streets, most doubts were settled. The headline was enough:

LECLERC'S TANKS
ARE AT CHEVILLY
AND CROIX-DE-BERNY

"Croix-de-Berny! It's only seven kilometers away!"

"Ten minutes from the Porte d'Orléans, five without traffic."

"Let's hurry! There's no traffic today!"

"It can't be true."

"Why not?"

"It's too beautiful!"

As the sun dipped behind the Arch of Triumph, casting a peach-colored glow over the façades of buildings, crowds of Parisians headed for the southern edge of the city, rushing toward the moment they could no longer wait for.

The evening air was soft; bars of gold spangled the violet horizon. From his perch on the flower-topped barricade before the restaurant Perigourdine, Gaudin watched the light slant across the twin-towered façade of Notre Dame and smiled as his gaze swept the Place St. Michel, where he saw a huge American flag draped over the fountain in the middle of the square and a sign in German offering the ironic assurance, LEBEN GARANTIERT!

Gaudin was in no hurry to go home. Although he was impatient to see Suzanne, he was reluctant to take leave of "his" barricade. He thought he was entering a new future, that all his past troubles would be washed away, but he also knew that he was leaving behind on the barricade what had briefly been the best and most meaningful moment in his life. This was the watershed, the point and the moment of change from one state to another. He wanted to leave the past and its unhappiness, illuminated by this final peak of experience, and enter the future and its promise with a full consciousness of his passage from one to the other. If he had any doubts about the promise he had created largely by himself, he did not allow himself to think about them. Good will, he thought, on his side and Suzanne's would be enough to settle most of their difficulties.

He dawdled. Certain that Suzanne would be at home waiting for him, he prolonged the moment, tasting it. He looked about him and thought that this was one time, one week in his life, when he had lived unselfishly, when he had had no thought of himself, no thought of his interests, no sense of his own feelings or even of his own life. He had fought at the side of men he loved and he had been happy to know that under the summer sun and in the simple camaraderie of battle men had loved him. It had not been much to ask, he thought. But he knew that here in the world of men he had won what before in the long years of living with a woman he had lost.

Only vaguely, if at all, did Gaudin realize that he had thrust himself into the underground labyrinths of the resistance to be swallowed up in a kind of voluntary self-immolation because of his need to fill the emptiness that resulted from his marriage. He did not realize any more clearly that the intensity of his joy during the past few days was as much a compensation for the failure of his life with Suzanne as it was the successful culmination of a struggle that had absorbed the full shock of his energy over a span of years. His tragedy was that he had not been able to live with, or without, Suzanne. He knew it. As he stood behind the barricade on the Place St. Michel, he knew that the world of men was fading away from him, that he was going back to an older struggle and to a woman who always had been and always would be his deepest life. He asked no more now than the peace of her arms. The rest would fall into place.

Gaudin sighed. Slowly, with a smile whose enigmatic lines expressed sadness as well as delight, he made the rounds of the barricade, shaking hands with each of the men. Then he left.

At first he walked slowly, carrying the joy of the last days with him. But he had not gone far before he was thinking of Suzanne and the joy that awaited him, and his step quickened. The sun had gone down and the air was cooler and filled with the evening smell of Paris. It was just like the early happy days of their marriage, he thought, when he had walked nightly through these Paris streets, returning from work, with the vision of Suzanne waiting for him, fresh and smiling, her arms open to him. His heart was full with a sensation of the mystery and romance of one woman out of millions waiting in one apartment out of millions for one man out of millions to appear. He hurried now, impatient to be with her after the long separation, and turned into "their" street with his heart beating faster and his mind racing ahead to the touch and smell of her.

A crowd was massed in front of his apartment house. He did not even notice it until he was upon them. Smiling good-naturedly, he pushed through the crowd. It gave way reluctantly, and he heard, without listening or thinking about it, fragments of what was said.

"I saw her when she came home, a big crowd following her and shouting and . . ."

"But what else could she do to get away from them but go home and lock the door? Many of them are still . . ."

"It's a shame!"

"What times! There's not enough gas to cook a meal but there's enough to cook yourself . . ."

"It wasn't gas. She shot herself."

"No, she . . ."

When Gaudin, still smiling, got to the door, with the new look in his eyes and his long, heavy nose an incongruous exclamation point in the middle of a happy face, the concierge was there, holding the crowd back. He noticed an odd look come over her face when she saw him.

"What's going on?" Gaudin asked, brushing past and not really interested.

"It's your wife."

Gaudin turned back. "My wife?"

The concierge held Gaudin's gaze only for a moment. Gaudin looked at the circle of silent faces around him and his smile dribbled away. A pained, puzzled expression came into his eyes. He did not move and nobody spoke. He seemed to be paralyzed. He started to say something to the concierge but instead turned and raced up the stairs.

The door of his apartment was open, and a number of people were on the landing and in the foyer. Somebody tried to stop him as he went in, but Gaudin roughly brushed the hand aside. The smell of gas hung faintly in the air. He went past the kitchen, through the salon and into the bedroom. Suzanne, or all that was left of her, lay stretched out on the bed. He stood over her, knowing that this strange naked face was the face of the woman he loved, a face he had never seen before and which he knew to be her real face. He looked down on the bare, unframed reality of her, and it was neither ugly nor obscene but so overwhelmingly sad that he wanted to weep and weep and never stop weeping. He felt now that all these years he had been joined together with her in the dark without ever having seen her, but that now, suddenly, the light had been switched on. His eyes reflected the agony and naked distortion of her face. He stood there motionless, but his body began to tremble. Suddenly he looked about wildly and shouted, "I did it! I did it!" He sobbed and cried, "I can't look at her! I can't look at her!" Two men who had been hovering at the door came in to calm him.

"Who are you?" Gaudin shouted. "Get out! Get out of here!"

But he did not seem able to hold an idea for more than an instant and did not wait to see whether the men got out. He said no more. His face closed down tightly over the death within him like the lid of a coffin being nailed over a corpse.

He hurtled back through the rooms of his apartment and fled.

†

PATRICE waited until five, as he had said he would, for Klaus to call. No call came. At five-ten Patrice called the bespectacled young man who had established the lookout on the Rue de Beaune. The young man told Patrice that nothing unusual had taken place during the day and that nobody had even appeared to look the street over, much less deploy infantrymen in doorways in view of a small coup. More than ever, Patrice was convinced that the story Klaus had told him was true. But his conviction did not lead him to abandon his precautions. Automatically, Patrice played it as if he required all the security he had prepared for the operation.

After speaking to the bespectacled young man, Patrice made three more phone calls: one to the café and two to apartments on the Rue de Beaune overlooking the rendezvous point. Everything was running perfectly. The men were armed with tommy guns. They were already in the positions assigned to them. The trap was set. All that was now needed was to wait for the mouse to appear and to spring it.

Patrice's plan was simplicity itself. As soon as he met Klaus he was going to suggest a quiet place off the street where they could talk. If Klaus showed any reluctance to go along, Patrice intended to point a revolver at him and force him into the near-by resistance command post at the rear of the bookstore. If Klaus was armed or appeared with men who were armed, that was a risk that could only be played by ear and with the help of the men Patrice had knowledgeably deployed to help him in just such an eventuality. Once in the command post, Patrice figured he would quickly learn where Danielle was. If Klaus really wanted to make a deal, he would find Patrice an easy man to do business with provided he was offering information on Danielle's whereabouts in exchange for whatever he wanted. If the man were a fake who had tried but failed to trap Patrice, then Patrice had a few ideas on how to persuade him to say where Danielle was.

After making his calls Patrice looked at his watch, saw he had plenty of time to get to the Rue de Beaune at the appointed hour and immediately set out on foot. Patrice was anxious, overanxious. He wanted nothing to go wrong. Too much depended on what was about to happen that night. He was nervous and, erratically and without apparent cause, his heart thumped wildly. Patrice tried to void his mind of all thought. In the past four years it had proved a helpful and calming little trick at moments of tension, when there was nothing to do but wait for the crisis to explode. This time, however, it proved harder not to think. And it would be a while yet before he would come to grips with the man he had never seen but would never forget. When Patrice reached the Rue de Beaune and the quai he looked at his watch. It was exactly seven-twenty-five.

While Patrice was making his preparations to trap Klaus, Klaus was making his preparations to bag Patrice. He had known that Patrice would not accept the meeting place he suggested and was prepared to accept any reasonable alternative Patrice offered. The spot on the quai across from the Tuileries and the Louvre was ideal for Klaus's purposes. He studied the corner on the map and in the early afternoon sped by in the black Citroen. To Klaus it looked like any other street corner. What was most interesting about it was that it was visible from the higher floors of the Louvre across the Seine. Klaus asked for and received further co-operation from the army. He placed a man at a window of the museum armed with a pair of binoculars and a walkie-talkie. Below the window Klaus stationed the armored car and the armed unit that had been assigned to him. The armored car was equipped with a walkie-talkie. That was all Klaus required.

He was delighted with the elegance of his plan. The man in the window would train his binoculars on the corner where he was to meet Patrice. At the instant the meeting occurred he would tell the men in the armored car. The car would dash across the river toward them. It could not possibly take longer than thirty or forty seconds, if that. Klaus anticipated that Patrice would be armed and that he would have some armed men strategically spotted along the street. He was prepared to do anything Patrice suggested, go anywhere he wanted to go, knowing that he could delay their departure for at least twenty seconds without arousing any suspicions and that before they had taken more than a few steps in any direction the armored car, under constant direction from the man with the binoculars, would overtake them. The car would sweep down on them and cut across their path, forcing them against the wall of the building. In this way it would protect Klaus from being fired upon. It would also cut off Patrice from any possibility of a running dash for freedom. Klaus did not want any of that kind of thing. He was interested in Patrice alive, not dead, and wanted him to be taken quietly and without fireworks. Klaus knew that he himself faced a certain risk, but he also knew that all operations of this kind involved risk. He was not worried. He felt that with the fine hand of the expert he had cut the risk to a minimum.

The entire plan depended on precise timing, and Klaus was determined that everything would be done with meticulous exactitude. He gathered his men early, tested the radio equipment, sat at the window in the Louvre and looked through the binoculars at the corner where he would soon be meeting Patrice. Everything checked. Klaus was pleased. He would give these amateur conspirators a lesson they would never forget and never be able to put to use. When he pounced on Patrice, the fellow would have no idea what had happened or how it had been done. Klaus was suddenly impatient for it all to be over. He looked at his watch. It was only six o'clock. He had given himself plenty of margin. The men were at their stations and Klaus left them there with instructions to relax until he returned. Then he went to the Meurice to eat his dinner and to wait out the interminable minutes before the moment came for him to walk across the Seine to the corner of the quai and the Rue de Beaune.

†

KLAUS knew that the atmosphere at the Meurice that day had been gloomy. But when he walked into the hotel lobby shortly past six, after an absence of a few hours, he saw that the gloom had suddenly thickened to an impenetrably black funk. By that time General von Choltitz knew that his reinforcements, due the following day, had little or no chance of arriving on time, and those close to the general suspected the worst: that on the following morning, for the first time since the occupation began, the swastika would not be hoisted over the Meurice or the other occupied hotels on the Rue de Rivoli. The Germans were holed up in their strong points, but Von Choltitz wanted to give some impression, as a last gesture, that he still dominated Paris. He sent out patrols.

The patrols fooled no one. From the staff officers at the Meurice, Klaus gathered during dinner that all hope of holding Paris was virtually gone. It was even doubtful that the garrison could be pulled out before Allied troops overran the city. Remnants would escape, of course, but the loss would be almost total.

The news did not overly depress Klaus. He measured the extent of the disaster against his own little castle in Spain and concluded that the fall of Paris could do him no harm and might do him some good. He would be among the remnants that escaped. It would have to be tonight, immediately after he took Patrice in hand. Nothing had amused Klaus these last few days, but he found an inordinate pleasure in visualizing the scene when he appeared in Berlin fresh from the catastrophe of Paris with two resistance leaders as an offering to the Fuehrer. To pluck victory from defeat, Klaus told himself with self-deprecating irony, was practically heroism beyond the call of duty.

When he left the Meurice he breathed deeply of the sweet evening air. It smelled good. Klaus loved Paris and was sad that he would be leaving it. He wondered when he would be seeing it again and had a presentiment that it would not be for a long time.

It was seven-fifteen when Klaus reached the armored car parked in the Tuileries. The men were now impatient to be finished with the job and back in their barracks. They did not like the tone of the city, which all of them sensed, nor the attitude of Parisians, who had observed them all day with a mixture of irony and satisfaction. Klaus was impatient too. He spoke to his observer at the window over the two-way radio in the armored car.

"Is anybody there yet?"

After a moment the lookout said, "Nobody at all."

"Keep looking," Klaus said. "He's due in fifteen minutes. Let me know when he shows up."

Ten minutes later the lookout called excitedly, "Somebody's there. A big fellow in shirt sleeves."

"Does it look as if he's waiting for somebody?"

"He's waiting all right, looking at his watch and waiting."

"This is it," Klaus said. "Keep your eye on him, and the second you see me walk up to him and nod my head, let the men down here know it. Have you got that?"

"I got it."

Klaus turned to the sergeant in charge of the unit on the armored car. "You know what to do," he said.

The sergeant nodded.

"You'd better have the driver start up the motor when I leave," Klaus said. "And remember: everything depends on speed and precision. Above all, don't start until you get the word from up there that I've made contact. Once you get the word come on as fast as you can."

As Klaus walked away from the sergeant and the armored car, he heard the motor grind to violent life and then idle placidly. He came out of the Tuileries and onto the quai of the right bank. The sinking sun was flat against the buildings lining the left bank of the Seine, transfiguring them. The gray stones were no longer gray; they were warm and alive and rose-gold and they might have been the façade of a long row of gilded palaces. He looked at his watch. It was seven-thirty. In about two minutes he would establish contact. Klaus looked around him as he walked, conscious of the beauty of the evening. The light was clean, the air soft. He looked down at his uniform and felt the lapels, automatically checking to see that he had left no telltale insignia. Then it happened. He heard the metallic crackle of rifles and machine guns close by, feeling they were on top of him, and felt rather than heard, with his entire body the zing of bullets all around him. He hit the asphalt as if he had been clubbed and, after feeling icy cold for a second, was drenched in sweat. When he looked up he saw a group of F.F.I.s at a bridge about a hundred yards downstream. The movement of his head brought a flurry of rifle shots, and he clenched his fists and tried to squeeze his body right through the asphalt as he heard the bullets sting the road beside him and leap away. He quickly wriggled up to the stone parapet along the quai, which turned slightly at that point and gave him cover. But as he started to edge his way backward along the parapet, a shower of bullets swept over him from the rear. He lay still as death. Miraculously, he had not been touched. But he was surrounded. He could not budge.

Klaus lay face down on the hard sidewalk, squeezed against the stone parapet, and for a while he hardly dared breathe. Not a sound broke the evening stillness. He breathed a little more easily now. They thought he was dead. Then he thought of his appointment with Patrice. He would be late. Klaus turned his left arm very slowly and carefully and ever so slightly. The movement was imperceptible. It was also unreasonably disappointing to a man in his position. His watch was smashed. Klaus did not know if a bullet had touched it or if he had battered the watch when he hit the ground. He felt as if hours had gone by, but he knew it could only have been a few minutes. He did not feel lost, though he was surrounded, nor was he frightened. Too much had happened too quickly for him to be able to afford that luxury. He was more stunned than anything else. In a state of shock, he lay still and thought, I will get out of this fix and get to the Rue de Beaune. The men in the armored car would have heard the shooting. They would come to help him.

They did not come immediately. Klaus figured that they were waiting for him to appear on the street corner, according to their instructions. Soon, when he failed to show, they would come for him. If only they came soon, he thought. He did not want to miss Patrice. It was at that point that he heard behind him the sound of a vehicle and knew it was a German armored car by the noise of the motor and the rattle of the chassis. He did not dare turn his head. Abruptly and violently the firing broke out again. Klaus was frightened now. The din was awesome. He thrust his head at the point where the wall met the sidewalk, trying to squeeze into it. Behind him he heard a tremendous explosion through the noise of battle and felt the sidewalk under him tremble from the concussion. Then he heard shouts in French and in German and heard a group of men wearing heavy shoes run toward him. He kept his head down, stiffened and held his breath. The men were beside him. A hand grasped his shoulder and shook him. Bullets were flying by. Then a voice spoke in German. Klaus did not know what it said. He did not care. He opened his eyes, turned and looked up at the sergeant in charge of the armored car unit.

"Where's the car?" Klaus demanded, feeling as if he were lost at sea and the armored car were a ship that would carry him to safety.

"They got it. It's blown up. Didn't you see?"

So that was the explosion. Klaus did not ask how it happened. He did not care.

"Are we still surrounded?" he asked.

The sergeant nodded. The other men of the unit had backed up to them, and there they formed a tiny island. But the firing, for some mysterious reason that none of them could fathom, had suddenly stopped.

"Can we get out?" Klaus asked.

The sergeant shrugged.

Klaus was infuriated. "We can shoot our way out!" He cried. "We have tommy guns."

"Not all of us," the sergeant said. "Two dropped their guns when the explosion came. One is dead. One gave up."

Klaus sensed that the sergeant wanted to give up too, but did not dare to suggest it. What could they do? He had to get to the Rue de Beaune. The shooting began again, but this time the German soldiers sent back an answering volley and the F.F.I.s took to cover.

"We're pinned," the sergeant said. "We can't budge."

They lay there, and for a long time Klaus's mind churned but produced no plan to unpin them. A strange thought flashed through his mind. He wondered briefly if he had loved Suzanne. It was the first time he had asked himself the question and he was unable to answer it. Indecision had always plagued him, and his life had consisted in floating along with whatever current bore him. The pattern dominated his personal life as well as his career. It occurred to him that he might be on the verge of losing his freedom, and, before violently dismissing the idea, he sensed that Suzanne would take on a new importance to him against the prospect of years of prison life, with no possibility of knowing any other woman. But he knew too that time would erode his feelings for her and indeed most of his memory. He was not a young man any more, and suddenly the absurdity of his situation, lying in a street with half a dozen younger men and being shot at, momentarily overwhelmed him. What am I doing here? he wondered. How and why did I get here? He felt a violent disgust, not only with what had happened to him, but with himself as well. He felt that he was decent, yet everything he had ever done was vile.

The twilight was deepening now and it seemed as if the city had withdrawn into itself. The firing on them was intermittent. Every now and then, under covering fire, they made a move to dash in one direction or another, and then the F.F.I.s poured bullets over them, forcing them to drop along the parapet for greater protection. Klaus noted that the men were with the sergeant, that they were all getting more and more sullen. He felt isolated from them and knew they wanted to surrender. Every minute that passed made them feel their situation was more desperate. Klaus started to tell the sergeant that with dusk they would have a better chance to make a break. He saw that what he said was unconvincing. He also began to wonder whether Patrice was still waiting for him at the Rue de Beaune. The sullenness and fear of the men began to infect Klaus. He knew that he would have to do something quickly if he were to keep control over the unit. They were already beginning to whisper among themselves, and God knew what plot they were hatching.

Suddenly they were aware of something miraculous and awesome that was happening all around them. The air was filled with the clanging of bells. It seemed that all the church bells of Paris were ringing at once. The sound seemed to envelop and choke them like a material and hostile force. The soldiers looked at each other and at Klaus. They were nakedly afraid. Hard metallic sound, loud and overpowering, pounded at them. They were surrounded by it. The hidden power of millions of Parisians appeared to take shape in the ringing bells, and, like the soldiers, Klaus felt he was being drowned in a sea of sound. Panic gripped the men. They looked nervously in all directions, their tommy guns cocked. But there was nothing to shoot at. All the while the bells pealed in a wild and violent rhapsody. Then lights went on in many windows along the left bank. They were perfect targets. A rage swept over Klaus.

"Fire on the lights!" he shouted.

The clatter of tommy guns counterpointed the many-tongued sound of the bells. Most of the lights opposite them went out.

"Down there!" Klaus roared. "Get those lights out!"

Again the crackle of tommy guns broke the sound of the bells. The F.F.I.s showered them with bullets. One of the men fell, a nasty wound in his thigh. He moaned quietly, but without ever stopping. The animal sound was unnerving.

"It's hopeless," the sergeant finally said to Klaus.

"What's that?" Klaus cried.

For a moment the sergeant flinched. Then he repeated, "It's hopeless."

Klaus was incensed. "I'm the only one here who can say that!" he bawled. "I'm in command and as long as I say we have a chance, we have a chance."

All of them disagreed with Klaus—silently. He felt their disagreement like a bag thrown over his head and pulled tight around his neck, choking him. Again the baffling question flashed into his mind: Why am I here? It made no sense. Neither the city nor the country nor the people were his own. He had no business there. He ought to be where he belonged. Again he thought of Suzanne and again, this time intensely, he regretted her. He went over the steps that had kept him here in Paris and searched for the points at which he could have left with her. It always went back to the murder of his informer, Adrien Lemonnier. Of course he could have left and, once in Berlin, he might have been able to patch things up. But what good would that have done? Here, now, lying in a Paris gutter with a group of men whose lack of will was helping to undermine his own, Klaus no longer believed that Germany had a chance. It is difficult for a man who believes in a regime to think it will fall when his interest demands that it survive. It is all the more difficult when he is surrounded by all the visible signs of its strength. For such a man in such a situation it takes a leap of imagination to foresee the collapse of all that holds a working society intact. But at the point where he sees part of that structure disintegrate it is equally difficult for him to imagine that the rest can survive without breaking. Klaus was completely frustrated. It was late now and he knew he had lost his chance to take Patrice. Everything seemed clear to him, in a quite different light, this one tinted black with pessimism. He had one desire: to survive.

After an interval of intense F.F.I. fire, Klaus said to the men around him, "We've had enough. We'll have to give up before they come in and slaughter us all."

"We ought to give ourselves up to regular troops, not to the terrorists," one of the men said.

"Do you want to get up and find regulars?" the sergeant asked sarcastically.

Klaus told himself that his captors would never know he had been a member of the Gestapo. He was sure he would hide it successfully.

But now that the end had come, he regretted all he had done in the past years. He regretted it for one reason: he had lost. There had been a miscalculation, and he knew that he could not have lost more completely. Yet he also knew, deeply, as he felt the hopelessness of his position, that if it were to begin all over again he would choose the same road. He could not help himself. It was the easy path he had to take—even if at the end of it he were to find himself lying on his belly in a city far from home awaiting capture or death.

"I'm giving up for all of us," he said.

None of the soldiers objected. Klaus tossed aside his revolver and waved his handkerchief. For a moment the F.F.I. fire redoubled, then it stopped.

Into the silence Klaus shouted, "We're giving up."

"Put down your guns and come over with your hands up!" one of the F.F.I.s shouted back.

Klaus translated and the Germans did as they were told. A minute later they were prisoners.

Some confusion followed while the F.F.I.s lined up the prisoners with their hands locked over their heads. While the prisoners waited, a Red Cross girl bound the wounded soldier's thigh. The soldier, a burly, heavy-featured man, kept saying abjectly, in pidgin French, between moans, "French not terrorist. French nice. German nice too."

One of the F.F.I.s blew up. "Shut it, you bastard!" he growled. "Any more of that and I'll put you away. We're no Nazis. We even treat sons of bitches like you as if they were human. Now shut up!"

Klaus was thinking, It's finished now. I'm a prisoner. He thought that his job was done, too, and he had a small regret that he had left one loose end untied. There was Danielle, he thought, in the villa on the Boulevard Suchet, and he wasn't around to do anything about her. He had not been able to use her after all. He remembered how Suzanne had pleaded with him to release her. It was too late now. The matter was out of his hands. He felt no sense of loyalty at all to the French fascists who were guarding Danielle and he was rather sorry for her, but it never occurred to him to say anything to his captors about her. If he did, he knew they would quickly find out who and what he was, and he had no illusions as to what they would do to him. The reason Klaus felt sorry for Danielle was that he knew what would happen to her. The city was going to fall and he would not be there to move Danielle east. The Frenchmen hated her. She was one of their own, but on the other side. That made her doubly hateful to them. He knew how they felt. He had heard them often enough. They had no use for her and they would have to flee. There was no question of their taking her along. But if they left her and were later caught, she could serve as a witness against them. Klaus knew that before they left they would kill her. He shrugged and looked around, thinking again, It's out of my hands.

The Red Cross girl finished her bandage, while the prisoners maintained a wary silence. After the F.F.I.'s outburst, they felt they were safe as long as they behaved themselves. So far as the resistance was concerned, they were safe. But that night they still ran certain risks.

As the F.F.I.s were about to march off their prisoners, Klaus saw a wild-eyed man with his arms dangling limply at his sides approach them. A large pendulous nose hung despondently in the middle of his haggard face, which, except for the eyes, seemed dead. Watching him, Klaus felt uneasy. Gaudin passed the line of prisoners, then, noticing them, retraced his steps. He walked down the line as if he were reviewing them, but looked through each of the men without seeing them. Suddenly his whole face became illuminated. A grotesque expression distorted it. Stepping back, he cried, "They did it! They did it!" He snapped a revolver out of his pocket and fired three shots into the line of prisoners before some F.F.I.s overpowered him. Two men fell. Klaus remained frozen where he stood. Held by the F.F.I.s, Gaudin babbled incoherently for a while, then quieted. The two soldiers were dead. Seeing that Gaudin was disarmed and calm again, the F.F.I. leader ordered his men to release him.

"What you did, comrade, is bad," the F.F.I. leader said. He paused, looked at the bodies stretched out on the ground and at the line of prisoners, then added, "But that makes two less. And two Boches less in the world, that's good."

A few minutes later Klaus and the remaining prisoners, their hands still folded over their heads, were led away.

From seven-twenty-five until almost nine o'clock Patrice waited for Klaus to appear. He heard the shooting across the Seine and wondered briefly whether the skirmish could be holding up the man who was to meet him. But he had no way of making a connection between Klaus and the firing. All he could do was wait on the street corner he had chosen. He waited until it was finally apparent even to him and against all the hope he had gathered to shore up his morale that the man who had phoned him was not going to appear. When he left the

Rue de Beaune, apologizing to the men for their pointless vigil, he was so dejected he could not bear to think about it. He could not understand what had happened; he had no way of knowing why the man had not appeared, and at least for the moment he did not want to speculate about it.

He checked in at the bookshop and the bespectacled young man gave him a lift to the Prefecture, in a battered, prewar Renault with "F.F.I." scrawled all over it. Everything was running smoothly at the Prefecture, where he was told that Leclerc's troops were expected that night at the Hotel de Ville.

Patrice was in no mood to remain at the Prefecture. By the time he got to the Hotel de Ville talk of the impending liberation was on everybody's lips. The place was in an uproar. Patrice had never seen anything approaching the turmoil and frenzy of activity that the expectation of Leclerc had fermented in the insurrection's nerve center. The mounting excitement was intense and palpable. From all over the city resistance leaders had gravitated toward the building. There they waited in an atmosphere of spiraling suspense for the arrival of Leclerc's troops. Sorel had an expression of bliss on his face that made Patrice think he momentarily expected the gates of heaven to open wide and admit him. But all their faces were alive with the same dazzling look of joy. It was impossible not to be carried along by their soaring spirits. Although Patrice was numbed by his evening's experience, he too found the mood of the resistance on this penultimate night irresistible.

Grinning boyishly, Lefort joined Patrice. He had been drinking and had reached a state of untroubled euphoria. "This newspaper is the best thing that ever happened to me," he told Patrice. Then, holding his hand up dramatically, he announced, "I'm changing its name."

"What's wrong with *Le Saboteur*?"

Lefort smiled indulgently. "*Le Saboteur,* old man, was a fine name until today. But now that the occupation is ending I can hardly call my newspaper *Le Saboteur du Soir*. I've decided to call it *Paris-Nouvelles*. How do you like it?"

"May it become the biggest paper in all of France," Patrice intoned.

"Amen," Lefort said reverently. "How did you know that was my nightly prayer? No, don't tell me." He was bubbling over like activated champagne. "Let me make some predictions. This is a wonderful time for predictions. Riviere, for example. In three years he will be out of politics and back in the Sorbonne, amazing and bedazzling students as he was unable to amaze and bedazzle those who are no longer students."

"Too clever for the multitudes. Let's have more."

"Bourbon. In one year, if my addition is correct, zero."

"Less than a year. Not clever enough, even for the multitudes. Next."

Lefort looked around and saw Sorel. "Sorel," he said. "Socialist deputy as long as he lives. A true representative of the multitudes."

"Bravo," Patrice said.

"Who else is there? Ah, yes, Reboussin." Lefort paused. "Well, we can't be too severe with him. He plays the game too well. I elect him Premier of France within five years."

Patrice nodded. "Of course, he will accomplish nothing, but he will, as they say, lead the nation."

Serenely, Lefort changed the subject. "You know that Hitler issued orders to destroy Paris. Three times." He held up the appropriate number of fingers. "Three orders to destroy Paris once, not one order to destroy Paris three times. Once is enough for him. Don't tell anybody I said so," he whispered conspiratorially, "but maybe the resistance ought to award Von Choltitz a medal." He burst into laughter. "After all, just imagine the shape Paris might be in right now if it hadn't been for the truce."

Sorel and a few others joined them, and suddenly Patrice felt so miserable he was unable to face anyone. He walked off into a large, crowded room and for a while felt alone there. The thought of Danielle tormented him. He was certain that he had missed his last chance of saving her and that at this very moment she was perhaps being driven out of Paris. There was no possibility of his doing anything effective about it. The city was big, the gates leading in and out of it numerous, and he had no idea when Danielle would be taken away. It was his impotence to help her and his anguish that in a sense he had lost her all over again that were driving Patrice to the end of his strength. He wanted to leave the Hotel de Ville and all its commotions, but he felt that if he were alone, he would feel much worse. He did not know what he would do alone and did not want to face it. He stayed. It was strange to find himself here, feeling the way he did. The best part of his liberation, he thought, was gone.

†

THAT evening Danielle stood disconsolately at the barred window of
her tiny top-floor room on the Boulevard Suchet. In the six days she
had been a prisoner a change had come over her. Her face was thinner
and more severe and her eyes were a darker, less communicative blue.
She had withdrawn in the mysterious way that people afflicted by a
deep personal sorrow withdraw behind the barrier of their suffering to
insulate themselves from the world. In captivity this inner withdrawal
was Danielle's dignity. The insulating wall she threw up between herself and her jailers was her instinctive reply to all that was humiliating
in her position. They could push her around, but they could not touch
her. She sensed from their attitude that they knew it. Despite everything, they came to her with a certain indefinable reserve; she also
noted, and shivered slightly when she thought of it, a special vindic-
tiveness in their eyes and a nasty, small kind of hatred that was capable
of things she did not want to think of.

What she did think of, standing at the window, was that there were
many things about her captivity that she did not understand. It baffled
her, for example, that they did not continue her interrogation and
bring it to an end. It puzzled her that she was being kept in a villa and
not in a prison cell. She could not grasp why she was being guarded
by French hirelings rather than by Germans, and she had no idea why
they were casually holding her here in Paris and not shipping her to
Germany to be corralled with others of her species behind barbed wire.
She assumed, correctly, that all of this had something to do with the
insurrection, but exactly what she did not know. One thing she was
sure of after her last talk with Klaus: he knew more about her than
he had indicated. She could tell now that she had not fooled him at all,
that evasiveness was not going to help her, and that the next time he
sat down with her to get any information she was going to be in trouble. It worried her. This thought poisoned her days and gave her
jittery, sleepless nights. She could not deaden her nerves or quiet her
imagination against the terror of that interrogation, and its endless
postponement made it all the more terrifying. She was afraid that she
would talk.

When she was not tormented by her fears of what Klaus might do
to her and what she might say, she thought about Patrice and the

insurrection. All she knew about the uprising was what she had been able to gather from chance remarks dropped by her guards. It was not much. Beyond her door, where the guards were stationed all day and all night, there was a small radio. It was on briefly every day with the intervals of electricity, but though Danielle listened to it through the door and eavesdropped on the talk of the guards, she heard almost nothing about the one thing that really interested her. She was not sure that it was good that the insurrection was continuing for so long. At least the Germans had not been able to suppress it. But they were still in Paris and that meant that there was no co-ordination on the uprising between the resistance and the Allies. It was the continuation of the insurrection that finally led Danielle to figure out what her immediate future depended upon. They must be waiting, she thought, to see how it would come out. If the Germans held Paris, they would probably hold her here for a while to be interrogated on the spot. If the Germans were forced to retreat, she would be taken along with them to Germany. No matter what happened, it would not be good for her.

She gazed upon Paris, sprawled before her. From the east, night was swinging over the city, but a luminous fringe of blue and gold edged the western sky as the dying day made one last effort to survive before disappearing forever. Danielle looked longingly at the city she loved. An enormous fire was blazing behind the Arch of Triumph, illuminating the sky with a red glare. But the City of Light was a city without light. Gloom invaded its buildings, and Danielle knew that all over the city millions of Parisians sat at their windows or on their balconies or stood in front of their doors to enjoy the last bit of light from the evening sky. Danielle remembered the hush of the streets, broken only by the low hum of voices at windows and doorways. It was the moment out there, she knew, when, somewhere, a switch was pulled and the electricity flashed on. At that moment, every night, an "Ah" of relief and delight rose from the streets. A moment later nobody was visible; the entire quarter, the whole city, was precipitated indoors. Shutters snapped closed; blackout curtains were drawn; and several million Parisians proceeded to commit a criminal offense: they listened to the radio—to the BBC. Danielle felt the same hunger for news as the rest of the city and left her post at the window to take up her post at the door.

How noisy the guards could be, she thought, with their *pinard* and their irrelevancies and their vulgarities. But there was something comforting about the noise; she was really afraid when they were quiet. At the moment they were even more noisy than usual because they were in the middle of a fierce argument. It had been going on all day, but Danielle had not been able to hear enough to gather what it was about. Every now and then, just when things started to make sense, one of them would shout, "Quiet! Do you want her to know about it too?" That always quieted them.

When she came to the door this time one of them was saying, "But what if he doesn't come back?"

And another said, "He will come back and if he doesn't, we'll do it my way. We have plenty of time. The main thing is not to leave any garbage behind when you leave a house." One of them laughed uproariously at this.

"That's right," another voice said. "Always leave a place the way you found it—spotless. That's what mother always used to say."

They all laughed at that, and Danielle could tell from the way they were talking and laughing that they had been drinking. She could tell that something important, something critical, was in the air. She had felt it all day. Now she was sure.

One of them said, "Let's give the dial a twirl. The lights are on. Maybe we can find out what's happening."

Another said, "You're out of your mind. You know they never tell the truth."

But Danielle heard somebody at the radio having trouble getting a signal. "*Merde!*" she heard him say. "All it can get is Paris, and there are no stations in Paris any more."

"Give it a twirl," another voice said.

Suddenly a strong signal roared out. "What do you know!" the man at the radio said in surprise. "They're on the air again."

Danielle was listening to the voice coming out of the radio. It was a new voice, yet it was familiar. Its accent was that of Paris and it was saturated with emotion. Some disjointed phrases crackled out of the loud background noises. The broadcast was coming from the street. Danielle found herself suddenly quivering with excitement. It's the resistance, she thought. Then the speaker cut in with an announcement.

"This is the Radio of the French Nation!" he said. "The hour of liberation is ringing!"

His emotion showered over Danielle. Pressing her ear against the door, she blinked back the hot tears.

"Parisians! We are bringing you news of the liberation of your city! Leclerc's army is entering Paris! Any minute now the tanks will be rolling by! In front of me, at the Porte d'Italie, the street is choked with people. They're drunk! All of us are drunk tonight; but drunk with joy! For the first time in four years we're drinking the red wine of freedom and it's gone to our heads. The crowd is shouting and singing and completely wild! Listen to them!"

Their roar burst out of the radio and exploded in Danielle's ears. The broadcast shot out of the loud-speaker, throbbing with the sound and touch and smell of the Paris street. The speaker rushed on. He was as uncontained as the crowd he was describing, and as they infected him he infected his listeners. He stammered and stumbled; his voice broke under his emotion; but he picked up and raced on, the words tumbling out of his mouth and onto the air. The blind exultation of the city and the shattering sense of the moment stabbed across the air and pierced Danielle's heart. She could not keep back the tears.

"There they are!" the speaker cried. "They're coming in now! Here are the tanks!"

He had to shout against the deep wild roar of the crowd and could barely be heard.

"The tanks are rolling down the Avenue d'Italie. In a few minutes they'll be crossing the Seine at the heart of Paris! Another tank just went by. Listen to the crowd! People are hugging and kissing each other. They're waving so hard you'd think they were going to shake their arms loose. The crowd is wild, absolutely wild with joy!"

Danielle listened to the unremitting roar of the crowd as it pounded out of the loud-speaker. How she yearned to be there and part of it!

"We've waited four years for this moment," the speaker cried, with the crowd roaring behind him. "We want all of Paris to know that we've just been liberated. Tell everybody you know! Telephone your friends! Tell your neighbors! Tell those who live on your landing and those who live on the floors above and below you! Open your windows and shout it across the street! Let the joy of the liberation burst across the city like a rocket and light up every street and every house! Put out the flags! Paris has been liberated and we are free men again!"

Danielle could not stand there a moment longer without moving; the tiny room was hardly big enough to contain her joy. She went to the window and looked over the city. Out of the indistinguishably black façades of the buildings of Paris came the strange, discordant counterpoint of ringing telephones, blaring radios and ecstatic voices. Danielle could imagine the doors opening, the excited voices rising and descending in stair wells, the people running up and down, laughing and inviting each other to their apartments for the liberation drink out of the bottle that had been hoarded over the years for this occasion. In every building in Paris, she thought, people who had been neighbors for years and who had never before said more than *bonjour* or *bon soir* to each other would now be toasting the liberation. She felt sad that it was not for her and went back to the door. The radio was still blaring. Hoarse but tireless, the speaker called for the attention of his listeners.

"I have just received a message from the General Secretary of Information," he announced. "He has asked me to tell all the curés who are listening in to ring the church bells immediately to announce the entrance into Paris of our liberators. I repeat . . ."

Danielle went back to the window. Less than two minutes later a single church bell, far off, tolled its lonely note over the city. An instant later it was answered by a quicker, gayer bell. Here and there other bells chimed in. The deep, Gothic tones of Notre Dame de Paris sounded their ponderous note into the mounting rhapsody. One after the other the bells of Paris rang out and the night was filled with their music. From Sacré-Coeur, from St. Germain des Près, from St. Augustin, from St. Eustache, from the cathedrals and the hundred churches of the city the bronze tongues of the bells smacked their bronze palates, and the bells clanged and hammered and beat and tolled their bronze cries of joy.

Then, while Danielle watched beneath the night sky and the pealing of the bells, blackout curtains were yanked clear and shutters clattered open; and one by one the lights blinked on, sparkling over the vast valley where Paris lay stretched across the bed of the Seine. From the topmost street in Montmartre to the far reaches of the fourteenth *arrondissement* the lights flashed on, illuminating the night. Millions of lights seemed to be laughing out of the city. All around, Parisians thrust their heads out of brightly illuminated squares of light. They sang "Madelon" and "Tipperary" and then shouted *vivas* for France, De Gaulle, the resistance, the Allies, the Americans. They laughed and they shouted to each other and drank toasts from one window to the next as the bells clamored above them.

Behind her, Danielle heard the sudden change in tone of the speaker. "We were a little hasty," he said. "Only a spearhead of

Leclerc's army has arrived. The Germans are still in the city. It is wiser to close your windows. . . ."

One by one the lights around the city went out and darkness closed in on it as before. Here and there German soldiers had fired into lighted windows and at men working the church bells. The speaker announced that the Germans were attacking the *mairie* of the eleventh *arrondissement* and sent out repeated calls for F.F.I.s to come to the aid of the besieged building. From the Longchamps race track and the heights of St. Cloud quick flashes of light tore the velvet sky as German batteries opened fire on Paris for the first time since the insurrection had begun. At Nanterre, west of the city, German gasoline dumps still blazed away, throwing a red glare into the sky.

Danielle stood at the window for a long time after the lights went out and the bells stopped ringing. She did not want to be alone again, feeling that as long as she stood at the window looking out over the city she was part of it and the experience of the night was still alive. Nothing had ever stirred her so deeply. A line of Victor Hugo's that she had not thought of for a long time kept running through her head: "Where the Sphinx says Chaos, Paris says Liberty."

Finally she went to her narrow bed and lay down on it. What would happen to her now? The question answered itself. They would have to move her to Germany. They would have to do it fast, too. By tomorrow the city would be liberated. They would be moving out tonight, then. For a moment she thought that maybe by now it was too late for them to get away, that they would be forced to stay and surrender and that she would be liberated. But the idea seemed too wildly dreamlike for Danielle to depend upon.

Suddenly she jumped to her feet and stood by the bed as if transfixed, listening as sharply as she could to what was going on outside her door. There wasn't a sound. It frightened her. She walked over to the door and put her ear to it. Dead silence. The radio had been turned off, but she had no idea when that had happened or, now that she thought of it, why they had let it run so long. She had the feeling that nobody was there. For one wonderful moment she let her imagination go and thought, They've taken off and left me behind! But then she told herself that they couldn't have done that. There was one way of finding out if anybody was on the other side of the door. She knocked on it. No answer. She knocked again, louder. Still no answer. She called out several times. There wasn't a sound on the other side of her door.

Danielle's heart began pounding and skipping beats. Once again she wondered, but this time seriously, if they could have left. Quietly, she turned the doorknob and pushed. She almost wept with disappointment. The door was locked. She bent down and looked through the keyhole. The key was in it. But just then she heard sounds in the house. They were far off, but so loud they carried right up to the top floor. Then she heard the shouts in the garden and raced from the door to the window. By standing on her tiptoes, she could make out one end of the garden. When she understood what was happening, involuntarily she said aloud, "No, no! Not that, not now; it isn't possible!" and she turned away from the window, standing with her back to it, weighed down by the deepest, most complete sense of hopelessness and despair. In a moment she heard a scattering of rifle shots in the garden below. She shuddered. Another volley and another one splintered the silence. Then she heard separate shots. She was numbed at the thought of what they were doing. All those lives at the very last minute. They would let no prisoner of theirs escape the butchery they had prepared. She understood now what she had overheard. This was their way of cleaning up the villa before they left.

The sounds in the house were louder now. She could hear them climbing the stairs. She wasn't afraid, not yet anyway. She was numb, completely incapable of feeling anything any more. All she could do was wait. She felt that at least she knew about the liberation, had even, in a way, gone through it. They couldn't take that away from her. But she didn't want to die. She wanted to see Patrice. She wanted to be in his arms and be comforted by him and weep, just weep, like the little girl she felt she was. They were climbing the last stairs now and were on the landing. She heard them come straight toward her room. Then the key turned in the lock and the door burst open. Bracing herself, stretched taut to face her ultimate moment, she stared at the men in the doorway. They stared back at her. At that instant she leaped violently back to life. These were not her captors. They were the resistance.

"Comrade," one of them said. "You're free."

Her heart flipped over. Never had she heard words as sweet as those. Her eyes filled with tears and she took a few blind, uncertain steps, reaching the door and throwing her arms around the man who had spoken. She felt weak; her knees gave. If the man, a dark, stocky fellow with a four-day beard, had not been there to hold her up, she would have collapsed. He patted her awkwardly on the back. It was like the gentle caress of an angel.

"Don't worry, little one," he said in a coarse, tender voice. "You're safe now. Are you all right?"

"Oh, yes," she wept, holding onto him, her voice muffled against his chest. "Oh, yes, I'm fine, fine."

"Then you're lucky," he said. "They have no hearts."

She had no voice to answer him, but presently she drew back and tried to wipe the tears away with her hands. He offered her a crushed handkerchief and she took it, laughing tearfully and saying through her tears and laughter, "I've never been so happy."

"They aren't so happy," he said grimly. "They were trying to get away, but we caught a few of them. These are the ones I've been waiting to get in this villa for six months. They caught it in the garden."

"I know," Danielle said. "I heard it."

His voice was suddenly gentle again. "Where do you want to go?"

"The Prefecture."

"Anybody you want to see there is at the Hotel de Ville tonight unless he's a cop."

"The Hotel de Ville then. He's not a cop."

"That's what I thought. I'll go down with you. We'll give you a ride."

Danielle sailed down the stairs and across the garden and into the street. The nightmare was over. She was free.

†

A LITTLE earlier on the Place de l'Hôtel de Ville, the spearhead of Leclerc's armored division pulled up with the church bells clamoring around them. Three medium tanks, eleven half tracks and four armored cars filed into the square and were deployed around it. Out of one of the tanks stepped a burly, bearded officer, the leader of the unit. A mass of F.F.I.s surrounded him, picked him up and carried him into the Hotel de Ville and up the grand staircase. The officer protested all the way. He could not grasp the merit of being the first Allied soldier in uniform to reach the semiliberated French capital.

"Please, please," he kept repeating. "It is nothing, nothing at all . . . Dronne is my name, Captain Dronne . . ."

Eager hands stretched over the heads of the crowd to shake the captain's hand. A hundred voices cried out their thanks. Limp with exhaustion after the forced advance to Paris, the captain was stupefied by the overwhelming welcome. His eyes were red with fatigue; his thick beard was matted. All day long dust had powdered his face and body, and sweat had coursed over him, caking the dirt and staining his face with smudged, sticky lines.

"Excuse me," he kept saying as he was borne through the crowd at the top of the stairs and into the splendor of the Prefect's office. "Excuse me. But I am dirty, really too dirty."

Hanging from the center of the gilded and scalloped ceiling of the Prefect's office was a magnificent chandelier. It was in full and brilliant illumination and sparkled from all its crystal facets. Beneath it the mass of shirt-sleeved F.F.I.s and resistance leaders, some carrying arms, crushed into the enormous room. In the middle of the jostling crowd the French captain was pushed face to face with Bidault. The leader of the resistance held the man in uniform by his shoulders and embraced him on both cheeks. Held in the arms of Paris, squeezed to the city's heart, the captain was incapable of words. His voice broke with emotion; he half sobbed. All he could say was, "I'm so dirty, so terribly dirty." He was whirled around, from one side to the other, the crowd crushing in on him. His hand was grasped at every instant and vigorously shaken, and all those who came close enough insisted on embracing him.

"Paris is yours," he was told. "Anything, anything at all. What do you want?"

The captain smiled radiantly out of his dirt-blackened face. "A bath," he said. "Just a bath."

Outside the open windows the church bells were joyfully ringing, while inside the room the shouts of acclaim for the captain and the delirium of victory rose to a shattering crescendo. Danielle had arrived a moment earlier. She pushed her way through the crowded room searching for Patrice, but was stopped by an ecstatic Sorel under the chandelier. All around them people were talking and laughing and they had to shout to make themselves heard through the din.

The celebration went on and on. Patrice doggedly stayed with it. But the longer he stayed the more depressed he became. He had waited for four years for this moment; it had come one week too late for him. All he could think of was Danielle.

He felt something fall on his head and picked a piece of crystal out of his hair. He looked up. The huge chandelier swayed, and he saw some of the crystal burst and spray. It was a second or two later, at the very instant that he realized what was happening, that he felt Lefort clutch his arm and cry, "My God, look!" He looked. For an instant he saw nothing but the swarm of humanity packing the Prefect's enormous office. Then he saw her. It was too much. He began to shout. He did not want to lose her again. "Down, down!" he cried, knowing she could not hear him. But as he shouted she saw him and the look on her face melted his heart. He could not hear her but saw her lips form the words, "Patrice, oh, Patrice!" They struggled toward each other through the massed groups of F.F.I.s. When they reached each other she was in tears and threw herself into his arms. To her amazement, as he pulled her to him, he flung her to the floor. At that moment she heard what he was shouting. The cry was all about them by then. Danielle lay in Patrice's arms with her head buried in his shoulder and, through the noises of the room, heard the flat detonation of rifle fire. Other cries cut through the celebration. "Put out the lights! They're firing on us!" A man near Patrice clutched his stomach and dropped. Then everybody hit the floor and a moment later the room was plunged in darkness.

"Oh, darling," Danielle wept, holding him tight. "Oh, darling," she sobbed, and could not say another word.

Patrice pressed her to him, feeling her warm, trembling body against his own. He held her face up and kissed the hot tears away. But then, as people began crawling through the confusion toward the door, he whispered to her, "Come on. Let's get out of here."

They groped their way out of the room and into the street. Hand in hand, they walked through the darkness to the river. They crossed a bridge and turned right along the Seine. All the time they walked they talked as if they never again would have another chance to say a word to each other. After they had gone a way along the quai they went down a flight of stone steps and strolled a short distance on the riverbank. The silence of the city was all around them, soft and gentle, like a caress.

"Here's a spot that I've been wanting to take you to for a long time," Patrice said when they stopped.

It was a grassy strip of ground where the dark waters of the Seine lapped softly at the edge of land.

"It's lovely," she said as they sat down.

Patrice put his arm around her. In the distance, before them, a dozen fires blazed as the German gasoline dumps at Nanterre went up in flames. The sky glowed like a giant furnace. But in the foreground Paris was black. Not a light, not a sound, except for a rifle shot now and then that intensified the deep silence. Across the Seine stood the Tuileries, their high gates etched against the red glow on the horizon and pointing up at a quarter-moon suspended in the middle of the night. Behind the gates German guards, wearing battle helmets and carrying rifles, were also outlined against the flaming curve of the sky. A short way down the Rue de Rivoli, in front of the Hotel de Ville, were the tanks of the Leclerc division. Swift, powerful darts of red light stabbed into the black belly of the night as the tank men fired tracer bullets to mark their arrival in Paris.

Holding each other closely, Patrice and Danielle sensed the conflict of the night, with the destiny of the city balanced between the German soldiers in the Tuileries and the French tanks at the Hotel de Ville. They knew that this moment was the climax of the past four years. Their jobs were done. It was the end and the beginning. The foretaste of freedom was sweet, but sweeter yet was the taste of being together.

For a long time they talked quietly. Then they were silent. When he pulled her down on the grass beside him, she curled up in his arms with a sigh, and they clung to each other as if all they were really sure of bringing out of their years of resistance was each other. A few feet away the gentle Seine lapped at the strip of land on which they lay. He cradled and caressed her and kissed her eyes, wild and tear-stained, in the sweet summer silence of the night; then he clasped her even tighter and kissed the tears away.

Long afterward, as Danielle lay back in his arms, he said, "They'll be coming in tomorrow."

"Yes, it will be all over then."

"We'll walk up the Champs Élysées—just for the walk, you understand."

"Of course. Why else should anybody walk up the Champs Élysées?"

The next day the troops of General Leclerc's Second Armored Division flooded into Paris. They were greeted with an explosion of joy. All day long troops, tanks and F.F.I.s fought the Germans as Paris wildly celebrated its liberation among flying bullets and bursting shells. It was one of the two or three maddest, happiest days in the city's two-thousand-year history.

By late afternoon the fighting was over. Soon after, when Patrice and Danielle walked arm in arm under the arcades of the Rue de Rivoli, all traces of the occupation had disappeared. There were no swastikas, no German military road signs, no barriers to keep Parisians off the sidewalks in front of hotels for German officers. The collaborationist books and the photographs and the propaganda posters were gone from shop windows. In place of the swastikas huge white bed sheets hung limply out of the windows of hotels recently occupied by the Germans. On a wall Patrice and Danielle saw an enormous poster showing a Marianne draped in the tricolor rising from a tomb and lifting up the stone that covered her. There was just one word across the poster: Liberation!

As they walked, Patrice slipped his arm around Danielle's waist. The façades of the buildings were blackened by smoke and flame; they were scarred and chipped by bullets, and deep gashes were torn in them by shell bursts. Windows were smashed and shutters were ripped loose and the iron curtains of shops were dented and pierced. In the gutters the black hulks of automobiles and trucks, still smoking, lay battered and twisted; burned-out tanks stood immobile, like the petrified corpses of deadly beasts. The pavement was broken, cobbles ripped out; at intersections, here and there, barricades were still half up and puddles of blood, part wet, part coagulated, stained the sidewalks. Like children at a fair, laughing and chattering, crowds upon crowds of Parisians streamed through the streets of their city, while fleets of U.S. Army tanks, trucks and jeeps swept into Paris and weaved in and out of the eight avenues leading to the immense square that circled the Arch of Triumph.

Patrice held Danielle closer; they smiled at each other. The smell of gunpowder hung in the air like an anesthetic, as proud, bloody and triumphant Paris held freedom, newborn, in her arms.

ABOUT THE AUTHOR

BERNARD FRIZELL *was born and educated in New York City. He was an undergraduate at Brooklyn College and a graduate student in philosophy on a series of fellowships at Harvard and the Sorbonne. Set for a university teaching career, Frizell branched out into journalism to stay on in Paris and lived there, on and off, for about 15 years.*

Between periods in France he has returned to the United States. At the outbreak of World War II he edited war news for the New York Post, *later became a propaganda analyst, then a radio news writer for the Office of War Information. He began his army career with the 691st Laundry Battalion (Mobile) as a specialist in drying clothes, ended it with the Psychological Warfare Branch in Paris. In between he wrote and broadcast news for Radio 7th Army and was a PWB war correspondent.*

After the war Frizell worked for Time *and* Life *magazines in Paris as a foreign correspondent, reporting on such cultural phenomena as existentialism, gastronomy and Lopism (an unlikely Latin Quarter form of political satire). He is now a staff writer for* Time *in New York, in recent years has written book reviews and covered cinema, theater and television for that magazine.* Ten Days in August *is his first book.*